YOU
CAN
DIE

YOU CAN DIE

REBECCA ZANETTI

ZEBRA BOOKS
Kensington Publishing Corp.

www.kensingtonbooks.com

ZEBRA BOOKS are published by

Kensington Publishing Corp.
119 West 40th Street
New York, NY 10018

All Kensington titles, imprints, and distributed lines are available at special quantity discounts for bulk purchases for sales promotion, premiums, fund-raising, and educational or institutional use.

Special book excerpts or customized printings can also be created to fit specific needs. For details, write or phone the office of the Kensington Sales Manager: Kensington Publishing Corp., 119 West 40th Street, New York, NY 10018. Attn. Sales Department. Phone: 1-800-221-2647.

First Printing: August 2023
ISBN-13: 978-1-4201-5436-8
ISBN-13: 978-1-4201-5437-5 (eBook)

10 9 8 7 6 5 4 3 2 1

Printed in the United States of America

*This one is for the Montana Tech 2022 football team,
which was an inspiration and tons of fun
to watch playing this year.
Here's also to your wonderful families,
whom we've been so fortunate to get to know.*

Acknowledgments

Thank you to Big Tone for being the best husband in the universe and for driving for hours and hours to football games this season while I wrote or edited in the passenger seat. Thank you to Gabe Zanetti for being such a dedicated badass on the football field and giving me plenty of inspiration. Thank you to Karlina Zanetti for being such a creative and unique adventurer, providing laughs and inspiration. I have the best family in the entire world;

Thank you to my agent, Caitlin Blasdell, whose brilliant ideas made this book so much better than it was when I first started. Where I see the trees, you see not only the forest but the mountains;

Thank you to my editor, Alicia Condon, for encouraging my crazy ideas and pushing me even further creatively. There's not a plot hole in the world that can escape you, and I'm so grateful to be working with you;

Thank you to the rest of the Kensington gang: Alexandra Nicolajsen, Steven Zacharias, Adam Zacharias, Lynn Cully, Jane Nutter, Lauren Jernigan, James Walsh, Ross Plotkin, Justine Willis,

Vida Engstrand, Elizabeth Trout, Kimberly Richardson, Kristin McLaughlin, and Rebecca Cremonese;

A special thank-you to Pam Joplin for the copy edits. I have no idea how you find everything you do and think you might be psychic;

Thank you to Anissa Beatty, whose enthusiasm, creativity, and hard work ethic make my life so much easier;

Thank you to Madison Fairbanks, Julie Elkin, and Katy Nielsen for your friendship, support, and all-around great times via Zoom and the Rebels;

Thank you to Leanna Feazel, Heather Frost, and Jessica Mobbs for the beta reads on this one.

Thank you also to my constant support system: Gail and Jim English, Kathy and Herb Zanetti, Debbie and Travis Smith, Stephanie and Don West, Jessica and Jonah Namson, Steve and Liz Berry, Jillian and Benji Stein, and the entire Younker family.

Prologue

A chilly mist hung low, almost to the rough pavement. Angry sleet pummeled the tent city, its roar muffling the rush hour traffic and the multiple honking horns above them. Vivienne Vuittron ducked her head and pulled her hood tighter over her hair as she scurried through the maze of temporary shelters, trying to keep as far from their openings as possible.

"This is crazy," Ryan muttered next to her, his hands in his pockets and his head down as rain slicked his hair to his head.

"I know," she whispered. "Come on. This way." She followed the beeping red dot on her phone, slightly extending it from her body as if she were in a landing party or something.

Ryan looked around. "This is not a safe place to be. Come on, Viv. Let's get back to my car."

"No." They'd left his dented old Subaru at the far end of the bridge; hopefully nobody would steal it.

"We're trespassing," Ryan hissed. "I think. Maybe not. Either way, this is so not safe."

Viv's chest tightened and her legs trembled. She could barely make out the number of tents under the overpass, but she kept following the blinking light—past the green tent with what smelled like marijuana smoke wafting out a top vent. She waded through mud puddles and was silently thankful she'd talked Ryan into this. It would be way too scary to come here alone. Cars zoomed by above them on their way to somewhere else.

She tiptoed over a couple of used syringes, wanting to run back to the car. "We're almost there."

"Where? We're in the middle of a fucking tent city. Your dad can't be here." Ryan frowned, looking kind of cute. They'd been dating for almost a month, and he was probably the best-looking boy she'd ever met.

"When he and Kirsti were cheating on my mom, I guess they parked his van anywhere to do it. If he's seeing somebody else and cheating on Kirsti, then I just need one picture." She'd planted a luggage tag disc in his oversized wallet over a month ago, and from what she could see, he often went odd places. There was a road on the other side of the tent city, and maybe her dad was parked there.

Somebody groaned inside a yellow tent, and she quickened her steps.

Ryan followed her. "You know we're going to miss first and second periods, right?"

"Probably third, too," she whispered. "What do you care? You skip class all the time." That was one of the things she liked about him.

"I only skip the first one because coach teaches it, and I don't really have to be there." He jumped over what looked like a pile of dirty baby wipes. "I understand health, baby." He wiggled his eyebrows.

She rolled her eyes. His sense of humor was something else she liked about him. Plus, he had sandy blond hair, spectacular blue eyes, and shoulders so wide, he played nose guard for the football team. Before she'd met him, she hadn't even known what a nose guard did. "Come on, it's this way. Mr. Big Shot Lawyer won't like seeing us here."

"I thought you said your dad was a dentist." Ryan pulled his hands out of his pockets to walk next to her.

She sighed. "Yeah, he sucked as a lawyer, so he went to dental school. That's where he met my mom. She worked to help him pay for it. Then he was a dentist for a while, but you know . . ."

"Oh, yeah," Ryan said. "Sorry."

"That's okay." Her father had left her mom for his dental hygienist, and he'd been fired at the same time. So he'd gone back to being a lawyer, which he probably still sucked at.

Ryan skirted a bunch of torn and bloody shirts. "At least he had something to fall back on?"

"Fell back on his girlfriend, if you ask me," she snorted. "That bimbo, I can't believe he's still dating her." It was sad because his cheating had hurt her mom so much, but it wasn't like her dad had been around that much anyway. Now he was probably cheating on Kirsti as well. "If I can't get a picture, I'll tape the note to his windshield. Then maybe we can make it to third period."

She kept slogging through the mud, her hair dripping rain down her face.

"Why don't we just call him?" Ryan asked.

"Would you call *your* dad?"

Ryan kicked a rock out of his way. "My dad's in prison."

That was one of the reasons they had bonded. Their fathers both sucked. "Yeah, I know. I'm sorry."

"No, it's his fault. He was the druggie who decided to

rob a construction trailer." Ryan nudged rolled-up socks to the side. "People on drugs do the dumbest fucking things."

"I know," Viv said. "My dad isn't on drugs. He's just an asshole."

The red light blinked faster, and Viv angled her head, staring at a purple tent. The fabric was bright compared to the other weather-worn tents, and the stitching was new.

Ryan gulped. "You think he's in there?" he whispered.

She winced, hating her dad more than ever. What kind of kinky crap was he into that he came here to do it in a purple tent?

Ryan coughed. "Oh, man. Talk about an 'I'm having a midlife crisis' situation. Geez, no offense, but this guy is just looking to get his rocks off. This is a crazy place to be."

"You have no idea," Viv muttered, stomping toward the tent.

Ryan looked around at the other tents as if scoping for threats. "He buys a tent and gets jiggy in a skeevy place like this instead of making money so your sister can get a new band uniform?"

"He's the worst," Viv muttered, her heart aching. She would not cry. Not again. "He has to pay his child support through the state because there's no choice, but other than that, he's not keeping up his end of the bargain."

The note she'd written felt heavy in her pocket. She hadn't been nice in it. She'd told him exactly what she thought, and she'd also told him that he needed to nut up and help out. Her mom was struggling to pay for everything right now.

Viv readied her camera, crouched, and yanked aside the tent flap.

Her mind went blank at what she saw. "Oh my God," she said, unable to move.

"What?" Ryan leaned down and then gasped. He grabbed her instantly and pulled her away. "Viv!"

"I know," she said, looking down.

Her father lay naked on his back with his eyes wide open, staring up at the top of the tent. Ripped clothes covered most of his tan wallet, which had been discarded in the corner. His chest was covered in blood that pooled on the ground around him. She couldn't look away from the terrifying sight of the colorful Valentine's Day candies shoved in his mouth and smashed all over his face. The heart shaped pieces fell out onto his bloodied cheeks and into the blood around his head.

From far away she could hear screaming, from very far away.

Ryan shook her. "Viv. Viv. Stop screaming."

She couldn't.

Chapter 1

The smell of marijuana clogged the dank air as Laurel Snow picked her way across the crumbling pavement in her mother's good navy-blue kitten heels. Blue tarps and small tents were placed haphazardly below the concrete ceiling of the bridge, their inhabitants remaining inside, protected from the pouring rain.

Yellow crime scene tape cordoned off the farthest section of the underpass, where two uniformed officers were going from tent to tent taking notes. An ambulance stood silently to the north, facing her with nobody in the driver's seat.

"Thank you for coming out today," said her escort, FBI Agent Sally Rodriguez, as if they'd just met for tea. After Laurel had received orders from DC, Agent Rodriguez had picked her up at the University of Washington, halfway through a planned lecture she was giving about behavioral analysis. Even though the lecture had started at eight in the morning, the entire room had been full of students.

She'd been secretly relieved to cut the class short. Public speaking was not one of her skills.

Laurel cinched her raincoat tighter around her waist,

acutely aware she wasn't dressed for a crime scene. Her simple blue jacket and skirt set with the white shell had been more appropriate for her role as a guest lecturer today. She stepped lightly over a smattering of used syringes as the rain flattened her hair to her head. Droplets slid down over her face, and she wiped them away. "I'm surprised I was brought in on this." She had inferred from her boss in DC that the head of the Seattle FBI field office wasn't pleased with Laurel taking over the Violent Crimes Unit and basing it out of Genesis Valley, which was two hours to the east.

"Don't ask me." Agent Rodriguez was around forty with grayish blond blending with the dark brown of her hair, cut in a sharp bob. Her light brown eyes shone with intelligence and a glint that said this wasn't her first day on the job. Her build was stocky, her jaw surprisingly delicate, and her hiking boots perfect for the terrain. "We have jurisdiction because we're at the tip of the Mount-Baker Snoqualmie Forest, but I'm hoping to pass the case to you because we're stretched way too thin in the Seattle Field Office." Above them, cars sped by on I-90.

Two men sat inside an orange-colored tent to the left, playing cards and smoking cigars. They watched Laurel walk by with flat eyes, their gray hair and beards long. Both wore torn gloves and layers of dirty clothing.

Rodriguez looked toward them and kept walking. "The counties and cities have been cleaning out these tent cities for the last year, but they spring right back up in a day or so." She pointed ahead at a bright purple tent set against scrubby bushes where white-suited crime techs were swarming. "The Seattle coroner is here but will transfer the case if asked."

A man moved from behind a pillar, his stance wide as he looked around the scene.

Rodriguez immediately pivoted to stride toward him, motioning for Laurel to do the same. "My boss has been waiting for you." .

The man had presence and a sense of command, wearing dark jeans, boots, and a black puffer jacket. An FBI badge hung at his belt. His chest was wide, his legs stocky, and his head bald. Piercing blue eyes were set in a boxer's face, complete with a nose that had been broken once or twice. He walked toward them, not seeming to notice the rain pummeling his smooth head.

Laurel tilted her head, curious. It was telling that he moved toward them. The power move would've been to force them to walk to him.

He held out a hand, his eyebrows raised and his gaze studying her face with interest—and surprise he did nothing to mask. "Special Agent Snow. It's nice to meet you." His handshake was short and professional. "I'm Special Agent in Charge Wayne Norrs."

Laurel shook his hand. She was accustomed to people taking a second look at her unusual features—dark, reddish-brown hair and heterochromatic eyes. She noted the strength in his grip. Norrs had to be in his early forties, and his stocky build showed muscle. "Deputy Director McCromby said you requested assistance from the FBI Pacific Northwest Violent Crimes Unit?" The unit had just become official a week ago when she'd been in DC. On a probationary basis, anyway.

"Yeah." He gestured toward the tent, where a crime scene photographer was snapping pictures. "My team is stretched thin with two RICO cases and seven drug trafficking cases. Take a look at the scene and then let's chat."

She blinked. He wasn't anything like she'd expected. After she'd been assigned to lead the PNVCU for a probationary year, McCromby had said Norrs was displeased, and that normally meant red tape and road-blocks in her experience. Though she hadn't practiced studying expressions lately, Norrs seemed to truly want her assistance.

"I'd like to bring my entire team in on this," Laurel said. Her small team was comprised of only four at the moment, but she had requested additional agents, and they should be arriving soon. She'd ignored management's suggestion that her team move to the city. She liked Genesis Valley.

"Take a look first," Norrs said easily, his voice scratchy as if he smoked a pack or two a day. "See if you want the case or if I should add it to my overflowing caseload. You're just back, right?"

"Yes." After working a serial arson case in New Jersey for more than a month, she'd spent two weeks in DC signing contracts, dealing with HR, and packing up her apartment. As it turned out, she hadn't had many possessions to bring here. Apparently, she'd never quite set down roots in the capital. It was good to be home finally. "What do we have?" she asked.

"Walk this way." Norrs led the way over to the purple tent, which was now shielded by a wide, white tarp.

Laurel crouched down to look inside, where a naked man lay covered in blood next to a balled up pile of clothing. A wallet had been opened, probably by the techs on scene, and placed atop the clothing. Several stab marks could be seen in the victim's upper chest, abdomen, and down his right leg.

"I called out our evidence response team to process the scene, and we'll use the Washington State lab for results. Assuming you'd take the case, I contacted the

Tempest County coroner, who is still on his way. That's good because I wanted you to see the body. It's protected from the elements by the new tent, but I have to release it as soon as he gets here," Norrs said. "There are too many stab wounds to count." The victim had brownish-gray hair and was clean-shaven. Heart-shaped candy had been stuffed down his throat and scattered across his teeth and around his head.

"Who is he?" She stood.

"His name was Victor Vuittron," Norrs said.

Laurel jolted. "Victor Vuittron?"

"Yeah," Norrs said, his gaze intense on her face. "You've heard of him?"

Her throat went dry. "Yes. He's the ex-husband of my office manager." She had to call Kate.

"So they were telling the truth," Norrs mused.

"Who?" Laurel asked, looking around and again noticing the too-quiet ambulance. She started moving that way before Norrs could answer. When she rounded the back corner, she found Viv, Kate's oldest daughter, inside and crying against the chest of a pale boy who was awkwardly patting her shoulder. They were both wearing hospital scrubs beneath the wool blankets that covered them. Had the police confiscated their clothing? "Viv?"

Viv turned her head and then pushed away from the boy, leaping down and rushing toward her. "Laurel!" she wailed, wrapping both arms around Laurel's waist and shoving her back a step. "My dad is dead."

Laurel hugged her back and smoothed her wet hair away from her face. "I'm so sorry, sweetheart." She studied the boy. He appeared to be about sixteen with broad shoulders, wet blond hair, and light blue eyes. No marks were evident on his face, neck, or hands. His face was pale and his eyes glassy as if in shock, his body shivering even though a blanket was wrapped around his shoulders.

Laurel straightened the blanket over Viv and gently nudged her back inside the ambulance. "Get out of the rain." When Viv wearily climbed back in, the boy put his arm over her shoulder. "Have you called your mom?"

"No." Viv leaned into the kid, her curly blond hair falling over his arm.

He cleared his throat. "The cops took our phones and separated us until they got our statements. Then they put us in here, but they still have our phones."

Norrs walked up behind her. "We have their phones and are awaiting warrants to search them."

Although she didn't think she'd see anything, Laurel double-checked that there were no cut marks on Viv's hands or face to indicate she'd stabbed anybody—often attackers cut themselves. "They're underage. Their parents need to be called before we interview them."

"Interview us?" the boy snapped. "That's crazy. We just found the body."

Viv sniffed. "Please call my mom."

Laurel nodded. "Do either of you require medical assistance?"

They both shook their heads.

She turned toward Norrs. "Have you interviewed all of the possible witnesses?"

"Yes," Norrs said. "As many as we could catch before they hightailed it out of here. How about we head to my office? I have a couple of agents trying to track down information about the tent as well as searching CCTV in the area. If there is any."

Laurel kept her expression bland. He seemed so cooperative. "That would be fine, so long as we take the kids with us and call their parents." She wasn't letting Viv out of her sight until she found Kate.

Norrs pointed toward the official vehicles. "My rig's over here."

Laurel fetched the kids from the ambulance, and they scrambled to stay close to her. Agent Norrs had been much more polite than she had been led to expect. They reached his light gray Dodge Ram, and he opened the passenger side door for her. She hesitated, then stepped up on the side rail to get in as the kids hopped into the back of the 4-door truck, both of them still pale and trembling.

He wiped rain off his head. "I'm sorry about that. You're not one of those women who dislikes having a guy open a door, are you? I know this is business, and I know we work together, but my mom would show up and box my ears if I didn't at least attempt it."

Laurel reached for her seatbelt. "No, I appreciate it. I just wasn't expecting it."

"Oh, good," Norrs said, shutting the door. Quick strides had him around the vehicle and jumping into the driver's side. He quickly started the engine and drove away from the crime scene.

The trip to the Seattle FBI office was quick, with very little traffic for once. Special Agent Norrs took them through the personnel elevator from the parking garage and walked beyond the reception desk. He handed off the kids to an agent, instructing that they be allowed to call their parents and then taken to different interrogation rooms.

Laurel tried to give Viv a reassuring nod before following Norrs.

"We'll make sure you have access to the building by the time you leave today," he said, winding through several offices until they reached a conference room in the rear. "I had everything set up in here for now."

She walked inside to find a murder board already set up, with pictures of the victim and surrounding area; the kids' pictures had been tacked on a second board.

"I sent those from my phone and had Sherry print them out," he said. "I'd like to offer you support on this, but I had to send Agent Rodriquez out on another case, and she'll be occupied for at least a week—if not two."

Laurel nodded. "She mentioned that your caseload is heavy right now." She studied the board. "I'm wondering about the significance of the Valentine's Day candy."

"I don't know. Valentine's Day was an entire month ago, and it appears as if Vuittron was killed last night, so . . ."

Laurel reached in her bag for a band to tie up her still damp hair. "The killing appears to have been fueled by rage, but the purchase of the tent and the location suggest otherwise," she murmured. She needed Kate's permission to speak with Viv about the case, but she wanted to be with the girl, comforting her. "Did you get anything out of the kids?"

"No, but they shouldn't have been there at all, so you have to wonder," Norrs said. "The officer on site did a quick interview with both of them to make sure the scene was safe. They said they just found the victim."

That made zero sense. Laurel sighed. Hopefully Viv hadn't lied to a federal agent.

A rustle sounded by the doorway, and an older woman with bright silver hair poked her head in. "Here are the first couple of witness statements from the scene, Special Agent Norrs, as well as identification and access for Special Agent Snow." She walked in and handed him two case files, before passing over an ID card for Laurel. "Also, we have a quick background on the victim—top file."

Norrs flipped open the file folder, sidling closer to Laurel so she could see. "Victor Vuitton, junior associate at Marshall & Cutting law firm."

"Yes. They've won some high-profile criminal cases the last couple of years," Sherry said.

Norrs sighed. "Dead lawyer. Gee. Wonder where we'll find suspects."

Laurel frowned. "I thought he was a dentist." She went back through her conversations with Kate. The first day they'd met, the woman had mentioned that she'd met her now ex-husband when he'd attended dental school. Then more recently, he'd committed adultery with his dental assistant, which had precipitated the divorce. Perhaps she hadn't asked enough questions of her new friend.

Sherry's bracelet jingled as she moved. "A missing persons report was filed this morning but didn't hit the database until about five minutes ago."

"Filed by whom?" Laurel asked.

"His wife, Kirsti Vuittron. She said that he didn't come home last night. Apparently her housekeeper found her in distress this morning and talked her into calling the police."

Laurel jolted. Victor had married his mistress? Was Kate aware of that fact?

Norrs studied the driver's license. "Run a background check on the Vuittron family as well as their housekeeper, would you? Please copy Special Agent Snow on that."

Laurel stiffened. "You'll need to interview Viv's mother, Kate Vuittron, when she arrives, Agent Norrs."

He nodded. "Understood. Anything else, Sherry?"

"You bet. Apparently Mr. Vuittron announced a month ago that he was running for Seattle City Council against

Councilman Eric Swelter. The primary isn't until August, but from the sounds of it, these guys hated each other." Sherry turned and strode away.

Norrs smacked his head. "I'm sorry, I should have introduced you. I've been working on my manners lately."

Laurel had to clear Kate of this, and fast. No way would Kate have stabbed her ex and then shoved candy down his throat. "I have to work on mine all the time. Don't concern yourself about it."

"Good. My guys are all knee-deep in other cases right now. I'll interview Kate Vuittron, considering your connection to the victim and possible suspects, but I'm hoping you'll work the remainder of the case and keep objective." He ran a broad hand over his smooth head. "I'm honestly so low on personnel right now that I don't have a choice."

She didn't want to be the one to interrogate Kate. "I concur and will be objective," Laurel said quietly. Her unit had been created for cases like these. "I'd like to check on the kids, even though their parents have not arrived yet. I won't ask them any questions related to the case."

"I'm sorry, but nobody speaks with the minors until guardians get here," Norrs said.

Another rustle sounded at the door, and Laurel partially turned, expecting to see Sherry. Instead, Dr. Abigail Caine stood in the doorway.

Laurel barely kept herself from taking a step back. "Abigail. What are you doing here?"

Her half sister smiled and sauntered over to Special Agent Norrs to lean up and kiss him on the cheek. She slid her arm through his as if she'd done it numerous times before. "Why Laurel, what a nice surprise," she purred.

Chapter 2

Laurel stared at her half sister. "This is unexpected."

Abigail leaned closer to Norrs's side. "If you would meet me for lunch once in a while, I would dish about my love life. But you always seem so busy. I didn't even know you were back in town."

Norrs slipped his arm around Abigail's waist and kissed her head. "I should have probably said something, Agent Snow. I just figured we should stick to business."

"Agreed," Laurel said, yet she couldn't help but study her half sister. Abigail's mahogany-colored hair was arranged up on her head with several tendrils escaping, and her eyes were sparkling. The left one was blue, the right one green, and a heterochromia green star glimmered in the blue eye. Exactly like Laurel's eyes. They could pass for twins, except that Abigail had several inches of height on Laurel. Today she wore a black pencil skirt with a white ruffled blouse and four-inch spiked red heels.

"You had your cast removed. How are you?" Abigail asked.

"I'm well," Laurel said. She'd suffered a distal radial fracture during her last case in Washington State, and she'd finally had the cast removed just a few days previous.

She was supposed to find a physical therapist now that she was back in town, but she'd studied the exercises she'd need to do to fully regain her strength and had already created her own treatment regimen. "It's nice to have the cast off."

"I'm sure it is. We do need to get together to deal with this nuisance lawsuit from Haylee Johnson."

Laurel hadn't had time to worry about it. The young woman had been engaged to Jason Abbott, a serial killer, and had been slightly injured during his capture. "The lawsuit isn't going anywhere. I've hired an attorney who's dealing with it." A good one out of Seattle with no ties to her hometown or her sister.

"Very well. It's close to lunch," Abigail said softly. "Why don't you join us, Laurel?"

Not in a millennium. Laurel's skin chilled. "Thanks, but I'm in the middle of a case." She studied the two. "How long have you been dating?" Could it possibly be coincidence that her half sister had shown up in the middle of another of Laurel's cases? There was no doubt in her mind Abigail had helped engineer the last serial case in town, and she'd participated in Laurel's first Washington State case, too, by covering for the killer, her brother. Of course, there had been no proof on either occasion.

Abigail chuckled. "Oh, when was it? Wayne? It's been months."

Laurel masked her surprise.

Norrs pulled her closer against his side. "Yeah. We met at the fishery banquet. Remember the charity function?"

"Oh yes," Abigail said. "Of course."

Laurel narrowed her gaze. Abigail's memory and IQ were as high as Laurel's, and she knew exactly when she'd met Norrs. In fact, she could probably repeat every word that had been said and describe every person who had been in the vicinity with great detail. "When was the fishery banquet?"

"Oh, I think it was around November . . ." Abigail murmured.

"No, December first," Norrs said.

"Yes, that's it," Abigail said. "It was the beginning of December."

Interesting. That was a mere four days after Laurel and Abigail had met, when Abigail had realized they were half sisters and Laurel still had no clue. Abigail had sought an FBI contact that early on? Laurel considered the last few months. "But Abigail, you've dated several men since then. Remember Officer Zello?" As far as Laurel was concerned, Abigail had used Zello as an alibi for an attack she'd perpetrated on a reporter, but she couldn't prove it.

Norrs shrugged. "That was my fault. I couldn't commit and didn't want to be serious, so I thought we should see other people, until very recently." He looked down at Abigail, his eyes shining. "I was an idiot."

"No, you were fine. I like to go slow," Abigail said, smiling widely.

"I have observed otherwise," Laurel said. There was no doubt in her mind that Abigail was manipulating Norrs, and she was doing a fine job of it. The question was why. Was it just to get closer to Laurel by having another contact in the FBI? Did she need a powerful ally should Laurel finally build a case against her? Laurel was perhaps closer to finding evidence than she'd realized. "What are you up to now, Abigail?"

Abigail feigned surprise so obviously that even Laurel caught it.

Norrs frowned. "You know, your sister told me about some of your suspicions concerning her, and I have to tell you, you're crazy." Abigail patted his arm and he seemed to soften. "I understand you had a difficult childhood and maybe even a tough adulthood, but you really should give her a chance."

This at least explained why Agent Norrs had been congenial with Laurel.

Abigail glanced over at the murder board. "Oh no, Wayne, you didn't tell me you had another bizarre killer out there."

"Yeah, honey, you don't need to look at that." Norrs quickly reached up and pulled down the screens to cover the boards.

She flattened her hand over his flat abdomen. "You are too sweet to me sometimes." Then she winked at Laurel, her face turned away from Norrs. "How about you call your totes adorbs, Huck Rivers, and we all go to dinner tonight after you wrap up whatever case you're on right now? It'd be nice for you to get to know Wayne in a more informal setting, since he's going to be around our family. What do you say?"

Norrs's chest puffed out. "I think that's an excellent idea. Abigail has told me about Captain Rivers, and I'm interested in Fish and Wildlife and all that they do for the state."

Laurel fought the urge to warn the agent off Abigail. He'd learn his lesson soon enough, unfortunately. But there was no time to figure out what her game was right now. Laurel felt helpless that she couldn't go comfort Viv until Kate arrived, especially as they were almost two hours from Genesis Valley, so the wait would be difficult. "I'm sure that Captain Rivers is busy." She claimed the case files. Being caught off guard was rare for her, but she had yet to discover the best way to handle Abigail.

Abigail preened. "The good news is, sweetheart," she nudged Norrs with her hip, "my sister is the best at catching killers. She never fails." Her chin lifted and her eyes glittered. "Do you, Laurel?"

Laurel met her stare directly. "Sometimes it takes time, but no. I never fail, Abigail."

Laurel exited the interrogation room, leaving behind Ryan Salisbury and his older sister June. Ryan seemed like a nice kid who hadn't wanted Viv to confront her father alone. Hours after finding the dead body, he was still pale and shaking. He'd asked more than once if he could see Viv and make sure she was okay.

His sister had been cooperative and bewildered, based on facial expressions and vocal tones. She was twenty-four and had custody of her brother, and both had readily admitted that their father was a criminal in jail. Their mother had died of cancer fifteen years ago, and they'd first lived with an aunt who had recently died. Then June had taken custody of Ryan. She worked as a hostess for a restaurant outside of Genesis Valley.

After interviewing them for over an hour, Laurel felt confident that Ryan had just wanted to help Viv, and that he'd never met Victor Vuittron. She held her case files close to her chest as she walked down the hallway to interrogation room number two, where she opened the door to see Viv and Kate sitting across a metal table—both pale with glassy eyes. Kate had her arm around Viv, whose nose was swollen. Her hair had partially dried to a curly mass down her back.

"Laurel," Kate said, tightening her hold on her daughter. "I can't believe this. Is it true?"

"Yes," Laurel said, walking inside and placing her materials on the table. "Did Agent Norrs interview you, Kate?"

Kate nodded. "Yes. I was in there for a good hour. Bottom line is I don't have an alibi except I was home with the girls last night. I had no idea that Viv was looking for her father and wasn't at school this morning. The problem is that, the only people who want him dead are probably me and Kirsti. Agent Norrs told me that Vic and that idiot had gotten married?"

Laurel took a deep breath. "I haven't spoken with her as of yet, but Kirsti claimed she was Vic's wife when she called in the missing persons report."

Kate gulped and Viv looked away. "I thought Norrs was lying, but apparently not," Kate muttered.

"Jerk," Viv said quietly. "Maybe she already wanted him dead. Also, Dad was running for city council against that guy he hates."

Kate's head lifted. "Oh, yeah, that guy. He's a jerk. Councilman . . . what's his name?"

"Swelter," Viv said, her eyes welling with tears. "I can't get the image of Dad out of my mind."

Laurel sat and took out a pen, although she didn't need to write anything down. With an eidetic memory, she could create a case file later. "All right, Viv. Kate, do we have permission to interview your daughter?"

"Of course," Kate said.

Laurel forced her muscles to relax. "Good. Let's get this over with and move on as best as we can. Viv, why did you skip school today?"

Viv cuddled into her mother. "I went to catch my father in the act. I saw on the tracking device I put in his wallet that he wasn't where he should be."

Kate groaned and put her forehead in her hand. "You didn't?"

Viv winced. "I did. I wanted to know where he was, and I figured he was doing stuff he shouldn't. I thought if I caught him, he'd give you money."

Kate paused and looked at her daughter, dropping her hand. "Give me money? What are you talking about?"

"Come on, Mom. I've seen you trying to find a second job so you'll have enough to raise the three of us. The child support doesn't go that far, and he's not contributing anything else. I just wanted him to help."

Kate sighed. "Honey, we will figure it out. We don't need his help."

Laurel watched the interplay. There was no doubt Kate loved her girls. She was glad she didn't have to interview Kate; it was hard enough questioning Viv. "When did you put the tracking device in his wallet?"

"It was just a luggage tag, and I planted it over Christmas," Viv admitted. "He's such a liar, I figured I'd catch him doing something wrong, and I knew I had to do it pretty soon because the battery on that thing hasn't been charged. But then I found him in that tent." Her eyes widened. "Who killed him, Laurel? Who would shove Valentine candy in his mouth like that? I don't understand."

Laurel shook her head. "I don't understand, either." She pulled out the note. "This is in your handwriting?"

"Yeah," Viv said. "That's my note."

Laurel read. "Dear Dad, you're an asshole, and while I wish you would just disappear, Mom needs help. You're a big shot lawyer now, and I heard that you're running for city council. So I'm sure the last thing you want me to do is to get on social media and tell everybody what a rotten person you are. Start giving Mom the money she deserves, or I'll tell everybody, you jerk."

Kate groaned.

Viv shrugged. "I meant every word."

Laurel sighed. "Okay, so let's run through this. Did you kill your father?"

"No!" Viv gasped. "Kirsti probably caught him with another woman and killed him."

That was entirely possible. "I'll speak with her next," Laurel said. "For now, run me through your entire day, and once you do it, we're going to do it again. All right? Tell me the truth."

"Fine," Viv said. "I have nothing to hide. I didn't kill him." She looked down at the table, appearing young and vulnerable. "I hated him, but I didn't want him dead."

Chapter 3

Case files and paper coffee cups balanced precariously in her hands, Laurel trudged up the stairs to her office. Her space was on the second floor above an ice creamery and coffee shop, and the smell of dark roast followed her. The walls had been decorated years ago with cancan dancers, and she made a mental note to order new wallpaper, now that she'd be here for at least a year. She reached the top and emerged onto a landing where Nester, her computer guru, sat behind a glass pastry display case piled high with manila file folders.

"Hey, Laurel," he said, looking up. "Kate took off like her hair was on fire, so I've been covering the front desk for her. What the heck is going on?"

Laurel shuffled the papers in her arms and handed him a vanilla latte. "Her ex was murdered, and her eldest daughter found the body."

Nester's jaw dropped open. "Seriously?" He was in his midtwenties with dark skin, intelligent brown eyes, and a penchant for winter sports. He'd remotely worked the arson case with her last month, and he'd done an excellent job. "Murdered? By whom?"

"We need to figure that out, and soon," Laurel said,

handing over the case files. "Begin conducting a deep dive on the victim and his entire family, including Kate and the girls. I'll set up a murder board in the conference room in just a minute." She lifted her shoulder sharply to keep her laptop bag from slipping. "What happened to the beauty school?"

Staggers Ice Creamery took up the middle of the first floor with the FBI on the second floor. To the right, both floors were occupied by Fish and Wildlife, and to the left, the two floors had been occupied by a beauty school.

Nester pulled his laptop closer to his body. "They moved out two days ago. I think they rented a newer space over by the mall."

"Good. Let's investigate moving to those floors so we have more room," she said.

"I can look into it," Nester said. "Now that our unit is a go, I received the directory of who to call for what." Now that they'd been granted a probationary year, they could finally acquire appropriate furniture, maybe even more space.

"Thanks." Laurel walked through an opening in the center of the wall, which led to a hallway that bisected the entire unit.

To the right was a conference room and an office. To the left, a computer room, a file room, and the restrooms. At the far end were three offices. One was hers, the next was vacant, and the third was Walter Smudgeon's, who was out on medical leave after being shot during the last case. He was on the mend and had called to say he'd report for duty the following day.

She glanced into the now empty computer room, where dented and mangled snowboards had been mounted on the walls, showing that Nester enjoyed taking risks. Her mind still reeling from her interaction with Abigail, as well as sympathy for Kate and her girls, she moved down to her office and dropped her laptop and the rest of her possessions on her makeshift desk, a weathered door on cinder blocks. It'd be convenient to have a desk with organized drawers. Hopefully Kate could requisition one now that they'd been assigned to the unit for at least a year. Then she removed her wool coat and hung it on a hook nailed into the back of the door.

Calming her mind so she could think, she strode down the hallway to the conference room, which held a gorgeous, high-end glass table held aloft by a copper sculpture of circles. On the other side of the table stood three green glass boards to use for cases.

"Hey Laurel?" Nester called out. "Seattle FBI just sent me all the pictures from the scene. What's up with the Valentine's Day candy?"

"I don't know yet. Could be something about a romance gone wrong," she mused. It was possible that Vuittron was cheating on his new wife as Viv had suggested.

She moved to the farthest board on the right, which was blank, and then slowly turned it over to see the other side, which she always kept hidden. A picture of Abigail was taped in the middle with ties to both the Snowblood Peak Killer case, as well as the more recent Witch Creek murders.

There was no doubt in her mind that Abigail had assisted her half brother, who had turned out to be the Snowblood Killer, with hiding his crimes until Laurel had come onto the scene.

More importantly, Laurel knew that Abigail had purposely triggered the perpetrator of the Witch Creek murders into starting to kill. Though his murders weren't Abigail's fault, she had definitely experimented on his brain and pushed him to indulge his fantasies. Why? Laurel couldn't quite be sure. However, when she drew the connections in her mind, she always came back to one fact. Abigail was attempting to make herself the center of Laurel's life. The idea was both terrifying and infuriating.

Nester popped up behind her and handed over several of the pictures for the new case. "I take it we're still going after your half sister after we help Kate?"

"Without a doubt," Laurel said. She wouldn't rest until Abigail faced justice.

Laurel sat on top of the pristine glass conference table and stared at the case board featuring her half sister. Lines upon lines and connections upon connections led from Abigail to the various crimes in both of the now-solved serial killer cases. Laurel let her subconscious work on the Victor Vuittron case while Nester conducted the background checks and tried to track down Kirsti Vuittron, after confirming that the marriage had, in fact, taken place. Kirsti was not at home and was not answering calls. Her phone went right to voice mail, and according to the FBI techs, had been turned off. In addition, while everyone apparently knew she had a housekeeper, nobody knew that person's name. Nester was also trying to track her down.

Where was Kirsti?

Movement sounded behind Laurel; she knew who'd entered the room before she turned around. A lot could be said about Captain Huck Rivers, and one of those things was that the man had presence.

"You're back," he said, his tone thoughtful.

She looked over her shoulder. "I returned last night but had an early morning class in Seattle." Should she have called him? She wasn't certain. They had started dating after the last case, about six weeks ago—a couple of dinners and a movie. Then they'd spoken or video conferenced at least every other day while she'd been on assignment in DC, and she'd looked forward to speaking with him each time. Now she was uncertain if their relationship required her to contact him once she had returned to town.

He moved closer to the conference table, his gaze on the board. "I was out checking snowmobile registrations and received a call from Jason Abbott's attorney that we can go speak to him."

She glanced at her watch. "It's after five."

"That's okay. His lawyer said we could come tonight if we wanted." Huck shrugged. "The county jail seems lax to allow that, but since you're FBI and I'm Fish and Wildlife, maybe they're just being cooperative."

Laurel stiffened. "I thought he was pleading not guilty."

"He is," Huck said. "For some reason he wants to talk to you."

It didn't surprise her. Jason was most likely a psychopath, and he'd enjoy any cat and mouse interaction they might have. But he was central to her case against Abigail. "Excellent. I'd like to speak with him while he's being held in the Tempest County Jail." Washington State had charged Jason with several homicides, so he'd be tried in the state court. It was possible he'd be held in the nearby county jail throughout his trial, but she wouldn't count on that.

"Me, too," Huck mused, his gaze still on the board.

She stood and faltered. "I should've phoned you last night?"

His smile was quick. "Only if you wanted to talk to me."

"Oh . . . well . . . good." She had been tired and unprepared for the class today, so she hadn't wished to speak with anybody.

The captain looked healthy. He was well over six feet, a strong man, packed hard with muscle. His eyes were brown, his dark hair a little shaggy around his ears, and his shoulders wide. He had rugged features, and as usual, he'd let the scruff on his face go beyond a couple of days since shaving.

She looked around his feet. "Where's your dog?"

"He's back in the office with Monty," Huck said. "They won't let him in the jail cell, so I figured he should stay at the office." Huck was a captain with the Washington State Fish and Wildlife office, a fully commissioned officer. He was also the head of the Karelian Bear Dog Program, but right now there weren't any bears to chase away from homes. "I'll drive." He pulled his keys out of his jeans pocket.

"I know," Laurel murmured, walking around the table. It had been a long day, and her body was fatigued. But she wouldn't refuse a chance to speak with Jason Abbott and build a case against Abigail.

Huck paused in the doorway. "Does it bother you that I want to drive?"

She blinked. "Why would that bother me?"

He studied her face for a moment and his grin was slower this time, but fuller. "It shouldn't bother you. Sorry I asked."

"It's okay to ask," she said, pausing as her ears rang. She hadn't eaten all day, and it was important to feed her brain. She understood Huck to a degree that gave her some comfort. He liked to be in control, something to consider when entertaining the thought of having a relationship with him. However, empirically speaking, his reflexes were about eight-tenths of a second quicker than hers, from what she'd observed. Considering the roads were icy and another winter storm was roaring into their small town of Genesis Valley, it made sense for him to drive.

Huck stepped back and let her precede him down the

hallway. They reached the main landing, where Nester looked up from scribbling on a piece of paper. "Hey, the deputy director called and left a garbled message on the machine while I was downstairs fetching a much-needed bagel for dinner. He said something about still looking for new agents for the unit. Didn't sound good."

"Darn it," Laurel mused. "We need at least two agents. Did he say anything else?"

Nester shook his head. "I could barely make out what he was talking about. There were horns blaring in the background, and I think he was chewing ice. I don't know." He looked down at his notepad. "Then he wanted me to ask you how many people you'd met in the last week with genuine green eyes."

"Okay, thanks," Laurel said, heading for the door.

"Well? How many?" Nester called out.

Laurel made her way gingerly down the stairs because somebody had left chunks of ice on each tread. "One hundred and twenty with true green eyes. Ten with colored contacts," she called back. "Go home, Nester. Tuesday will come soon enough."

"Don't you have a pair of boots here at the office?" Huck asked from behind her.

"No, but I need to acquire a pair," Laurel agreed, continuing to step carefully in her heels. She crossed the vestibule and pushed outside while pulling on her wool coat. It was mid-March, and while it had been raining near Seattle, the snow in Genesis Valley hadn't let up any, which was normal for the mountains this time of year. A warm spring was forecast, but so far she was finding it difficult to believe. The wind pierced her skin, and she hurriedly buttoned up her coat. "I need to get a scarf," she murmured.

"Your gloves are sticking out of your pocket." Huck pressed the fob for his truck, and it beeped.

She pulled her gloves out and slipped them on. "Thanks."

"No problem." He reached the passenger door before she did and opened it. She faltered as always, caught off guard by the brusque man's gentlemanly moves. She had a feeling even if they hadn't decided to date, he would still open the door for her, agent or not. He'd asked her once if the courtesy bothered her, and she still didn't understand why it should bother her. Why would it bother anybody? It was intriguing that Agent Norrs had asked the same.

She stepped up into the cab and sat, grateful to be out of the wind.

They were well underway toward the county jail when Huck looked over at her. "I thought tonight I could make you dinner. A very late dinner."

"Dinner sounds lovely," she said. Did that mean it was a date? Did that mean he would like for her to stay the night, or did he want to talk about the case? She bit her lip.

He sped up to pass a logging truck. "I would like for you to stay all night until breakfast, at which point I'll take you to work."

"I would like that as well." She couldn't help but smile. "Thank you for explaining."

"Absolutely," he said. "I'm getting good at this communication thing."

In fact, he was.

Chapter 4

The early evening wind ruffled Laurel's hair and she pushed strands out of her face as she approached the county jail.

Genesis Valley police officer Frank Zello exited the building abruptly, nearly running them over. He skidded to a stop, his uniform pressed, his mustache as full as ever, and his eyes alert. "Whoa. Sorry."

Laurel paused. "Officer Zello? What are you doing here?"

The officer stepped aside. "I escorted a prisoner here for detainment." His tone was level, but a note of uneasiness lay beneath the surface.

"Demoted?" Huck asked, reaching for the door to hold it open.

"Yep," Zello muttered.

Laurel faltered. As a patrol officer, Zello had appeared proficient at his job. Yet he'd made irresponsible miscalculations in failing to report a sexual relationship with a victim of their last case as well as one with Abigail, when she'd been either a potential victim or a suspect. Even so, it was surprising the local sheriff had demoted Zello. Sheriff York was notoriously incompetent. "I'd heard you were on leave." Kate's penchant for gossip was coming in handy.

He nodded. "I took two weeks off to deal . . . with everything. Then I had a death in the family." He cleared his throat, looking as if he'd aged in the last month. He had to be midthirties at the most. "I was hoping to speak with your sister, but she's not answering my calls."

When Abigail was finished using people, she moved on.

Laurel wanted to be sympathetic. "Have you remembered anything more about the night Rachel Raprenzi was attacked?" She knew Abigail had drugged him and then gone out to attack the reporter, who was harassing Laurel, but Zello had stuck to his story that they'd had a nice dinner, drank an abundance of wine, had terrific sex, and then fell asleep together.

"No," Zello said, his jaw firming. "Your sister is not capable of violence. Why won't you see that?" His gaze softened. "I know you're not close, but she really needs you. I promise she didn't attack anybody."

Yes, she had. There was no question in Laurel's mind.

"Now, would you please let her know that I need to see her?" he asked.

There was no way to help the unfortunate man. Maybe he'd find somebody else and forget her manipulative half sister. "You need to move on. It's nice to see you again, Officer Zello," she said. If nothing else, she could fall back on good manners.

"Thanks." Zello released the door, and Laurel and Huck walked inside, checked in, and followed an officer to a room with a guard on duty. The guard opened the heavy, blue metal door for them, and she entered with Huck right behind her.

Jason Abbott didn't look any the worse for wear after having spent the last six weeks in prison. His hair was cut short, and his dark blue eyes still shone with intelligence. If anything, the beard he'd let grow a little longer made him look more studious. For some reason, the orange jumpsuit suited him as if it had been made just for him.

Laurel chose the chair directly across from Jason, knowing that Huck would try to get there first. Huck sat next to her, his arms crossed, his expression stone-cold. He angled his body in such a way that he could lunge across the table at Jason without needing to shift position.

Jason's lawyer sat beside him. She was a small blonde with bright blue eyes, wearing a threadbare beige-colored suit. She placed a phone on the table and pressed record. "I'm Amy Lotsom with the public defender's office. I'd like it on the record that my client is not confessing to anything and is, in fact, still professing his innocence in the Witch Creek murders."

"Then why are we here?" Huck asked, sounding bored but looking dangerous.

"We're here because I wanted to talk to you, Laurel," Jason said softly, his lips curving in what most people probably considered a charming smile.

Even though Laurel had spent hours upon hours studying facial expressions and nuances in order to read people better, she failed to see the charm. All she saw were facial movements and teeth. Jason had nice teeth, but she directed her statement to the lawyer.

"You've asked us here because you're probably contemplating a not guilty by reason of insanity plea, and you hope that I can help because I've been investigating Dr. Abigail Caine."

A glimmer entered Jason's eyes, but she couldn't decipher it.

He lifted his sculpted chin. "If it can be shown that Dr. Caine manipulated her subjects and used drugs in such a manner that they may have committed crimes they wouldn't normally have committed, then that might be a valid defense for the jury." He reached out and placed his hand over Laurel's. "Especially a jury of women."

Huck stiffened, but before he could move, Laurel turned her wrist, captured two of Jason's fingers, and shoved them back until one popped.

He yelped and pulled his hand away.

"You shouldn't touch people without an invitation, Jason," she said calmly. "It's a good way to get your hand broken. We might both want to see Dr. Caine brought to justice, but I'll never forget that you brutally murdered several women before cutting off their hands." Those women deserved justice, and Laurel would make sure they received it. While she wanted to put her sister away, she wouldn't let this killer go free to do it. However, she might be able to find a way to succeed in both endeavors. Jason Abbott wasn't as smart as he thought.

He stretched his fingers and one popped again. Oh, she hadn't really hurt him, but she could have. She watched him, waiting to see how the killer in him would react. His jaw hardened and his nostrils flared. He was a narcissistic, type two psychopath, and he wouldn't like being bested by a woman, any woman.

So now she smiled, forcing her facial muscles to comply. "You know, it must bother you that someone like Dr. Caine, a successful, intelligent woman, so easily bested you. She got into your mind enough that you killed other successful women." Laurel shook her head. "You basically just did her bidding."

Huck's chuckle was low and derisive. "You were just her bitch, weren't you, Jason?"

Jason shoved himself away from the table. "You stop it or I won't help you."

"You want us to help you?" Laurel asked, leaning toward him. "I am more than happy to investigate Abigail, and you could get all the payback you want."

His breathing quickened as his chest rose and fell. "Oh, I want revenge," he said. Red stained his cheekbones, and his hands clenched into fists, even though he was shackled to a bar on the table.

The lawyer patted his arm in an obvious attempt to soothe him, her nails short and pink against his bare skin. "Jason, you need to calm down," she said almost gently.

He seemed to relax, but his expression remained hard as he flattened his hands on the worn table. "What do you want to know?"

"Tell me everything from the first moment you met Abigail until you were arrested," Laurel said.

Jason tapped his fingers on the table. "I answered an advertisement to be a case subject in a study at the university. Something about neurobiology, how the brain works, and how to control my impulses. I showed up because the pay was good, and I needed cash."

"But then?" Huck asked.

"Then I filled out a bunch of questionnaires about how I felt about life, my parents, my childhood, my everything, just everything," he said. "After that I met with Dr. Caine, and we started a regimen exploring how I'd react in certain cases. Like if somebody made me angry, how I would react versus how I *wanted to* react. Then she would give me what she said was a vitamin B shot."

Laurel leaned forward. "Tell me about the injections. How'd they make you feel?"

Jason looked away as if trying to remember. "I guess, relaxed. And at the same time, more focused, as if I could get past any questions or inhibitions and really focus on what I wanted and what I needed. Then we'd watch different movies, a lot of action movies, some serial killer movies. Afterward, we'd talk about how I felt, what I thought, and how I could do it better."

Laurel thought back to her investigation of Abigail's office. After conducting a search pursuant to a valid warrant, she had found nothing like the materials Jason described. Knowing the narcissism inherent in Abigail, the woman would not have been able to destroy her own research. So Laurel just had to find it. "After you started killing, did you tell her about it?"

The lawyer grabbed Jason's arm. "Do not answer that question."

Laurel swallowed. Her stomach had been off all day, and the smell in the room wasn't helping. Sweat and orange cleanser. "Let me ask it this way. After the first woman was brutally killed, did you speak to or meet with Abigail Caine?"

Jason flashed a smile. "What date was the first killing?"

Laurel didn't have time for games. "You know the dates of all the killings. Answer the question."

Jason looked at his lawyer and winked. She released his arm. "I remember reading about the murders in the paper, and I was so sad for those poor women. I did not speak with Dr. Caine after that first murder, although I surely plan to meet her again someday."

Laurel's money was on Abigail in that situation. She continued questioning Jason, and Huck did the same, but no additional information was forthcoming.

Finally, they concluded the interview and left the room. Laurel started to walk toward the exit.

"Just a sec," Huck said.

"All right," Laurel said, pausing.

The attorney soon walked outside. "Can I help you?" Her gaze was hard on Huck.

Huck faced her. "I just wanted a quick word with you. He's charming, and he's smart. You're making a mistake."

The woman reared back. "I have no idea what you're talking about."

"Yeah, you do," Huck said. "I've given you a warning. You should take it." With that, he turned toward the door.

Laurel walked with him, wondering what she'd missed. While she admired Huck's gut instincts and the way he seemed to know things that other people missed, she still couldn't see what he'd noticed as she replayed the entire interview in her mind. "What did you discern?"

His phone buzzed and he lifted it to his ear. "Rivers." He listened as they walked out into the snowy night. "How many hours? Okay. I'll grab Aeneas and meet you at the base. I'll lead the search on the northern trail." He clicked off. "Two lost hikers up on Snowblood Mountain, and there's another blizzard headed that way." They reached the vehicle, and he unlocked the passenger side door. "Chances are I'll need a raincheck on that late dinner."

Chapter 5

Tuesday morning, Kirsti Vuittron finally surfaced and agreed to meet with Laurel just after nine. She and Vic lived on the southern side of Genesis Valley near Potterton Mountain, and Laurel pulled into their driveway around nine thirty. The house was a two-story with light beige siding and white window frames with dark blue shutters. The interior of the home was spacious and undoubtedly remodeled within the last year or so.

It was much nicer than the home Kate and the girls were currently occupying.

Laurel sat on what appeared to be a new white leather sofa as Kirsti brought over an antique tea set to pour two cups.

She sat across from Laurel in a matching white chair and crossed her legs. Her hands shook as she poured the tea and the cup clattered against the saucer as she handed it across the modern, low wooden coffee table.

"Thank you," Laurel said, accepting the tea. The smell of hibiscus wafted up and she took a sip. It was nowhere near as good as one of her mom's teas. "I'm sorry to bother you at a time like this. I understand you're recently married?" She cataloged the interior of the home to draw out later and think about.

Kirsti sat back, leaving her tea on the table. "Yes, I'm the new Mrs. Vuittron. We went to Vegas a few weeks ago and made it official." She held out her left hand to show a cluster of diamonds.

Those diamonds could pay for several teams worth of band and volleyball uniforms. "All right, Mrs. Vuittron."

"Call me Kirsti." She appeared to be in her early twenties with thick black hair to her shoulders. Her eyes were light blue and her bone structure Nordic. "I just can't believe that he's dead."

"I'm very sorry for your loss." Laurel took another sip and then placed the cup and saucer on the table. "We had difficulty locating you. Where have you been?"

Kirsti sniffed. "I freaked out when they notified me that Victor was dead and just didn't want to talk to or see anybody. I was here but didn't answer my phone or the door."

That was possible but unprovable. "I noted that you called in a missing persons report, but you waited until yesterday morning?"

"Yes," Kirsti said, her hands fluttering in her lap. She wore dark jeans and a burnt-orange sweater. Her hair was up; no makeup hid the ravages of a rough night. "I just kind of fell apart when he didn't come home all night. I thought—"

"What?" Laurel asked.

Kirsti's gaze hardened. "I know who you are. That you work with that hag, Kate."

Laurel's eyebrows rose. "Hag?" An unusual rush of emotion swept through her. This bratty woman who'd helped to split up a family was calling Kate a derogatory name? She was Laurel's friend, and it took a shocking amount of self-control to refrain from striking out. "Kate Vuittron works for my office and does an admirable job.

Why didn't you call in a missing persons report Sunday night when your new husband failed to return home?"

Kirsti sniffed. "I thought he was cheating on me, okay? You know that old saying—if they'll do it with you, they'll do it to you."

Laurel hadn't heard that expression, but it seemed apt. "Did Victor often stay out all night?"

"Lately a few times, but he said he was just working late at the law firm. You know, since he's the newest lawyer there and he wanted to impress his friend and boss."

"His friend?"

"Yes. Frederick Marshall is, I mean was, Vic's friend as well as boss. He's a named partner at Marshall & Cutting, obviously." She reached for her tea and took a sip. "Victor had to make a lot of money to pay child support for those kids he didn't even know very well."

Laurel considered the interview with Viv. "Victor wasn't close to his children?"

Kirsti's eyes flared. "Kate turned them against him. He wanted to know them, but they were all so mad that he left her. He didn't love her. What was he supposed to do?" She shook her head and tears dropped from her eyes. "Some people shouldn't have kids."

That was harsh. "Why did you finally call the authorities?"

She held a hand to her chest. "Our housekeeper comes in to clean every morning and then returns to bring dinner every evening. When she got here, I was sobbing, and she thought we should call. So we did."

Laurel sat back, trying to appear casual. Most FBI agents would be taking notes, but she would type everything later. She found that interviewees responded better if she didn't obviously write down what they said. They were freer with their answers and appeared to be more relaxed. "So you called in a missing persons right away?"

"No. First I called his law firm and spoke with Melissa Cutting, who is the other named partner at the firm. She said she hadn't heard from him."

"Okay," Laurel said. "The police report states that there was no sign of a struggle in your home."

"No. There was no sign whatsoever." Kirsti threw up her hands and then looked around. "Everything's just as it should be, even his car, which you are more than welcome to check."

Laurel already had Nester working on obtaining a search warrant, but the woman's offer would make things easier. "I appreciate that. We have a good crime lab with the FBI in Seattle, and I'll have them pick up the car later if that's okay with you."

"That's fine," Kirsti said, sniffing. "In fact, they're free to search the home and our small backyard if they want. I already looked around, and there's nothing out of place. I just . . ." She held her hand to her forehead. Tears gathered in her eyes.

Laurel let Kirsti compose herself. "I'm sorry I have to put you through this right now."

"No, it's okay," Kirsti said. "I really want to know what happened to him. Either Kate or one of those bratty kids killed him. Nothing else makes sense."

"I think we should look at his entire life, including his work as a lawyer." Laurel again fought the urge to defend Kate. "Did Victor have Valentine's Day candy around the house? The heart-shaped kind with all the sayings on it?"

"No." Kirsti wrinkled her nose. "Don't be silly. He gave me a diamond bracelet for Valentine's Day."

Of course he did. "Did Victor have any enemies?"

"No." Kirsti pressed her palm against her left eye and pushed in hard enough to create a white ring around the side of her face. "Just Kate and those kids. Well, and Councilman Swelter, I guess. They knew each other from childhood, and they really didn't like each other."

"Why not?"

She shrugged. "No clue. Victor mentioned that he had some sort of juicy dirt on Swelter that he was going to use in the campaign, but he didn't say what. You should ask Melissa Cutting—she was friends with Victor for years."

Interesting. Was there something odd in Kirsti's voice? "Is Ms. Cutting married?" Laurel asked.

"Her husband died years ago." Kirsti looked down at her lap. "I suppose she was a good friend to Victor."

That was something Laurel would have to follow up on. "Not to you?"

"No. We never really mixed, if you know what I mean."

Laurel had no idea what that meant. "Could you elaborate?"

"We're just different people." Kirsti reached for her tea and took a deep gulp. "It's hard to explain. I work hard but like to have fun, and Melissa is just a frigid bitch."

Laurel blinked. "Was there more than a professional relationship between Melissa and Victor?" She didn't like asking the question, but it was necessary.

"Who knows?" Kirsti took another drink. "She's such a cold fish, it's hard to imagine."

"Kirsti? Do you have a current copy of Victor's will and any life insurance information?" Kate hadn't had any of the documents.

Kirsti again shook her head. "I don't know any of that but assume he left me everything. His will is probably at the firm." She picked at lint on a sofa pillow. "I'm tired and need to rest now."

Laurel wasn't finished. "I'm surprised your house-keeper isn't here."

"I know," Kirsti said, looking at the clock. "She requested the day off because of everything, but I asked her to drop by this morning to give a statement to you. I don't know where she is. She's usually much more responsible than this."

As if on cue, a rap echoed on the door and then it opened. "Hello. Sorry I'm late," a woman called out.

Laurel turned to watch an eighty-something-year-old woman hitch slowly up the stairs before removing the plastic covering from her spiraling gray hair.

"I'm so sorry I'm late. I slept in. I can't believe I slept in. I was up all night worrying about Victor, and then, I don't know, I fell asleep. Hi, I'm Mrs. Mosby." She walked toward Laurel and held out a hand.

Laurel shook her hand and then moved over on the sofa.

"Oh, thank you," Mrs. Mosby said, dropping down as water cascaded off her Wellingtons to dampen the white fluffy rug protecting the wooden floor. Kirsti didn't seem to notice. "I can't believe somebody killed Victor. Who would do something like that?"

"I don't know, ma'am, but I will find out." Laurel studied the housekeeper. The woman might be closer to ninety than eighty and had to weigh about a hundred pounds, if that. She had rough, gnarled hands that looked as if she had worked hard her entire life.

"I just knew something was wrong," Mrs. Mosby said. She wore a bright green raincoat over pink slacks. Faded green eyes shone in her weathered face, which was also brightened by glossy orange lipstick. "When he wasn't here, I just knew it."

Kirsti gave a small sound of distress. "You were right. I wish you weren't, but you were."

Mrs. Mosby nodded. "I am so sorry. You have to find who did this to him."

"I'll do my best," Laurel promised. "Can you think of any enemies he might have?"

"I can't think of enemies, but I sure didn't like that barracuda he worked with," Mrs. Mosby said.

Kirsti giggled. "Florence, you sure know how to read people, don't you."

Mrs. Mosby leaned toward Laurel. "You need to talk to that trollop."

That was a word Laurel hadn't heard in a very long time. "I will. Now let's go through the events of Sunday again, and you take me through the entire day. All right?"

"I'd be happy to," Mrs. Mosby said, reaching out and lifting Laurel's cup of tea. "You don't need this, do you?"

"No. Go ahead," Laurel said. "Start at the beginning."

Mrs. Mosby went through her activities on Sunday, once and then again, rapidly answering all of Laurel's questions. Finally, Laurel wrapped up the interview without gleaning any additional relevant information, and the older woman walked her out into the chilly March day.

"At least it has stopped snowing for a short time. I'd move to the city, but it just rains there," Mrs. Mosby said, pulling the plastic cover over her curly hair again. "Your eyes are something spectacular. Are those real or are you wearing Halloween contacts in March? That'd be weird."

"They're authentic." Laurel looked around the snowy front yard, not seeing any signs of a struggle. "They're heterochromatic, meaning two different colors, and I have another heterochromatic burst in one eye. It's rare."

"It's very pretty." Mrs. Mosby began ambling toward an older Chevy Cavalier next to Laurel's SUV in the drive. "I found them one time, you know."

Laurel walked briskly along the icy sidewalk, wearing boots today. "Found who?"

"Victor and Melissa, that barracuda tramp. They were all ruffled, coming out of the bedroom." She sighed and turned to look back at the house. "I never said nothing, because why? Kirsti wasn't exactly a nun."

Laurel reached around the older woman to open the driver's side door for her. "You believe Victor and Melissa Cutting were having an affair?"

Mrs. Mosby shrugged.

Laurel helped the housekeeper into the vehicle. "What about Kirsti?"

Mrs. Mosby's wrinkled jaw firmed. "What's good for the goose, if you know what I mean."

"I don't."

"She likes to work out a lot with her trainer." Mrs. Mosby reached for her door. "That's all I'm saying."

Laurel stepped back so she could shut the door and watched the woman drive slowly away. When she turned back to the house, a figure stood in the living room window. Kirsti Vuittron. Without waving, the homewrecker slid out of sight.

Chapter 6

Laurel walked up the stairs to the second floor of Seattle City Hall and turned right to enter the councilmembers' offices. A young female receptionist with several face piercings sat behind a wide desk. "Can I help you?"

"Yes. I would like to see Eric Swelter," Laurel said.

The woman craned her neck. "He's in there right now, but I think he's headed out to a meeting."

"That's all right," Laurel said, moving swiftly beyond the reception desk toward the office. "Excuse me, Councilman Swelter."

A man looked up from his desk and smiled. He stood. "Yes, I'm Eric Swelter. Can I help you?"

"I think so." She took his measure. He was about six feet tall, perfectly groomed, hair parted on the side, white-capped teeth, and strong bone structure, wearing a slick gray suit with a darker tie in the same hue. He appeared to be in his early fifties. "I'm wondering if you could tell me about your relationship with Victor Vuittron."

Swelter's eyebrows lifted as he remained standing. "I didn't know the guy very well. We played football against each other in high school, attended a camp or two at the same time, but we never really knew each other. He challenged me for city council, and he was going to lose. I heard he died Sunday night."

"Yes. What else did you hear?"

"That's about it," Swelter said, walking over to a tree stand to fetch a heavy overcoat. "I'm sorry, but I have to be going. Who are you, anyway?"

Laurel took her badge from her back pocket and flipped open the flap. "Special Agent Laurel Snow. I'm investigating Mr. Vuittron's death."

"It's nice to meet you, Agent Snow." This close, the councilman smelled like expensive cologne. He'd apparently bathed in it. "I'm sorry I can't help you more, but I really don't know much about Mr. Vuittron other than he filed the paperwork and had started fundraising for his campaign."

She tilted her head to the side. "It's my understanding that Mr. Vuittron said he had, and I quote, 'dirt on you'."

Swelter threw back his head and laughed. "If I had a nickel for every time somebody said they had dirt on me, I'd be a very wealthy man, Agent Snow." He glanced at his watch, which appeared to be a Rolex. "All I can tell you is I didn't have anything to do with Victor's death."

"Where were you Sunday night?"

"Now that's really none of your business, is it?" Swelter asked, still smiling. He moved toward the door.

"Is there any reason you won't tell me?" she called out.

He looked over his shoulder. "I'm not a big fan of the police. In fact, many of us in this building aren't. You might want to take note of that fact."

She held her ground. "We all work for the same system, don't you think?"

"No. I'm happy to defund all of you," Swelter said. "For now, if you want to talk to me, call my lawyer." With that, he turned and walked away.

Interesting. She might have to do just that.

* * *

Around midnight, after nearly a twenty-four hour search on a freezing mountain, Huck said good-bye to the last of the volunteers and kicked back at a Formica-topped table with his shoulders against the far wall, finishing a piece of pizza. Old Lou's had always been where officers hung out after a rescue like the one he'd just been a part of, and this time, the entire crew had headed down for pizza. Lou made the best pizza in Genesis Valley, and he usually gave the team a steep discount.

Plus, the ambiance wasn't bad. A fire roared to the right in a heavy stone fireplace. At this time of night, most of the booths and tables had cleared out.

He checked his phone again to find an update from the local hospital about the two hikers. They were both doing well and were expected to make a full recovery. He glanced down at his dog sleeping peacefully at his feet. Yet another reason he liked Old Lou's. Lou let the dog stay.

"Night," Monty said, zipping up his parka and standing next to the table. He'd directed the teams from head-quarters since he was still recuperating from radiation treatments for cancer. "You did a good job on lead."

"Thanks." Huck took a drink of his beer. The search had taken so long he was seeing double. "It's late. You should head home and stay there tomorrow. I've got the office."

Monty pulled gloves free of his pocket. "I might just do that." His hair was a mix of gray and white, still thick despite the cancer treatments. He was in his late fifties and usually ran the office, even though he and Huck were both captains. Huck wasn't a fan of most people. "Think we should charge them?"

Huck shrugged. "We have enough statements from their friends that they ignored the posted signs and went off trail on purpose. They should either pay the state back for the cost of the rescue or at least get a fine." He had no problem putting his life on the line for lost hikers, even those who got lost on purpose, but they did owe the state for the time and resources. "It's up to you and the prosecutor."

"I'll think about it." Monty turned and loped out of the restaurant, letting snow blow inside as he went.

Huck stretched his neck, noting his calves cramping. He'd had to slog through thick snow on the mountain to find the young adults, and he'd had to use the litter to carry one of the men out. The kid probably had a broken ankle but would be all right.

The outside door opened but he didn't look up. It was well after midnight, and he should probably get home.

"Well, Captain Rivers, how nice to see you."

He lifted his head, keeping his expression blank. "Dr. Caine, it's rather late for you to be out, isn't it?"

She pulled out a chair to sit without being invited. The cold air had turned her cheeks rosy, and snow dotted her dark red hair. While she and Laurel had the same characteristics, in fact the exact same coloring, there was no way anybody could mistake them for each other. At least there was no way he could. Tonight Abigail wore a puffy white coat with a fur-lined hood. Diamonds twinkled at her ears and from a gold necklace with a large round diamond at her throat. "It is late, isn't it?" she crooned.

"Why are you in Genesis Valley at this time of night?"

She smiled and her heterochromatic eyes sparkled. "I had a late meeting in town and thought I'd drop by. I heard on the news that there were two lost hikers. I do hope you found them."

Yeah. Like she cared about lost hikers. "We did and they're expected to make a full recovery." He cocked his head, wondering if she was following him. There was no way to ask that. So he didn't. "I was just getting ready to leave," he finally said.

"That's too bad." She reached out and ran her nails over his knuckles. "I thought you and I could become friends, and we could start by you calling me Abigail."

He doubted very seriously the woman knew the definition of the word "friends." "That's nice of you, but I have enough friends."

She blinked once, masking whatever she was feeling, although it had to be surprise. It was doubtful many men turned down the beautiful woman, but he'd known danger in his life, and he'd known true predators. She had the instincts of a rabid fox. "Call me an infracaninophile, but I'm hoping you and Laurel make a go of it. You're a good match," she said.

"Why do you do that?" he drawled.

Her eyes widened. "Do what?"

"Use words other people don't know." Did she expect him to pretend he knew what infracaninophile meant? He probably couldn't even spell it. Or did she want him to feel stupid? "I have no problem with your vocabulary being more expansive than mine." Like most predators, she didn't look away. "I don't care what you think or feel, *Dr.* Caine. Not at all."

"I apologize," she said smoothly. "I just meant that I root for the underdog, which would be you."

His body was tired and his limbs heavy. The last thing he had time for was games with a psychopath. "Like I said, I don't care."

"But you should." Her fingers were cold on his knuckles. "Laurel has taken another case, this one with a murderer strong or smart enough to heft a grown man into a tent in the middle of nowhere. It's not a Washington State case, which means you won't be there to cover her back. To protect her." Abigail lightly scratched her red nails across his hand. "She's alone on this. You won't be able to handle that."

Everything inside him wanted to yank his hand free, but he wouldn't give her that satisfaction. "Special Agent Snow is more than capable of protecting herself." In fact, she'd saved his life once by jumping out of a crashed truck and firing at a killer.

"Ah, well." Abigail's dimple twinkled in her left cheek. Beauty could be deadly. "Logically, that makes sense, right?" She patted him, glee curving her lips. "But you're not a logical man. No. You're an alpha male—a throwback. She's your *woman*." She leaned in, bringing the scent of dark spice with her. "If she's harmed, you fail. Much as you did with that boy who drowned a few years back."

It was a direct hit, and he took it to the gut. But his expression didn't change, and his body didn't move. He had lost a kid during a case, and that pain had sent him into the woods with his dog to live as a recluse for far too long. Laurel Snow had brought him back into the world. The idea that she was in danger spurred something dark inside him, as Abigail no doubt intended. "You've overstayed your welcome tonight."

She pulled her hand back. "That is not kind. Considering you're dating my sister, don't you think we should at least try to get along?"

"We get along fine," he said. "I don't think we need to go any further than that."

She tilted her head very slightly and studied him. He met her gaze levelly.

"I don't understand your animosity," she said, keeping her voice light.

"I think you do." It was enough. He didn't need to say anything more. They both understood who she really was beneath the beautiful facade. Laurel knew what she'd done, and Laurel was smart enough to catch her half sister and put her away.

Abigail widened her eyes in a look that probably would've fooled most people. "I truly have no idea what you're talking about. Obviously this has something to do with the search warrant that was unjustly executed on my office several weeks ago. Laurel has all of my research. She knows I didn't do anything to harm Jason Abbott."

The hell she didn't. There wasn't a doubt in Huck's mind that Abigail had engineered the entire situation. Oh, Abbott was a killer and probably would've found his way down that path anyway, but there was no way to know for sure. What he did know was that Abigail had shoved Abbott right into killing.

"I really must be going." He nudged the dog to wake him up.

Abigail sighed. "I wish things could be different."

"Is that what you wish?" Huck knew he was poking the spider.

She drew back. "Of course it is."

"Hmm. I don't know," he murmured.

When he'd first met her, she was a blonde with blue eyes. Apparently she'd worn different wigs and eye colors through most of her life. Part of her desire to disguise herself wasn't her fault—her father had forced her to hide her true colors when she was younger, and yet part of it was most definitely by choice. "I find it interesting that once you met Laurel, you decided to go natural."

She leaned back. "Why wouldn't I? When I saw how beautiful my sister looked, I realized that I'd been wrong all these years to hide my true self. That wasn't my fault, you know."

"Maybe," he allowed. Most of it was her father's fault, and yet she had made plenty of bad decisions as an adult.

"Besides," she purred. "Don't you like the way I truly appear? There are two of us."

Huck glanced down at his sleeping dog and then back up. The animal had never liked Abigail. Was Aeneas pretending to be asleep? "That's just it," he murmured. "There aren't two of you. There's you and there's Laurel."

"Excuse me?" she muttered, her voice haughty now.

"You'll never get what you want," he said softly. "You can be anybody, and you have tried several identities already. You've been a blonde. You've been an adventurer. You've been an eccentric scientist. You've been a brunette. You've traveled the world and you've been whomever you wanted to be, but you know what?"

Sparks flashed in her dual-colored eyes. "What?"

"You can't be Laurel Snow."

She inhaled, lifting her chest and flaring her nostrils. "I know that."

"Do you? I don't think so. You're incapable of loving people the way she does. Her feelings are real . . . yours are just a mirroring of the people around you. No matter how hard you try to get to know her, to be in her world, you will never truly belong. You're lacking, and I think that you might actually feel *enough* to acknowledge that dark hole inside you. To at least realize it exists. But nobody can fill it, not even Laurel."

Abigail's eyes flared and she slapped a hand on the table. "I wouldn't if I were you."

"Too late. Already did," he said, striking back hard and fast, the only way he knew how. "You can't be her and you know it. So why don't you just leave her alone?"

Abigail stood then, a dark flush covering her patrician cheekbones. "Someday she'll have to choose one of us, Captain Rivers. I guarantee it won't be you."

Chapter 7

Early Wednesday morning, after a night of tumultuous dreams in which Laurel found herself chasing Abigail with a lime-green, fluorescent bow and arrow set decorated with tiny red hearts, she knocked on Kate Vuittron's door. While she fully understood the ability of the subconscious mind to work through issues, she didn't appreciate that all of her problems seemed to be narrowing in on one figure, Abigail Caine.

Kate's door opened. "Morning," she said, dressed for the day in dark gray leggings and an oversized white T-shirt. Her blond hair was up on top of her head, her eyes were red and her face pale. "Come in, Laurel. What are you doing here at this hour?"

Laurel stepped inside. Kate had rented the small cottage in Genesis Valley upon moving here last year and the place was both warm and welcoming, as well as strewn with her teenaged daughters' belongings. There was a violin case and a volleyball in one corner and several pairs of shoes scattered over by the fireplace ledge in the living room, which led to an open kitchen.

The place wasn't nearly as high-end or sterile as Kirsti and Vic's home.

"Here. I brought you cookies," Laurel said, awkwardly

handing Kate the foil-wrapped dish. "As well as some of my mom's new spring solstice tea." She transferred the glass jar. "It won't go out to the tea club until next month, but it has some good organic, natural pomegranate extract and matcha that's supposed to help boost energy and mood."

Kate took the gifts, and a small smile lifted her lips. "This is very kind of you. You didn't have to bake me cookies."

"I believe it's the proper protocol when somebody is in mourning." Laurel appreciated the warmth in the house because it was still snowing outside. "My mother bakes much better cookies than I do, but I followed the recipe to the exact amount, so they should be good."

"I'm sure they're wonderful." Kate reached over for an impulsive hug. "The girls are all sleeping. I'm letting them stay home from school this week." She paused. "Oh, I didn't even ask if I could have the week off."

"Of course you can have the week off." Laurel followed Kate into the kitchen, where she deposited the cookies and the jar of tea. "You can take as much time as you need. I'm sorry about Victor's death."

"Yeah," Kate said, rubbing a hand over her eyes. "It's so bizarre. We were married and had three wonderful kids, but he was such a jackass. As you know, he was older than me, and then I became too old for him, which is nuts. I'm really confused about my feelings. I am sorry he is dead. More sorry for the girls than anything else. They won't have their dad to someday walk them down the aisle."

"I'm so sorry, Kate," Laurel said.

Kate turned to the coffeepot and poured two cups, adding just a little bit of creamer to both. She handed one to Laurel. It was nice that Kate knew how Laurel preferred her coffee.

"Thank you," she said, taking a deep drink.

"You're pale. Are you all right?" Kate asked.

The warmth of the coffee splashed into her stomach. "I am. The team in DC had the flu, and I had a touch of it. I still haven't gotten enough sleep since arriving home to beat it completely."

"I know. You had to dive right back into another case. I hope you get some rest, though. Sometimes it's hard to find a balance." Kate looked at her wide-open kitchen with its cheery yellow walls and white cupboards. "I don't know when the funeral's going to be because I don't know when the coroner will release the body."

"I don't know that either," Laurel said. "And I can't discuss the case with you. For me to be able to work it at all, we have to keep some sort of separation between us. If you have anything you want to report, call Special Agent in Charge Norrs. He seems like a decent human being, although he's dating Abigail."

Kate's eyes widened. "Are you kidding me?"

"No," Laurel said.

Kate blew out air and looked around again as if she couldn't believe her ears. "That woman is psychotic. I mean she is *literally* psychotic. Correct?"

"Psychopathy is a descriptive term versus a diagnostic term, but yes, if I had to guess based on my experience with Abigail, I'd surmise she's psychopathic with malignant narcissism tossed in. She's also ingenious. Anybody close to me needs to be prepared for her to try to make friends."

Kate snorted. "I wouldn't be friends with that woman on a bet. Does she have any friends?"

Laurel took another drink of the delicious coffee. "Not like you and I think of friends. She mirrors relationships and she's charming, but she doesn't feel friendship the way we do. People are a means to an end for her."

Kate shook her head. "I can't believe she's cozying up to an FBI agent now, just like she did with that poor cop during the last case. I think that dude was in love with her."

"I can't believe it either," Laurel said, except she could. It would make perfect sense in Abigail's twisted mind. "Just be careful, Kate. If she contacts you for any reason, let me know and then ignore her."

Kate opened the foil and smiled at the snickerdoodles. "I will. Don't worry about that."

Laurel sighed. "There's something else. Nester did confirm that Vic married Kirsti, and I spoke to Kirsti about it yesterday. Apparently they headed to Vegas about three weeks ago."

"Oh," Kate said, drawing back. "I can't believe he didn't even tell his own kids." Her face fell. "Does that mean anything he had left goes to Kirsti and not the girls? I don't want his money—I'm just worried about them."

Laurel wasn't certain she had the right to talk about the will, but nothing really prevented her, either. "I'll find out for you. Hopefully he took care of the kids, at the very least."

Kate ground her palm into her right eye. "That's something we're going to worry about another day."

"I agree," Laurel said. "For now, I need to get back to the office and figure out who killed your ex."

"While also chasing your sister and your absent father," Kate said. "Laurel, you have to do me one favor."

Laurel placed her empty mug on the granite kitchen island. "Anything."

"Let somebody help you," Kate said gently. "You do so

much on your own. I know Walter's coming back. Let him help you. It'll mean a lot to him, and I'll rest easier."

What an odd request. "Of course I'll let him help."

"No, you'll *kind of* let him help because you're worried about his recovery. He's a grown man and he can make his own decisions. In addition, feel free, even though it's not a Fish and Wildlife case, to draw on Huck and his officers during this case. We're short-staffed and it's okay to ask for help." Kate emphasized the last.

Laurel took a deep breath. "I understand what you're saying, and I will definitely think about it."

"Fine," Kate said, giving in graciously and putting down her cup. "Please keep me informed as much as you can, and I promise I'll get back to work as soon as possible."

Now this time Laurel leaned in for an impulsive hug. "You take care of yourself and your girls. That's all that matters right now."

Agent Walter Smudgeon took a moment to settle his breathing as he reached the top of the stairs leading to the second story of the building. It had been more than six weeks since he'd been in the office, and yet everything looked the same.

The glass ice cream case still stood in for Kate's desk, and the cancan girl wallpaper still lined the sides of the stairwell. Yet somehow, everything felt different. He straightened his drab gray jacket and pants and made sure his belt was securely in place. He'd lost more than twenty-five pounds since being shot in the abdomen during their last case, and even though his gut still hurt from the three bullets he'd taken, he was probably on the mend to a healthier place than he'd been in more than a decade.

If only the nightmares would end.

He smoothed his thinning hair back and then strode through the center door and down the hallway as he had so many times before, hearing voices from the main conference room. He liked this office space. Kate had mentioned on the phone that Laurel wanted to perhaps rent the far-left suite, so they'd have more room, but there was something about this place that really worked for him.

He paused at the conference room. "I'm back."

Laurel looked over from her seat at the head of the table and smiled. "Walter." She stood and walked to him.

He hadn't seen her in several weeks, and as usual, her stunning looks caught him off guard. Oh, he'd seen redheads before, but nobody with the true, dark auburn color of her hair, and her eyes always caught his attention, one blue and one green with a burst of color in the blue one. She was only about five foot two, but the woman had presence.

He leaned down and patted her shoulder. "I'm back, Boss. Put me to work." She smiled, and he felt that he'd come home.

"Walter, it's so good to see you." She tucked her arm through his and pulled him inside the room.

Nester sat at the other side of the table and gave him a chin jerk. "It's good to have you back, Walter. We missed you."

"Thanks, kid," Walter said, turning his attention to the boards visible on the other side of the table. One was all about Abigail Caine, one for the missing Pastor Zeke Caine, and a new one that took up the middle board. "Looks like we got three cases going."

"We do," Laurel said, escorting him to a chair and then retaking her seat at the head of the table. "Right now, we're looking at the main case, which involves the murder of Victor Vuittron, Kate's ex and an attorney at Marshall & Cutting in Seattle."

He looked at the suspect list. "I talked to Kate last night. That's why I'm back permanently. None of this two-days-a-week crap. So, let me see. You're looking at Kate Vuittron, which is crazy, Kirsti Vuittron, who must be the home-wrecking shrew, law partner Melissa Cutting, Councilman Eric Swelter, and a big question mark as suspects." Seemed to him a lawyer like Vuittron would have a lot of enemies.

"I'm going to the law firm now to interview Melissa Cutting. Would you like to accompany me?" Laurel asked.

Absolutely. "Yes." Walter stood straighter. It felt good to be in the swing of things again. Oh, he still hurt, but he was alive and that meant something. The guilt he felt at not being able to prevent the death of the woman he'd been assigned to protect would always haunt him, but that was for late at night, alone in the dark. Right now, he was here, and he had a job to do.

He looked at the photograph of Melissa Cutting. She was a pretty woman. "You think she was having an affair with Victor Vuittron?" He noted the line drawn between them.

"We think it's possible," Laurel said.

Walter studied the picture of the victim. What a way to go. "What's the significance of the candy?"

"I don't know yet," Laurel said, her lips pursing as she thought it through in that way she had. Sometimes her intelligence was frightening. "It could be anything. The murder took place a month after Valentine's Day, so the candy may simply have been handy, or it may signify a romance gone bad, love gone bad, or something unrelated to either. It is too early to create a hypothesis."

Walter's gaze remained on the three boards. "There seems to be something ritualistic about the killing."

"Perhaps," Laurel allowed. "We'll know soon enough if we get another murder. For now, we're pursuing this one. It appears that the victim was possibly having an affair with his partner at work, and there's some indication that his wife was also having an affair."

Walter nodded. "It's usually sex or money, right?"

"Usually," Laurel agreed. "I have warrants submitted for phone and bank records but probably won't be given one for the councilman."

"I'm on it," Nester said.

Laurel's phone tinkled a happy tune and she sighed.

Walter's eyebrow rose. That so did not sound like her.

"For some reason, my mother's new pastime is changing my ringtones." She clicked the speaker button. "Snow."

"Hey, it's Huck." His low voice rumbled across the line.

"Hello. You're on speaker with my team," she said.

Her team. Walter's chest filled with warmth as if he'd eaten a fresh-from-the-oven chocolate chip cookie. Even after his screw up, she claimed him. A lump filled his throat.

"Hi, team," Huck said.

Laurel stacked her file folders together and lifted them against her chest. "I heard you found the lost hikers."

A printer whirred over the phone line. "Yeah, they purposely went where they shouldn't have, but they're going to be fine," Huck said. "We're checking access passes out on Fish and Wildlife lands today. You want to meet for lunch?"

She glanced at her watch. "I think we'll be back in time."

"Okay. At the Center Diner?"

Walter kind of liked the grumpy Fish and Wildlife officer, and it was nice to see Laurel stepping out of her comfort zone a little bit. She was too smart and pretty to be alone.

"Sure," Laurel said. "I may run a couple of thoughts by you."

"Great. I had an interesting talk with your half sister last night. I think she's on the move—the entire team should be on alert."

Laurel paled. "I agree. Abigail is going to become more persistent." Laurel looked at Nester and then at Walter. "I haven't had a chance to tell any of you that she is dating the special agent in charge of the Seattle FBI field office."

Huck sighed audibly. "That just figures, doesn't it? You need to be careful. She's hiding it fairly well, but she's furious that you executed that warrant on her office before you left town. When somebody like her gets enraged or insulted, don't they strike out?"

"Affirmative," Laurel said quietly. "They absolutely do."

Chapter 8

Marshall & Cutting took up the top three floors of a shiny glass and chrome building on the outskirts of Seattle. Laurel had taken advantage of the drive to fill Walter in on all three of the current cases. It was nice to have him back, but she didn't want him to negatively impact his recovery, so she'd have to ensure he didn't overtax himself.

The security guard at the bottom floor checked them in and they rode the elevator to the top floor, where they were met instantly by an efficient-looking woman with coifed white hair and a mint-green St. John suit. She strode on three-inch, candy apple heels to greet them. "Hello, I am Roxanne, Ms. Cutting's personal assistant."

Laurel showed her badge. "I'm Special Agent Laurel Snow and this is Agent Smudgeon."

Walter flipped out his badge and then put it efficiently back in his jacket pocket. When he moved, his weapon became visible in its shoulder holster beneath his jacket.

"Come this way." Roxanne preceded them through a wide reception area with sparkling gold accents that matched the wide, gilded frames bordering what appeared to be original C.M. Russell paintings. "Ms. Cutting will see you in just a moment." She led them past several offices to a conference room already prepared with a water pitcher and glasses in the center of a solid oak table.

"There's coffee and tea on the credenza to your right," Roxanne said.

"Thank you very much. Did you know Victor well?" Laurel purposely used his first name.

Roxanne halted and her eyes filled. "He'd only worked here for six months, but I thought he was a kind man. I can't believe that . . ." Her hand shook as she lifted it to her head and pushed a wayward strand of hair away from her eyes. "We're all stunned. We don't know what to think. We don't know what to say."

Laurel studied her body language. Her shoulders were hunched and her lips down. "I understand this kind of thing is shocking. Do you know of any enemies Mr. Vuittron might have had?"

"No." Roxanne leaned against the doorframe as if she couldn't hold herself up any longer. "Nobody. He seemed to get along with everyone. When my son got in a car accident last month, Victor was the first one at the hospital to bring him some baseball cards."

"Is your son all right?" Walter asked, turning away from pouring himself a cup of coffee.

"Oh yes, he's fine. He just broke his ankle," Roxanne said. "Thank you for asking."

Interesting. Laurel liked that. She cared about people but would not have thought to ask. She appreciated that Walter did. "Mr. Vuittron's new wife thought we should look at Councilman Eric Swelter as a suspect because Mr. Vuittron had some dirt on him." She disliked the vernacular, but it was exactly what Kirsti had said.

Roxanne nodded. "I was aware that Victor was excited about the debate in June, but I didn't know why. If he had negative information about Councilman Swelter, he didn't share it with me."

That was unfortunate.

"I know this is indelicate," Laurel started, "but we've heard rumors that Victor and Melissa were . . . well, I'm not quite sure how to put it." She knew exactly how to put it, but she'd also been studying how to draw information out of people and how to put them at ease.

The woman wrung her hands together. "I don't know what you mean."

Walter stepped closer, towering over Laurel's five foot two.

"I think you do know," he said conversationally. "You also probably know that lying to the FBI is a federal offense." He took a sip of his coffee, looking congenial but serious.

"I don't know anything," Roxanne said, straightening. "If I did, I surely wouldn't engage in rumors." With that she lifted her head and moved back into the hallway. "Ms. Cutting will be ready for you in a moment. Please have a seat." Her tone became curt, and she turned away a little too forcefully and stomped out of sight.

When they'd come down the hallway, Laurel had noticed that most of the office doors were closed. Was it because everyone was in mourning or just busy? Or even at work today? Perhaps most of the office workers had taken the day off. It was eerily quiet on the floor.

"Did I come on too strong?" Walter asked, moving around the table to take a seat.

"I don't believe so. I think you approached her correctly." In her experience, personal assistants very rarely engaged in gossip about their boss unless there was a TV camera nearby. Just speaking to FBI agents probably wasn't enough to do it for this assistant.

Laurel poured herself a glass of water and took a sip, then sat. The conference room was understated. The chairs were leather but not ostentatious, and the artwork was Western but not pretentious. She recognized a Seltzer painting of a sunrise on one wall and a Wieghorst mountain landscape on the other. She believed she'd passed a Donald Teague on the way in.

A woman silently entered the room. She was young, maybe in her late twenties, with long coiled black hair, dark eyes, and burnished brown skin. Her lips were full and red, and she stood to at least five foot seven. "Hello. I'm Thema Sackey, and I was Victor's associate." She pushed her hair behind her ear. "Ms. Cutting is in a meeting and will be a few moments late, so she thought I could answer questions in the meantime." Thema pulled out a chair and sat gracefully, her posture straight and her tone level.

Laurel signaled for Walter to begin. It'd be good for him to take the lead and get comfortable again in his role.

Walter kept one hand wrapped around the coffee cup. "First, we're very sorry for your loss, Ms. Sackey."

"Thank you, and please call me Thema." She crossed her legs, but her posture remained at attention. Perhaps she had been a dancer before becoming an attorney. Her name, surname, and coloring showed a Ghanaian heritage, and she certainly had the symmetrical bone structure and high cheekbones associated with such an ancestry. From an objective standpoint, she was beautiful.

"All right, Thema," Walter said. "Do you have any idea who'd want Victor dead?"

Thema shook her head, and her hair escaped from behind her ear. "No. Our division practices criminal defense, so we defend people accused of crimes, but we usually win."

"What about victims' families?" Laurel interjected.

Thema nodded. "We have received a few threats the last couple of months. I'll compile a list for you and send it right over." Her eyes filled with tears. "Victor was a good guy." She held up a hand. "I know, you probably won't believe that since he defended the accused, but he spent his free time helping others. He was an inspiration."

Walter smiled, looking gentle. "We heard he was having an affair."

Thema jolted, and her brows drew down. "I have no idea what you're talking about."

"Did Valentine's Day have any significance to Victor or any of his cases?" Walter asked. They'd decided to keep the detail of the candy being shoved down Victor's throat concealed from the public at this point.

"No. Sorry. That was a month ago. Why do you ask?" Thema asked.

"I'm sorry to keep you waiting." A woman bustled inside, her thick brown hair down around her shoulders. "I'm Melissa Cutting."

Laurel stood. "I'm Special Agent Laurel Snow and this is Agent Smudgeon."

Walter stood as well.

Neither Laurel nor Ms. Cutting offered a hand, so nobody shook. It was a good arrangement as far as Laurel was concerned.

"Please, sit." Ms. Cutting pulled out a chair. She wore a black suit with her skirt hemline at least two inches above her knee and a low, peach-colored silk shell that revealed the tops of her breasts. She was thin and appeared to be in good shape. Her jewelry was comprised of an emerald necklace and matching earrings. She wore a plain, gold wedding band on her left ring finger and a mammoth, emerald-and-diamond ring on her right ring finger. "Can I get you anything other than coffee or water?" she asked.

Laurel retook her seat as Walter did the same. "No, thank you."

"We're sorry for your loss, Ms. Cutting," Walter murmured.

"Thank you," Ms. Cutting said. "You can call me Melissa. There's no need for formality when we're talking about a brutal murder, now is there?"

Walter straightened and Laurel tried to read the woman's expression. She saw grief and something else that she couldn't identify. She needed to start practicing with the computer programs again at reading cues and facial expressions. "We were hoping to also speak with Frederick Marshall today."

"He's on sabbatical," Melissa said, waving her hand in the air. "He and his wife separated over a month ago, and he's not doing well. So he went off to the wilds of Alaska where he has a hunting cabin and is completely unplugged. I'll make sure he calls you when he decides to return."

Walter gulped his coffee. "Why did he and his wife separate?"

"I'm sure I don't know," Melissa said.

Laurel didn't like the phrasing of her statement. It was time to throw her off a little. "Were you and Victor having an affair?" she asked.

Melissa jerked back as if she'd been slapped. "Of course not." She had to be in her late forties or early fifties with sharp brown eyes. Her eyelashes were obvious extensions of the wild variety. Her eyebrows had been filled in symmetrically with expert microblading, and her forehead and her cheeks didn't move. Botox? Quite possibly. It was very difficult to read someone's expressions when they'd had injections. Closer examination showed that Melissa's lips were also probably enhanced. Her technician had overestimated what was needed for the top lip, so it hung quite a bit past the bottom lip. "How can you ask something like that at a time like this?" She wiped a tear out of her eye.

Laurel sat back. "As you know, I'm sure, it's a crime to lie to a federal agent. We don't care if you were having an affair, Ms. Cutting. We just want the truth. We're trying to discover who killed Victor."

"Victor and I were not having an affair." Melissa rolled her eyes. "Seriously. That twit Kirsti was jealous when she accused him of that. The woman even called and left a message on my phone here at work, accusing me. If you ask me, she was misdirecting."

"How so?" Walter asked quietly, taking another drink of coffee.

"Oh." Melissa sighed and looked down at her hands. She tapped her bright pink nails on the table. "About a month ago, we were working on a DUI defense for one of my business clients. Anyway, we worked late, and we opened a good bourbon a client had given me. Victor started going on and on about how Kirsti wasn't interested in him anymore and how she had the hots for some guy named Boyd. I figured he was just drunk and sounding off, and I really just kind of ignored it. The next day, we both pretended it hadn't happened, but I think Victor up and married that moron as a way to keep her."

"So you never got together?" Walter asked.

"No," Ms. Cutting said. "We've been friends for years. All of us. A group of us went to college together, and Victor and I were in the same major. I don't know, after college we all stayed in touch. In fact, he and my late husband, Rich, had been friends since childhood. Rich passed away from an aneurism four years ago."

"I'm sorry for your loss," Laurel said.

Melissa's face pinched obviously enough to be visible despite Botox. "Thank you. We didn't have a clue." She looked down at her ring, the emerald one, and gently rubbed the stone.

"Your ring is lovely." Walter noted.

"It was my grandmother's," Melissa said. "It reminds me of her."

That was sweet, and a smart observation from Walter since the woman seemed to look at it for comfort. Laurel admired the ring. "Victor's housekeeper said she caught you and Victor in a compromising position." More or less.

"The housekeeper?" Melissa laughed now. "I assisted on a couple of Victor's cases, although I mainly practice civil litigation rather than criminal. We worked out of his house a few times, and she did come in once after we'd pulled an all-nighter. One that involved case law and strategy . . . not sex. Grumpy woman."

The rest of the law firm employees might provide insight on whether or not she was being truthful. "Did Victor have any enemies?" Laurel asked.

"No." Melissa frowned, or at least it looked as if she tried to frown. "I can't think of anybody. Victor won the cases he took on, and I have no doubt he would've become very successful if he'd lived. I can't think of any death threats."

Thema sat forward. "I'll compile a list of any threats or angry emails we did receive."

Walter took out a light blue notebook and started writing.

Laurel would type notes later from memory. "Do you have a copy of Victor's last will and testament?"

Ms. Cutting pressed a hand to her neck. "I drafted it, and I'm happy to hand it over to you. His divorce cleaned him out, and he was barely paying his bills. He did have life insurance in the amount of two million dollars."

"Who are the named beneficiaries?"

"His three daughters. The trust set up for his children with steps that include college, and so on. Final payout is when they reach the age of thirty." She winced. "Though the will and trust were created before he married the bimbo, so . . ."

It was good that he'd made arrangements for his children, and yet, that was another motive for Kate, darn it. Plus, Kirsti might try to overturn the will, but that was a worry for tomorrow. "Since your husband and Victor were friends for years, do you also know Councilman Swelter?" Laurel asked.

"Not really. I've seen him on television but that's all. Rich never mentioned him." Melissa brushed away tears. "Thema will walk you two out, and, fair warning, the media has just arrived and now is camped outside the building. A dead defense lawyer in Seattle makes for good news, especially with the few details that have emerged about the death."

How unfortunate. Laurel had hoped the media wouldn't discover the story for a while longer. Now she had to deal with reporters. "Do you have any idea who would want to harm Victor?"

Melissa shook her head and her hair feathered around her shoulders. "We worked long hours, won cases or drafted excellent contracts, and then he went home to his twenty-something bride. I don't think anybody wanted him dead."

Laurel finished her water. "We know that's not true."

Melissa nodded. "You're right. I guess his ex-wife probably hated his guts."

Chapter 9

The Corner Diner held a prominent position in the quaint square of Genesis Valley. The booths were burgundy colored, the tables scratched, and the ambience cheerful during the late afternoon. Laurel sat across from Huck in a booth and munched on her Cobb salad. The dressing was homemade, and she'd enjoyed it last time. The combination was just as good on this blustery afternoon. She'd missed breakfast and lunch and had actually felt her blood sugar bottom out, but a midafternoon meal could still count as lunch.

Huck was watching a video on his phone. "You did a good job avoiding answering questions when the media jumped you outside of Marshall & Cutting."

"Thank you." Laurel sent a quick email updating Special Agent Norrs about the case. "Walter can appear very dangerous when poked." It was an attribute Laurel admired.

Huck whistled. "He does look tough. That slight hip check he managed with the guy from Channel Four is impressive, and I'm glad he's back on the job. Who's the woman in the green suit?"

Laurel didn't need to look. "That's Thema Sackey, an

attorney who worked with my victim. She walked us out of the building. She's beautiful, right?"

He turned off the video and slid the phone away. "My type is brainiac redheads with multicolored eyes who I find beyond beautiful."

The man could be very charming. "Did you catch anybody in the park without access passes today?" she murmured, taking a drink of sparkling water.

"Not today," Huck said thoughtfully, his dog at his feet under the table. "Helped a couple of people having problems with snowmobile engines, but all in all it was a pretty good day." He more than filled the large booth with his bulk and sleek muscle. His hair was wind tousled and his eyes tired.

"Did you get any sleep?" Laurel snuck the dog a piece of chicken and he took it delicately off her fingers without scraping her with his sharp teeth. Aeneas was a Karelian Bear Dog, who excelled in both fighting off bears and search and rescue.

Huck rolled his neck. "Some. I got home later than I thought last night and then was called out early this morning about a lost hunter. We found him and he was fine."

It was odd that they were working such different cases. She had become accustomed to working alongside him even though they'd only had two cases together. "Walter needs to get recertified with his weapon."

Huck finished his cheeseburger. "Good. He needs to be a good shot."

"I'm certain he is proficient."

"I hope he shoots your half sister," Huck muttered.

Laurel's mind was still running through the discussion that Huck had had with Abigail the night before. He'd given Laurel the details after they'd ordered. Her stomach ached every time she thought about her half sister being in Huck's vicinity. "It sounds as if Abigail is angry."

"You think?" Huck asked. "I wish we could get her on attacking Rachel last month, but she didn't leave so much as a fingerprint."

"She's probably not finished with Rachel," Laurel murmured. Abigail had threatened Huck's ex-fiancée, a reporter, during the last case. Probably to mess with both Laurel's case and Huck's mind. "Or maybe she is. I don't know. I'm usually able to follow the progression of her thoughts, but I lack the anger that drives her."

Huck munched on a fry. "I thought psychopaths just didn't care. I thought they didn't get angry."

"She's most likely a narcissist, too, and they get very angry." Laurel took a bite of her potato salad. It was phenomenal as well. There was something about small town diners that she'd always really enjoyed. Of course, when she'd been eleven years old and left for college, she'd ended up studying in the diners where her mother worked. It had been a good upbringing, and sometimes she wondered if she'd be more like Abigail if she hadn't had her mother's love her entire life. "I wonder if I'd be more like Abigail without my mom." Then she jolted. She normally censored her thoughts.

"That's crazy," Huck said. "You'd be you. You're not someone who kills people, and you're not somebody who hurts people. Abigail is, and that's just a fact."

The terrible thing was, Abigail probably didn't even care if she hurt people. She was simply bored or looking for a challenge. Unfortunately, right now, the challenge seemed to be gaining Laurel's attention.

Huck cleared his throat. "I wanted to talk to you about this case that you're on."

"What about it?" Laurel asked.

The dog sneezed under the table, and Huck dropped a hand to pet him. "Obviously the killer is dangerous and has made murder a game. I'd like to know that you have backup with you." He shifted in the booth, not quite meeting her gaze. "I know that Smudgeon might have been a decent agent, but he was shot in the gut, and he's not going to be at full capability for quite a while, if ever."

"He's more than capable," Laurel said, frowning. She was missing something in the conversation but couldn't figure out what.

"So you'll take him with you when you're working this case?"

Now Huck sounded a little bit like Kate. "I don't know. Maybe," Laurel said. "I usually have backup with me, but sometimes we have to split up. Why?" She was perfectly capable of doing her job.

He slipped the dog a bite of burger that had remained on his plate. "I don't know. It was something Abigail said. I let her get in my head. Forget it."

That did sound like Abigail. "I always take precautions, Huck. I promised my mother years ago when I decided to become an agent that I'd always be careful."

"Good." His grin revealed a dimple in his right cheek. His eyes were a mellow topaz in the diner and he more than filled out his long-sleeved green shirt. She was struck again by the symmetry of his rugged face. She liked things that balanced, and Huck Rivers definitely balanced.

"You want to come over tonight?" he asked. "I was thinking about barbecuing something. My deck's covered so it shouldn't get too snowy."

She smiled. "Dinner sounds lovely." She'd have to stop by the store and pick up a bottle of wine on the way.

His phone buzzed and he sighed, lifting it to his ear. One of his eyebrows rose. "Seriously? How close to the house?" he asked. "Yeah, I can be there in about five minutes." He glanced at his watch. "All right, thanks." He clicked off.

"What happened?" she asked.

Huck's brow wrinkled. "Hunter got too close to a house, shot the siding near the front window." He tossed his napkin onto his plate. "It's still bobcat season for two more days, but they shouldn't have been shooting that close to a dwelling, regardless. I need to go see what happened, take a report, and then find this guy."

"I'll take care of the tab," Laurel said. "You go ahead."

"Thanks." He stood and his dog bounded out from beneath the table. Then he hesitated, leaned over, and placed a quick kiss on her forehead. "Sorry I'll have to reschedule dinner."

"That's all right." She watched him go, bemused. That was both awkward and endearing. She turned to scroll through recent emails on her phone as she finished her lunch. Movement sounded behind her, and then all of a sudden, Abigail Caine was sitting in Huck's vacated seat.

"Well, hello sister," Abigail said.

Laurel clicked her phone off and leaned back. "Are you following me?"

Abigail's cheeks were rosy, and snow dotted her thick hair. "Of course not. I had a meeting with Pastor John at the church and popped in here to grab lunch. They have phenomenal potato salad, you know."

"Why were you meeting with Pastor John?" John had taken charge of the Genesis Valley Community Church for their father years ago and was actually the person who'd filed the missing person's report on Zeke Caine.

Abigail shrugged. "I come by to see the good pastor every once in a while. I wanted to know if he's heard from our father. I used to date John, and we're business partners, as you know. Plus, I'm quite curious about the new venture he's on."

"Venture?"

Abigail's eyes sparkled. "You haven't heard? The church is going national with a televised sermon every Sunday as part of new programming for the Christian Network. Something about small towns and values. Anyway, it'll make Pastor John famous and the church wealthy."

So that explained why Abigail wanted to be involved, although the woman was already wealthy. "I thought Pastor John was in your past. Aren't you dating an FBI agent now?"

"I surely am," Abigail said, her smile widening. Her lipstick was a deep, dark red that matched her hair and brought out the startling hues of her blue and green eyes. Her coat was a thick white parka and her mittens blue. She pulled them off. "This is nice, us talking about boys. Would you like to have dessert?"

"No, I really wouldn't," Laurel said. "In fact, I should be going."

Abigail tsked her tongue. "We need to talk."

"Why?" Laurel asked.

Abigail slapped the mittens onto the table. "You're investigating me, aren't you?" she asked. "I would think you'd want to interview me."

"I'd like for you to come in for an official interview at my office." Did Abigail have that much of an enlarged ego? Yes, she probably did.

"No, I think this is fine." Abigail lifted a finger to wave at the waitress, who instantly brought over a mug and poured coffee into it. "Thank you. I'll have the apple pie," she said. "And one for my younger sister here."

Laurel tucked her phone into her laptop bag. "No, thank you."

"You're no fun," Abigail muttered, lifting her cup to her mouth.

Laurel tilted her head. "Was Jason Abbott fun?"

Abigail's eyes sparkled. "Not really. His brain was, well, mushy."

"Are you admitting that you manipulated him into killing those women?"

Abigail chuckled. "Of course not. Jason was a participant in my study regarding neurobiology and reactions to emotional stimuli across a wide spectrum. I didn't have any idea he was a killer and would've called you immediately if I'd had a clue. Honestly, he was just a test subject."

"You can read people, I think," Laurel murmured. It was a talent she admired. Abigail would have to be more than proficient at the act in order to appear so charming when she was actually so deadly.

Abigail wiped snow off her coat. "I do read people well. In fact, you know you and Huck Rivers aren't going to last, right?"

"Because I'm no fun?" Laurel asked mildly.

"Well, that's one reason," Abigail said. "Plus, I mean, come on. It's Huck Rivers. He doesn't want some straight-laced, logical federal agent for the long term."

This could get interesting. "Oh no?"

"Of course not. That man's about hearth and home and dog and kids. He's going to want some sweet woman who maybe teaches kindergarten but is home every night to cook a hearty dinner for him and his animal-loving, mountain-hiking, rule-following progeny."

Laurel finished her sparkling water. "That doesn't sound like Huck. I think he's perfectly capable of making his own dinner."

"I'm sure he is, but that's not what he wants long term. You know that. After that kid died a few years back, he may have become a recluse for a while, but he's back now. He's off chasing down bad guys and rescuing animals from beneath porches. Soon he's going to want to build that little home for himself. He's going to want a woman who can love him and his kids wholeheartedly. Not someone reserved. You deal with reality." Abigail took another drink of her coffee.

Laurel hadn't really thought about it. She and Huck had just started dating. "What's your point?"

"I'm just giving you some sisterly advice," Abigail said, smiling even wider when her pie was placed in front of her. "Oh, this looks delicious." She reached for a clean spoon and dug in. "Oh my gosh, this is good. Do you want some?"

"No." Laurel's stomach was swirling after this conversation.

Abigail took another bite and then sighed. "As your older sister, I just feel like I should, at the very least, give you a heads-up about a man like Huck. You don't seem all that experienced to me, and I've known a lot of men in my life. That one is all about protecting and defending. He's not going to want the mother of his children out shooting people or being shot at either."

The mother of his children? They'd had fewer than a handful of dates. Laurel kept her expression stoic. "You may be able to get into most people's heads, but not mine, Abigail. You're wasting your time."

Yet that was untrue. Now, Laurel had all sorts of doubts. Was it worth the time and confusion to build something with Huck if they were wrong for each other? She'd never thought about having children. Huck probably had. Laurel set her napkin on her mostly cleared plate. "Why aren't you in school anyway? Don't you ever teach?"

Abigail hummed in what sounded like pleasure. "School is in session, yes. I'm just as smart, if not smarter than you are, sister. I always accomplish my work early."

There was something ominous in Abigail's tone, but Laurel couldn't quite place it. Even so, she shivered.

Chapter 10

Laurel spent the remainder of the afternoon wrapping up the paperwork associated with her last case in DC as well as completing all the documents she needed to make the unit permanent for at least a year. She had sent Walter with Nester back to the Marshall & Cutting law firm to interview the rest of the employees, with the exception of Frederick Marshall, who still hadn't been located. While they were gone, she reviewed the background documents that Nester had provided for the Victor Vuittron murder. The only sounds around her were the snow and sleet pelting the window.

It was March and hopefully soon the snow would turn to rain and then spring would arrive, but it was supposed to be a late spring, so who knew? She glanced out the window at the darkening day and the misty gray. She wasn't prone to the dramatic, but if she were, she would say the landscape outside looked haunted.

Her neck ached and her head hurt, so she packed up the manila file folders; she'd review them after dinner. Throwing on her heavy parka, she walked through the office to find Kate behind the glass ice cream display case packing up her own bag. "What are you doing here?"

Kate's eyes were bloodshot. "I popped down to the office to grab some of my files so I can at least get us some decent furniture while I'm working from home. The kids have decided to return to school tomorrow, but I could use one day at home by myself, you know?"

"Absolutely. Also, I discovered that Victor left two million dollars in trust for the girls before he married Kirsti." Laurel had no idea if Kirsti would challenge the will and trust, and if she did, whether she had a case or not.

Kate's jaw went slack. "That's wonderful. College will be paid for, at the very least." She clapped her hands together. "I'm sure Kirsti will challenge the trust, but that's a worry for another day."

"Agreed. For now, my mom made chili and has left me three messages not to be late. Would you like to join us for dinner?"

Kate tucked her file folders into an overlarge bag. "I would love to join you for chili at your mom's house, but Vida has a music recital and Val has a volleyball game, both starting in thirty minutes. If they want to try to return to normal, I'm going to let them. For now, I'm trying to figure out how to be two places at once. I'll probably just have to run between them."

Laurel paused. The woman managed three teenaged girls while also working full time, and she seemed to be proficient at running her life. Laurel thought through her conversation with Abigail. "Did you always know you wanted to be a mother?"

Kate buttoned up her wool coat. "Yeah, I always planned on it. Then when I married Vic, the girls came pretty quick. You know how that turned out."

"Yes, I do."

Kate frowned. "You don't usually ask personal questions. Where's this coming from?"

Laurel didn't ask personal questions? No, she probably didn't. "It was just something that Abigail said about my commencing a relationship with Captain Rivers."

Kate rolled her eyes. "Oh, please. You can't let that woman get in your head. You have to know better than that."

"I do," Laurel said. "But it doesn't mean she's wrong. It doesn't make any logical sense to begin a relationship with somebody when you want different things, does it?"

Kate shrugged. "I don't know. Sometimes temporary's fun. Besides, why do you think you want different things? Do you know what he wants?"

"No," Laurel said. "But I never really considered what I want either. I've only ever wished to pursue knowledge and then dedicate myself to taking criminals off the street. In other words, I think I've only wanted to work."

Kate tilted her head. "But you dated before, right?"

"Yes. I've dated before," Laurel said. "Usually not very long, though. I either get bored, or whomever I'm dating gets irritated. I'm not the most emotional of people."

"I don't think that's true," Kate said. "I think you lead with your brain because it's so big. But you have a big heart, too."

Warmth bubbled through Laurel. "I think that's the nicest thing anybody's ever said to me."

Kate patted her arm. "That's sad. We're going to have to work on that. My advice for now, though, is to stop letting Abigail Caine mess with your head. You and Huck have just started dating and there's no reason to borrow trouble. He's a nice guy with a few trust issues, but there's no hurry for you to figure everything out."

Laurel smiled. It was nice having a friend. She wasn't accustomed to having girlfriends. When she was in college, everybody had been six to ten years older than her. Then she'd entered the FBI young and had never quite taken the time to form friendships. "I've become accustomed to talking over my days with the captain during the last six weeks. It's interesting. It's as if we've learned about each other while I've been away from home."

"Yeah, but you started dating before that."

Laurel nodded. "True. We did engage in—"

"God. For the love of all that is holy, please do not use the word *coitus*. Please don't tell me that you and the extremely sexy captain engaged in coitus. Please. I'll give you anything." Kate's eyes sparkled despite the exhaustion on her face.

Coitus was the correct terminology. "You're right. We engaged in hot, passionate, wild sex. Twice."

"Excellent. Much better put." Kate hefted her bag over her shoulder.

Laurel chuckled. "Yet we've become more intimate just talking on the phone than we did getting naked."

"Sounds like somebody is falling for the hot officer," Kate mused. "That's good."

Was it? Laurel had never found success in relationships. "I'll walk you out. By the way, I appreciate your friendship." She trusted Kate, which was rare for her.

"As I do yours. For now, if you could tell me how to be in two places at once, so I can watch both volleyball and the recital, I'd really appreciate it."

It was an intriguing proposition. "According to quantum mechanics, microscopic systems like cells, atoms, and even molecules can be in two places at the same time by a principle called superimposition." Laurel sighed. "But we're probably too big to be able to exist in two places at once."

"Are you sure?" Kate asked, shaking her head as they walked down the stairs.

"Well, there are several theories that could put you into a couple places at once," Laurel said, warming to her subject. "You could talk about multiple universes where a superimposition collapses, which would form another universe, or you could induce the quantum state to collapse and—"

Kate snorted. "I'm out. You left me behind. I'm going to have to go study my quantum mechanics before we go further." She nudged Laurel in the side. "But I do appreciate the attempt."

"You're very welcome." Laurel pushed open the door to the vestibule and allowed Kate through before she turned and locked their door. "It is a fascinating hypothesis. If you could be in two places at once, would you truly want to be? Maybe tonight, but in most instances?"

"Raising three girls, absolutely I would," Kate said. "One of the places I'd like to be is sleeping cuddled up in my warm bed." She opened the outside door, and the snow instantly blew against them. A heavy mist hung low, obscuring most of the parking lot.

Laurel ducked her head and followed Kate out into the already dark night.

Kate's hair blew against her face. "Man, I'll be happy when it starts getting lighter in the evening."

"Excuse me, Agent Snow." A woman jumped out of an idling Volkswagen Bug with thick snow tires.

Laurel stepped in front of Kate and reached for the weapon in her purse until she realized it was Thema Sackey from Marshall & Cutting. She relaxed. "Ms. Sackey, what are you doing here?"

"I have my paralegal compiling a list of possible threats made against Victor." Thema tucked her overcoat more securely around herself. "Those have to be vetted by Melissa Cutting before I can share them."

Kate stilled next to Laurel. "Oh."

This was awkward. "The sooner, the better. We need

those records." Laurel swiped snow out of her eyes. "If you don't have information for me, then why are you here?"

Snow dotted Thema's dark hair, and her eyes narrowed in a way that indicated intensity. "I was just retained to represent Jason Abbott, who was savvy enough to fire his public defender. We met for several hours this afternoon."

"Ah, crap," Kate muttered. "Guess who must've been watching that news video of you outside the law firm this morning, Laurel?"

Laurel quickly calculated the problems this created. How had Jason seen the footage? Obviously he was being given recreation time he didn't deserve. "Ms. Sackey, you're a possible witness in an FBI investigation, and while there's no legal conflict of interest with you representing Mr. Abbott, surely you see the difficulties that would create."

"I don't care. Jason deserves a good defense, and I'm the best." Thema's chin lifted.

"Jason?" Kate muttered. "He's already *Jason* to you after meeting once? That man is a charmer, and you've been caught in a very intricate web. Get out now, lady."

Thema cut her gaze toward Kate. "I know exactly who he is. Any perceived conflict is your problem, not mine." She brushed snow off her blue designer wool coat. "Not that I'm unaware of the dangers. I've already received a death threat—less than an hour after I filed my notice of representation with the court. An hour." Her eyes blazed. "Nobody is going to scare me off a case. Not some coward leaving death threats on my car and not the FBI. Do you understand?"

Laurel tilted her head. "Why do you think I want to frighten you?" How did that make any sense?

Thema returned her focus to Laurel. "I just thought we should be very clear."

"Then let's be clear," Laurel murmured. "Mr. Abbott hired you to cause problems for me. He most certainly saw you on the television with me outside of your office as we ignored those reporters and their cameras, and it appears as if he called or had somebody call you at that point." Jason wanted to play games with her and this case, but his manipulations wouldn't work.

"That matters little to me," Thema returned. Ambition glowed in her eyes. "I want this case."

Laurel studied the woman. "You also fit the profile of his victims perfectly. You're beautiful, accomplished, and have a doctorate."

Thema stilled. "Again. I don't care."

Fair enough.

Kate sighed. "He raped and murdered successful women, then cut off their hands. Do you like your hands, Ms. Sackey?"

Laurel partially turned. "Sometimes you say the quiet part out loud, Kate."

Kate shifted her overlarge purse to her other shoulder. "We all have character flaws. I'll work on that one."

Thema grasped Laurel's arm. "You have to reconsider Jason Abbott's case. Your testimony would go very far toward clearing him."

"I'm not going to clear him," Laurel said, her ears heating. The audacity of the woman was stunning. "He stalked and killed innocent women."

"Yes, but it wasn't his fault." Thema tightened her grip. "He was treated horribly by his mother. He was abused. Then he was manipulated by Abigail Caine. He never would've killed without the cognitive realignment or the injections she subjected him to. I've been doing my research and none of it was his fault."

"Oh, he killed," Kate said, edging up next to Laurel. "Even if he was manipulated, he murdered those women and left them naked and dead in the snow, frozen over. How can you defend him?" Her voice rose on the last.

Laurel interceded. "Everybody deserves a defense, Ms. Sackey, but I'm not going to help you free a killer. I will tell the truth on the stand, the justice system will do its job, and that murderer will be put away for life to protect the rest of society."

"You telling the truth is all that I need," Thema said. "I think the truth helps him. I would like to depose you."

"Then you'll need a subpoena," Laurel said. She was about to be late for dinner with her mother, and she didn't have time to soothe her mom all night. She needed to read through several case files and also knit a pair of booties for a nonprofit organization she'd created years ago for premature babies. "If you want the case file, we'll need a subpoena, but will accept service so you don't have to hire a process server."

"Fine," Thema said, turning on tall black boots toward her car. "I'll let you know when the subpoena is headed your way."

With the sound of screeching tires, an older Chevy truck careened into the parking lot and the sound of gunfire ripped through the stormy evening. Wood chips flew from the building.

"Get down," Laurel yelled, tackling Kate to the ice. Pain exploded through her elbows as they impacted the ground and her head jerked back hard enough that her neck zinged with pain.

Thema screeched and ducked beside her vehicle, flattening herself on the frozen ground.

Laurel rolled over and yanked her weapon from her purse before getting to her knees and firing toward the truck. The Chevy slid to the right and zoomed out of sight.

"Is everybody okay?" Laurel asked, standing and sweeping the entire parking lot with her weapon.

Kate groaned. "I think I've been hit."

Chapter 11

Huck skidded into the unplowed parking lot and slowed down near an ambulance. Yellow crime scene tape blocked off the front of his building, and emergency personnel scurried in every direction. He stopped the truck and jumped out, striding toward the ambulance through the blowing snow.

Fish and Wildlife vehicles were scattered as normal around the lot with other vehicles, while state police cars were lined up on the left, several with their lights still spinning blue and red. To the right of the tape were two Genesis Valley police vehicles, also with lights engaged. He'd gotten the call nearly thirty minutes ago but had been across the county working on a poaching case that'd he'd taken on after arresting the man who'd shot too close to a home.

"Status," he barked upon seeing Ena Ilemoto, one of his officers. She was tall with long dark hair in a ponytail, and she was much better at dealing with people than Huck—without question.

"I texted you already." She looked up from sketching the scene on a white pad. Several spotlights had already been engaged and lit up the entire area. "Nobody shot, one injury, building hit mainly on the Fish and Wildlife wing."

Jerking her dark head toward the sputtering sign in the center of the building, she shrugged. "Except for the sign. Shooter hit that."

Huck flicked his gaze to the Stagger's Ice Creamery sign in the middle of the building. It was an electric yellow, and the bullets had impacted the "Cream" section. A loud buzzing emerged with sparks. "Somebody turn that off."

Ena started walking toward the building. "On it."

He didn't ask why she was at work so late. Her most recent boyfriend had been a jackass, according to her. He rounded the ambulance to find Kate Vuittron sitting on the back bumper with her arm bent against her chest and a thick blanket wrapped over her shoulders. Ice and dirt marred the side of her face, and her eyes were glossy. "You okay?"

She nodded, scattering loose gravel from her hair. The granules were used to provide traction on ice and currently covered the sidewalk. "Yeah. I thought I was shot, but I guess my shoulder is just dislocated."

The paramedic, a tough guy named Bert, gently helped her up. "Let's transport you to the hospital." Bert was in his sixties and built like a linebacker. He glanced at Huck. "You should get your girl checked out as well. She hit the ground hard, and didn't she just get her damn cast off?" Without waiting for a response, he eased Kate up into the ambulance.

Huck turned toward the building and spotted Laurel near the doorway. The twisting cop car lights danced over her dark auburn hair and highlighted her pale skin. Something inside him settled. She was all right. Even though his people had reported in while he'd sped this way, he needed to see for himself.

He moved toward her across several inches of snow blanketing solid ice and started to duck under the crime scene tape. The wind chilled his exposed skin above his long-sleeved T-shirt, but he wasn't going back for his coat.

"Hey Huck." Monty moved his way, snow covering his silvery-white hair.

Huck didn't waste time arguing that Monty shouldn't be in the cold. "Who was the target?" His gaze moved beyond the agent to watch Laurel over by the building, talking to Genesis Valley Sheriff Upton York.

"Unknown at this time," Monty said. "Do you have any idea who'd want to shoot at our office these days, supposing that we were the target?"

"No." Huck continued ducking under the tape and strode over the icy parking lot to reach the sidewalk fronting the office.

"That's all I can tell you," Laurel was saying to Sheriff York.

York was an ass. Huck walked right into their space, facing Laurel. "You okay?"

"Yes." Her hair was a wet mess around her shoulders. A few of the gravel pellets used to cover the ice on the walkway were caught in her hair, and a bruise was forming on her chin. Her dual-colored eyes were clear, but she stood as if her legs hurt. Probably her knees from the impact, considering her pants were torn and her skin visible and bloody. "The shooter was in an older Chevy truck, probably circa 1970 or so. The color was dirty yellow, and the license plates had been removed. The entire vehicle was one long dent but otherwise, I witnessed no identifiable markings."

Huck looked at the bullet holes in the building. "How many shots?"

"Eight," Laurel said. "Two hit that Volkswagen Bug and the rest impacted the building."

"Did you return fire?"

She nodded. "Yes. Five shots at the truck, and I think I hit the bed of it. There was no sound of breaking glass, and the vehicle didn't pause before driving away, so I don't believe I hurt the driver." She shivered.

He wanted to reach over and zip up her parka, but he fought the instinct. She needed to be in charge of the scene, and his treating her like a wounded, delicate female wouldn't help. The woman was strong and smart, but she had a fragility to her that fought with every good instinct he owned. "You protected Kate, which was what mattered."

She stuck her hands in her pockets. "I need to practice firing with my healed wrist again."

Huck glanced at the bright yellow Bug, a crazy vehicle to be using at this time of year. "Who owns the Bug?"

Laurel removed one hand and rubbed her shoulder, rolling it and stretching her neck. "Thema Sackey. She's both Jason Abbott's lawyer and an attorney with Victor Vuittron's legal firm."

Huck lifted his chin. "She's Abbott's attorney?"

"Affirmative," Laurel said.

He didn't believe in coincidences. "How the hell did that happen?"

"He must have caught sight of us on the news earlier and apparently hired her immediately. The woman is ambitious." Laurel stared at the Bug. "I believe there's a bullet hole in the right rear tire. The shooter wasn't accustomed to firing from that distance or from a vehicle. He wasn't a good shot."

That was a good thing. "Is there a way to get Abbott's attorney fired?" She created too many complications.

"I can't think of a legal way," Laurel admitted. "There's an appearance of conflict of interest, but it's not strong enough for me to file any legal action."

"Damn it," Huck muttered. Jason Abbot was a parasite that wouldn't go away. He'd made plenty of enemies during his crime spree, so Huck couldn't fault anybody for wanting him to face justice. But shooting at his attorney wasn't the way to do it. "Was the shooter aiming for her, do you think?"

Laurel brushed the few pieces of remaining gravel out of her hair. "I don't know. He seemed to aim at all of us." She looked back toward the damaged wood. "The probabilities point to Thema, and she did receive a death threat almost immediately after filing the paperwork to act as Jason Abbott's attorney, but I've also gained notoriety from the last couple of cases, and Kate's ex was just murdered. Plus, the FBI and Fish and Wildlife offices are both located in the building, so . . ."

Huck nodded. They weren't even sure of the target, much less the shooter. He'd need to have his people look over any recent complaints or threats against the office, but he couldn't think of anything offhand. "Where is Ms. Sackey?"

The sheriff's chest puffed out. In his late thirties, he had beady brown eyes, a large torso, and now a slight belly but was still built like a wrestler. The sleet had matted his hair to his rapidly receding hairline. "I sent her to the hospital to be checked out. She hit her head on her car when she ducked."

"Is she covered?" Huck asked.

The sheriff rolled his eyes. "No, Captain. We sent a possible shooting victim to the hospital without any protection. I have one of my guys babysitting. But if you ask me, the FBI has chased the press too much and probably pissed somebody off." He sniffed and turned back to Laurel. "Everyone knows that you acted unprofessionally in the Jason Abbott case, considering your sister was involved somehow. I've heard you're being sued because of Abbott?"

Laurel's gaze sharpened on the sheriff. "Interesting. To my knowledge, the lawsuit hasn't made the news yet. How are you so familiar with the details?"

York snorted. "Keep your friends close . . ."

Laurel's eyebrows rose as she obviously completed the old saying. "I don't consider you an enemy." Her voice was factual, and she probably didn't realize the insult lurking in the statement. However, her tone did indicate that she didn't consider the sheriff at all.

The sheriff's nostrils flared, and his shoulders squared.

Huck kept his expression bland. "You're being sued?"

"Apparently. The FBI and my attorney in Seattle are handling the situation. It's a nuisance case, Captain Rivers." She shrugged and ice fell from her coat. "Jason Abbott's ex-fiancée, Haylee Johnson, is suing me for emotional distress."

Huck frowned. "You saved her life." Abbott had kidnapped the woman and threatened to shoot her in front of Laurel, and Laurel had saved them all—despite having a broken wrist. Was Haylee angry enough to shoot at Laurel? Or was Abbott manipulating yet another woman? The man had a chilling gift.

Huck motioned Ena over, and she hurried his way. "I want CCTV from all businesses and traffic cams in each direction as well as from our building." Why hadn't Laurel told him about the lawsuit?

"Already on it," Ena said. "Monty took a look at our footage of the parking area a few minutes ago and just went back upstairs with a tech trying to make it clearer. There was ice on the cameras and the parking lot was dark, so we can't see much more than what Agent Snow has described. Yet."

Huck bit back a sigh. Monty had just finished radiation treatments for prostate cancer and should've been taking it easy. "How is Monty doing?"

"He needs to work, Boss," Ena said gently. "Somebody shot toward our building from our parking lot, so he called everyone in. This is an attack on all of us, regardless of the intended target." She glanced at Laurel as she spoke.

Upton edged closer. "This was a shooting in Genesis Valley, so it's our jurisdiction."

Irritation heated Huck's ears and he subtly moved to put his body between Laurel and York. "Fish and Wildlife was shot at in our own building, which makes it a state matter. In addition, the possible target was an FBI agent, which makes this federal." He wanted to get Laurel to the hospital just to make sure she was fine.

She was surveying the area, no doubt memorizing the placement of everyone and everything. "We can all share jurisdiction right now," she suggested. "There's a lot of legwork to do, and if the sheriff will provide protection for Ms. Sackey tonight, that'll free my agents and your officers."

It was a decent olive branch. "That works for me," Huck said. "Let's let our folks process the scene, and how about you go see a doctor?"

"I'll go to the hospital." She moved past York as if forgetting the sheriff was even there. "I would like to interview Ms. Sackey while events are fresh in her mind."

Good enough.

Chapter 12

Laurel's wet boots squeaked across the sparkling clean tiles of the hospital as she and Huck dodged around the reception desk, which was currently empty. She knew her way well enough through the hospital after having visited Walter several times when he'd been shot.

Ahead of them, Kate turned a corner and stopped short, her arm in a sling. Her face was pinched but her eyes were clear. "Hey."

"Hi," Laurel said, relief filtering through her. "Where are you going?"

"Viv is outside to pick me up," Kate said, a stack of papers in her good hand. "Thanks for saving my life." She was pale but stood tall. "I owe you one."

Laurel winced. "I'm sorry about the shoulder."

Kate snorted. "I'm happy I don't have bullet holes." She looked toward the reception area. "If you're planning on talking to your witness, you should get going before the cranky nurse returns. She won't let you go back."

"I know," Laurel said, edging closer to a wall. She didn't want to fight with that nurse again. Not tonight. "Did you get a look at the shooter?"

"No. Sorry." Kate scrunched up her face. "I just heard

shots and then was on the ground. You have pretty quick reflexes, Laurel."

She was just well trained. "Do you know of anybody who'd want to shoot at you?"

Kate's eyes widened. "Me? You think I was the target?"

"No. It's improbable that you were the target, but we have to examine all possibilities. Is there a chance Kirsti Vuittron would want you dead?" Laurel asked.

Kate snorted. "The bimbo hates me, but I can't see her bothering to shoot at me. As for whoever killed my ex, I just don't see it." She turned even paler.

"Are you sure you're all right?" Laurel asked.

Kate leaned in and hugged Laurel with her good arm while Huck looked on. "I'm fine, my friend. Do your job, and I'll see you tomorrow."

"No," Laurel said, gently returning the hug before leaning back. "You take the day off tomorrow. In fact, take the rest of the week off." Heavy footsteps sounded down the adjacent hall, and she jerked.

"It's that nurse. Run," Kate whispered, turning and moving quickly toward the reception area.

Laurel pivoted and hustled down the opposing hallway with Huck at her side. She reached the examination rooms at the end of the hall and paused at seeing Officer Zello standing tall at attention outside the farthest door to the left.

"Man, you did get in trouble," Huck said.

Zello nodded, his uniform perfectly pressed and his mustache neatly groomed as usual. "You have no idea. The sheriff wanted to demote me to dog catcher, but that position is occupied by one of his cousins and the guy seems to like it. So at the moment, I'm on transport and apparently, babysitting duty." He looked at Laurel's wet and bedraggled clothing. "But at least I'm inside."

"There is that," Huck said dryly. "How's our witness?"

"The doc gave her a clean bill of health," Zello said. "Sounds like she has a concussion, but she's been yelling orders into her phone for the last ten minutes about different court cases. Lady didn't like getting shot at, and I can't really blame her."

"No kidding," Huck said. "All right, let's talk to her." He pushed open the door after knocking and getting permission to enter. He started to move inside.

Officer Zello shifted his weight. "Agent Snow, may I have a word?"

"Certainly." Laurel stopped.

Huck gave her a look, one she couldn't decipher, and walked into the hospital room before shutting the door.

Laurel tilted her head. "Did the witness say something or do you have any information to assist with this case?"

"No," Officer Zello said, standing taller. "It's not that, and I know this is inappropriate, but have you talked to your sister lately?"

Laurel blinked. "Why would you ask me that?" Whatever could Abigail have to do with this shooting?

"Because I've been calling her, and she won't return my calls. Weeks ago we bought tickets to attend the rare vehicle auction in Vegas next week, since we both collect, but I haven't heard from her." He straightened his already straight duty belt. "That's not like her and I'm worried."

That was exactly like Abigail. Laurel knew to choose her words carefully, but the truth was the truth. "It would be wise for you to move on. Abigail doesn't care about people the way that you do. She uses people and she used you." Maybe adopting a softer tone would help him accept reality, but Laurel didn't know how to do anything other than be honest. "Right now she's already romantically involved with another man."

Zello paled and his eyes widened. "She's seeing

somebody else? Does she care about him? I mean, is it serious? Will he protect her?"

"No," Laurel said. "I don't think she cares about anybody, but she's using him just as she used you. For your own peace of mind, you really should move on."

"You don't understand. She's vulnerable in a way you would never understand, and I can take care of her. We had a real connection."

Laurel sighed. "She doesn't connect with anybody, Officer Zello." There had to be a way to make him understand. "Abigail is dangerous, and if you continue pursuing her when she wishes to be left alone, she might turn on you. There's no line she won't cross if angered."

Fighting the urge to pat his arm, she turned and pushed her way into the examination room where Thema Sackey sat in a hospital gown under covers with an IV attached to her inner elbow. A Band-Aid had been placed above her right eye, and the swelling extended down around the side of her temple to form a dark bruise on the upper part of her cheekbone. Her phone was in her hands, and she was looking at Huck with her eyes widened and her brows lifted. Keen interest? He was quite handsome.

Fascinating. Laurel was learning to read people better. Those lessons from the Internet were paying off. Huck lounged against the far wall as if giving the woman space.

"Ms. Sackey, how are you?" Laurel asked, approaching the bed.

Thema smoothed her blanket. "I'm fine. The doctor says I have a slight concussion but can be discharged in an hour or so. I also have a bunch of scratches and bruises on my hands, but it's not a big deal. Have you caught the shooter?"

"Not yet," Laurel said. "We're not even certain of the target."

Thema paled a little. "Considering I received a death

threat just a few hours before the shooter opened fire, I was probably the target."

"It's a good possibility," Laurel agreed. "However, you also work, or rather worked, with Victor Vuittron. We can't fail to investigate that aspect of your life either. Were you and Victor working on any cases together?"

Thema twirled her phone back and forth in her hands. "Yes. I was Victor's associate. I worked on all of his cases."

"We'll have to go through them," Laurel said. "It's my understanding that you and your firm are compiling a list of possible threats for us." It was doubtful that the firm would give the FBI much information, considering all of Victor's cases were criminal defense. "It would be very helpful if you could encourage them to be fully transparent."

"I'll do my best," Thema said dryly. "But we're not going to give up client information to the government. You have to know that."

"I do. I just want a list of who might possibly want to hurt you and/or Victor Vuittron," Laurel said. "You've had time to consider the issue since we last spoke at your office. Does anybody immediately spring to mind?"

Thema pursed her lips together. "We did lose a case a month ago. Our client was convicted of embezzlement of almost five million dollars, and she paid the firm a healthy sum for her defense. We lost the case, and her husband screamed some threats at the U.S. Marshals who took her into custody immediately after the sentencing."

"What kind of threats?" Huck asked.

"The normal. That we were incompetent and deserved to be in shackles," Thema said. "His name was Sal Lewis, and he also threatened the judge and jury. I believe he was held in contempt of court. I doubt it went beyond that, but I'll make sure you have all of his contact information."

She rubbed a slight bruise on her chin. "I would find it hard to believe that guy stabbed Victor to death."

Laurel nodded. "The ritualistic nature of Mr. Vuittron's murder is far different from being fired upon at night. If the shooter is also the killer, then Mr. Vuittron's death was far more personal to him, or her. If that's the case, then I suspect that you are a threat to the killer. Please send me that list as soon as possible."

"I will," Thema said. "You know the shooter could have been after you as well, and I might just have been in the wrong place at the wrong time."

Huck shifted his weight.

"I'm well aware of that fact," Laurel said. "Still, you are the most likely target, and we're going to keep a protection detail on you while you're in the hospital. You might need to hire private security after you're discharged just to be safe. I promise we will pursue all avenues to find this person. Did you happen to see anything of interest before the firing commenced?"

Thema shook her head. "No. I was looking at you, heard bullets, and then just dropped to the ground and hit my face on the car door. I didn't see the shooter or notice anything out of place before it happened."

"That's understandable," Laurel said. "We do have CCTV of the area, but so far we can't decipher much about the shooter. I would like for you to think back over your professional life, and even if it's insignificant, please let us know if there's anybody who might wish you harm. What about your personal life?"

Thema frowned. "No. My life is at the law firm. I love to work." She looked over at Huck. "Captain Rivers, I fail to see how Fish and Wildlife is involved in this case, although I do appreciate your checking up on me."

Huck studied the woman. "It was my building that was shot at. Plus, Fish and Wildlife personnel are fully commissioned state officers in Washington State. We pursue all state matters, although I prefer a good poaching case, to be honest."

His smile caused Thema to smile in return. "I see," she said. "Is there any way you could be put on protection detail?"

Huck shook his head. "Sorry. No."

"That's a pity," Thema murmured, pink filtering across her cheekbones. "But it's all right. If your officer would escort me home, my apartment building has security, as does the law firm. So I'm covered both at home and at work."

Laurel watched the interaction. Thema was proficient at flirting. For a short time in Laurel's late teenage years, she'd attempted to learn how to flirt by watching different television shows, but she never managed to accomplish it. In the end, she decided that flirting wasn't one of her talents and that she would just go with honesty.

Perhaps the captain liked flirting. He seemed to be getting a response from Thema, although Laurel couldn't decipher if he was enjoying it. The captain had a good poker face and was quite difficult to read, even under the best of circumstances.

So she cleared her throat and focused on Thema again. "Let's go through your entire day. I'd like you to concentrate on the time from when Jason Abbott called you until the shooter opened fire in the parking lot. All right?"

Thema looked toward Laurel and then settled back against the pillows. "All right. So, about an hour after I escorted you from the law firm, I received a call from the county jail. I could hear sincerity in Jason Abbott's voice and decided I was going to help him be treated fairly, considering that all he'd had so far was subpar counsel. He was smart to fire her and lucky to find me."

Chapter 13

The snow had softened to a lazy drift of flakes as the weather changed by the hour in the mountains. Laurel shed her outerwear in the cozy vestibule of Huck's cabin. He and Aeneas were still outside in the darkness shoveling the walkway, and the dog's happy yips echoed through the quiet every few moments. Her phone buzzed and she lifted it to her ear while kicking off her boots. "Snow."

"Hi. I'm calling to check on you and on Kate," Deidre said, a whistling teapot in the background.

"I'm still fine, Mom." Laurel had already spoken with her mother twice. "Kate is already home with her kids. She has a dislocated shoulder but will be all right. Viv drove her home, and though I told her to take the rest of the week off, I expect I'll see her at the office tomorrow anyway." Laurel checked her socks, noted they were wet, and toed them off as well. Her knees were smarting, and she needed to take a look at the scrapes after having refused medical attention. She didn't require a doctor's time for such inconsequential injuries. "I'm sorry I missed chili night."

"Me, too," Deidre said. "I do wish you'd come home tonight so I can see for myself that you're all right." There was a tone in her voice, probably motherly guilt.

Laurel wanted to take care of her small hurts before worrying her mother. Plus, she wished to talk over the case with Huck while all the facts were still spinning around in her mind. She padded barefoot across the burnished oak floor to the kitchen, where she began filling the dented and slightly rusty coffeepot with water and then hunted for the filter and coffee in the nearest cupboard. She had no idea when Huck's birthday occurred, but a thoughtful gift would be a Keurig. If they were still dating, of course. Or, if they were just friends, a new coffee maker would be a decent gift. Her phone vibrated with another call. "I have to go, Mom. I'll call you in the morning."

"Night," Deidre said, ending the call.

Lauren pressed the button on the coffee maker as she answered. "Snow."

"Hi, Laurel. It's Nester."

Laurel leaned against the counter. "You're working late."

"We just received the coroner's report on Victor Vuittron. You must have some juice to get our case put to the top of the list."

"Dr. Ortega is efficient," Laurel mused. "What did he conclude?"

Papers rustled. "The manner of death is listed as homicide, and the cause of death as exsanguination due to multiple stab and incised wounds in the neck, trunk, right leg, and upper extremities."

That was what Laurel had expected. "How many stab wounds?"

"At least forty-eight," Nester said, coughing. "His blood alcohol content was 0.12, but there were no other drugs in his system. Rigor mortis was generalized to late, and liver mortis was posterior and slightly blanching, so he'd been dead several hours. There were no other significant findings."

"No trace evidence?" Laurel asked.

More papers rustled. "Blue paint chips on the back of the body and imbedded into the heels. They've been sent to the state lab in Vancouver," Nester said, his voice hoarse. "I spoke with the coroner, and his best guess was that the chips came from a truck bed when the body was dragged out and dumped on the ground. He's seen it before."

That made sense, considering the witnesses at the tent city had noted a truck. "Anything else?"

"Negative."

"All right. You need to get some rest, Nester. That cough doesn't sound good. I hope you're not getting the flu." The outside door opened. "I'll see you tomorrow. Good-bye." She ended the call and turned to find the captain removing his boots and coat as Aeneas bounded over to his pillow by the fireplace to snuggle down. Kindling and logs were already perfectly placed inside the wide cavern.

Huck's gaze swept her from head to toe before he followed the dog and bent to ignite the fire. He looked tall and strong in his wet jeans and dark green shirt, and both of his gray socks had holes in them. "How's the face?"

She gingerly touched the bruise on her chin. "I have a small contusion but nothing serious. I believe I hit the back of Kate's head when I tackled her."

The fire ignited and started to crackle almost instantly. He rose and dusted off his hands before flicking on an old stereo, which started crooning a Florida Georgia Line song about dirt. Then he stalked toward her. "You caught yourself with your knees as you took her down." Reaching Laurel, he moved suddenly and swept her up.

She yelped and planted a hand against his hard chest,

trying to regain her balance. Heat poured off him. "What are you *doing*?"

"Taking care of you." He strode easily across the living room and into his lone bathroom, which was attached to the master bedroom by another door, making it also a master bath. He settled her gently on the wide granite counter near the sink and reached for her pants, quickly unzipping them. "Lift."

She obediently clutched the countertop and lifted her hips to allow him to drag off the soggy pants, leaving her in her sweater and pink panties.

He crouched and studied her knees, his breath warm on her skin. "I'm going to have to dig some of this gravel out."

"I can do it," she said, bemused.

He looked up, his topaz eyes more bourbon colored than brown in the soft light. "I've got you."

Her chest felt heavy. "I don't know how to do this," she murmured.

He stood and opened a drawer to the right of her thigh to remove a small first aid kit. "Do what?" His thick brown hair had started to dry and curl beneath his ears.

"Let somebody take care of me." Or rather, let a man take care of her.

His grin was quick. "You don't have to *do* anything, Special Agent Laurel Snow. Just relax and tell me if I need to stop." He crouched again, placed the kit on the ground, and flipped it open. "You landed hard," he mused, taking out tweezers and efficiently plucking gravel out of her swollen flesh.

"Hard enough to dislocate Kate's shoulder," Laurel said, leaning back against the mirror.

He looked up. "Not your fault."

"I know." Yet she ran the scenario over in her mind,

trying to discern how she could've tackled Kate without injuring her. There hadn't been time to think. "We need to investigate the relatives and friends of all of Jason Abbott's victims." It was possible one or more of them had decided to take their anger out on Jason's new lawyer. There were few secrets in a small town. "I don't like the timing of the shooting."

Huck continued plucking debris, and though his movements were gentle, pain pinged through her knees. "I texted Ena to contact Abbott's public defender. I want to see if she had any death threats during the short time she represented him."

"I'll have to speak with him again," Laurel said.

"I'm going with you." Huck turned his ministrations to her other knee.

She didn't require him to accompany her, but they had agreed to share jurisdiction, and his observational skills were exceptional. "You'd like to attend because you're also working the case?"

"No." He tossed the tweezers aside and drew out antibacterial spray to coat both knees. Then he looked up, strong and sure, even crouched below her. "I'm going to make sure a psychopath doesn't lunge at you." He held up a hand before she could protest. "I know you're trained and smart. Even so, I'd like to be there."

She grinned, even though the spray had stung. "You want to put your big body in between me and danger?"

"Every fucking time." He ducked and pulled out bandages to cover her now clean knees. Standing to his impressive height, he reached for her hands and turned them over to view the scratches on her knuckles. "These look okay." Gently, he kissed one bruised hand and then the other, sending warmth and heat to her lower abdomen. "You need to strengthen this wrist now that you're out of the cast." He turned over her right hand and nuzzled the inside of her wrist.

"It feels better already," Laurel murmured, heat flowing through her as her neurons released serotonin, dopamine, and acetylcholine. "I'm not good at dating, Huck."

He released her arm and tangled his fingers in the hair at her nape. "You don't have to be anything or anybody but you, Laurel." Moving in, he leaned down and pressed his mouth against hers. His lips were firm and warm, and then he kissed her, tipping her head to the side and taking her under.

She opened her mouth and returned his kiss, sliding her hands up his abs to his torso and over his deltoids, which were as hard as solid rock beneath her palms. It had been six long weeks since she'd touched him, and this time felt different. They'd gotten to know each other during their time apart, and that distance added both an intimacy and a vulnerability to this physical exchange.

He wrapped his free arm around her waist and lifted her off the counter, turning almost immediately toward the bedroom. Not once did he break his kiss.

With their height and weight difference, it was logical that he could easily carry her in such a manner. Even so, her nipples hardened and her sex softened and swelled at his obvious masculinity. Biology dictated the emotional and physical responses of even a logical woman such as herself. Butterflies in the abdomen didn't exist, but the nerves flaring to life inside her felt just like beating wings.

He placed her on the bed and ripped her shirt over her head, releasing her mouth only long enough to do so. Then he was on her again, pressing her back, kissing her so that the blood rushing through her head drowned out all other sounds.

She pulled on his shirt until he relented and leaned back

to let her pull it off. The sound she made when she filled her palms with all of that smooth muscle, scars and all, was one she'd decipher later.

He chuckled and kissed her neck, fumbling to tear off his jeans while licking his way down her body. The captain knew what he was doing with female anatomy, and all too soon she was gyrating against his talented mouth before spiraling into an orgasm so powerful she stopped breathing for a second. Then he lazily wandered back up her body and reached for a condom from the bedside table.

She dug her nails into his flanks, noting how much stronger her left hand was right now. Then she helped him with the condom, and soon he was inside her, full and pulsing.

He drew in air, holding them both still for a moment as her body adjusted to him. The captain was well endowed. "I missed you."

She swallowed and her eyes widened. "I missed you, too." As an admission, it was massive. Perhaps for them both.

As if he realized that truth, he started to move, powering into her with a strong rhythm. Then there was no more thinking. Only wild, passionate, wet sex.

So much better than coitus.

She awoke the captain once more during the night, and that time, he went slow in a way that had her wanting to express feelings she couldn't recognize. Finally, she fell asleep cuddled into his side, all of her hurts banished for the night.

The buzz of her phone awoke her from a dream in which she chased Huck Rivers over the side of a mountain, trying to stop him from falling into an avalanche. She reached for the phone and then realized it wasn't hers ringing. Her back was pressed against the very warm front of Captain Rivers, and she snuggled closer, noting dawn arriving outside the glass door that led to his deck.

"Rivers," Huck answered, running his hand down her arm. He stiffened. "All right. We're on the way. Yes. I'll pick up Agent Snow."

Laurel pushed away the pleasant night. "What happened?"

"That was Monty. We have another body—Valentine's Day candy and all."

Chapter 14

Genesis Valley Community Church looked like a nightmarish version of a Norman Rockwell painting set against a frosted mountain as the wind blasted snow in every direction. Laurel jumped out of Huck's truck and walked toward the side of the white clapboard building to where a myriad of colorful tents were bundled together.

Captain Monty Buckley strode away from an already cordoned-off crime scene toward them, his hair a grayish white, his face wan, and his shoulders hunched inside his Fish and Wildlife jacket. In the dawn hour, the dark circles beneath his eyes were readily visible.

"What are you still doing out here?" Huck asked, moving toward the man. "I told you to head on home. I've got this."

Monty shrugged. "Pastor John called me, and I called you and wanted to wait until you arrived. Our team is already here taking the lead, but it's my understanding that the FBI has a similar case."

"It sounds like it," Laurel said.

Laurel looked over to see Pastor John standing outside the yellow crime scene tape, staring at the tied-down tents and wide tarps, stacked together. She'd met him during her first case in town, during which he'd been a suspect for a short time. Tall and broad with dark skin and intelligent brown eyes, the pastor was a man she couldn't quite read, but that could be because he had both known her father and taken over as pastor of the small church when her father had left to go on, as he put it, walkabout. Then her gaze caught on Ena Ilemoto, who stepped out from behind the pastor. She wore a heavy Fish and Wildlife parka. How had she gotten there so quickly?

"What's with all the tents and tarps?" Huck asked.

Monty turned and surveyed the officers still working to protect the scene before the crime lab arrived. "The church was getting ready for the Windy River Fishing Derby this coming weekend," Monty said. "They have a bake sale and a bunch of carnival games for the kids as well as some raffles and other fun snow-filled events."

Laurel looked at the older man, wondering if he should be out in the cold. Monty had been undergoing radiation treatments for cancer, but she didn't want to overstep her boundaries with him. Her mother and Monty had been spending time together, and she would do nothing to interfere with her mother's happiness after all this time. Even if the two were just friends, Laurel didn't want to cause a disturbance between them.

"Why did Pastor John call you?" she asked.

Monty kicked a chunk of ice out of the way. "I attend the church, so when the pastor came upon the body, he called me."

Laurel hadn't known that Monty attended the small church.

He caught her gaze. "I joined after I was diagnosed with cancer. I didn't know your father or attend when he was the pastor."

That made sense. Many people turned to religion when

faced with a crisis, especially a medical one. "Let's view the scene," she said. "Why do you think it's similar to the murder in Seattle?"

"Follow me." Monty ducked under the crime scene tape and led them through the tall tents that had been pitched to protect different carnival-type games. Right in the middle of the maze sat a bright purple tent just like the one that had held Victor Vuittron's body.

Laurel snapped several pictures to send to Nester. The Vancouver lab would test the tent along with the other one to find out its exact material composition and where it was made and sold. Maybe Nester's research could uncover something online as well.

The state police were busy stringing a tarp over the tent to protect it from the elements until the crime techs and coroner arrived. The tent flap was open, and Laurel crouched, accepting a flashlight from Huck to point inside.

Cold brutality met her gaze. A naked man lay on his back with blood covering his body and his mouth open with what appeared to be heart-shaped Valentine's Day candy stuffed in it. Several of the pieces had disintegrated into a mushy mess. The candy also was stuck in the blood on his neck and the ground around him. It looked similar to the Victor Vuittron murder. Balled up clothing was in the corner.

She didn't move any closer because she didn't want to contaminate the scene. From this distance and with that much blood on the man, it was impossible to tell how many times he'd been stabbed.

"This look like the Victor Vuittron crime scene?" Huck asked.

"Affirmative." She stood and glanced around, noting marks across the snow. "He was dragged."

Huck moved closer to the marks and bent down, careful

to stay to the side. "Looks like heel drag marks." He pointed to an area down the path. "The killer kicked snow in every direction, and it snowed all night, so I don't see a way to take molds. We can have the techs double-check." He stood. "Was there evidence that the other body was dragged?"

"Not at the last scene, but the body had paint embedded in the heels as if pulled from a vehicle," she murmured. "At the last scene, it appeared as if the truck had driven right up to the tent, but the rain had erased any tire impressions. There, it would have been easy for somebody to pull a body out and just shove it inside the tent." Unlike the first victim, it appeared as if this one had been killed right here instead of being moved. The splatter of blood showed rage. "Perhaps the killer isn't as strong as we surmised," she said.

"Even so, it would take strength to pull this guy through this whole encampment." Huck looked around. "With the naked body, candy hearts, and stabbing . . . could the killer be a very physically strong woman?"

"It's possible, although female killers statistically prefer poison or a gun as a weapon. Knives are more difficult." Laurel turned and kept to the side of the barely visible drag marks, following the trail back through the tents to the main road serving the church. "There's a lot of rage in these killings."

Officer Ilemoto approached, notebook in hand. "The pastor would like to speak with you."

Laurel looked several inches up at the agent's face. In the early hour, snow dotted her dark hair. "Could he identify the victim?"

"Called the guy Ricky but only wants to speak with you," Ena said evenly.

All right. Laurel brushed snow off her nose. "Who called you in, Officer Ilemoto?"

Officer Ilemoto looked over Laurel's head at Huck. "I heard the call come in on my radio and wasn't sleeping." Dark circles were visible beneath her even darker eyes. "My boyfriend dumped me last month, and I don't sleep a lot. He found somebody new."

That was a lot more information than Laurel needed.

Huck tucked his hands in his jacket pockets. "Did you see anything odd or interesting as you looked around?"

"Negative," the officer said, drawing out her phone. "I took pictures for you."

"Thank you," Laurel said. "Who's been called in to process the scene?"

"We called in the medical investigators from Tempest County," Officer Ilemoto said.

Laurel eyed the pastor, who was staring at her. "Have the investigators send everything to the state crime lab in Vancouver. I want one agency processing all of the evidence. Also, call in Dr. Ortega to do the autopsy." He was the best, as far as she was concerned. It was difficult to earn Laurel's trust, and Ortega had more than accomplished the feat.

Officer Ilemoto typed on her phone. "Also, I know you're short-staffed, so if you need any assistance in the field, please call on me. I'd like to get more field experience."

"Okay." Laurel would discreetly ask Huck about the woman to determine if she was qualified to work in the field. She then turned and walked outside the crime scene toward Pastor John, with Huck in tow. "Pastor," she said.

"Agent Snow, I'm sorry to see you again under such terrible circumstances." The pastor had a low, soothing voice that could no doubt reach the far corners of the church. He probably had a nice singing voice as well.

"Did you know the victim?" Laurel asked.

"Yes." Pastor John looked back toward the multitude of tents.

"Who was he?" Laurel asked.

The pastor took a deep breath. "His name was Ricky, and he has attended the church for as long as I've been here, probably longer. I believe he grew up in Genesis Valley."

Ricky had appeared to be Caucasian at about fifty-something years old with white-blondish hair, maybe medium-sized at about five foot ten. She hadn't taken a good look at the body, but he also appeared to be in decent shape. "What can you tell me about him?"

"He was a nice guy," the pastor said. "Helped out during the drives we had here for the church, and he attended regularly with his wife until they separated."

Huck looked toward the tents. "How did you find the purple tent? I can't see it from here."

Pastor John shrugged. "I heard something—some sort of weird noise. So I came outside and saw a truck drive away."

"What kind of truck?" Laurel asked.

Pastor John looked down the long drive. "I don't know. It was idling at the far end of the drive and just took off. It might have been green. I honestly didn't pay attention."

"Did you see a person? Did you see the driver?"

"No," he said.

Laurel switched topics rapidly. "What time did you get here?"

"I stayed the night," the pastor said. "Sometimes I get working late on a sermon, and I have a couch in my office. Last night I was working hard on the sermon plan for the new television show I'm heading. Did you hear about that?"

"Yes," Laurel said.

The pastor stretched his neck and his eyes gleamed. "That kind of publicity will be amazing for the church and its coffers. After working until well after midnight, I fell asleep, and something awoke me early this morning."

"Why did you go out to the middle of the tents?" Huck asked, working easily with Laurel.

The pastor shook his head. "I don't know. I saw the truck, and I can't explain it. I thought I heard something, so I walked out there. The caterwauling wind made the open tent flap slap against the fabric, and I followed the sound."

"Was it still dark?" Laurel asked.

Pastor looked to the right as if trying to remember. "The sun was just coming up. It was only about an hour ago, so it was a little dark. I did take my flashlight, and the purple tent caught my attention right away. It wasn't supposed to be there."

Huck pivoted slightly, blocking the wind from blasting Laurel's face. "When was the last time you checked that area?" he asked.

"It would have been yesterday," Pastor John said. "That purple tent was not there yesterday, and I finished double-checking everything right before it got dark last night."

Laurel scrutinized the area. The killer no doubt had brought the tent at the same time they'd dropped the body.

"What does the Valentine's candy mean?" Pastor John asked.

Laurel shook her head. "I don't know. Does the candy hold significance to you or the church or this upcoming celebration? Is there anything to do with Valentine's Day, even though it was a month ago?"

"No," Pastor John said. "I don't understand any of

this." He shivered, even though he was wearing a heavy white sweater beneath a rain slicker.

"Can you tell us anything else about Ricky? We need his last name, address, vocation, and anything else you have," Huck said.

Pastor John's shoulders hunched. "Ricky was a great guy. I have his contact information in the church. I'll get it for you." He sounded weary and his mouth had turned down.

"I am very sorry for your loss," Laurel said. "Do you know of a Victor Vuittron, by any chance? Was he a member of the church?"

Pastor John brushed snow off his knees. "Victor Vuittron is not a member of the church, and I've never met him. However, I have heard of him from Ricky, whom I counseled."

"Counseled about what?" Huck asked.

Pastor John wiped the remnants of melted snow off his dark head. "That's confidential."

"He's dead," Huck returned.

Pastor John shoved his hands in his pockets. "Clergy-penitent privilege outlasts death, as does my oath. However, just so you know, I often counsel parishioners about their marriages if they're having trouble."

So Ricky was seeking help after he and his wife separated. Laurel needed to discover why that had happened. "How did Ricky know Victor Vuittron?" she asked, her heart rate increasing slightly. "You can tell us that much."

Pastor John sagged against the building. "Ricky's full name was Frederick Marshall, and he was a named partner at the Marshall & Cutting Law Firm. He was in charge of the entire antitrust division and also practiced family law."

Chapter 15

Laurel's phone buzzed on her way back from the crime scene.

"Snow," she said, pressing a button on her dash.

"Hi Laurel. It's Kate."

Laurel squinted to see through the snow smashing against the windshield. "Hi Kate. How's your shoulder?"

"Not great. It still hurts," Kate said. "But I have bigger problems than that. I know I shouldn't call you."

Laurel's mind spun. "You can always call me. What's going on?"

"Agent Norrs has asked me to come in today for an official interview with the FBI," Kate said, her voice rising. "Something about Frederick Marshall being killed."

Laurel slowed down for a bend in the road. She was driving Huck's truck so she could swing by her house to change her clothing. Huck had caught a ride back to the office with Monty. "Why would Agent Norrs want you to come in today?" The woman had been shot at last night, for goodness' sake.

"Frederick Marshall represented Victor in the divorce against me," Kate said. "But, come on. They worked for the same law firm. Victor did all of the paperwork. Frederick just put his name on it so it looked like Victor had an attorney. I never even met Frederick."

"Okay," Laurel said. "Let me think about this." It was proper procedure for Norrs to want to interview Kate, but he seemed to be trying to scare her at the same time. Laurel didn't appreciate the tactic, especially since Kate worked for the unit.

"Do I need a lawyer?" Kate asked.

Laurel chewed on her lip. Her stomach was churning and she really needed to eat something. The morning scene had been chilly, and her body was still shivering in an effort to warm up. "I don't know if you need a lawyer. We both know you didn't kill anybody. Besides, it would be nearly impossible for you to have dragged a body through the snow last night with your dislocated shoulder. Let me call Norrs, and I'll call you back."

"Okay, thanks," Kate said, her voice trembling.

Laurel clicked off and dialed a number. A receptionist at the Seattle FBI office answered and then put her immediately through to Special Agent in Charge Norrs.

"Hi, Agent Snow," Norrs said crisply.

"Good morning," she said. "Kate was injured last night and dislocated her shoulder. There is no way she could have dragged a body through the snow to that tent by the church."

"Maybe not, but maybe one of her kids helped her," Norrs said.

Laurel reared back even though she was driving. "That's insane. You're telling me that Kate killed her ex-husband and let her oldest daughter find his body, and then she conscripted her kids into helping her kill another man? That's ridiculous."

"From what I could tell, the daughter was out on her own when she found her father, and her mother had no idea where she was." The whirring of a printer sounded over the line. "You need to be objective."

Laurel took a deep breath. She was not being objective, but for the moment, she was absolutely fine with that fact. Her brain still worked even if her emotions were slightly involved. Maybe more than slightly. "I take your point, but you're wrong."

"Perhaps these are revenge killings, and the ritualistic aspect is to throw us off. Or Kate is angry about her husband's betrayal. Wives get angry when husbands leave them for younger women. The newest victim helped with the divorce, and from the sounds of it, Kate didn't get a lot in the settlement. I've seen people kill for a lot less."

Laurel turned away from the main road. "I have, too," she said. "But you're barking up the wrong tree here."

Norrs sighed. "I've always hated that expression. What kind of dog barks up the wrong tree? The saying has to do with hunting, right?"

"Actually yes," Laurel said. "It happened often in the 1800s when hunting with packs of dogs was popular. Small animals like raccoons would make dogs believe they were up a certain tree before they jumped to the next one and escaped. Raccoons are pretty intelligent, you know."

Norrs was quiet for a moment. "Why are we talking about raccoons?"

Laurel hunched over the steering wheel, gripping it tightly. This conversation was unravelling. "You asked."

"Okay, back to business," Norrs snapped. "I do need to interview Kate and you know it, so I'm bringing her into the Seattle office to do it."

Kate was still injured and dealing with the fact that her ex-husband had died. Laurel thought through her next move carefully and then followed instinct, or most likely, a carefully thought-out plan that she was pretending was instinct. "I'm going to have Kate lawyer up unless you interview her at my office."

"You're an FBI agent, Snow," Norrs barked, like those dogs from long ago.

"I'm aware of my job, Special Agent in Charge Norrs," Laurel returned softly. "Kate Vuittron is on my team and in my unit, and I'm going to protect her as you would any of your employees. Please call me back with a time that you would like to meet with her in my office."

Norrs sighed heavily. "Fine. I'm actually about thirty minutes away interviewing a witness in my RICO case and will meet you at your office. Tell Kate to be there, or I'll have my guys bring her to Seattle."

Laurel drew in air. "Thank you and have a good day." She clicked off and immediately dialed Kate.

"What did he say?" Kate asked by way of greeting.

"You need to come into the office to be interviewed. I'll be there the entire time." Laurel couldn't imagine that Kate would say anything to incriminate herself, especially since there was no way Kate had killed either man. But if she did, Laurel would insist upon the interview ending until Kate could meet with an attorney. "We'll play it by ear as to whether you should hire legal counsel or not."

"That's such a weird expression," Kate said unexpectedly. "Whose ear?"

Laurel appreciated her attempt at humor. "The expression derives from the music world. A musician would re-create a song by listening to it rather than by reading music, and the phrase caught on."

Kate chuckled, but she sounded strained. "It figures you'd know that." Then she gulped. "I appreciate your help, but Agent Norrs won't let you be present for my interview, remember? You're supposed to be impartial."

Laurel took the turn toward her mother's house so she could change into warm clothing. "I'm your supervisor, and as such, will be present for any interview. I'll stay quiet and in the background, but I will be there for you, Kate." She might not have a lot of friends in this world, but she'd protect the ones she had.

"Okay. I'll meet you at the office." Kate's voice trembled as she ended the call.

Laurel gripped the steering wheel tighter. She had to find this killer.

Now.

Death scented the air, even though several candles flickered in the apartment. It would be necessary to burn the bloody clothes to dispatch the smell.

The flat-screen television sat on the polished table, rapidly flashing through different stations. Not one showed the newest murder. It might be too soon for reporting on Marshall's death. It was fitting he'd been found in a tent by the church. Talk about a man going straight to hell. He could watch the church go by as the devil took him.

There was no doubt that Victor Vuittron's murder still should be front and center in the news media. It was a pity how many murders occurred in Seattle and the outlying areas. His death had barely made a blip on the news, and then the reporters had moved on and forgotten about him. This was unacceptable.

Fury felt like red ants crawling over skin, biting and burrowing deep. Unbelievable. How many people would have to die before the news finally caught on? This wouldn't do. A quick Internet search on the battered laptop revealed several local podcasts. *The Killing Hour* was an obvious choice, and the contact would be easy. Plus, toss in a bit of politics, and the story would go viral.

For now, the pain of frostbite nipped at the fingers as death loomed closer. It had a presence, it had a feeling, and it had a purpose. For so long this path was one to avoid, but now there was no choice. These people had to pay, and pay they would.

The heat was off in the apartment, but that was all right because sometimes feeling cold, feeling the devastating chill of northern Washington, was better than feeling nothing at all. Those dark hours, the ones when the knife had plunged into the flesh so many times over and over and over again, only came back during dreams. There was no memory of those, but they had happened. The bloody clothes, now in the bathroom turning the white tiles red, were proof of that.

Why did it have to come to this? All these events had been set into motion years ago. So many heartbeats between then and now. Fate was fate and justice was justice, and sometimes there was absolutely no choice. The need to seek vengeance was growing stronger already—it was time to get back to work.

The pile of boxes holding Valentine's Day candy sat proudly in the closet, waiting to be used. Laurel Snow was smart, most likely brilliant. Would she figure out the significance of the candy?

The woman had stopped killers before, but those had been evildoers just seeking attention. This was different. This was justice.

Justice for all of the victims out there, not just the ones harmed by these men. This was a mission, and it was important. The only one that truly mattered. Sure, Vuittron and Marshall's deaths were personal, but there was a bigger message. Those who victimized others could become victims themselves. More must die in order to balance the scales.

Lady Justice never slept. Those two men, in their profession, should've known that one simple fact.

For now, it was time to go wide with the message.

It was easy to print out a quick notecard to send to the podcaster along with photographs of the dead sinners. Soon everyone would know about Vuittron and Marshall. Both men deserved to have their evils exposed to the world. They thought they could live normal lives, pretending they cared by volunteering time in soup kitchens and at churches? What liars. The sheer hypocrisy of their entire lives was enough to make a sane person puke.

A quick clicking of the keys on the laptop brought up a picture of perfection. Reddish-brown hair, sharp features, and heterochromatic blue and green eyes. The printer burred and spat out the photo. It was time to place her on the wall as an inspiration of sorts. Oh, she might be brilliant and beautiful, but in the end, she was just like the others.

Another victim.

Chapter 16

Huck tried to readjust his damn chair so it didn't destroy his back, while his dog snored on the thick, round bed in the corner. Although he'd only taken over the office two months ago, it already looked as if a tornado had gone through it. Papers and case files were stacked all across his desk and even on one of the two chairs across from it, and the top drawer of his file cabinet could barely shut, thanks to the papers poking out the top.

"Hey, Huck." Ena poked her head in the door. "Howdy, sweet Aeneas," she said, tossing him a biscuit. The dog lifted his head, snatched the biscuit out of the air, chewed happily, and dropped his nose back to his paws. Within seconds, he was snoring softly again.

"That's impressive," Ena said.

"Don't I know it," Huck muttered and then tried to smile. He needed to work on his communication and office skills. "How are you doing?" Was she still having trouble sleeping?

Her shoulders went back. "Absolutely fine and ready to work."

That's exactly what he wanted to hear. "What do you have for me?"

"Nothing new on the CCTV from our building last night. We can send it to the Seattle techs, but I don't think we're going to get a better picture. No license plate, no picture of the shooter or the weapon. The vehicle looks like an older Chevy, and we're running the description through the database now, but I'm not hopeful." Ena turned from the dog.

Huck scrubbed both hands down his face. "Fair enough. Just keep on it, would you?"

"Absolutely." She bustled away.

A shuffling sound emerged, and then Monty walked inside. His face was still pale and he looked tired, but his shoulders were back and his posture straight. "Hey, did you hear about the CCTV?"

"Yeah, I just talked to Ena," Huck said. "Why don't you go home and get rest? I can handle anything that comes in today." He had a staff of five to send out on poaching or injured animal calls, but he'd be the one to go on any search and rescue mission. Aeneas was that good, and Huck could track almost as well as the dog. "You're on the mend, and I'd hate to see you get sick. Take a break for the rest of the day."

Monty leaned against the doorframe. "That's my plan. I have some intel about poachers on the other side of Snowblood Peak hunting bobcats and maybe fox. My source will call tonight after his trail camera catches them in the act today. Want to head over there with me tomorrow and check it out?"

"Sure," Huck said. The hunting season for both bobcat and foxes had now ended, and anybody hunting was poaching. They had to protect natural resources for future generations. "How about I pick you up around five in the morning? We can catch them if they're still at it, or if not, we can start questioning witnesses." Many folks in that area were helpful in reporting poachers, who usually came from out of town. Then, after they worked a few hours, he could send Monty home to rest. It was a good plan.

"No problem. But I wanted to tell you, you have a visitor."

Huck's eyebrows rose. "Who is it?"

"Haylee Johnson." Monty frowned.

Huck paused. The ex-fiancée of serial killer Jason Abbott? "Why is Haylee Johnson here?"

"If I knew, I'd tell you, buddy. Do you want me to send her back?"

Huck nodded. "Yeah, definitely send her back. Then go home," he added sternly.

"I'm headed," Monty said. "Don't worry." He quickly disappeared from sight.

A couple moments later, Haylee Johnson hovered in his doorway. Huck stood, gesturing her inside. "Ms. Johnson, this is a surprise."

"I'm sure," Haylee said, walking inside and sitting in the one chair that didn't hold a bunch of case files. The woman was in her early twenties with long blond hair, soft blue eyes, and a nervous twitch in her shoulders. "I know this is weird, but I was hoping that maybe my attorney could contact you about the case I have going on."

"You mean your lawsuit against Laurel Snow and the FBI?" Huck couldn't believe how clueless the woman was behaving. "They saved your life."

"I know, but Jason and I have been talking, and everything that happened was unfair."

Huck kept his face placid and prevented his jaw from hitting his desk. "You're talking to Jason Abbott? You can't tell me you're still engaged." The woman had seemed to be yet another of Abbott's victims, since he'd used her for a cover. Then he'd held a gun to her head and threatened to kill her.

Haylee fidgeted nervously. "Listen, I know what Jason did was wrong."

"Wrong?" Heck exploded. "Are you kidding me?"

She paled and shrank away from him.

He immediately calmed down. "Haylee, he's a serial killer. He would've killed you if Laurel hadn't saved you. How is any of this not clear to you?"

"You just don't understand," Haylee said. "Jason was abused horribly by his mother, and then he was manipulated by Agent Snow's sister. She shot him full of drugs that messed with his brain, and then and only then did he go out and kill. I really don't think what happened is his fault."

"Oh, it's his fault," Huck said. "I don't care what was injected into him. You can't tell me that if I shot you full of drugs and made you watch some movies about killing that you'd go out and actually kill people, would you?"

The woman blinked. "Well, no."

He waited and let her work it through on her own. She looked toward the dog and then down at her feet.

"Do you have family?" Huck asked. "Is there anybody I can call to help you?"

She wiped her nose with the back of her hand. "My aunt is my lawyer, and she knows I'm fine."

"Who's your aunt?"

Haylee shuffled on the seat. "Melissa Cutting."

Huck's chin lowered. "From Marshall & Cutting?"

"Yeah. She refused to take Jason's case, but when he called Thema, she jumped at it. I don't think Melissa even knows yet."

Oh, there were circles upon circles here.

Haylee rolled her eyes. "How do you think I met Jason?

I came out here to attend the community college, knowing I could stay for free with Melissa. Then I met Jason, and I guess you know the rest." She swallowed. "My cousin is outside waiting for me right now." She shrugged. "He's really smart, and he's the one who talked to his mom about suing the FBI for compensation. He's been a great help. I miss Jason. We were starting a good life here, Captain Rivers. Then he met Abigail Caine, and everything just went"—tears filled her eyes—"so wrong."

Huck tried to be as gentle as he could. "You need to leave town and move on. Jason Abbott is going to prison for the rest of his life, and if Washington State still had the death penalty, he'd get it. We don't, so he'll be in prison. Cut yourself free now." It was the best advice he could give the young woman.

She wrung her hands together. "I don't think it's fair, and I have to do what I think is right. Laurel Snow and her sister hurt Jason."

Huck stiffened. "How angry are you at Agent Snow?"

"Very," Haylee said, her eyes widening. "You don't get it. Jason's the only person who's ever loved me, and I have to help him. If it wasn't for Laurel and Abigail, he would not be in prison right now. He would not have killed. I'm positive of it."

Huck had no doubt that Abbott would've murdered people at some point in his life. He was a serial killer. "Are you angry enough to have shot at Laurel?"

Haylee jerked. "What?"

"Did you shoot at Laurel Snow last night?" he asked.

"No," Haylee said. "I've never shot at anybody. What are you talking about?"

Huck studied her, his gut whispering that she was telling the truth. "What are you driving these days?" Hadn't she and Jason driven a truck for their landscaping business?

"I had to sell everything from the business. So I don't really have a car right now." She wiped her nose with the back of her sleeve. "My cousin has a new blue Subaru, and we've been using that."

So no truck. "What's his name?"

"Lance Cutting," she said. "Not that it matters."

It might matter. "Do you know anybody with an older, cream-colored or dirty yellow Chevy truck?" Huck asked.

"I don't know. Maybe. It sounds like a regular vehicle to have around here, right?"

Huck nodded. "Yeah, that's true. Do you know why Jason switched lawyers?"

Pink crept onto Haylee's wide cheekbones. "His public defender sucked, so I'm thinking that was the first reason."

"What about the second reason?"

Haylee chewed on her thumbnail. "Even though Aunt Melissa didn't want Jason's case, Marshall & Cutting is the best criminal defense law firm in the state. Jason wasn't interested in hiring them until the other day, though. I don't know why he changed his mind finally."

Huck barely kept from groaning. "I don't know how much to tell you or what you can handle, but here's the deal. Agent Snow is working on a case about the murder of an attorney at Marshall & Cutting, and that's why Jason wanted to hire that firm and that particular lawyer. That's the only reason."

Haylee frowned. "What do you mean? What are you talking about?"

Huck wasn't sure about her mental stability, so he didn't know how far to push her. The woman obviously had issues. "Jason hired Marshall & Cutting to mess with Laurel. It's that simple. You're being manipulated by your fiancé. You need to get away from him, and you need to get away from him now."

Haylee stood, her shoulders trembling. "You're just as mean as the rest of them, Huck Rivers. You all deserve what you get." With that, she turned on her heel and stomped out of the office.

The dog looked up from his bed and whined.

That was an interesting tantrum. Huck lifted the phone and dialed Ena.

"Yo, Huck," Ena said. "What's up?"

"Have our computer guys do a deep dive on Haylee Johnson as well as Melissa Cutting and her son, Lance," he said. "In fact, give me the entire background on every person of interest in the case. We might as well do that now. Thanks." He paused and remembered that this wasn't his case. It was Laurel's, and he wasn't involved. Even so, there was nothing wrong with conducting a couple of background checks, especially since Haylee Johnson had approached him. Then he could turn over any information he discovered to Laurel.

He hung up and looked at his dog. "Remember when we used to just hang out in the woods and catch poachers?"

The dog snorted and went back to snoring.

Yelling from outside the office had them both snapping to attention. Huck shoved his weapon into his waistband and hurried out of his office with Aeneas following him. He ran alongside a series of file cabinets to where Ena was already pushing open the door to the vestibule.

Haylee cringed against the side wall while a tall man with long blond hair shouted at Laurel at the base of the stairs to her office. "Lance, stop it!" she screamed.

Walter stood next to Laurel, hand on his weapon.

Huck moved to intercede just as the guy lunged toward Laurel.

Walter instantly moved forward, ducked his head, and flipped the blond over his shoulder. The attacker landed hard on his side, and Walter grabbed his arm, flipped him onto his belly, and planted his worn boot in the small of his back, holding the arm at a painful-looking angle. Walter then looked down curiously, his breath even and steady.

Huck's body relaxed and he grinned. "Welcome back, Walter."

Chapter 17

The interview between Agent Norrs and Kate had given Laurel a headache. By the look of Norrs when he left, his temples were pounding as well. He hadn't gone easy on Kate, but she'd held fast, saying she had no idea who'd killed either victim. She'd also invited Norrs to search her home and vehicles as well as speak with all of her neighbors, which he'd apparently already done. Nobody had seen Kate leave at the right time to kill either man.

It wasn't an ironclad alibi, but it would hold up. After the interview, Laurel had sent Kate home for the rest of the day.

Her head still hurting, Laurel tapped papers into place and then flipped open the file folder in front of her to read a preliminary background check on Frederick Marshall.

Walter lumbered in and placed a warm mug of tea on her desk. "It's the December Brew I found in the kitchen. You look peaked."

"I think I'm fighting the flu." Laurel looked up and inhaled her mother's fragrant blend. "Thank you for interceding when Mr. Cutting attempted a battery earlier today." It was unfortunate that Haylee Johnson's cousin had allowed himself to become so angry. From the nonsense he'd spewed, he truly believed that Laurel and Abigail had purposely set up Jason to harm Haylee.

"Just doing my job," Walter said, hitching up his belt. "Do you think he'll be charged?"

"I don't know." Laurel had arrested Lance Cutting for assault and attempted battery of an FBI agent, and he was being processed in Seattle right now. The man had been upset and was no doubt being manipulated by both Jason and Haylee, so Laurel could have compassion. But it was up to the federal prosecutor whether or not to charge him. "We'll see. His mother is a lawyer, after all."

A rustle sounded by the doorway. "Hey, Laurel." Nester poked his head in and then stood straighter. Today he'd worn a new black sweater over dark slacks and appeared more dressed up than usual. He'd also cleanly shaven his attractive face. "Hey, Walter. Want to walk later today?"

"Sure," Walter said. "I'm leaving hiking boots and outerwear here at the office so we can walk any time."

Nester grinned. "How about snowboarding? We could go this weekend."

Walter winced. "I think I should wait on that kind of thing—just until all of my wounds heal completely."

Laurel nodded. "Let's not overdo it, men. Walter, you still need to rest." The wind picked up, scattering ice against the window behind her.

Nester stared at the storm outside. "Laurel? How many more days of snow should we expect?"

"We're on a sliding scale here in March. We should continue to receive an inch of snow a day, descending until about a third of an inch at the end of the month. On average, of course," she said.

Walter's cheek creased. "You know that off the top of your head?"

"I live here." Of course Laurel was aware of the daily weather. Who wouldn't be?

Nester smiled as if he'd been given a present. "Cool, thanks. That means tons more snow in the mountains, and it's going to be a long season." He hustled inside and handed over a stack of papers. "I dumped the phones of Victor Vuittron and his wife, as well as that of his assistant. Those are the only three phone lines that the warrant covered, and I've applied for warrants for the Marshalls."

"What did you find?" Laurel asked, perking up.

"Nothing of interest with Victor's assistant," Nester said. "Mrs. Kirsti Vuittron had many calls with her personal trainer, a guy named Boyd McElhenny, and in looking through the text messages, they weren't about fitness." He lifted a shoulder. "Or I guess you could call it fitness, but they were definitely getting naked."

Laurel glanced over the documents. It figured that Kirsti hadn't remained faithful. "We'll need a background check on Boyd."

"Already on it," Nester said. "Also, on Mr. Vuittron's phone, there were a lot of phone calls to Melissa Cutting, his law partner, as well as Thema Sackey, his junior associate."

"That's normal," Laurel said.

"Yeah, but some of the texts with Miss Cutting were, I would have to say, flirtatious, and the ones with Ms. Sackey were downright lusty." He wiggled his eyebrows. "After reading one of the text chains, I'll never look at strawberry ice cream the same again."

Laurel stilled and then looked up at Nester. Those two women had lied to her the other day? "Do you think Victor Vuittron and Thema Sackey were having an affair?"

"Based on their texts, they were having more than an affair. They were planning a life together. Victor was seeing

Thema long before he married Kirsti. That guy was some jerk." Nester scratched his left eyebrow. "Also, Victor accused Thema of having feelings for Frederick Marshall. Apparently those two bumped uglies after last year's office Christmas party, and Thema regretted it. Victor still seemed irritated about it."

Laurel sighed. Was the entire law firm a hotbed of sex and lies? "All right. Please get a warrant to dump the phones of Thema Sackey, Melissa Cutting, and the personal trainer. We don't have enough to seek a warrant to search anybody's homes yet, but let's keep compiling info." She cocked her head to the side. "Agent Smudgeon, how do you feel about bringing a witness here tomorrow morning and being a mite grumpy about it?"

"I like the idea," Walter said, straightening. "Who do you want?"

Laurel thought about it. "Why don't you bring in Thema Sackey? I'd like to make her a little uncomfortable. She's a lawyer and will know she doesn't have to accompany you, though." It'd be interesting to see if Sackey threw up a protest or not.

Walter's smile lacked warmth. "I'll just mention strawberry ice cream and see if that changes her mind."

"Exactly," Laurel mused. "After that, we'll interview Melissa Cutting and Kirsti Vuittron again. Let's ask those two to come down to the office at the same time within the next few days." Right now, she needed help with legwork. Where were those additional agents the deputy director had promised? And she needed to update Special Agent in Charge Norrs.

Nester lifted his chin. "You want them at the same time?"

"Absolutely," Laurel said. She'd speak with Melissa first about the flirty texts with Victor Vuittron, then she'd talk with Kirsti. One or both of those women might be angry about the love triangle. "We also need to interview Frederick Marshall's wife."

Nester cleared his throat. "Mrs. Marshall was located at a spa retreat over on Vancouver Island. She confirmed that she and Mr. Marshall separated because, according to her, he was a 'lowdown, dirty, cheating sonofabitch.' She's agreed to come and speak to you this afternoon."

Jealousy might be a decent motive. "Push hard for the warrant to dump the phones of the Marshalls."

"I will. Also, Thema Sackey emailed us a list of potential threats to Victor, but she indicated that nothing appeared very serious to her. She wanted me to let you know that Sal Lewis, the guy she told you about who yelled threats in the courtroom, has been in county lockup for burglary since that day." Nester glanced down at his notes. "So it's back to affairs and sex in the law firm?"

Laurel tapped her foot. "I don't know. There are a lot of complications within that law firm, aren't there?"

Nester snorted. "Is that what the kids are calling it these days?"

Mrs. Marshall was on time, showing up at precisely three in the afternoon. They settled her at the conference table with Laurel and Walter sitting across from her. The woman was in her late forties with thick brown hair cut bluntly at her shoulders. She wore a designer black dress with black Jimmy Choo heels.

"Mrs. Marshall, were you aware that your husband had a one-night stand with Thema Sackey after the firm's holiday party in December?" Laurel asked.

Mrs. Marshall didn't so much as twitch. "I am well aware that my husband slept with that twit, as did half the firm, if you ask me. That's why we separated right after the holidays." She looked toward Laurel. "You should know that already."

"I did," Laurel said. "I merely sought confirmation from you. Do you have any idea who'd want your husband dead?"

"Besides me?" Mrs. Marshall asked. "I don't know. Half of his clients, at least the ones he charged a fortune to. The guy was in antitrust, and he wasn't very good at it."

"Tell me more," Laurel said.

"Sure. He lost tons of money for clients and . . . I don't know. The guy was a schmuck. What do you want me to tell you?" It was odd hearing someone so well dressed using the word "schmuck."

"Do you know what significance Valentine's candy had to your husband?" Laurel asked, changing topics to keep the witness off guard.

Mrs. Marshall frowned. "Valentine's candy? No. Frederick wasn't a very romantic guy. I can't see him buying candy for anybody. Why?"

"Your husband never bought you candy?" Walter asked.

"No, never," Mrs. Marshall said. "Frankly, I don't really care. You probably want to know where I was last night. Here's my alibi. I was at a yoga retreat near the Sound, and I believe the whole place had cameras." She quickly wrote a note and handed it to Laurel. "If you ask me, I'd look at his clients, although . . ." She frowned and glanced at her hands.

"What is it?" Laurel asked.

Mrs. Marshall shrugged. "I don't know. I spoke with Frederick about a week ago and he said that somebody was following him. I thought he was full of crap, to be honest with you, and I thought he was looking for sympathy from me a little too late. I'd already hired a lawyer, and we were going to serve him next week with divorce papers."

"Yet now you're a widow?" Walter asked cheerfully.

"I surely am." Mrs. Marshall looked at Walter. "Which means I get all the money instead of half. Is that what you're insinuating?"

Walter didn't back down. "Yes, it is. Did he tell you anything about this person who was supposedly following him?"

"No, just that he believed he was being followed from home to work and then around town. Perhaps I should've taken him seriously." Mrs. Marshall bit her lip, which was covered in light pink gloss.

Laurel tapped her nails on the top of her wooden desk. "Did Mr. Vuittron and your husband share any clients?"

"I wouldn't know," Mrs. Marshall said. "Victor practiced criminal law and Frederick antitrust, but some of their client lists may have crossed. I didn't pay much attention."

"Was Frederick involved in the city council race with Victor?" Laurel asked.

Mrs. Marshall rubbed her left eye. "Not really, but I know Frederick did some work for the guy Victor was challenging."

Walter straightened. "Your husband represented Councilman Swelter?"

"Yes," Mrs. Marshall said.

Laurel pushed papers to the side. "Did Frederick have confidential information about Councilman Swelter?"

"How should I know? Frederick was his attorney, so you'd think so. But I don't know what it was. As I've said, I paid little attention to the firm."

"Do you know the current Mrs. Vuittron very well?" Laurel asked.

Mrs. Marshall's brown eyes sparkled. "I do know that twit Kirsti. Is she still banging her tennis coach? Or was that last year?"

Laurel tilted her head. "No. I believe she might be seeing her personal trainer. In your experience, did Kirsti or Victor often have affairs?"

Mrs. Marshall leaned toward Laurel as if sharing a secret. "Listen. We've all been friends since Fredrick attended law school, Victor and us. He could never keep it in his pants. I was as surprised as anybody when he told us he'd decided to forget the law and become a dentist. Actually, he told us at our wedding. He looked so handsome in the groomsman tux."

"Victor and Frederick were close enough to be in each other's weddings?" Walter asked.

"Sure. They go back to grade school." Mrs. Marshall sighed.

Laurel drew connections in her mind. "It's my understanding that Councilman Swelter and Victor played football against each other in high school and maybe before that. Did your husband know the councilman as well?"

"I have no idea. If he did, he never mentioned it." Mrs. Marshall tugged on her gold necklace. "History is weird, right? You wouldn't believe who my maid of honor was."

Laurel studied the woman. "Something tells me it was Melissa Cutting."

"Yep," Mrs. Marshall said. "Even in undergrad, those two had big plans for creating a firm. They all went to UW Law School and then did exactly that. Look where they ended up. Except for Vic. He wanted to fix teeth." She shuddered.

Laurel's chin rose. "Do you know Kate Vuittron?"

"Not really. We all lost touch when Victor left to go into dentistry and just sent each other holiday cards every year. Victor had a beautiful family, but I wasn't surprised he gave it all up for a twentysomething-year-old. Darn midlife crisis."

Laurel's stomach rolled. Poor Kate. She closed her file folder on the table.

Walter shifted his weight and winced as if his gut also hurt. Had his bullet wounds healed enough for him to be back at work full time?

"It probably wouldn't surprise you that Victor was having an affair, even though he'd just married Kirsti?" Laurel asked.

Mrs. Marshall looked toward the now closed file folder. "Not in the slightest." A half smile lifted her upper lip. "That's what his home-wrecking new wife deserves, right?"

"Would she be angry enough to want him dead?" Laurel asked.

"Who knows? It probably depends on whether she gets the life insurance money or not," Mrs. Marshall drawled.

Laurel clasped her hands on top of the file folder. "Where were you the night Victor was killed?"

Both of Mrs. Marshall's eyebrows rose. "I assume I was home. Why?"

Laurel smiled. "You have an alibi for your husband's murder and Kirsti has one for her husband's. You both were victims of a cheating spouse."

Mrs. Marshall's chin dropped and then she burst out laughing. "You think I killed Victor, and she killed Frederick? We were in on it together?" She held a hand to her designer dress. "That's hilarious."

Yet was it?

Chapter 18

Laurel's headlights cut through the falling snow as she drove home after dark, watching both sides of the road for deer. They seemed to be plentiful this March and frequently jumped right out in front of cars. She'd nearly hit one just the other day.

Reaching her family's property, she turned down the main road and drove for several minutes toward her mother's home. She pulled into the driveway and noted the cheerful twinkling of the lights on the eaves. Since it was March, they were green and white to reflect St. Patrick's Day. In addition to the lights, there were leprechauns and pots of gold strewn across the wide deck that fronted the home.

She stepped out of her car, noting the gold coins caught in the snowy shrubs. It was nice that her mother was so fanciful because Laurel lacked any sense of whimsy. Fighting the wind, she hurried inside and removed her wet clothing in the front vestibule before locking the door. The smell of something delicious wafted from the kitchen and she instantly headed that way. "Mom?"

"Oh, hi honey." Deidre poked her head out from the pantry and then stepped all the way out. As usual, she was dressed in yoga gear. This time pink. "I'm trying a new recipe. It's ground-beef-stuffed peppers with just enough cheese to be absolutely delicious. I think. I haven't tried them yet." She quickly set two places as Laurel walked to the cupboard and took down a bottle of Silver Oak Cabernet.

"Ooh, it's a wine night," Deidre said.

Laurel smiled at her mother, who was several inches taller than Laurel. She had short blond hair and sparkling blue eyes. "You seem happy," Laurel said.

"It's nice for you to notice," Deidre said. "You've been studying facial expressions again, haven't you?"

"I have," Laurel said, pouring them both a glass of wine. "I think I'm getting fairly proficient at it."

Deidre laughed. "That's good. I'm glad. How are your cases going?"

They sat at the table. "I don't know. I'm in the middle of three and don't seem to be making much progress with any of them. Thought I'd take the night off and knit for a few hours." Her mother had a knitting room off to the side of the kitchen and they often sat there together and created booties, hats, and little outfits for premature babies. It was for a good cause and knitting always helped her mind to relax.

"Sounds wonderful," her mom said. "I need to warn you that Rachel Raprenzi called me earlier today asking for a quote about your current cases."

Laurel sat back as irritation pricked her skin. "Why is a reporter calling you?"

"Probably because she can't get to you," Deidre said.

Rachel was a thorn in Laurel's side. The ambitious reporter had recently started up a new podcast called *The Killing Hour*. She was also Huck River's ex-fiancée.

"I hope you told her 'no comment.'"

"I may have said something a little more direct than that." Deidre smiled as she stood and walked past the counter. She reached into a drawer for pot holders and opened the oven.

A knock sounded on the outside door, and Laurel stood and walked casually through the living room. "Are you expecting anybody?" she called back.

"No," Diedre said. "I did invite your Uncle Carl for dinner, but you know he rarely comes."

Laurel opened the door and then stepped back at the sight of Councilman Eric Swelter standing on the porch. "What are you doing here?"

"I need your help," he said. "I'm being unjustly accused, and you're the only person who can help me."

Laurel stepped closer to him, forcing him back onto the porch before shutting the door behind her. "This is not the appropriate way to gain my attention, Councilman. If you like, you can make an appointment to see me tomorrow morning, but you will get off this property and you will do it right now."

He took a step back as if he wasn't a complete moron and held up both hands. "Listen, I don't want to make you angry, but a reporter just contacted me on my personal phone number, and I have no idea how she got it. She's going to run a story tomorrow saying that I'm a possible suspect in the Broken Heart Murders."

"The what?" Laurel asked, putting a hand to her head.

"Yes, apparently the media has named the recent killings the Broken Heart Murders because of candy. She wanted to know why I shoved Valentine's Day candy down the throats of Victor Vuittron and Frederick Marshall. I don't know why you gave her my name, but I will sue you for slander."

"I didn't give any information to the media," Laurel

said. How in the world had a reporter gotten hold of the details she'd been keeping back?

"The leak definitely came from your office, Agent Snow. So unless you expect the lawsuit from hell, I suggest you take care of this."

Laurel rubbed her chilled arms. "Take care of it how?"

"You need to tell the reporter that I'm not a suspect. Either that or I will sue you, and I'll take everything you have."

She ignored the threat because she didn't have time for it. "You *are* a suspect, and you refused to speak with me. That's the truth, not slander." She watched him carefully. "Would you like to tell me what Frederick Marshall had on you that he shared with Victor Vuittron?" There was more to the story or Swelter wouldn't be standing on her front porch right now.

"Nothing." Red blazed across his bland features. "My legal pursuits are none of your business. They're nobody's business."

He was definitely hiding something. "Who's the reporter?"

"Rachel Raprenzi."

Yes, that's what Laurel had surmised. The woman had excellent sources. "Nobody on my team has spoken with a reporter. You might want to check in with your lawyers."

"Just take care of it." Swelter turned and stomped down the stairs, headed toward a tall white Chevy truck. It looked new and gleamed in the snow. Laurel tilted her head and watched him drive away. At a distance, was it possible that the truck could look like an older Chevy? She didn't think so, but she needed to review the CCTV drive of the shooter firing at her building.

Her phone buzzed and she pulled it from her back pocket. "Snow," she answered.

"Hello, Agent Snow. This is Rachel Raprenzi with *The Killing Hour*. We're going live on the podcast with a story that Councilman Eric Swelter is your main suspect in the Broken Heart Murders. That he shoved those little Valentine's candies down the throats of the victims and they broke right in two. Would you like to comment?" Rachel asked cheerfully.

Laurel sighed. "Where did you get your information?"

"None of your business. Comment or not?"

Had the killer contacted the media? "I have no comment, Ms. Raprenzi. I can also inform you that you're risking both slander and libel if you run this story."

"I think I've got it covered," Rachel said. "Are you sure you wouldn't like to give me a comment?"

"No comment," Laurel said, ending the call. She blew out a breath and leaned against the chilled wooden siding of the house. She knew her team hadn't talked to the press. So it appeared the killer had reached out to the media.

Fantastic. That was all she needed.

After a sleepless night, Laurel drove to work with snow smashing against her windshield. Instead of following the statistical probability model that predicted snow accumulation would decrease, this March appeared to be going in the other direction. As she drove into her parking lot and slid several spots before coming to a stop, she took a moment to glare at the swollen underbellies of the clouds. They were purple and gray, and the snow was falling in large chunks instead of the dreamy drifting flakes of the day before.

She stepped out of her car and ducked her head against the brutal wind before running toward the door on the right side of the building. Shoving her way inside, she stopped short at seeing Rachel Raprenzi waiting by the Fish and Wildlife door to the right, a cameraman behind her, already focused on Laurel.

"Agent Snow, I'm sorry I couldn't get your full statement last night," Rachel said.

"What I said last night was 'no comment.'" Laurel moved past her toward the doorway to her stairwell.

Rachel lurched forward to intercept her. "Councilman Swelter is blaming your office for leaks concerning his involvement in the Broken Heart Killer case. Did you know that?"

Laurel disliked that case name immediately. She also doubted that Councilman Swelter had bothered to speak with Rachel about anything. "Again, no comment," she said. Darn it. Where was Walter? At the thought of Walter throwing Rachel across the room, Laurel smiled. It wasn't a kind thought, but she forgave herself almost immediately. "If you'll excuse me."

She opened her door, stepped through it, and sharply shut it. Shaking her head, she climbed the stairs, ignoring the dancing cancan girl wallpaper.

She was startled to find Kate standing at the top of the stairs, one arm in a sling and one hand on her hip, her eyes wide. "You are not going to believe this," Kate said.

Laurel paused and then shifted her heavy laptop bag from one shoulder to the other. "Why are you here? You should be taking it easy."

"Nobody is stopping me from working. The kids are at school and I'm here. Again, guess what has happened now?"

"What?" Should she send Kate home?

The downstairs door opened, and Laurel immediately turned to tell Rachel to vacate the premises. She stopped as Huck Rivers stomped up the stairs, his face set in a frown and his shoulders back. His jaw was clenched tight enough that he had to be giving himself a headache.

"You are not going to believe this," he muttered, reaching the landing.

Laurel pivoted to keep both of them in sight. "That's what Kate just said. What's going on?"

Kate visibly vibrated. "Remember when you told me to call and see if we could rent the left side of the building so we could have two stories?"

"Yes," Laurel said cautiously.

"Well, I did. And guess what?" Kate snapped.

A sinking feeling swamped her gut. She was eating Tums like candy these days. "Oh no," Laurel said, looking back down the stairs.

"Oh yes," Huck said. "Rachel Raprenzi and *The Killing Hour* podcast have rented out the top floor. They're going to be right next to your office."

Laurel took a deep breath and tapped her forehead with her fingers—a nervous habit. "Well, it makes sense."

"What do you mean it makes sense?" Kate all but yelled.

Laurel had to admire the woman's temper. It was something to see. "We were just made a permanent unit, and we handle violent crimes. Rachel has a crime podcast. Locating herself next to us where she can see our comings and goings is a smart move." She hated to admit it.

"It's a terrible move," Huck said. "I don't want that woman anywhere near any of our cases."

"You're the one who was engaged to her," Kate retorted.

Laurel held up a hand. "Listen, we all have to work together, and we all have to strive to refrain from giving her any facts. Right now, she has her teeth in the Valentine's candy case, and she has a source. It might be the killer, or it might be somebody from either your office or mine. We need to figure it out, Huck."

Huck lifted his hands. "Nobody knows anything in my office. We're not involved in your case except to the extent that we were called in on the last murder. I don't know any of the facts."

That was true. "I did poke around Seattle City Hall and briefly saw the councilman the other day. That might've alerted Rachel, and she could've drawn her conclusions from there," Laurel mused. However, that didn't explain how Rachel knew about the gruesome details of the murders.

Huck's frown, already deep, deepened even more. "She's rented the top floor. We have to find a vet or an animal groomer to lease the bottom floor. The woman is allergic to cats."

"Nice." Kate held up a hand to give him a high five. "Sorry I snapped at you."

"I didn't notice," Huck said.

A knock sounded on the door below, and then it slowly opened. Laurel craned her neck to see to the bottom of the staircase.

Rachel Raprenzi looked up. "Agent Snow, I was wondering if you were available for a quick interview. I'd like a few background facts about the murders before I go live."

"No comment," Laurel snapped. Oh, this was a disaster.

Chapter 19

Early Friday morning, Laurel sipped a latte in her office as she finished signing the paperwork approving Walter's status to full time again. He'd need to recertify within the next month, but he could do it. As she reached for the last document, the sleeve of her sweater caught the rough wood of her desk, and she gingerly released the wool. They really did need to acquire appropriate office furniture. She'd love to have a drawer or two.

Walter poked his head in the door. "Hey, Boss."

"Walter. Good morning," Laurel said. "Were you successful?" It was nice to be relying on him again.

Walter's eyes twinkled. "Yes. Thema Sackey is right now waiting for you in our conference room with her bodyguard holding up the wall outside. I'm uncertain, but I think steam might be pouring from her ears."

Laurel set her pen down. "Partial blackmail will do that to somebody."

"Is it blackmail or extortion?"

"In blackmail there's a threat of release of information, and in extortion, there's a threat of violence or unfair use of power," Laurel said. "So it's closest to blackmail, which we didn't actually commit, since you didn't make a threat. Correct?"

Walter set his hand on the butt of his weapon. "True. I said the words 'strawberry ice cream' and she was more than happy to come talk to you." He smiled again and straightened his black jacket. He wore it over jeans and thick boots with a badge and gun at his waist. It was the first time she'd seen him in jeans, and he'd definitely lost weight. Good for him. "Want me to bring in that councilman next?" It was nice to see him so engaged.

Laurel shook her head. "He won't come without a warrant, and I don't want to push him yet."

"Okay, but that guy is smarmy, if you know what I mean."

Laurel had no idea what that meant. "Please explain."

Walter stretched his shoulder. "He's just one of those guys who . . . well, he's a politician. Full of snide comments and those polished teeth. I guess he's been rude to several of the workers at City Hall, from what I could find out by making a few phone calls to buddies last night. Nothing actionable, though."

Nester came into view behind Walter. "Hey. I just confirmed that Frederick Marshall never went on his trip to Alaska. I spoke on the phone with his neighbor, a nice elderly lady named Lilly, and she said that Frederick had been home all week, having a staycation. She knew because he shoveled her walk every day, including Wednesday."

"He must've been kidnapped Wednesday night," Laurel mused. "Has the warrant for his home come in?"

"Just now," Nester said.

Laurel mentally clicked through her rapidly growing to-do list. "Walter? Would you execute the warrant?" She held up a hand when he nodded and quickly hit speed dial on her phone.

"Hey. I'm in the middle of nowhere and might lose you," Huck said by way of answer.

She tried something new. "I, ah, I need help."

He was silent for a moment. "What's wrong?"

She rolled her eyes. "Nothing. We're short-staffed, and I wondered if you had an officer who could help Walter serve a search warrant on the home of one of my victims." She didn't want to send Walter out without backup, and she needed Nester on his computer. "If not, no worries."

"Sure," Huck said. "I know that Ena wants more time in the field, but tell Walter he may need to listen to a litany of why men suck. I'll call her now." Wind whistled, muffling his words.

"Thanks." She ended the call. "Ena will accompany you. Teach her everything you know about serving a warrant and searching a scene, would you?" It sounded like the woman was new to the field.

Walter stood even taller. "Of course." He moved back into the hallway. "I'll call if we find anything interesting." He turned and strode away.

"I'm back on the warrants," Nester said.

"Good. Also conduct a search for any suspicious deaths in Washington State, would you? I want to make sure we haven't missed any."

Nester turned to follow Walter down the hall before ducking into his computer room.

Laurel walked out of her office and was surprised to see Officer Frank Zello standing across from the conference room, dressed in civilian clothing. He stood tall in jeans and a green sweater with his gun secured in a shoulder holster over the sweater. His hair was slicked back, and his mustache was as thick as ever. "Agent Snow," he said.

"What are you doing here?" she asked.

He gestured toward the conference room. "Thema

Sackey hired me as a protection detail during my off hours." He held up his hand. "I'm off today and am just covering her back during that time. She's pretty safe in the office and in the courtroom, so I'm more involved when there's transportation."

"Have you seen anybody following her?" Laurel asked.

"No. It's been pretty uneventful." The officer lifted his shoulder. "But I don't blame her for being scared. She was shot at, and she is defending one of the worst murderers in Washington State history." His lips turned down in distaste. Even so, he seemed to be a good officer, so Thema would be safe while he was covering her.

"I have her now while she's in the conference room, if you want to run down and get a latte."

"Great. Thanks." The officer turned and strode back down the hallway.

Laurel turned into the conference room where Thema Sackey awaited, texting rapidly on her phone with very sharp stabs.

Laurel didn't see any steam coming from her ears, but her heightened color and the tapping of her foot showed she was angry. "Ms. Sackey, how nice to see you," Laurel said, walking inside and shutting the door.

"How dare you!" Thema burst out, slamming her phone on the table. "I could have you arrested for blackmail."

"I don't think so," Laurel said. "I do appreciate your coming in and agreeing to speak with me."

Despite the stormy day, Thema had worn a blue suit with matching jacket and pants and a white silk blouse. Her jewelry was understated and silver. Her thick, coiled hair was piled up on her head, and bright red lipstick covered her generous mouth. With her heightened color, she looked stunning. "What do you want, Ms. Snow? I have to be in court this afternoon."

"It's Agent Snow." Laurel pulled out a chair and sat. "I want to know if you killed Victor and Frederick."

Thema's mouth gaped open, but she quickly recovered. "Of course not. Why would I kill either of those men? They were my bosses and they paid me well."

"Were you in love with Victor?"

Thema blinked. "No."

"But you had an affair with him?" Laurel asked.

Thema sat back and narrowed her gaze. Smart woman. She knew she shouldn't lie to a federal agent again, or she'd face perjury charges. She could still refuse to answer.

"If you didn't kill him, I just want to figure out who did," Laurel said. "I don't care that you were having an affair with him, and I'm willing to forget the fact that you lied to me last time we spoke."

Thema sighed. "How did you find out?"

"Phone records. I've read your texts, obviously. Remember the strawberry ice cream?"

Thema blanched. "Oh, I remember the strawberry ice cream." Her shoulders slumped. "Fine. Yes. Victor and I were in love." She held up a hand as if expecting Laurel to protest. "Honest. He was the sweetest guy. He was smart and funny."

"In love? Then why did he marry Kirsti?"

Thema inhaled and her nostrils flared. "That bitch told him she was pregnant. Can you believe it?"

This was news. "I take it she lied?"

"Yes," Thema spat. "Victor didn't want any more children, but he really didn't want to pay child support to another woman since he had to pay so much already. So he married her and then found out she wasn't pregnant." She shook her head. "Some people aren't made to be parents."

That was the truth.

Thema's shoulders slumped. "I know there was an age gap between Victor and me, and I know that I worked for

him, and it looks bad, but honestly, he was a nice guy who
made me laugh."

"Did you have plans for the future?" Laurel asked.

"I don't know." Thema looked at the windows in front
of the conference room, facing the hallway. "Maybe? I
think he definitely did. I was just enjoying the moment,
to be honest."

Laurel kept the case file closed on the opulent table.
"What about Frederick Marshall?"

"What about him?" Thema asked.

So much for complete honesty. "You were having an
affair with him, too, weren't you?"

"No." Thema leaned back. "Man. How'd you find out
about that?" Once the attorney started talking, she didn't
seem to be guarding her words as carefully as Laurel
would've expected.

"Phone records. Victor was, to put it mildly, jealous?"

Thema nodded. "Yeah, he was jealous. At the Christmas party a few months ago . . . I don't know. Victor and
I had gotten in a big fight, and I had too much to drink,
and Frederick could be very charming. It was just one
night. It wasn't even that good."

Laurel tilted her head. "What do you mean? Sexually,
it wasn't that good?"

Thema's chin dropped and her brows drew down.
"Yes, Agent Snow. The sex was not that good." She spoke
slowly as if addressing a small child.

Laurel flattened her hand on the file. "How did Victor
discover that you'd had coitus with Frederick?"

"Coitus? Seriously?" Thema rolled her eyes. "They got
in an argument and Frederick threw that fact in his face.
He knew Victor and I were seeing each other, and he just
said something he shouldn't have."

"What was the argument about?"

Thema shifted uncomfortably on her chair. "I can't really answer that."

"How about off the record?"

Thema looked to the side as if considering. "All right. Off the record? Victor might have done something he shouldn't have."

Laurel perked up. "Do tell."

Thema sighed. "As you know, Victor was running for city council against that rat bastard, Eric Swelter."

Now "rat bastard" was an expression Laurel had never been able to trace back to its source. Intriguing. It was, however, a vivid descriptor. "I am aware of the city council race."

Thema scratched her chin. "Frederick was engaged to do some antitrust work for Eric Swelter, and I believe he found discrepancies within Swelter's company and books. The councilman owns a construction company with his cousin. I don't know the details," she hastened to add. "But Victor may have gone through files that he shouldn't have had access to."

"How did Frederick discover Victor's breach of conduct?"

"I don't know," Thema said. "All I know is that I was working late about a month ago, waiting for Victor to finish up so we could go to a late dinner together, and I heard yelling. I ran down to the conference room and . . . oh, man. I have never seen Frederick that mad. His face was so red I thought he was going to have a stroke. I walked in and asked what was going on. That's when Frederick yelled at Victor, 'I've already tapped your current piece of ass.'" She rolled her eyes. "It was juvenile and stupid. And then Victor punched him."

Laurel sat back. "Victor punched Frederick?"

"Yeah. Victor yelled that he loved me and then struck

out. It was one punch to the jaw. Frederick pushed him back and that was the end. It wasn't a very impressive fight." Thema drummed her nails on the tabletop.

"Do you have any idea what Victor discovered in the files?"

"No. And if I did, I wouldn't tell you," Thema said. "Anything in those case files is protected by attorney-client privilege. Victor basically broke both that privilege and the law when he looked into case files he shouldn't have and then threatened to use them."

"Did he threaten Councilman Swelter?" Laurel asked, leaning forward.

Thema reached for her phone and read the face. "I don't know. He didn't tell me. I think he planned to use the information to win the councilman's race, but I don't know if it was to get Swelter to step down or if he would've released it to the media."

"If it had been released to the media, we'd already know about it," Laurel said.

Thema's phone zinged as she no doubt sent off a text. "I know." Her voice became distracted. "But the primary election isn't until August, so I think Victor was probably going to sit on it for a while."

"Have you thought of any other people who wanted to harm Victor? Or hurt Frederick?"

Thema winced. "No, not both of them. I can see unsatisfied clients in the criminal world wanting Victor dead, and maybe people who lost money wanting Frederick dead. But not both of them."

"Except for Councilman Swelter. He's the only one I can think of who has a connection to both men, at least right now. Besides you," Laurel said softly.

Thema leaned back and crossed her arms. "Yeah. Besides me."

Chapter 20

Laurel escorted Thema into the hallway after concluding the interview; Officer Zello was back at his post with a latte in his hand. She smiled at him and then turned to her office. Just then, Abigail burst through the opening at the other end of the hallway, hurrying toward Laurel.

"Laurel, I need you," she shouted.

Laurel paused. "Abigail, what are you doing here?"

"We have to talk." Her sister was dressed in wide-leg, winter-white pants, high-heeled black boots, and a green sweater beneath a short-fitting white puffer coat. Snow covered her hair, and she brushed it back. Her eyes were wide and sparkling, and a flush darkened her high cheekbones.

"Abigail," Officer Zello said.

Abigail paused and looked toward him. "Frank." She looked over his civilian clothing. "What are you doing here?"

He gestured toward Thema. "I provide protection detail on my days off." He stepped toward her. "How have you been? I've missed you." His ears turned red.

"I've been busy. I'm sorry I haven't returned your

texts." Abigail cut her gaze toward Laurel. "We really need to speak."

"Wait," Zello said hesitantly, reaching out and touching Abigail's coat. "I've called you several times."

"I was out of town for a while." Abigail leaned slightly away from him. "I chose not to call you about the car auction because collecting is no longer a hobby of mine. Frank, I don't have time for this. Laurel. Now," she said, starting to move toward Laurel's office.

Zello turned around to watch her go. "Hey, Abigail. I'm serious. I really do need to talk to you. Could we please meet for dinner tonight?"

Abigail stopped moving and blew out air, looking over her shoulder. "Sure. I'll meet you for dinner at Old Lou's diner around seven." Without waiting for his agreement, she brushed past Laurel and stomped into Laurel's office.

"Ms. Sackey, I'll be in touch," Laurel said, turning and then following Abigail. She walked inside and shut the door to find Abigail already seated behind Laurel's desk.

"Move," Laurel said. Abigail rolled her eyes and stood, crossing around to sit in one of the guest chairs. "You can't burst into my office like this," Laurel said. "This is an official FBI office now." Thinking of which, they really did need to get some security in place.

Abigail tapped her expensive boot. "You're my sister. I can come see you anytime I want."

Laurel crossed around the desk and took her seat, dropping the case file on the rough wooden door. "I'm busy, Abigail. What do you need?"

"What I need is to talk to you about our father," Abigail said, lines cut into the sides of her mouth.

"What about him?"

Abigail yanked her cell phone out of her jacket pocket

and plunked it on the desk. "He's back." She pressed a button, and a recorded message started to play.

"Abigail, it's your father. I'm back in town, and I would like to see you. From what I can tell, you have a half sister. I'm a little upset nobody told me about her. I will handle you later." The message ended.

"See?" Abigail slapped her hand on the desk next to the phone. "He's back. He knows about you. This is exactly what I did not want to have happen."

Laurel's entire body flushed with heat and she nearly swayed. "Why not?" Finally. She could face the monster. "I've been seeking him for months."

"You don't want to find him." Abigail leaned toward Laurel, bringing the scent of spiced apples with her. Was that a new perfume? "He's not a good man. He tormented me my whole life. For goodness' sake, Laurel! He raped your mother."

The perfume was making her nauseous. "I'm aware of that," Laurel said.

"Then you have to make him pay," Abigail sputtered.

"I would like to make him pay," Laurel agreed. "Unfortunately, the statute of limitations for rape in the first degree in Washington State is twenty years after commission of the offense. We are past that." She leaned forward. "However, I am more than happy to investigate him. If he's raped one woman, he's raped more. Or, at the very least, he's broken the law in another way. I will get him."

Abigail tapped her foot on the ground. "You don't understand. You think I'm bad? He's a thousand times worse. He has no soul, Laurel. None."

A chill crept down Laurel's back. "Good. Then I won't mind taking him down completely."

"You don't understand," Abigail repeated softly, looking away.

Laurel wasn't close to this half sister of hers, but she could still feel empathy for the child who'd been raised by Zeke Caine before being sent off to boarding school and then college at an early age. "Did he hurt you?"

Abigail scoffed and looked back at Laurel. "He didn't rape me or touch me inappropriately, if that's what you're asking."

"It was," Laurel admitted.

Abigail shook her head. "No. However, he was unkind, no, downright cruel."

"I know," Laurel said. "I'm sorry about that." Would Abigail be a different person if she'd been raised by a loving mother as Laurel had been? Or would she still be a malignant narcissist? Was her psychopathy born or made?

Abigail lifted her chin. "I've always wondered if he killed my mother."

Laurel had entertained the thought that perhaps Abigail had killed her mother. "She died during a rafting trip, correct?"

"Yes. She fell out of the boat and drowned. We were all there. But she was behind me in the raft, and then she was just gone." Abigail played with her necklace. "I've always wondered if he just killed her, but I never had the courage to ask him."

It was difficult to imagine Abigail lacking courage to do anything. Laurel studied her sister's facial expressions and couldn't discern any falsehood. But then again, Abigail was a master at lying and hiding her feelings. "Do you know where he'd go now that he's back in town?"

"My best guess is the church, but Pastor John would've called me had our father shown up. I always wondered if he knew about you."

"As did I," Laurel said. She had lived in Genesis Valley until moving away for school at a young age, but she'd stayed on the family farm, and her mother had rarely taken her into town. It was quite possible that Zeke Caine had had no idea that he'd fathered another daughter.

"You know how lucky you are, don't you?" Abigail asked.

Laurel nodded. "I've had that thought many times as I discovered more about our father. Again, I'm sorry you were with him for so long."

"Oh, he sent me away soon enough," Abigail said. "It was lonely, but I guess it was better than being with him."

Laurel looked down at Abigail's phone. "Could I borrow your phone? See if we can trace the call?"

"No." Abigail chuckled low. "There's nothing helpful on my phone. If our father's back in town, and if he called and left a message, he used a burner phone. It's already crumpled and dead and gone."

"Why?" Laurel asked. "He was a successful pastor in town. I don't think anybody knew of the crimes he undoubtedly committed. Why did he leave? To stay under the radar?"

"Oh," Abigail said. "I think people did know about some of his crimes. But he didn't just leave, you know."

This is the first time Abigail had given Laurel any sense of why their father had disappeared five years ago. "Was it you?" Laurel asked. "Did you threaten him?"

Abigail shrugged. "Does it matter?"

"Absolutely, it matters."

Abigail exhaled and then brushed the last bit of snow off her dark red hair. It had already melted in most places, leaving the strands wet around her shoulders. "No, it wasn't me. I think that he and my brother, Robert, got into it one time. About what, I don't know. And then, all of a sudden, Father left. I was happy about it. I think Robert was actually trying to do the right thing, for once."

Laurel tapped a pen on the old wooden door. Robert Caine had been Abigail's half brother, who had turned out to be the serial killer in the Snowblood Peak case. "Why do you think Robert threatened our father?"

Abigail met her gaze directly. "It was just a gut feeling. A couple things Robert said. I know that Robert wanted me to be close to him and his family, and I wouldn't be around while our father was still at the church. So I think he took care of it the best way he knew how. He probably threatened our father in some way. I have no idea where he's been these last five years. And frankly, I don't care."

It was unfortunate that Robert was dead and couldn't be asked. "Do you think we're in danger from him?" Laurel asked evenly.

"Absolutely," Abigail said. "He's evil. How are you not understanding this? I think I've been very clear." She threw up one perfectly manicured hand. Her nails were red, a stark contrast to her pale skin. "I've killed for you once, Laurel. I think it's your turn to protect me."

"I will," Laurel said. "If Zeke Caine is a threat to anybody, I will make sure to take him down. You will be protected."

Abigail had shot her half brother in order to save Laurel during the Snowblood Peak case, and sometimes Laurel wondered if it was out of sisterly duty or to hide the fact that Abigail had most likely helped to hide Robert's crimes. At the moment, it didn't matter.

Abigail's nostrils flared. "Think outside of your perfect world right now. Our father is a sadistic dick, and he will play games with you that you can't even imagine. He'll be everywhere in your life, and you won't be able to find him, much less prove it. Maybe we should run."

"Not a chance. Tell me absolutely every place you think Zeke Caine could be right now." Finally. Laurel was going to come face-to-face with the monster whose DNA she shared.

After an unfruitful day of searching for her father throughout Genesis Valley, Laurel was tired, hungry, and downright irritated. She'd spent time at the church, visited each business within the unofficial town square, and had even spoken with several parishioners who had been long-standing members of the church. Though nobody had been contacted by Zeke, many seemed thrilled he was back. They obviously didn't know him.

The storm had finally lightened up, but the temperature had dropped, freezing the recent snow to the ground and the trees around her. She drove slowly away from her office building and pressed a button on her dash to call Huck. The call went immediately to voice mail. He had left her a message earlier that he was working a poaching case that night and might not be back, so she wasn't worried.

She hesitated and then turned left instead of going straight, taking a long side road and winding around a snowy hill to park in front of a wide, log building illuminated with bright lights. There were cars scattered around the snowy parking lot.

Her phone buzzed and she answered it. "Snow."

"Hi, Boss. We didn't find anything of interest at Frederick Marshall's house," Walter said. "No signs of struggle. Ena did a good job helping me search, and I think we should ask her for help until we get the new agents."

"All right. Thanks and have a good night." Laurel ended the call and sat in her quiet vehicle for a moment, staring at the establishment.

A sign adorned the area above the double door. OLD LOU'S. She shouldn't do this and get involved, but there was something inside her that just couldn't help it. Shaking off her unease, she jumped out of her SUV to pick her way carefully across the icy ground and push open the door.

As expected, her sister was nowhere to be seen. Instead, Officer Zello sat hunched over a beer at the far end of the bar.

She moved toward him, knowing she should just turn around and go home. It was almost nine at night, and she was tired.

He looked up, his eyes blurry. "You know, you're just as pretty as she is." His voice slurred.

"Thank you," Laurel said dryly, putting her purse on the bar. "Do you have a ride home?"

"I do."

She looked at his half-empty beer but could smell tequila. "I tried to warn you about Abigail."

"I know. It was kind of you to warn me, but . . . I don't know, there's something about her. She's wounded and she's lost."

There were many adjectives Laurel could use to describe Abigail Caine. Wounded and lost were not two of them. "She's deadly and she's dangerous. There's no doubt she's a threat to you if you don't let her go."

Zello shrugged. "It's not her fault. She had a rough childhood and she's doing the best she can. She could really use a sister."

Laurel didn't know how to help him. "If you would just keep your personal life away from the job, then I think you would find success." He'd worked a scene efficiently in the Witch Creek murders, but his love life had harmed his credibility.

Zello snorted. "Like you have?"

Laurel paused. "What do you mean?"

"You and Huck Rivers. There's no doubt you guys are burning up the sheets. Abigail told me all about it."

She didn't appreciate her half sister discussing her with anybody. "I don't owe you an explanation, but I will say that the captain and I don't work together. Sometimes we collaborate on cases, but we don't let that interfere with the job. Ever."

"Right. It's easier to get caught up than you think, lady."

Unease wandered through her. That was probably true. She retrieved her purse. What was wrong with her? Was she so thrown off by her sister and the return of her father that she ignored all logic? It wasn't her place to get involved here, and Officer Zello's decisions weren't her business. "I strongly suggest you get an Uber home."

"Wait." He looked up, his eyes so bloodshot it made her own itch in pain. "I saw your father."

Laurel straightened. "Where?"

"Here. About an hour ago. I recognized him from the missing persons report." Zello threw out an arm toward the main door. "The guy walked in, winked at me, and then ran back out. I chased him but he jumped into a green truck and sped away."

"He winked at you?"

Zello snorted. "Yeah. It was creepy."

Zeke Caine playing games. Perhaps Abigail had been right, and even her ex was a target. "Thanks for telling me."

"Of course. Now would you call your sister for me? We can both talk to her."

For goodness' sakes. "No. Please move on." Laurel turned on her heel and left him staring into his beer. She'd known better.

She was halfway home when her phone rang, so she hit the Bluetooth button. "Agent Snow."

"Hi. It's Norrs," Norrs said with the sound of a television set droning in the background. "I wanted to call and update you that we haven't found any connection between Kate Vuittron and the newest victim, Frederick Marshall, other than his name atop her divorce papers. We've confirmed from searching Victor's computer that he actually drafted all of the documents. We're still looking, but so far, she's clear. Thought you'd want to know."

"Thank you," she said, an ache in her chest finally dissipating. Kate needed to be free of this.

He cleared his throat. "Also, I was wondering if you and Officer Rivers would like to go to dinner tomorrow night with Abigail and myself? A Saturday night double date?"

The last thing Laurel wanted was to deal with the train wreck of Abigail's love life. "I don't think so, Agent Norrs."

"Maybe next weekend, then. Have a good one, Agent Snow." He ended the call.

Not in a million years.

Chapter 21

It was much more satisfying to leave a mangled body in the snow than in a place like this one. Must be something about the contrast between pure snow and dirty blood.

Whidbey Island was snow-free this time of year, although a blustery wind swept across the area closest to the beach. Our Lady of the Waves Catholic church stood proudly on the western side of the island. At this time of the morning, before the sun had started to climb, the place was deserted.

This church was a combination of brick and stone with tall arches and powerful lights along the eaves that cast their beams out toward the churning and deadly water. The parking area was on the other side, but luckily enough, there had been a trail to the beach wide enough for a truck.

This side, where the waves crashed against the rocks, was the perfect place to leave this sinner. The purple tent was easy to set up even in the wind, although the howling through the eaves of the church was eerie. Once the tent was erected, it was simple to move to the back of the truck and pull out the sinner by the ankles. His flesh was rapidly chilling, and the blood had stopped flowing from the multiple stab wounds.

It was difficult to remember the actual stabbing. There had been such rage and such pain; the knife had plunged wildly in and out.

The blood was sticky but could be ignored for now. The body thumped off the truck and was more solid than it looked, but not too difficult to drag into the tent. It was interesting how heavy sinners were, even in death. Must be the putrid evil living in their very pores.

Men like this made others victims. It was a fitting end to a monster.

A sound ticked outside of the tent, hopefully just more of the waves against the rocks. A quick glance showed no one out there. Good. The naked body looked peaceful, which wasn't right. This body shouldn't be peaceful. It had done wrong, and the sinner should pay.

Tears made the interior of the tent blurry, even with the flashlight pointed at the body. But there was nothing that could be done about that. It was time for the hearts. There were piles of them making each jacket pocket heavy.

Pain flashed to agony, and then the world went dark again. Seconds, minutes, perhaps hours later, that same pain echoed in a loud scream. A quick glance confirmed that the candy had indeed been shoved inside the dead man's throat and spilled all around his bloody head. How had that happened? When had it happened? The urge to back away from the body, snarling and crying, was overwhelming.

The sun was starting to peek up over the other side of the little island. There wasn't much time. There was blood in the back of the truck, and it was imperative it be washed out before anybody noticed.

Silent and judgmental, the church stood in strict vigil as

the waves pounded the shore and the wind assaulted the water.

Alone in the tent, the sinner lay with his eyes open, his body bloodied, and his little hearts crammed down his throat.

There was no need to look back.

The call came in just as Laurel pulled into the parking lot in front of her building. She'd arranged to meet her team on the blustery Saturday morning so they could go over the case again, without any interruptions. "Snow," she answered through the Bluetooth.

"We have another one," Agent Norrs said.

Laurel caught sight of Walter as he exited his vehicle and motioned him over. She lowered her window. "Just a sec," she said to Norrs.

Walter approached her door. "What's up, Boss?"

"Hop in," she said. "I have Agent Norrs on speaker phone."

Walter lumbered around the vehicle and climbed into the passenger seat, slamming the door and tossing his backpack into the back seat.

"What do we have, Agent Norrs?" Laurel asked.

Rain muffled Norrs's voice. "Male body stabbed several times, Valentine's Day candy stuffed in his mouth and sprinkled around his head."

"Where?" Laurel asked.

"Whidbey Island on the west side," Norrs said.

Laurel glanced at the drizzly day outside. While the snow had stopped for now, a heavy rain fell, and soon, it'd freeze. "It'll take me two point one hours to get there."

"I know. The agents on the ground can't hold the body

that long because the wind has really picked up. They can't secure it. Do you want me to send it to Dr. Ortega at Tempest County?"

It was convenient that Agent Norrs was working so collaboratively. How much would his attitude alter when Abigail inevitably discontinued their romantic relationship? "Yes, thank you," Laurel said. "Is there anything else of interest at the scene?"

"Same purple tent, I think," Norrs answered. "Agents on scene reported signs of dragging the body. Also, the body placement was right behind the Our Lady of the Waves church. My guys think it's creepy."

Another church? She ran through the other two murders. Had she missed something with Victor Vuittron's murder? Was there a place of worship near where his body was dumped? "Any identification on the victim?"

"Not yet. They ran his fingerprints, and he didn't pop."

Laurel backed out of the parking area and drove onto the main road. "If he was a lawyer, his prints would have been in the system after taking the bar exam."

"I'm aware of that," Agent Norrs said. "This isn't a lawyer. My team is all out on that RICO case right now. Can yours handle this? I was just called in because I've worked with the local sheriff before."

"Yes, we can handle this. Please send the pictures, and I'll have my team start trying to identify this victim."

"I'd start with the law firm," Norrs said.

Walter rolled his eyes and mouthed. "No shit."

Laurel tried to hide a smile. "Would you please have the scene preserved as much as possible? I'd like to view it before the crime techs remove the tent."

"Sure thing," Norrs said. "Drive carefully. It's a hell of a storm out here."

"Thanks," Laurel said, clicking off.

Walter fastened his seatbelt. "So we have a nonlawyer as a victim this time. That's interesting, right?"

"I'm more intrigued by the fact that the body was staged by a church." She pressed the button to call the best computer expert in the FBI.

"This is Nester," Nester answered.

She hadn't seen his car in the parking lot. "Hi. Are you in the office?"

"Yeah, I am. I had a friend drop me off."

Walter snorted.

Laurel frowned, and then Walter shook his head.

"All right. Has the lab found anything on the purple tents or the candy?" she asked.

"No," Nester said. "The lab's backed up. We won't hear anything about the tent or the candy for probably a week, if that. I've done research, and it looks like, just based on a preliminary search, it's a common camping tent found in stores all over the world. I've been calling different outfitting places in the Seattle area during my off time, just to ask if anybody bought them in bulk. So far, nothing."

She appreciated his initiative. "Okay, please keep trying. Also, will you conduct a quick search for a church or community center near the area where Victor Vuittron's body was found beneath the underpass?"

"Just a sec." The sound of typing came over the line. "Huh. Yeah, there is. It's actually pretty close to that place, just a block away."

"What kind of church?" Walter asked.

More typing echoed. "Let me see. Lutheran. It's a Lutheran church, with a community center next to it."

"Nester?" Laurel said. "I know that Richard Marshall attended Genesis Valley Community Church, and he was found near church grounds in a tent. Make some calls and find out if Victor Vuittron attended church, and if so, where."

Walter shifted in his seat. "You think churches have something to do with it?"

"It's possible," Laurel admitted. "All three of the victims have been found near churches, and I don't like that coincidence."

"What does it mean?" Nester asked through the phone. "Like they were sinners and deserved to be stabbed a zillion times? What does it have to do with Valentine's heart-shaped candy?"

That was the pivotal question. "Could be nothing," Laurel mused. "We need to examine these murders from different angles. They're ritualistic, true. But that could be an attempt to hide the true motive behind the crimes."

"Gotcha," Nester said. "I'll start making those calls now, and I'll get back to you."

What else did she need? "Any news on the warrants for the additional phone dumps?"

"Not yet, but I'll start calling the judge in about an hour."

She had full faith Nester had chosen the correct judge to ask. "Thanks." Ending the call, she looked at Walter. "What did I miss about that friend dropping Nester off?"

"You didn't miss anything, Boss," Walter said. "Nester has a new girlfriend, that's all."

Nester seemed to have a new girlfriend every month or so. Good for him. He was young and smart, and no doubt enjoyed his time off. "How are you feeling?" She turned onto I-90 and sped up, careful of the icy conditions.

"I'm a lot better. Nester and I have been walking, and I'm losing weight just like the doc ordered. It's good to be back on full duty."

"Good, I've missed you," Laurel said, meaning it. Walter was a good partner.

Walter shucked her on the arm. "I've missed you, too, Boss."

Her phone dinged as Norrs texted the pictures from the newest scene. "Send those to Nester so he can work on identifying the victim, please."

"Sure," Walter said, taking her phone.

Laurel turned to concentrate on the road. They drove in companionable silence for about half an hour until her phone buzzed. She hit the button on the dash. "Snow."

"Hey, it's Nester. We have an ID on the newest vic."

She looked at Walter. "Already?"

"Yes. I teleconferenced with Melissa Cutting at the law firm and showed her the picture, figuring that was a good place to start. Apparently she works on Saturdays, too."

"What did you find?" Walter asked.

Nester sneezed. "Excuse me. The victim's name was Jiro Makino, and he was a videographer."

"A videographer? Was he a client of the firm?" Laurel asked.

"Yes. He utilized the firm to draft contracts and actually exchanged services to do so. He filmed a couple of ads for them." Nester coughed. Was he getting sick? "Ms. Cutting also told me that Jiro was a client of Victor's for two DUIs."

Laurel slowed down to allow a careening Subaru to pass her. "Were there any victims in the DUIs?"

"Negative," Nester said. "I also asked her if she had any idea who would want Mr. Makino dead, and she did not." The young man was turning into a good investigator.

"Okay. Thank you," Laurel said.

Rapid typing sounded. "Ms. Cutting has no idea if Victor Vuittron attended a church."

So much for that idea, but the churches were still a key.

"Please find out if Mr. Makino had any family and see if they'll meet with us later today. Walter and I will have time after viewing the scene on Whidbey Island."

"Sure thing," Nester said. "I'm on Jiro's website now, and it looks like he did a lot of work within the Pacific Northwest. He even filmed footage of the Karelian Bear Dog Program, but I don't see Huck Rivers in it. Ena is in there, though. She looks happy." Nester's voice turned thoughtful. "The guy filmed everything from documentaries to weddings. He was pretty talented." Then Nester gave a short whistle.

"What is it?" Laurel asked, speeding up to pass a logging truck.

"Guess whose campaign video he filmed earlier this year?"

Laurel cut a quick look at Walter. "Don't tell me."

"Yep," Nester said. "Councilman Swelter's."

Chapter 22

"This is creepy as hell," Walter said, bending down to look inside the purple tent.

Laurel cocked her head to the side and had to agree. The body had been removed. Mushed Valentine's candy was scattered throughout and covered in blood, creating a paste of heart-shaped remains. The state crime lab techs bustled around, so she backed away to let them finish their work. The church stood tall and silent above them. "I can't connect the dots between the churches and the Valentine's candy," she mused.

Walter's thin hair blew in the heavy breeze, and he looked down at the tumultuous ocean as it smashed against the rocks. "I don't know, love and light? Good and evil? Life and death?" He scratched his chin. "All of it seems weird. It could just be somebody had the Valentine's Day candy left over and wanted to shove something in their throats to choke them."

Laurel looked toward him. "You mean so they couldn't speak?"

"Yeah, think about it. Maybe they were liars or maybe

this killer thought they were liars. They talked about love, and it wasn't true."

Laurel shook her ahead. "It could be something as obscure as this killer seeing a heart-shaped candy years ago. We don't want to get too caught up in it, but it is a clue." She shivered in the cold.

"Let's get going," Walter said. "There's nothing here for us."

Laurel followed him back to the car, started the engine, and turned the heat on full blast even though it wasn't raining or snowing on Whidbey Island. The chill off the ocean was piercing. Her phone rang and she hit the Bluetooth. "Agent Snow."

"Hi, Agent Snow. It's Dr. Ortega."

She warmed. "Dr. Ortega, it's good to hear from you. How are you?"

"I'm excellent. Thank you for asking." The doctor was as efficient as any she'd ever met.

"Do you have the autopsy on Frederick Marshall?"

Papers rustled and Dr. Ortega cleared his voice. "Yes. It's similar to the autopsy on Victor Vuittron. I also found flecks of paint on the heels and the back of the legs on Frederick Marshall, and I sent them to the lab. We're probably two weeks out from receiving more details though."

Laurel drove away from the church and turned onto a main street. "Do you still think it was paint flecks?"

"I do. I've seen it before, and they look like paint flecks to me. Also, in the wounds on Marshall's body, I found leather."

Walter leaned toward the speaker. "Leather? What do you mean you found leather?"

"Leather was imbedded in several of the stab wounds. My guess is your killer's wearing heavy leather gloves."

Walter nodded. "It makes sense. When you stab somebody like that, you'll also often cut or hurt yourself. If this killer has half a brain, he'd wear gloves. It's odd that you didn't find any leather in the first body."

"Maybe the killer was more careful with the first body or in less of a rage," Laurel mused.

"I don't know." Dr. Ortega cleared his throat. "The third body just arrived, and I'll do the autopsy later tonight. Just so you know, Frederick Marshall was stabbed fifty-two times."

"So it's not the number," Laurel said out loud. Fifty-two and forty-eight times. It was similar, but it wasn't exactly the same. It was more like a rage killing—but also a well-thought-out plan considering the tent and the Valentine's candy. "Anything on the candy?" she asked.

"No," Dr. Ortega said. "It appears to be just regular Valentine's Day heart-shaped candy. I did send several samples to the crime lab, but again . . ."

Walter groaned. "They're way behind with backlog."

Laurel turned again and then drove around a neighborhood until she reached a craftsman-style home with stained redwood siding. There were light green accents on the door and the eaves. "Please keep us informed," she said.

"You bet," Dr. Ortega said, finishing the call.

"Nice place," Walter said.

Laurel noted the precise and relaxing layout of the landscaping. Nester had sent her Jiro Makino's aunt's address while she'd been examining the scene earlier.

"Has the aunt already been notified?" Walter asked.

"Yes." Laurel stepped out of the SUV. "She was notified a few hours ago, according to Agent Norrs."

Walter shuffled from the car and quickly buttoned up his overcoat. "Good. I hate doing notifications."

Laurel strode up the cobblestone walkway and unlatched the gate, which she opened, allowing Walter through before shutting it. Well-tended shrubs adorned the front yard. She walked up the two stairs, noting the perfectly aligned green pots housing potted daffodils before knocking on the door.

A woman, probably in her early seventies, her dark gray hair askew and fresh tear tracks on her face, opened the door. "Can I help you?"

Laurel showed her badge. "Good Afternoon. I'm Special Agent Laurel Snow."

"Oh, yes," the woman said. "Come on in. Your office called and said you would be coming."

"Thank you." Laurel followed her inside a living room decorated with a blue tweed sofa and white chairs. In the center was a gold and glass coffee table, and the area was open to the kitchen, which smelled like warm strawberries. The heat was turned on full blast.

"Please sit down. I am Himari Makino. Jiro was my nephew."

"I'm very sorry for your loss," Walter said, walking around the sofa to take a seat. "Thank you for speaking with us."

"Of course." She sounded confused and bewildered.

Laurel noted the red and green, traditional Japanese ukiyo-e hanging scroll on the other side of the dining room. "That is beautiful," she murmured.

Himari nodded. "Thank you. My mother brought that over from Japan when she immigrated here decades ago. Please sit."

Laurel took the seat on the sofa next to Walter so Himari could have some space in a chair. "Do you have any idea who would want to harm your nephew?" she asked as gently as she could.

Himari's hands trembled as she clasped them in her lap. She wore black leggings and a deep blue sweater. Her feet were bare and surprisingly long for her small stature. "No. I can't imagine. Jiro had friends everywhere. He was an artist."

Laurel unzipped her parka in response to the heat flowing from the vents. "Did he have any angry ex-girlfriends or wives or anybody romantically involved with him?"

"He was divorced last year after being married for just three years," Himari said. "That's why he moved in with me here. He and his wife lived in Olympia."

"Tell me about his wife," Walter said.

"No, it wasn't Beth. They weren't happy together, so she moved to Europe. She's been in Berlin for the past year and was more than pleased to leave him." Himari sighed. "Jiro was a true artist dedicated only to his work. I'm afraid he wasn't the best of husbands."

"Did they have any children?" Laurel asked.

Himari picked a pillow up off the floor and put it on her lap to hug against herself. "No, they didn't. I think that was part of the problem. Beth wanted children and Jiro didn't, so they got divorced and he's been living here." She looked around. "Why don't people ask that about each other before they marry?"

Laurel agreed with the sentiment. Should she and Huck ask such questions now that they were dating? Did she want kids? He seemed to want them, but she wasn't good with people. What if she couldn't be good with children? "It's nice you let your nephew live with you."

Himari's lips trembled in a smile. "I traveled quite a bit during his childhood, and it has been nice getting to know him as an adult."

Walter unbuttoned his jacket and sweat dotted his upper brow. The heat must be set to eighty degrees. "Are his parents still living?"

"No," Himari said. "My brother and his wife both passed a couple of decades ago. I can only pray that Jiro has found his way to them."

Laurel discreetly tried to open her jacket to cool off a little bit. She could feel sweat prick along her back. "Do you know of a Victor Vuittron or Frederick Marshall?"

"Yes," Himari said. "I think I know those names. They're with that law firm, and they were in the news?"

Laurel wiped a dot of sweat off her forehead. "Yes. They worked for the Marshall & Cutting Law firm and, unfortunately, both were killed in the same manner as your nephew."

"That's terrible," Himari said, a tear sliding down her face. "I just don't know what to say. What is the connection among the three?"

"I don't know. We were hoping you could help us with that," Laurel said. "Have you met Victor or Frederick?"

Tears gathered in Himari's eyes. "I met Victor at a fundraiser for his campaign. Jiro helped create a video for him. He was running for city council, and I was my nephew's date." She smiled and the sight was sad. "I met Victor, and we had a good time."

Walter took his coat off.

"Oh, is it too hot in here?" Himari asked.

"No. No, not at all," Walter said, his face beet red. "It's fine, really. I just needed to take my coat off." He cleared his throat. "How did Jiro know Victor?"

Himari put a hand to her head as if trying to remember. "They were boyhood friends. They went way back."

"Did they go to elementary school together, or high school?" Walter asked.

Himari shook her head. "I don't think so. Jiro went to private school in southern Washington, and I'm fairly certain Victor attended school in Seattle."

Laurel tilted her head. "Then how did they know each other?"

"I believe they first met at summer camp and then stayed in touch, reconnecting at the University of Washington." Himari stood and walked over to a beautiful oak desk to rifle through the bottom drawer. She pulled out a photo album. "This was my sister's. I kept it after she died. Jiro didn't seem interested in it, but I figured someday he'd get married and have kids and want them."

She reclaimed her seat and flipped through the overflowing pages before pulling out a photograph. "There you go. It was Sunrise Camp over on Sunrise Lake. Jiro went his sophomore year in high school." She pulled out a picture and handed it to Laurel.

Laurel looked at the photograph of what appeared to be about thirty smiling teenagers with five older camp counselors standing behind them. She tried to make him out. "There's Victor," she said. Her heart began to beat faster. "And that's Frederick Marshall." He was thinner and obviously looked younger, but there was no doubt it was Frederick.

"Jiro's standing in the front row," Himari said.

Laurel quickly spotted him, smiling and looking carefree. The boy standing next to him made her catch her breath. "That's Councilman Swelter."

Himari shrugged. "I don't know him."

But Laurel did. She had to get him to speak with her. She had no warrant, but she was about to become very annoying to him. "May I keep this?" she asked.

"Sure," Himari said. "What does it matter now?"

Chapter 23

His feet finally warming up, Huck walked up the stairs to the FBI office and found Laurel sitting on top of the glass table in the conference room, staring at the middle case board. At the bottom, she'd taped pictures of the three victims.

"Hey," he said.

She looked over her shoulder. Her eyes were tired, and her hair was messy around her pale face. "Did you catch your poachers?"

"We did," he said. "That'll teach them to poach here." He walked around the table to pull out a chair. "Looks like you have three victims now."

"We do," she said.

"It's after seven, and it's Saturday night, Laurel. Why don't we grab dinner and then head home?"

The woman had that unfocused look he'd learned to recognize as the one she wore in the middle of a case. He'd seen it twice before, and he couldn't even imagine how fast her brain was running.

She looked back at the board. "I'd love to, but my mom is leaving for a retreat tomorrow with several of her employees, so I should stay home tonight. I mean, it's not home. I'm building my own home, but I should be there tonight."

God, she was cute when she got flustered. He nodded. "Then tomorrow night you're all mine."

Her smile was sweet and a little tentative. "That could be arranged."

"Don't you own part of your mom's company?"

"Yes, but I don't get involved with all the worshiping the moon and channeling the energy of the sun. I just came up with the idea of mass producing the teas and creating a subscription service," Laurel said.

Deidre Snow owned a subscription service for teas, and her success was probably owed to her daughter, who would never take the credit. But, if anybody needed some quiet time away from murder, it was Laurel Snow. "Are you sure you don't want to go on the retreat?" he asked, already knowing the answer.

She smiled. "No, thanks. But that will give us time together. Now that we're dating?" Her hesitation was endearing.

He needed to get a grip on himself. "I'm looking forward to it," he said.

"Good. By the way, Ena was in a video about the Karelian Bear Dog Program filmed by one of my victims. Why weren't you?"

He half remembered the promotional video. "I said no."

"I figured." Her phone buzzed and she pulled it out of her back pocket. When she saw who was calling, she set it on speaker. "Agent Snow."

"Agent Snow, this is Councilman Swelter. You called three times this afternoon. Don't you even take weekends off from harassing people?" The councilman sounded irritated. The hackles rose on Huck's back, but he didn't let his expression change.

Laurel straightened. "Yes. I've been trying to reach you. Are you familiar with a filmmaker named Jiro Makino?"

Swelter sighed. "Yes. Why?"

"How do you know him?" Laurel asked.

Papers rustled across the line. "He's the guy who filmed one of my campaign videos. When I asked him to film the second one, he said no because he'd decided he was better friends with Victor Vuittron, who was running against me. Victor and I have had a problem since we were kids. The asshole was only running because he didn't like me," Swelter snapped.

"Why not?" Laurel asked.

Huck wished the jerk was face-to-face with them right now. It was difficult to imagine anybody liking Swelter.

"Because he was an ass. We've never gotten along— football rivalry and all of that. Wrap this up, Agent."

Laurel tapped her fingers on the glass tabletop. "Did you know Jiro in any other context?"

Swelter was silent for a moment. "Why? Is Jiro dead, too?"

"Just answer the question, please."

Now his sigh was long suffering and a little too loud. "Apparently he was at one of the many summer camps my folks shipped me to when I was a kid. My assistant hired Jiro because he saw one of the documentaries that Jiro did. I didn't even remember him from when we were kids until he reminded me. The guy didn't make an impression on me, and I haven't talked to him since he filmed what could only be considered a mediocre video. Okay?"

Huck wanted to punch this guy in the nose. Instead, he just sat back and stared at the board.

Laurel also stared at the board. "Was this camp the Sunrise Camp?"

"No clue," Swelter said. "Could've been. My folks fought

all the time and liked me gone in the summer. Can't remember half of the names of the places I learned to be one with fucking nature."

"Where did you grow up, Councilman Swelter?" Laurel asked.

"What the hell does that have to do with anything?" Swelter snarled.

Laurel glared at her phone. "If you'll just answer the questions, we can get through this now. Or I can come down to your office again and wait till you speak with me."

"Fine. I grew up in Spokane and moved to Seattle right after college. Now I really have to go." He ended the call.

Huck whistled. "What a complete ass. Tell me he's a suspect."

Laurel pointed at the board where the Councilman's picture was taped next to one of Melissa Cutting, partner in the law firm. The other pictures were of Mrs. Kirsti Vuittron and Mrs. Marshall, both now widows, and Thema Sackey, the junior associate at the firm. "Yes, he's a suspect, but I'm not getting a real strong hit on him." She scrubbed her hands through her hair. "The victims are connected by a summer camp as well as the law firm. Though the law firm provides more suspects for now."

"It's possible they all just met at a summer camp, which led to at least two of them working for the same law firm. There seems to be quite a bit more intrigue going on at the firm. Or perhaps within the councilman's race?" Huck tried to examine the board from a different angle. "What's the chance that this is just a serial killer choosing victims at random? That he or she has a problem with successful men in their mid-fifties who might have a secret or two?"

Laurel stretched her neck. "It's possible. The victimology

just changed, however, with Jiro Makino being full Japanese."

"Does that matter?" Huck asked.

"Sometimes the victimology varies a little bit. These three men were successful, and all of them attended the same summer camp when they were kids. That's how they knew each other." Laurel pulled a picture out from beneath a file folder. "The camp went out of business about ten years ago, according to Nester's research earlier today. So far, that's all I know about it."

Huck looked at the pictures of all the kids. "What about posting the picture on social media with requests for information?"

She twirled the picture around with one finger. "That's a possibility down the line. Right now, we don't want to post it and let the killer know we've found this link. Especially if this is the link rather than the law firm. Who knows? I'm hoping to find one person who'll lead us to names for the rest of the kids."

Huck looked again at the photo of the kids in front of a lake, all smiling and in some sort of swimwear. About fifteen boys and fifteen girls with three male and two female counselors standing behind them smiling. "You need somebody to identify those kids."

She nodded. "Nester is searching for somebody who can do that. If he's unsuccessful, I'll take the picture to Swelter. We could also have the techs in DC run facial rec, maybe."

"You just need one person to start with," Huck mused.

She examined the photograph. "I don't trust Swelter and would rather find somebody else to confirm identifications. That guy lies for a living." She taped the picture to the board alongside the suspects and the victims. "This is one link between the victims, and the law firm is the other." Her phone rang again, and she pressed the speaker button. Apparently work never stopped for Laurel Snow. "Agent Snow."

"Hi, Agent Snow. I'm glad I caught you. This is Thema Sackey."

Laurel's eyebrows rose. "Ms. Sackey, hello. Do you have news for me?"

"No. But I do have a request for you. Jason Abbott would like to speak with you on Tuesday morning if that works with your schedule."

Huck straightened and almost rejected the offer, but he didn't want to interfere.

Laurel shook her head. "No, that doesn't work with my schedule. I don't have anything to discuss with Mr. Abbott."

"He thinks he can help you with your current case," Thema said. "I told him that he should not speak with you, but he's not listening to me."

Laurel looked at Huck and pursed her lips. "How can he help?"

Thema sighed. "I have no idea. Again, he's meeting with you against advice of counsel."

Laurel bit her lip. "Very well, I'll meet him at nine on Tuesday morning." She ended the call.

Huck shook his head. "That's a mistake."

Laurel turned back to the board. "Most likely."

The clouds hung low as another blistering storm pounded the mountain village around her. Laurel drove home after eating pizza with Huck for a Saturday night date of sorts, her mind occupied with the links between the victims. She'd called Ena, who'd said that Jiro was a nice guy while filming the promo spots, but that she hadn't gotten to know him at all.

So Laurel was no closer to finding the killer.

The lights of a vehicle glimmered through the darkness behind her as she drove the country road, keeping pace almost perfectly. Awareness ticked down her spine. She kept a close eye and then turned down the private road that bisected the family farm. She drove just far enough that she could still see the outside road, and the vehicle drove by. This case was getting to her. She was starting to see phantoms everywhere, which was not like her.

Taking a deep breath, she continued on her way, making a sharp left toward what used to be an old barn. She was turning the place into a barndominium and couldn't wait to see it finished. Leaving her car running, she jumped out and slogged through the snow to open the main door and look inside. The architect had finished drawing up her plans nearly three weeks ago, and she'd hired a company to move out equipment that had been left. They'd have to wait until spring when the ground thawed to begin constructing the wings off the main area.

She could see it all in her head. It would be the perfect place for her to live. It was close to her mother and to town, and yet it had privacy surrounded by trees up against the creek. If she was transferred after this year, then she could rent the place as an Airbnb. But for now, she could only smell possibilities.

The contractor was supposed to have started the framing inside to shore up the structure, and she hoped they'd gotten as far as she wanted.

She breathed in the cold air and looked at what might be her home. So much progress had already been made that she smiled. The framers had finished half of the west wall. Moving inside, she inspected the work. It looked good. The contractor was somebody recommended by her uncle, so she felt confident of the quality. The idea of having her own place on the family farm filled her with more delight than she'd expected. It was a logical move, and yet she truly was looking forward to building this two-story home with its large office and small closets just for herself.

A plaintive meow caught her attention and she turned to face the far corner. Another one came. Frowning, she hurried toward the back of the barn to find a wounded animal curled up in the corner.

"Hello there." She crouched but made no effort to reach him. He looked up and one of his damaged ears twitched. He appeared to be a gray and white cat, probably around a year or so old. His eyes were a luminous green and clear, and his front paw was bloody.

"How badly are you hurt?" she asked, looking around. Where had this cat come from? A couple of open boards to the left showed cat hair clumped in the wood. The barn was acres upon acres away from both the main road and her mother's house. Her uncles lived even farther toward the mountain, and none of them had a cat. Had somebody dumped the poor guy out at the main road? He'd been smart to seek shelter.

He meowed and then slowly stretched, limping toward her, shivering in the cold.

She tugged off her parka and gently wrapped it around him. "It looks like you and I are going to the vet." She picked him up, careful to keep her hands away from his sharp little teeth. She had his legs trapped so he couldn't claw her, but she also didn't know that he was free of disease. His coat was a little bit mangy, and he was sopping wet.

"Come on, friend," she said. "I'll take you to the vet and they can handle you from there. I'm sure they can find you a good home." She hustled back outside and placed him gently on the passenger seat before turning on the heat. He gave one more meow and snuggled down in her coat, going right to sleep. She stared at him, bemused. For a wounded cat, he seemed surprisingly trusting. That was odd. Even so, she had to get him to the vet.

Movement by the tree line caught her eye and she stiffened. What was that? Silently, she reached for her laptop bag on the floor and drew out her weapon, sliding from the vehicle.

Nothing moved. The snowstorm blasted her, while heavily weighed tree bows shook in the wind. Were the shadows playing tricks on her? Or had somebody been out there watching her? Her breath created tendrils in the cold. She remained in place until she was too cold to effectively shoot. If there had been somebody out there, he was gone now.

Chapter 24

Early the next morning, Laurel placed her mother's two suitcases near the door. "Are you sure you're only going for a week?"

"Very funny," Deidre said, bustling out of the kitchen to drop another tote on top of the bags. "I'm bringing all of the ingredients for the different ceremonies. You know that."

Laurel fought the urge to sneeze at the strong scent of lavender. "Mom, it's a yoga retreat."

"It's a business retreat," Deidre returned. "You made sure of it."

Actually, it was smart tax planning. "It'd be nice if you just relaxed."

"I will. I promise." Diedre's gaze shifted to the cat sleeping soundly on its new pillow by the fireplace. "I can't believe you brought a cat home."

Laurel pushed her hair out of her eyes. "I know. That wasn't my plan."

Deidre laughed. "It's nice when something upsets one of your many plans." She winked at the cat. "I have to admit, I love your big brain, but when your huge heart shows up, it makes me even prouder as a mother."

Laurel rolled her eyes and stared at the cat. "I think he has gifts."

Deidre chuckled. "Yeah. He's a cutie."

At the vet, the little guy had looked at Laurel with those big eyes and then meowed. It was almost as if he'd been talking to her. Oh, she knew cats couldn't talk to people, but she also knew she couldn't just leave him there. The veterinarian had stitched up the cat's paw and said his ear would heal. He was in good shape, and somebody had already neutered him, but chances were they'd dropped him off on the road in the middle of nowhere. The mere idea was infuriating.

"We could use a pet around here," Deidre said. "Never thought it'd be a cat. I would've guessed you were more of a dog person."

The last thing she had time for right now was a pet. "I do like dogs," Laurel agreed. "But that guy charmed me." She could admit that he charmed her, at least to her mother, if nobody else.

"What are we going to name him?" Deidre asked.

His name was rather obvious. "I was thinking Lacassagne after Alexandre Lacassagne."

Deidre fetched her wallet off the table by the door. "Of course you were. He invented ice cream, right?"

Laurel snorted. "No. Lacassagne founded a criminology school. He looked at both biological and societal factors to determine criminality. In fact, he also was an early pioneer in toxicology."

"Sounds like ice cream to me. I was thinking Fred for a name." Deidre tossed her wallet into a large slouchy bag. "What do you think?"

"Fred Lacassagne? I find that name befitting our brave hero who found his way into the barn through the snowy night." Laurel looked out the front window at the clear day. The sun sparkled on the freshly fallen snow, shining like diamonds. "Mom, it's a clear day now, but there's another storm moving in tonight. You should probably get going."

"Oh, don't you worry. Dolores is going to pick me up in an hour. I want to go meditate and mentally prepare myself first."

Laurel didn't ask what her mom was preparing herself for because it no doubt had something to do with the moon. She purchased the best teas she could and grew a few of her own in greenhouses during the summer, but her mother believed that the spells and chants she cast over the tea boosted their medicinal qualities. Laurel thought it was a good marketing idea, and she was open to the possibility that her mother knew something she did not. "All right, you go meditate. I'll clean up the kitchen."

They'd celebrated adopting Lacassagne by making huckleberry pancakes for breakfast.

"Thanks," Deidre said, laying a hand on Laurel's arm. "I wish you'd come with me. It's a whole week unplugged from the rest of the world. Just because you don't believe our ceremonies strengthen our teas, or that the moon can heal hurts, doesn't mean none of it is true."

Laurel looked up at her mom's clear blue eyes. "I know. But I'm in the middle of a couple of cases and being unplugged for a week might just cause me to go insane."

Deidre snorted. "At least have some fun and sneak that Huck Rivers upstairs to your bedroom while I'm gone."

"I thought you didn't like Huck." There weren't many men she did like.

Deidre shrugged smoothly muscled shoulders beneath her mint-green yoga jacket. "He took a bullet for you, and Monty says he's a good guy, so I'm willing to give him a chance." She leaned in and kissed Laurel's forehead. "You deserve some fun, sweets. I wish you could find it with me at a relaxing retreat." Turning, she headed to the rear of the home and their yoga room.

Laurel cleaned the kitchen, enjoying the simple task. Once finished, she poured herself another cup of her mom's emerald tea and had started to move toward the living room when a knock sounded on the door. Dolores wouldn't be this early. She set the mug down and walked to the door, opening it and barely holding back a gasp.

In front of her stood Zeke Caine.

For the first time in Laurel Snow's entire life, she acted on instinct instead of thinking things through. In her stocking feet, she burst outside of the house and shoved him with both hands against his chest, pushing him all the way across the porch and down the three steps.

"You cannot be here," she said, her voice shaking. Intellectually, she knew that adrenaline and cortisol had just flooded her system, but she didn't care. She didn't need her weapon to handle him. She felt she could break every bone in his body, beginning with his left eye socket.

He took two steps back, his boots scraping on the salt-covered, icy walk. "So it's true," he said, his gaze hard on her face.

"Affirmative," she said, looking up several inches to meet his stare.

The man was bald, no longer set apart by the reddish-brown hair that had at one time matched hers. She looked into heterochromatic eyes, the exact same as hers and Abigail's. Apparently he'd hidden his for years while Laurel had been encouraged to just be herself. He had also forced Abigail to hide her true coloring, saying it was the mark of the devil, or something just as ridiculous.

"I would think you'd want to know me," he said, putting his hands on his hips. For this first fatherly visit, he had worn dark slacks and a thick black parka that covered whatever else he had on beneath it. His jaw was square and his cheekbones high, and he might have been considered handsome if he wasn't evil.

"I don't want to know anything about you," Laurel said. "What I want to do is take you down. If I had met you nine years earlier, I'd have arrested you for rape."

He chuckled and his upper lip curled. "Your mother lied. She may have had an overactive imagination, but she was willing."

Anger flashed through Laurel so quickly her ears heated and then tingled. Yet she forced herself to remain calm. She didn't know when, and she didn't know how, but she would make him pay. "Pastor John filed a missing persons report on you, saying you'd been absent for the last five years. Where have you been?"

"Look at you, doing your job no matter what." His gaze remained on her face as if he couldn't look away. "It's irrelevant where I've been. I have returned now."

"Why now?" She thought through what she knew of him. "Oh. You heard about Pastor John taking the church national and getting famous. You want your job back."

The muscles in his cheeks barely tightened. "It's my church. If anybody is going to be on television making millions, it's me."

"Spoken like a true narcissist." The snow and ice cut through her thick socks, but she ignored the pain. "I'll need a witness statement as to where you've been in order to file the matter away."

"That's a secret I plan on keeping."

She had no doubt he had many secrets. "Why did you leave?" He'd been a successful pastor in a popular church, yet one day he'd left his entire life behind him. "It's Abigail's belief that Robert scared you away."

Zeke's eyes hardened. "Robert couldn't scare a butterfly away. Turns out he was a serial killer, huh? It's interesting, isn't it?"

Laurel widened her stance, acutely aware of her mother in the house behind her. She could not let Deidre see this monster. Deidre was finally on a path to healing, and confronting Zeke Caine would set her back. "What's interesting?" She couldn't help but ask.

His lip curled even more, giving him an asymmetrical appearance. "My son turned out to be a serial killer. One of my daughters is an FBI agent who *chases* serial killers and the third, well, you know Abigail has most certainly killed, right?"

Laurel forced her facial muscles to show no emotion. "Who do you think she's killed?"

"Oh, please. You must have a brain in your head. I knew Abigail was on the path to becoming a very charming killer when the freaky brat was only four years old, the first time she pulled the legs off a bug." He shook his head. "I do hope you haven't made friends with her."

Laurel just stared at the man she wanted to hurt more than anybody else in the world. The violence coursing through her should be shocking, but instead, she embraced the fury. "I don't know how, but I will see you behind bars. I'm sure you've abused other women besides my mother."

He threw his head back and laughed. "I haven't abused anybody, including your mother. In fact, I'm the victim here. She never told me she got pregnant and had a child."

"Why would she?" Laurel asked. "You raped her, and besides, you were horrible to Abigail."

"Abigail's a horrible person," Zeke returned. "I thought maybe five years apart would mellow her hatred toward me, but I was wrong. She's just as vile and angry as ever, and if you think she has true feelings for you, you're wrong. There can only be one princess and she's it. You should watch your back."

Laurel lifted her chin. "I take it you've seen her?"

"I just came from her place. She told me where to find you," Zeke said.

That just figured. And Abigail would know exactly whom Laurel would call after this visit. "You need to leave, and you need to leave now, or I will have you arrested for trespassing." She tried to keep her voice level, but she couldn't prevent a tremor.

He looked behind her to the house. "I see. You don't want me to force your mother to tell you the truth, huh?"

"I know the truth," Laurel said. Bile rose in her throat. She wanted to vomit. "Leave." The rage inside her was new and she stopped to examine it. Shooting him would provide her with a moment of relief and then years of regret. But she could have him arrested for trespass instead. Maybe planting him behind bars even for a short time would help her build a case against him. He surely had transgressed more times than she knew about.

"Fine. I'll leave on one condition," he drawled.

Laurel waited, her legs trembling.

He looked at the fanciful leprechauns and pots of gold strewn across the colorful porch. "You meet me at the church tonight so we can talk. I have things to tell you about Abigail that you should understand."

Laurel needed to get him away from the house. Her nape itched. She could tell her mother was coming close. Deidre would only meditate for so long. "Fine, I'll meet you at the church. Six o'clock."

"Make it seven," Zeke said. "I have work to do first, and then I'll return home to my flock and retake my place in *my* church just in time." He turned on his heel and strode back down the driveway.

Laurel watched him go, clenching her fingers into a fist. She craned her neck as she watched him climb into a vehicle parked at the end of the driveway beneath the bows of snow-laden pine trees. The vehicle was an older green truck with no license plate. The engine caught after coughing, and then her father drove out of sight.

She'd had no justifiable cause to detain him. Even if she had, she didn't want her mother anywhere near that man. She couldn't even put out a BOLO on him because he wasn't wanted for a crime, and as a missing person, he'd apparently been found.

Movement sounded behind her, and the door opened.

"Laurel, what are you doing out here?" Deidre asked.

Laurel took a deep breath and smoothed out her expression before turning around. "I was just checking the weather. You should get going, Mom. There's a storm coming."

Chapter 25

The winter storm roared in around five that Sunday evening, and it didn't appear to be slowing any. Laurel drove carefully through the Genesis Valley center square toward the river and the church, once again pressing the button on her phone to call Abigail. Once again, the call went to voice mail.

"Call me," Laurel said, ending the call.

She'd already left a detailed message earlier, but Abigail didn't seem inclined to either answer her phone or return a phone call. Laurel flipped her windshield wipers on faster as punishing sleet hindered visibility. She took the turn for the church and headed toward the looming mountains, barely able to make them out through the blustery weather.

It was unthinkable that Zeke had just appeared on her porch this morning. As she drew closer to the church, adrenaline ticked through her system, and her heart rate increased. Her palms grew damp. She tried to relax her hands on the steering wheel. All day she'd run through different reasons to arrest him, but she hadn't found one that actually worked. She needed to investigate him, and the first step toward doing that was to discover where he had been the last five years.

Her phone buzzed and she hit the button on the dash. "Abigail?" she asked.

"No, it's Huck," Huck said through the speaker. "Where are you? Right now, I'm about an hour away but thought we could meet for a late dinner before the workweek starts again tomorrow. Not that we get weekends off."

"I can't," Laurel said, turning the windshield wipers up even faster. "I tried to call you earlier but didn't get an answer." She'd surmised he was out on a call.

Aeneas barked in the background. "Yeah, I got called out to the south side of Blarneys Creek. An ice fisherman wandered off after drinking too much moonshine in his coffee, and it took all day to find the guy."

That was dangerous terrain in which to get lost. "Did you find him?"

"We did. He has frostbite but is probably going to be okay. Aeneas found him. He did a good job." Huck's voice lowered on the last as he addressed praise to his dog. "Where are you?"

She squinted to see better through the sleet and could barely make out the church at the end of the road. "It's a long story, but I'm going to meet Zeke Caine."

"You're doing what?" he burst out.

She flicked her lights on low beam to better see the road. "He showed up at the house earlier and then agreed to meet me out at his church tonight. I need to find out where he has been, Huck." She would never refer to Caine as her father.

The sound of a coat zipper being secured came loudly through the phone. "Please tell me you have backup with you."

She straightened in her heated seat. "I have my gun—

I don't need backup." Perhaps. She didn't know Zeke Caine, had no idea why he wanted to meet with her. He was a predator, and based on his treatment of not only her mother but Abigail, he suffered from psychopathy as well as narcissism. Or rather, he made others suffer. "I don't believe he wants to hurt me right now." That might change, especially since she wanted to put him behind bars.

"Are you sure about that?" Huck asked.

"Yes. He has no reason to want to harm me. I think he's curious about me, which would be natural. He also most likely wants to confound me because he won't be able to help himself."

Huck groaned. "What happens when he fails at fucking with your head?"

Then he'd probably turn to other means, and who knew what that would entail. "Right now, that's irrelevant. He wants to discuss Abigail, and I am interested in his insights as well as his knowledge of her childhood. He seemed angry with her, and I plan to utilize that emotion."

"You're not great with emotions, and I don't think you're seeing the entire picture here. Take a breath, Snow. Your feelings about having this asshole back in town might cloud your thinking."

She still wanted to vomit. "I agree. But the reward is worth the risk in this situation. He might have relevant information regarding Abigail. And I'm going to discover where he has been these last five years because I believe there's something in his past that could lead to a conviction." There was no way Zeke would talk to her with anybody else around. But if he was as narcissistic as she believed, he wouldn't be able to stop himself from bragging to her. It was just a matter of manipulating him, which admittedly was not one of her strengths. "I'm armed and can take care of myself."

The sound of brakes squealing came over the line. "I understand you can take care of yourself. In fact, you've saved my life more than once, but this isn't a situation you should be in alone."

Caution ticked through her. The captain was intelligent and his instincts sharply honed. She swerved around a chunk of ice in the road. "I'm aware of that, but he won't talk to me if there's anybody else there, and I know it. I'm taking all safety precautions. You can trust me." Her gaze caught on what looked like a truck off the road in the area used for volleyball in the summer. She squinted and slowed down. "There's a truck in the field to the west of the church."

"Like in an accident?" Huck asked.

The vehicle was still running, its engine rumbling loudly and smoke pouring from its tailpipe, but she couldn't see a driver. The lights were also off. She couldn't see much of anything. Something flashed and bullets pinged against her car. "Damn it!" She swerved.

"What's going on?" Huck yelled through the phone.

"Shots fired. Shots fired," she called out just as her front tire blew. The SUV jumped and then skidded wildly. She let up on the gas, hit the brakes, let up on the gas again, and turned into the field, spinning around. Dizziness attacked her. More bullets pelted against the car. She released her seatbelt and ducked her head, flattening herself to the seat. Panting, she shoved open the passenger side door and scrambled out the other side, falling to the snow and pulling her gun from her bag. The cold instantly attacked her. Levering herself up, she fired rapidly toward the dark form of the truck, barely able to see it through the storm though it was only yards away.

The vehicle bucked and then sped across the field and turned by the tree line. There was a figure in the driver's seat, but other than that, she couldn't identify anything. Whoever it was had hunched over the steering wheel, and the cab was darkened. She kept firing and had turned to jump back in her car when she noticed something on the ground where the truck had been.

"Laurel, report in," Huck yelled through the speakers.

She grabbed a flashlight from her glovebox and pointed it at the form on the ground, every part of her wanting to pursue the truck. The light illuminated two bluish feet. She gasped. "Huck, send an ambulance, send paramedics right away." Ignoring his shouted questions, she rummaged in the back of her car and grabbed a blanket, then ran toward the body. She slipped on the ice covered grass and went down, landing on her knees but keeping hold of her weapon in one hand and the flashlight and blanket in the other.

Sleet bombarded her and she blinked it away to see. Then she forced herself to stand, fighting the wind as she ran toward the body again.

It wheezed and shuddered on the icy ground. As she grew closer, she could determine it was a male body, a naked male body. She skidded on her knees and threw the blanket over his bloody chest, sucking in frozen air as she pointed the flashlight at the victim's face.

It was Zeke Caine.

"Zeke," she gasped, tucking the blanket around him and pressing a hand against the wound in his neck. Shock and cold slowed her movements, and she forced herself to move faster. His eyes were open, and his mouth tried to form words. The star in his blue eye glowed in the flashlight's glare. "Don't talk," she said, covering more of his freezing flesh with the blanket. From the look of his chest, he'd been stabbed several times.

Blood poured from a wound in his temple, and she

shoved her gun in the back of her waistband and pressed one hand against his head, trying to stem the flood. He groaned and then his body went still. "Just hold on," she snapped, pressing harder. She looked over her shoulder to make sure the truck was gone. Not even its headlights were visible any longer. Her hands shook as she tried to save his life.

His mouth formed words again. She leaned closer to hear him, her hair brushing his chin.

"Abigail," he said quietly.

"Just breathe. Just concentrate. Don't fall asleep." She couldn't determine how many wounds he'd endured, so she pressed the blanket over his entire torso. She hadn't noticed any blood on his feet or legs, and they were now covered by the blanket. His blood saturated the material beneath her hands, and she attempted to apply more pressure where the wool was the wettest. "Just try to breathe," she ordered.

He wasn't shaking any longer, which was a bad sign. Laurel pressed against as many of the wounds as she could, keeping the blanket on him. She vaguely noted Valentine's Day heart-shaped candy strewn around the area by his head. There weren't any pieces near his mouth. Had the candy fallen out of the attacker's pockets?

His body bucked and his eyelids closed. She was losing him.

"Don't go to sleep." She leaned in. This might be her only chance to find that shooter. Where were the paramedics? "Who did this to you? Who stabbed you?"

He was turning blue, even though red soaked the snow around him. He opened his eyelids and focused on her face, his eyes widening. Then he coughed several times, partially turning on his side. She pulled him back and applied more pressure to his thorax area. His lungs sounded full of liquid. He looked at her, tears filling his eyes. "Abigail," he croaked.

"No, it's Laurel," she said. Or did he mean that Abigail had done this? "Did Abigail stab you?" His eyes slowly started closing again. "Keep your eyes open. Stay awake," she ordered, pressing even harder on his torso.

He groaned but kept his eyelids shut.

She had to save him. The blood pounded loudly through her ears as sleet and snow beat down on them. She partially leaned her body over his head to protect him from the elements, pivoting her hips so she could continue applying pressure to what she guessed were the most serious wounds. One of her knees slid onto several pieces of the candy, snapping the hearts in two and embedding them in the ice and blood.

His mouth opened as if he couldn't breathe.

"You'll be all right," she said, willing him to continue breathing. The sound of sirens competed with the storm behind her, and she held tight, trying to keep him alive. Soon the paramedics skidded to a stop along with an ambulance, and then so many red and blue lights lit up the night that she could see across the entire field. Zeke Caine gave a rattle that sounded hollow.

She shook him. "Stay awake, Zeke. You don't get to die now."

Chapter 26

Huck barreled through the emergency room doors with his dog at his heels and quickly swept the waiting room, his gaze landing instantly on Laurel. She sat in a chair in the corner, blood covering her torso and hands and even part of her neck as well as the knees of her jeans. Her hair was back, and her face was pale.

He quickly clocked the other people in the room. Walter Smudgeon paced alongside the far wall. Kate sat against the window in a green plastic chair beside Nester, who was rapidly typing on a laptop, hunched over with his shoulders up to his ears.

Huck let his chest settle. She was okay—everybody was okay. He strode inside and caught her attention. She looked up and he could swear relief crossed her face.

"Hi," he said.

"Hi." She looked down at her bloody hands.

Huck moved toward her and took the chair next to her just as the door opened again and Sheriff Upton York bustled inside with two uniforms behind him. One was Officer Zello. The guy must've been forgiven for his mistakes.

York moved straight for Laurel. "You need to make a report right now," he said.

"She's not making a report to you," Huck retorted, standing and edging himself in front of her.

York's chest puffed out and he glared up into Huck's face. "There was a stabbing and shots fired, and she's the only witness who's conscious right now, so she will talk to me. I have jurisdiction on this, and you know it."

"The hell you do," Huck retorted. "The stabbing and shots fired occurred on county, not city land. The state is taking this case." He had no idea if the state could take the case, considering an FBI agent had been shot at, but he wasn't letting this moron have the lead.

"You can't take the case because you're fucking her," York said.

Fury gripped him faster than thought did. Huck grabbed York by the lapels and lifted him before slamming him hard against the wall.

The first officer moved to intercede, but Zello grabbed his buddy and pulled him back. "Hold on. The sheriff was out of line," Zello said.

"Huck," Laurel said, standing and grabbing his arm.

He looked down at her. "What?"

York struggled to get free. His face turned beet red, and his toes scraped against the tile.

"Let him go," Laurel said.

"Happily." Huck released him.

York straightened his uniform; even his ears had turned an ugly crimson. With his receding hairline, the furious color could be seen all across his scalp. Was the guy going to have a heart attack or what? "I should have you arrested for battery," he sputtered.

"Go ahead," Huck said. "I'm sure the press will have a great time with that. Big, bad sheriff crying because he was called out for being disrespectful to a female FBI agent who'd just been shot at and was still covered in a victim's blood after she'd saved him." He didn't like calling Zeke Caine a victim, but he also didn't want to be arrested right now.

York turned on his officers. "You're on leave, Zello," he spat. "I don't give a shit if you have a high-powered lawyer who's going to make my life miserable. She's only helping you because you promised to protect her ass, which we both know you're incapable of doing. I never should've offered you a job, you loser. You go ahead and tell that witch to bring it on."

Huck's eyebrows lifted.

Zello took a step back. "I'm a good officer."

His buddy, a tall blond guy with a short goatee, nodded. "Let's just forget this entire incident." He looked at Laurel. "Nobody meant to disrespect you, ma'am."

York stood taller, vibrating with what looked like fury. "Watch yourself, Pentagoe. I have no problem putting you on leave as well." He glared at Zello. "The leave will be temporary as I initiate the process of firing you." He stormed toward the door.

Officer Pentagoe winced and looked at Zello before following his boss.

Zello sighed and glanced down at Laurel. "I don't suppose you have a vacancy in your unit?"

A speck of dried blood fell off her cheekbone. "Not at the moment."

"That's what I thought." Zello sighed and strode out of the hospital into the stormy night.

Laurel visibly shook herself. "Listen, this is an FBI case." She gestured toward Walter. "You need to take the lead and approach it as if I'm not your boss. You need to question me, and you need to take my clothes as evidence."

Walter's jaw firmed and he strode toward the reception area. "I'll get evidence bags as well as something for you to change into."

Huck sat and pulled her back down. "Are you injured?"

"No, I'm fine. My car was hit—the FBI will take it in for ballistics."

"What happened?" he asked, focusing on the case. The number of suspects who'd want Zeke Caine dead were probably vast.

"Somebody fired on me when I went to investigate that truck." She sounded confused, maybe bewildered.

Walter returned and handed her a bundle of scrubs before crouching down to face her, his gaze serious and his notebook already in hand. "Tell me about the person who shot at you."

"I didn't see the person," she said. "The shooter was behind the truck. I just saw the flash of a gun, and then I jumped out when they hit my tire, and returned fire. It was so dark and there was no visibility. The shooter entered the truck and drove away into the trees." She sounded dazed. "Then I saw the body on the ground."

"Tell me about the truck," Walter said gently.

"It was a dark truck, maybe an older model? I think green, black, or blue . . . maybe brown. The vehicle was just a dark blur, and I didn't get close enough to it at any point to really see anything. There was no visible license plate." She frowned. "For the record, Zeke Caine came to my house this morning, and he was driving a green truck. I have no way of knowing if it was the same vehicle or not."

Huck wanted to groan.

Walter's expression didn't change. "The victim came to your house today?"

"Yes." Laurel focused on Walter's face. "He surfaced this morning."

"What did he say?"

Laurel picked at the dried blood on her hands. "He said he wanted to talk, but I didn't want to encourage his presence at my mom's house because she was there."

Huck stretched an arm over her shoulders for support. "Are you sure you didn't hit your head?" He gently ran his fingers through her hair and down her face.

She leaned into his touch. "I may have bumped my head falling from the car, but then I grabbed the blanket and just tried to stop Zeke's bleeding."

Walter cleared his throat. "I understand that the victim was stabbed. Did you see a knife?"

"No." She looked around the waiting room, her pupils enlarged. There was no doubt she was in shock.

Walter's gaze dropped to the blood on Laurel's knees. "Walk me through everything that happened, step-by-step. Let's talk about why you have so much blood on you."

Laurel ran through her evening, giving an exact account of every detail. Good. Her focus was back. "Then the paramedics arrived, and I stepped out of the way to allow them to work."

"What was Caine's status when you arrived at the hospital?" Huck asked.

She looked toward the vacant reception area desk, her face so pale that dark circles stood out under her eyes. "He's in surgery now. He was stabbed multiple times."

"Just like the other deaths?" Walter asked.

She nodded. "Yes, and there was Valentine's Day candy around his head, but it hadn't been shoved into his mouth."

Walter took notes and then looked up. "It sounds like you interrupted the killer."

The idea made everything inside Huck go cold. She should have taken backup with her, but he understood

why she hadn't. She'd probably been searching for Zeke
Caine her whole life, not just the last few months.

Walter shook his head. "This is odd, don't you agree?
With the stabbing and the Valentine's Day candy, this
looks like our killer. So what's the connection between
Caine and the other victims?"

"I don't know of one right now," Laurel said thoughtfully. She focused on Walter. "Zeke said the name 'Abigail' to me twice, but I don't know if it's because I look
similar to her or if maybe she stabbed him. You should
have somebody bring her in for questioning."

Walter's chest filled. "I will."

She seemed to focus even more. "You should also call
Agent Norrs with an update on this. Walter, you take the
lead on the Zeke Caine case because I have a conflict of
interest. In the meantime, I plan to work on the other
cases."

"Do you think they're related?" Walter asked.

She swallowed. "I don't know. There was candy but
no tent. As you said, I may have interrupted the killer,
but why Zeke Caine?" She craned her neck to look around
Walter to where Nester sat. "Nester, are you searching
for any sort of connection between Caine and the other
victims?"

Nester kept typing. "I'm on it, Laurel. So far nothing.
Do you have any idea if Zeke attended the Sunrise Camp?"

Laurel shook her head. "I don't know anything about
him, but I think he's older than the other victims. We can
examine the picture again. I didn't recognize him when I
looked at it before."

"Doesn't mean he wasn't there," Nester said. "I'll keep
investigating the matter."

"I don't like this," Huck said. "I think it's too much of
a coincidence."

Laurel looked toward the reception area. "I agree. The Valentine's candy case has garnered media attention but nothing in-depth yet. Even so, anybody could've seen the coverage and chosen to copy the crime."

Huck scrubbed both hands down his face. "Great. There are only three people we know of right now who might've wanted Caine dead."

Laurel jolted. "Abigail and myself for certain. Who's the third?"

He didn't want to say it, but any decent investigator would connect the dots. "Your mother."

Laurel stiffened. "My mother—"

The doors opened and Rachel Raprenzi strutted inside with her cameraman behind her.

Walter handed the clothing to Laurel and then intercepted them before Huck could. "Get out," he spat.

"Sorry, this is a public hospital," Rachel said as the cameraman filmed the entire room and landed on Laurel.

Walter put a hand over the camera lens and grasped Rachel by the arm. "You're trespassing and you're leaving right now. You don't have official business here. I'm more than happy to arrest you."

Rachel smiled at Huck. "That's okay. I got what I needed." She turned on a three-inch heel and strode back into the storm with her cameraman following her.

The doors that led into the ER opened and a doctor in blue scrubs walked out. He pulled the cap off his head and looked around. The man looked exhausted. He was in his sixties with thick, gray hair, mellow brown eyes, and a thin frame.

Laurel stood. "How is Mr. Caine?"

The doctor rolled his neck. "The pastor came through the surgery successfully."

Laurel didn't outwardly react. Huck kept an eye on her to make sure she wasn't going to go down.

"Could you tell how many times he was stabbed?" she asked.

"Five times. I had to remove his gallbladder and appendix. He was able to keep his spleen." The doctor looked around. "He's in the ICU, and he's not up to speaking with anybody now. Tomorrow is out as well."

"All right," Laurel said. Her voice sounded firmer now.

Walter held up a hand. "You can't talk to him, Laurel. I will."

Huck looked at the doctor. "Did he say anything?"

The doctor shoved the cap into his back pocket. "The pastor was a little out of it when they brought him in, and it was touch and go for a while, but before we put him under, he did say one word."

"What was that?" Huck asked.

"Laurel."

Chapter 27

Fatigue weighed down Laurel's shoulders as she climbed the stairs to her mom's house with Huck on her heels. The wind pierced the thin scrubs she wore, and she wanted nothing more than to take a shower and get the blood off her skin. She'd been able to wash her hands after samples had been taken, but she'd only managed to completely clean one of them.

"Do you want to go to my place, or should we stay here tonight?" Huck asked.

She paused in unlocking the door and noted that the lock wasn't engaged. Had she forgotten to lock it? It was quite possible considering how nervous she'd been to meet Zeke Caine. "You don't need to stay with me, Huck."

He stepped closer to her and the warmth from his body heated her back. "I think I do."

It was difficult to concentrate on anything right now, so she pushed open the door. "Let's stay here." It felt like it would take too much energy to pack a bag.

"All right," he said. "I'll release Aeneas from the truck and let him run around a little. Then I'll be in. You take a shower." He dropped a kiss on the top of her head and moved away.

Surprising tears pricked the backs of her eyes. She was not one for emotion, but at the moment she felt overwhelmed. "That's a good plan." She could use a few moments alone.

That reminded her she probably needed to feed her new cat. She should buy a book on how to properly take care of the young feline. She walked inside and kicked her shoes off, wincing as she placed her bare feet on the wooden floor. Walter had taken all of Laurel's clothing to send to the crime lab, and the hospital had been lacking in surplus socks. Didn't hospitals always have socks?

She walked inside and turned to look for the cat in the living room. Her entire body jolted at the sight of her sister waiting in the light of the fire. "Abigail," she breathed.

Abigail sat on the comfortable floral sofa near the blazing gas fireplace. She held a pillow on her lap and a pair of yellow booties in her hand. "Please tell me you don't waste valuable time actually knitting booties. These are your mother's, correct?"

Laurel looked toward the knitting room and back to the living room. She'd knitted those booties last week, and she'd left them near the boxes to be mailed to her nonprofit. "Did you search the whole house?"

Abigail smiled, her expression catlike. "As a matter of fact, I did. And you know what? I was bored. There's nothing of interest here. Even the teas are herbal—no kick."

Laurel tried to focus on the moment. She'd never had this much difficulty. Though she understood she'd been in shock and her body had been flooded with both fight or flee chemicals, it was surprising how much the withdrawal of those hormones was affecting her physically. She comprehended the phenomena on a mental level, but experiencing it was different. "You're trespassing. I'm happy to have you arrested."

"You're not going to arrest me, sister. Why don't you come in and sit down? You look like you're about to fall over."

She felt like she was about to fall over. Gravity was not working in her favor right now. She looked around for Fred.

"Are you searching for your cat?" Abigail asked.

Laurel's hair rose on the back of her neck. "Yes. Where is he?"

Abigail tossed a hand in the air. "For some reason he didn't take to me. He snarled and ran away. I assure you he's somewhere in this cozy little home."

Cats had good instincts. Laurel walked inside and sat on the matching floral chair before reaching for a blanket to cover her legs. "What are you doing here? The FBI is looking for you."

"Did you do it?" Abigail sat back on the couch, the fire-light dancing over the reddish highlights of her hair, which was secured in a ponytail.

Laurel coughed. "Do what?"

"Stab our father."

Laurel stared at her for a moment, trying to gauge her angle. "No, I didn't stab him. Did you?"

"No." Abigail drummed her nails on the arm of the sofa. "You can tell me, Laurel. Honest. I'm your sister and I would never ever betray you."

Laurel had no doubt that Abigail would betray her in a heartbeat should the right circumstances arise. "I didn't stab him, Abigail. I tried to save him. In fact, I did save him."

Abigail blew out air. "Well, that's unfortunate. You had a chance to let that old bastard die and you didn't take it?"

Laurel looked down at the dried blood still on her hands "No, I didn't. I need to take a shower." But she didn't move.

Instead, she focused on her half sister. "If you didn't stab him, and I didn't stab him, who else wanted him dead?"

Abigail laughed, but the sound lacked any humor. "Who doesn't want him dead? The guy is a psycho. He's hurt a lot of people."

Laurel looked at the powerful fire as it blew out heat. Her feet were finally starting to thaw. "We don't know that to be true except for you, me, and, of course, my mother. So far as I can tell, Pastor John and all the parishioners at the church genuinely like him."

"Many of them are probably lying," Abigail said carelessly. "I have no doubt your mother wasn't the first woman he abused."

"I agree," Laurel said. "But I haven't found another."

Abigail crossed her legs, bringing attention to her thick green socks.

Laurel looked over her shoulder to see Abigail's boots tucked under the bench. The woman had made herself right at home. "There have to be other women he hurt. Do you have any idea where he's been the last five years?"

"No," Abigail said. "Nor do I care, and neither should you."

Zeke Caine had to pay for at least some of his crimes, but first Laurel had to discover what they were. "He said he spoke to you before coming to visit me."

Abigail tilted her head to the side for a moment. It reminded Laurel of one of her own mannerisms and she shivered. "When did he say that?" Abigail asked. "I thought he was badly wounded when you found him."

"He came by the house earlier today."

Abigail's eyes gleamed. "Is that a fact? What did you say to him?"

"I told him to leave, and I agreed to meet him later," Laurel admitted. "I didn't want him anywhere near my mother." The wind spiked ice against the windows, and she jumped. "Zeke said you gave him directions to my home."

"He lied."

Fred started padding in from the kitchen. "There's your kitty," Abigail drawled. "So you wanted to protect your mother from our big bad father, huh? You know the best way you could've done that?"

Laurel watched the cat move closer.

"Yeah," Abigail said. "You should have let him die. How many times was he stabbed, anyway?"

"I'm not sharing those details." However, Laurel needed to glean integral facts from Abigail before Huck returned. The woman would stop talking and start flirting the moment he entered the room. "When did you become aware that Zeke was back in town? What did you talk about when he came to see you?"

Abigail shook her head. "He showed up last night at my place. Somehow he got past the security at the gate. He always was smart."

"What did he tell you?"

"Not much," Abigail said. "He asked me questions and guess about whom?"

The cat jumped onto Laurel's lap and purred, snuggling down on top of the blanket. Laurel reached out to gently scratch behind his ears, using the hand that was free of blood. "What was the focus of his questioning?"

"Oh, he wanted to know everything," Abigail said. "He wanted to know what you did for a living. What I thought of you, how you'd investigated the Snowblood Peak murders, who you're dating, what you're like in general . . ." She uncrossed her legs. For her visit she'd worn black yoga pants and an oversized black sweatshirt with a hint of turquoise underneath. It was as casual as Laurel had ever seen her. "He also wanted to know what questions you were asking about him and who you had spoken with at the church."

Laurel zeroed in on this new information. "Did he mention anybody in particular from the church?"

"No. He just wanted to know who you'd spoken with. I told him that I had no idea because, Laurel, I have no idea." Abigail emphasized the last several words. "You don't talk to me, so I really couldn't tell him anything. Could I?"

That was part of Laurel's plan. She didn't want Abigail to know about her investigation or her life in general. "I assume he spoke with you to brag about his success in disappearing for such a long time. Where has he been these last five years?"

Abigail's eyes sparked. "I already told you, I don't know. I asked him and he refused to tell me. He did say that it was none of my business."

"What was he driving?"

Abigail frowned as if trying to remember, which was just an act. Her memory was as good as Laurel's. "He was driving a green truck with no license plate. I also have no idea where the truck came from. I've never seen it before."

Laurel sighed. "Do you know of any property he owns in the county?"

"Nope," Abigail said, glancing at her watch.

Laurel thought Abigail knew more than she was telling. Abigail liked to keep her secrets close. "Please account for your whereabouts all day today into the night."

"Excuse me?"

Laurel tried to read her sister's facial expressions, but there weren't any. "Where were you?"

"Not where you were," Abigail returned. "Unlike you,

I was not at the scene of an attempted murder. Are you sure you didn't finally just lose your temper and stab that bastard? There is blood all over you."

Laurel wasn't in the mood for Abigail's cat and mouse games. "Either tell me something useful or get out of my house."

Abigail reared up.

The cat lifted its head and turned to watch her as if sensing a predator in its vicinity.

"I'm here to check on you to make sure that you're all right after the ordeal I heard you went through," Abigail said through clenched teeth.

Laurel soothed the animal by petting his head and caressing her hand down his body. He slowly relaxed on her lap. "How did you hear about the stabbing?"

Abigail flicked invisible lint off her yoga pants. "Rachel Raprenzi teased an upcoming episode of *The Killing Hour* from the hospital. There was a lovely shot of you sitting in the corner of the hospital waiting room all bloody. You looked like a damn Victorian heroine. Even I wanted to rescue you."

Laurel wanted to groan but instead kept her body relaxed and her expression serene. "Rachel announced the identity of the victim?"

"Oh, yeah. She knew it was Pastor Zeke Caine who used to run the Genesis Valley Community Church. My phone has been absolutely blowing up with parishioners calling for information. I, of course, have let them all go to voice mail. Buffoons."

Laurel continued stroking the cat. His purring was calming her. She'd read a report once that petting a cat could reduce the level of cortisol in a body and bring down blood pressure. Perhaps it was true. "Did any of the callers sound worried or concerned for themselves?"

Abigail watched the cat. "They all sounded worried and concerned. Who knows or cares why."

Laurel swallowed. Her throat hurt from being out in the cold. She should make some tea. "Would you turn over your phone to the FBI?"

"Not a chance," Abigail said.

Laurel wasn't surprised. "Would you let me listen to the messages?"

Abigail tilted her head. "You know, I think I would. Not tonight because I am tired. With the stress of my father being stabbed, I really can't deal with this questioning any longer. Unfortunately, I have a faculty dinner tomorrow night, but if you'd like to join me for dinner Tuesday night after work, I would be more than happy to let you listen to my messages."

The door opened and Huck walked in with Aeneas jumping around his feet. The dog bounded into the living room and then tried to stop, skidding across the wood floor when he spotted Abigail. He backed away and then turned his head to see the cat on Laurel's lap. His muscles bunched.

"Down," Huck ordered. Aeneas instantly dropped to his belly and put his nose on his paws.

"How laudable. That's how you train a dog," Abigail said, her gaze wandering from Huck's boots up to his face. "Captain Rivers, what a pleasure it is to see you again."

Huck glowered. "How did you get in here?" He looked at Laurel.

"Oh my," Abigail stage-whispered. "Look at you casting a belgard at my baby sister."

Huck's jaw visibly tightened. "Was she here when we arrived?"

"Yes," Laurel said.

Huck's smile wasn't the one Laurel normally saw. "Excellent. Dr. Caine, you're under arrest for trespassing. You have the right to . . ."

"No," Laurel said. "Huck, not this time." She needed to listen to those messages. Abigail surely would erase them before Laurel could get to them if she didn't play nice. She certainly didn't have enough evidence to obtain a warrant for Abigail's phone. Cooperating with the woman was the only way she could pursue this case right now.

Abigail stood. "Sorry about that, Captain Rivers. I'm sure you'd *love* to see me in handcuffs."

Huck pivoted to the side and gave a hand motion for his dog to follow him. The dog instantly jumped up and walked behind him.

Abigail sauntered past Laurel and paused to reach for the cat. Fred snarled. She laughed. "Your animals sure do love you." Holding her head high, she walked past Huck, slipped her feet into her boots, and opened the front door. "There's not a doubt in my mind you were the only person within miles of our father when he was stabbed. Why you called the authorities, I can't imagine. A lapse in judgment? A sense of guilt?" She stepped outside onto the porch and partially turned. "I'll see you Tuesday, dear sister."

The door slammed shut and Laurel jumped.

Chapter 28

Laurel awoke to the sound of purring. She opened her eyes to find Fred on her chest, his nose close to hers. "Morning." She petted between his ears and stretched. The bed was still nicely warm from Huck's muscled body. It wasn't bad being awakened by a cat.

The smell of pancakes caught her attention. She gently set the cat to the side and stood, stretching her neck and body. She wasn't experiencing any ill effects after falling out of the car the night before, although her left shoulder was still a little sore. She used the facilities, brushed her teeth, and then threw on yoga pants and a T-shirt before walking downstairs to find Huck in her mom's kitchen with a pink apron tied around his waist.

"Morning," he said. He looked good in the morning. His hair was tousled, and his torso was bare, but he'd thrown on a pair of jeans. Her mouth watered. He glanced at her phone, charging on the counter. "I called in for both of us, saying we'd be in sometime in the afternoon, if we didn't decide to take the day off. I hope that's okay."

She stopped to ponder the question. "I think it is." Her brain could use a break. The doorbell rang and she paused, frowning.

"I've got it," Huck said.

"No. Your pancakes will burn." She walked by him and moved to open the door. Special Agent in Charge Norrs was waiting on the other side. "Agent Norrs," she said, stepping aside. "Come on in."

"Thank you." Even off duty, he looked official in cargo pants and a puffer jacket with his posture ramrod straight. "I'm sorry to disturb you—I heard you were taking the day off."

She'd been expecting him. It was the correct procedure to follow, and it's what she would've done in his shoes. "Agent Smudgeon had orders to contact you."

"He called last night, but I thought I'd give you until this morning to rest up. The sooner we get you clear of this, the sooner we can move on to the other aspects of the case."

Huck walked out of the kitchen and looked at Norrs. "We're taking the day off," he muttered.

Laurel quickly made the introductions; neither man moved to shake hands.

"Please sit down, Agent Norrs," Laurel said, gesturing toward the living room.

Huck gave her a look and returned to the kitchen.

She walked inside and took the sofa, leaving Norrs to sit on the chair. "Can I get you anything? We have tea," she offered. "A copious amount of it."

"No thanks. I'm good," Norrs said. "I appreciate that you made Agent Smudgeon the lead on your father's stabbing, which will allow you to continue working the other murders." He shifted his bulk on the chair, making it look tiny. "But since Smudgeon is under your command, I'm taking the lead in your father's assault."

Laurel crossed her legs, her body chilling. "Let's refer to him as Zeke Caine or Mr. Caine or Pastor Caine. All right? That man is not my father."

"Fair enough," Norrs said. "I'm sorry about that." He frowned. "But I do need to ask you some questions."

Laurel stared at the man, wondering how he could be fooled by her sister. He seemed intelligent. "Considering you're involved with Abigail, I don't think you're the appropriate person to lead this investigation either," she said. "Surely you know that."

He stilled as if he hadn't considered that angle. "Abigail didn't have anything to do with the stabbing of your . . . I mean, Pastor Zeke Caine."

"How do you know that?" Laurel asked. "Were you there?"

"No, I wasn't there," he said.

The man was blinded by his feelings for Abigail. "Have you asked for her alibi?" Laurel asked.

His jaw firmed. "She was at her home last night. We spoke on the phone, fairly close to the time of the stabbing, I would think."

"Good. Then you won't mind getting her phone records and double-checking." Laurel had no idea if Abigail was involved or not, but the more she thought about it, the more it made sense.

Norrs leaned forward. "I don't want to be confrontational, but surely you understand that you're a suspect in the stabbing of the pastor. I know about his history with your mother."

"Then I would assume you know that Abigail's just as likely a suspect."

Norrs's face reddened. "Okay. I take your point and recommend that Agent Smudgeon should take the lead on this case, so long as he reports back to both of us."

Interesting. "Why are you here, then?"

He glanced toward the kitchen, where Huck was out of sight, still cooking. "I thought you and I could just talk it out this morning. It's my understanding that there was heart-shaped candy found around the pastor's head, and it was sent to the lab."

"Yes," Laurel said.

"Have you found any connection between Zeke Caine and the other victims?"

She shook her head. "As of last night, Nester hadn't found a connection."

"Where were you the night Victor Vuittron was killed?"

Laurel remained in place, but the question still surprised her. "You know I had just arrived home from DC the night before the killing."

"I've checked your flight information. You returned around five in the afternoon on Sunday night."

She considered the Vuittron crime scene. "Your premise is that I flew home and then murdered Mr. Vuittron early in the morning before continuing to the university to teach the class that your agent interrupted?"

"Where were you the night that Frederick Marshall was killed?" he asked methodically.

"I was with Huck Rivers at his home," she said. "I got the call in the morning and headed out to the crime scene, as you know."

He nodded. "I see. Boyfriends don't make the best of alibis. Do you have an alibi for Jiro Makino's death?"

"I was pulling into the parking lot at work when I received the call from you that there'd been another body," she said. "You can't seriously be looking at me for these crimes."

There was absolutely no expression on his face. It was admirable really. "You're brilliant, aren't you?" he asked softly.

"Brilliant isn't actually a term that anybody uses when dealing with IQ, but if you're asking if I'm known to be intelligent, then the answer is yes." She stood and walked to the fireplace, turning it on. "You do know that Abigail is also, in your terms, brilliant?"

He looked toward the kitchen and then back. "If you wanted to kill somebody, and if you wanted to hide that fact, wouldn't it make sense to create a serial killer type situation? You are an expert on those, aren't you?"

Laurel could easily follow his line of thinking. "Yes, but in that scenario, it wouldn't make sense to choose three men who are easy to connect and then one who isn't. Especially if the odd one out is the main target," she said thoughtfully.

"Unless that would be a defense? That it was illogical to choose connected victims except for the main one. Wouldn't you say?"

She frowned and returned to her seat. "I'd say that's too risky for a murder plan. If one wanted to use three victims as decoys for one target, then those three should be as random as possible. Otherwise, the target is too obvious."

He leaned back as if settling in for a long discussion. "Did you want Zeke Caine dead?"

"No," she said honestly. "I wanted him in jail behind bars paying the price that he should pay for the crimes he's committed. Did Abigail want him dead?"

Agent Norrs held up a hand. "We're not discussing your sister. We're discussing you and your possible motivation for stabbing the pastor. There was nobody else out there that night, was there?"

"I saw someone drive away in a truck," Laurel said.

"Did you call for help?" Norrs returned.

Laurel jumped as the cat leaped onto her lap. She settled him down and petted him behind his ears until he relaxed. "I was on the phone with Huck when somebody opened fire on my car. You do realize there were bullet holes in my vehicle?"

"True." Norrs unzipped his jacket. "I have no doubt that you could stage any scene you wanted to protect yourself, Agent Snow. What I'm trying to do is get to the truth so we can move past this. Did you or did you not stab your father last night?"

"I did not."

Norrs drew out a notebook and took several notes before looking up. "I can get a warrant to dump your phone and your computer, but I'd rather just ask."

She continued petting the now loudly purring cat. "I have no problem submitting my phone and computer to our lab technicians." This was an intriguing line of questioning; Norrs was more thoughtful than she'd imagined. "Following your reasoning, if Abigail killed the three decoys and then tried to kill Zeke Caine, commencing an affair with an FBI Special Agent in Charge would be a smart move. Correct?"

Norrs jolted and then quickly recovered. "It'd be best if you told me now if you had any connection to Victor Vuittron, Frederick Marshall, or Jiro Makino."

Laurel scrubbed the cat behind the ears, appreciating how loud his purring was. "I'd heard of Vuittron but never met him."

"Ah, yes. Your assistant's ex-husband? He's better off dead as far as she's concerned, right?" Norrs leaned forward. "Logically, what if you and Kate were in this together? Both getting rid of men you didn't want around?"

"As I already said, I wanted Zeke in prison, not dead." Laurel had to help clear Kate. "Kate wanted her children to have a father, even an absent one. Neither of us ever met Marshall or Makino." She watched him carefully. "I wonder if Abigail has any connection to them?"

Norrs slammed his fist on his thigh.

Laurel jumped. "What's wrong?"

His lids half lowered. "What's wrong? Seriously? You just accused the woman I love of murder."

"I thought we were discussing possible motives for the crimes," she murmured.

He shook his head. "You're unbelievable. I'm questioning you for murder."

She was missing something here. "I'm freely answering your questions." Why was his face turning so red?

He sucked in air and slowly exhaled. "You're not even a mite mad or scared right now, are you?"

She frowned, this time not following his line of thought. "No."

"Why not?" he snapped.

She considered his question. "I'm not angry because you're doing your job, and I'm not frightened because I didn't do anything wrong."

Huck emerged from the kitchen. "The pancakes are ready." He glared at Agent Norrs. "You can't seriously be considering her as a suspect in this, can you?"

Norrs looked from Laurel up to Huck and then back. "Agent Snow wanted her father dead."

"Then why did she call for help?" Huck asked.

Norrs looked down at his notes. "My guess would be timing. She was on the phone with you, correct?"

"Yes. When shots rang out," Huck said. "That was before she found the body."

Norrs looked up at him. "It's possible she timed it perfectly. For now, I'm doing all the legwork I need to until Pastor Caine is cleared to speak with us. He was still asleep last time I checked." He stood. "After all, your name was the last he spoke, Laurel."

Laurel also stood. "Zeke Caine will give his statement

to Agent Smudgeon, not to you. If I have to call the deputy director, I will, but we both know you need to excuse yourself from this investigation, just as I have." She followed him to the door and waited until he'd stepped outside onto the porch before continuing. "There's something else you should consider."

"What's that?" he asked, looking over his shoulder as he descended the steps.

She chose her words carefully. "Whereas I'm neither angry nor frightened while discussing this case and possible suspects, *you* are. Very much so. You might want to contemplate why."

Chapter 29

Tuesday morning, Laurel sat in the leather chair in the conference room as Walter walked out, his head held high. He'd performed an admiral job of questioning her, and she was pleased with how tough he'd been. Before commencing the interview, Walter had removed the glass board with Zeke Caine's case on it and taken it to his office. Until they discovered who'd stabbed him, Laurel would remain away from his office.

She'd already checked in with the hospital, and Zeke still wasn't well enough for visitors, so she hadn't yet sent Walter there. Standing, she reached for her laptop bag. "I'll be back in about two hours, maybe three," she called out, striding down the hallway and stopping to see Kate.

"Are you going to speak with Jason Abbott again?" Kate asked. "I saw your calendar."

Laurel nodded. "Yes. He says he has information regarding the current candy murders, and he may be able to provide insight." She was driving her mom's car.

"That's not why you're going," Kate said. "You're hoping he'll give you information about Abigail."

Laurel switched the laptop to her other shoulder. Apparently her left one was still sore from when she'd jumped out of the car. "Yes. I'm hoping he'll trip up. There's something he has been holding back, but I can't figure out what or why."

"Do you think he remembers everything?" Kate asked.

"I don't know. Whatever she injected him with may have caused memory loss. I don't think he's playing with me, but I can't say for sure. If he doesn't provide relevant information this time, I'm not visiting him again."

Kate reached for a pencil. "Good. I can't stand that guy."

"Agreed," Laurel said. "I'll be back." She walked down the stairs and emerged into the vestibule, just as Huck did the same. She wasn't surprised. "Kate called you?"

Huck pulled on a Fish and Wildlife jacket. "She texted me. I'm not letting you speak with Jason Abbott alone."

That was fine with her. She and Huck had worked the Abbott case together from the beginning. "I take it you're also driving?"

"You can drive if you want." Huck strode to the outside door and opened it for her.

"We both know that you'd much rather drive, Captain Rivers." She blinked at the brightness of the day as she walked outside. Most of the clouds had disappeared. The sun was a mellow star in the sky, sparkling off the snow, but not providing any warmth. Finally, for the first time in weeks, the sky was a dark blue.

"Then I'll drive," Huck agreed readily, heading toward his truck.

That was acceptable to her. Part of dating somebody was accepting their foibles, and one of his was that he liked to be in control. They'd spent a mellow Monday off together, and she was starting to feel even more comfortable around him. She hauled herself up into his truck and they made the drive to the county jail in silence, both lost in their own thoughts.

When they arrived, he parked. "I like that we don't have to talk all the time."

She looked at him. "Are there people you've dated that you've had to talk to the whole time?"

"Yeah," he said.

That sounded difficult. "I'm glad we don't have to talk all the time, too." With that, she jumped out of the truck, sliding on the ice. Being more careful, she picked her way across the parking area and walked inside with Huck. After identifying themselves, they were led to the same interrogation room as last time. In addition to the guard on duty, Officer Zello stood outside, wearing civilian clothing.

"What are you doing here?" Huck asked.

"I'm on Thema Sackey," Zello said. "After the sheriff put me on leave, I called her, and she hired me for twenty-four-hour protection. She's been getting death threats."

Laurel's eyebrows rose. "I'd like to see those."

"You've got it. I'll send them over later today."

"Do you think any are viable?" Laurel asked.

Zello lifted a shoulder. "I don't know. There are a couple that are fairly descriptive, but people sending death threats anonymously are usually just cowards."

"I agree," Laurel said. The smell of the jail was of orange cleanser and body odor, and she grimaced. She opened the door to find Jason Abbott on one side of the table with Thema Sackey next to him. Abbott wore another orange jumpsuit.

Thema was in a light gray suit with a pretty blue shell. Her earrings were made of rubies, as was her necklace. She partially stood. "Thank you for coming."

"Jason, give me viable information about Abigail Caine, or this is the last time I'm speaking with you," Laurel said, pulling out a chair as Huck did the same.

Jason's eyes were bloodshot, and he looked tired compared to last time. He sniffed. "Sorry, I caught a cold. I won't shake your hand and give it to you."

Laurel hadn't been planning on shaking hands with him anyway. "What information do you have?"

Huck crossed his arms and just stared at Jason.

Jason glanced at him and then looked back at Laurel. "I want to help you on your current case."

She didn't have time to play games with him. Even so, he might have insight into the criminal mind of a serial killer that she lacked. "How so?"

"I think you're missing the ritualistic aspect of it."

When she didn't reply, he continued. "It's the candy that's the key. The candy in the throat. Don't you understand?"

Laurel narrowed her gaze. "How do you know about the candy in the throat?"

He pulled against the handcuffs that attached him to the bar on the table. "Thema told me."

The attorney blushed. "I watched Rachel Raprenzi's *The Killing Hour* last night, and she had a lot of details. Jason asked for them because he truly wants to help you."

Laurel studied the young woman. "You probably shouldn't share details about other killings with your client. It's counterproductive and just supplies fodder for his fantasies."

Jason vigorously shook his head. "No. I do want to help you. It's all about the candy with this guy. The way it was crushed down the victims' throats and scattered around the head, it's like it never was where it should be."

"This is bull," Huck said. "Let's get out of here."

Laurel eyed Jason. There was no logic to the way his mind worked, and that intrigued her. "Why do you want to help me?"

"Because we're friends," he said.

Huck shifted his weight while Laurel studied the killer. "We are not friends, Jason."

"I don't know. We have the same interests. Killing fascinates us. You and I are the same, Laurel," Jason said, his voice almost a whisper.

She leaned toward him. "If we're the same, then why don't you help me punish Abigail for what she did to you?"

Jason blanched. "Because you don't *want* me to help you with Abigail. She's your sister. At the end of the day, you don't want to put her away."

Was there any truth in that statement? Laurel considered it carefully. "No, you're incorrect. If she helped you to become a killer, if she pushed you into murdering those women, she deserves to face justice." She very pointedly looked at her watch. "Either provide me with relevant facts about Abigail and her practices with you, or I'm leaving and I'm never coming back." She meant every word.

Jason's smile was wide. "I fascinate you too much for you to abandon our friendship."

She pushed her chair back. "Huck, we're leaving."

"Wait," Thema said. "If he agrees to give you information, will you agree to testify on his behalf?"

Laurel cocked her head and looked at the lawyer. "I agree to testify to the truth, and if Abigail Caine is charged with facilitating murder, that can only help your client. Correct?"

Thema's eyes gleamed. "That's correct. Tell her what you know, Jason."

Jason cleared his throat. "Abigail has another lab. It's a place we went when she wanted to spend more time than just a few hours and dig deep."

Laurel's breath quickened but she hurriedly calmed her expression. "Where is this lab?"

Jason sighed. "You promise you'll help me?"

"I promise I'll tell the truth and, during the sentencing phase, I'll inform the judge that you cooperated." She'd also describe the brutality of his kills in great detail for the judge. "That's all I can do."

Jason looked down at his hands. "The lab is in an older part of the university. It's in a building at Maine and Granite in the basement room, sub B3."

Laurel looked at Huck.

He shrugged. "I don't believe him."

Jason shook his head. "I have no reason to lie. I need all the help I can get."

"Why are you providing me with these details now?" Laurel asked.

Jason looked at his lawyer. "There are probably records there that incriminate me, but even against legal advice, I've realized it's better for you to find proof that I was exploited with drugs and cognitive manipulation. I'm a victim here, too."

Laurel asked him a few more questions, but he had provided everything that he would for today. She finally stood and exited with Huck at her back.

Officer Zello straightened. "Agent Snow, can I have a word?"

Huck looked from the officer to Laurel, and she nodded. "I'll go start the truck," he said, striding down the hallway, past the guards, and through the door.

"What can I help you with, Officer Zello?" she asked.

"You can call me Frank, for starters," Zello said. "I'm not sure I'll be an officer again. I may go into private security."

She wanted to be kind to the man, but if this was about Abigail, she was going to shut him down fast. "Okay, Frank."

"I just wanted to say thank you for the other night when

I was crying into my beer. You were nice to me, and you didn't have to be."

She patted his arm, relaxing. Good. He was getting over Abigail. Perhaps he could get on with his life now. "It's all right. I know that Abigail can be manipulative, and it's probably easy to fall for her charm. I'm sorry that it impacted your career so detrimentally."

"Eh, I've always had terrible taste in women. Even so, I wish she'd at least call me."

Thema walked out of the room and shut the door behind her before motioning for the guard to come and take Jason Abbott.

"Are you ready?" Zello asked her, his gaze warming.

"I am." She smiled and patted his arm more intimately than Laurel had.

Laurel watched the interaction. Maybe Officer Zello's taste in women had improved. Her phone buzzed and she smiled a good-bye to them both before putting it to her ear as she walked toward the outside door. "Snow."

"It's Nester. I'm working on witness scheduling while my computer runs an update. When do you want Melissa Cutting and Kirsti Vuittron coming in for interviews?"

"Let's try for tomorrow afternoon." Laurel checked out with the guard on duty. "For now, would you find somebody to show me around the Sunrise Camp? I know it's out of business, but I looked at Google Maps yesterday, and it appears as if the buildings are still standing. Check property records. If possible, I'd like to go this afternoon."

Nester whistled. "That's about a five-hour drive southwest, Laurel."

Her head ached. "I know."

"I'll start making calls right now. Also, I heard back about Jiro Makino's ex-wife. She has a pretty good alibi in that she was in the hospital giving birth to triplets in Berlin the day he was killed. Apparently she was there for a week. I've spoken to cooperating witnesses and am trying to get the hospital CCTV, but there's a lot of red tape to go through."

Triplets? Incredible. "Nice job tracking those details down." Laurel needed more agents to conduct all of this fieldwork. "Please also draft a warrant for a lab at Northern Washington Tech located at Maine and Granite in the basement room, sub B3. It's related to the Jason Abbott case. I'll fill out an affidavit of cause as soon as I'm back in the office."

She definitely needed more agents. Now.

Chapter 30

Laurel took a latte into the computer room at the office and handed it to Nester. The room had no windows and was decorated with mangled snowboards from some of Nester's more disastrous times on the hill. Apparently he was an adroit snowboarder, but he liked to take risks. The wall behind him was filled with his diplomas.

"Thanks," he said, his gaze locked on one of his computer monitors. "I found the guy who caretakes the area around the Sunrise Camp during the winter, although the property was just sold at auction three months ago to a venture capitalist out of Texas. Running a background check on him now, but nothing interesting pops yet."

"Will the caretaker show me around?"

"Yeah, but not until tomorrow at noon. You should make it fine if you leave about seven in the morning."

She nodded. While she could send Walter, she wanted to see the place for herself. The case might be centered there.

Walter lumbered out from his office. "Hey, Boss." He looked bright eyed today and his hair was slicked back in a different and somehow younger look. His blue suit also looked new, and the green tie was a nice addition. "What do we have going on?"

"Legwork," Laurel said. "As soon as Nester acquires the warrant for Abigail's secret lab at the college, we're a go." She considered calling Agent Norrs with an update but discarded the idea almost immediately. Hopefully he was reconsidering his choice in women and examining why he'd been so upset the day before.

Nester grimaced. "I'm having trouble finding a judge so it might be tomorrow. But the second I get it, I'll let you know. Even if it's late tonight."

Walter glanced at his watch. "It's almost lunch. I'll run downstairs and get us all something quick to eat."

Nester took a big gulp of his latte. "Also, I have the printout of suspicious deaths in the Pacific Northwest within the last year."

He reached to his side and pulled papers off a printer. "I narrowed them down to deaths without gunshots. I have the full list, too, but it's pretty big so I thought we'd narrow it down. I looked particularly at stabbings and anything that seemed suspicious." He handed a stack of papers to both Laurel and Walter.

Laurel scanned her top sheet. "Why are the names in different colors?"

Nester looked back at his computer. "The red ones are ones I think you should look at. The blue ones already have viable suspects and don't seem worth our time. For example, the first blue one is a woman whose ex-husband was released with no bail after beating her up, and he went immediately home and stabbed her to death. The police are still putting together a case, but it doesn't seem like one of ours."

Laurel reached for a pencil on Nester's makeshift desk

to cross that one out. "I agree. Are any of the male victims in the same age range as ours?"

"There are three, but one is a suspicious heart attack, whatever that means. One is a strangulation that looks like it could be a suicide since he was hung off a building, and the third is a stabbing but without the candy, the nudity, or the tent. And that guy was in his seventies and only stabbed twice." Nester blanched. "I shouldn't say *only* twice, but you know what I mean."

"Yes," Laurel said. "All right. I'll go through this list, and then let's do a deeper background and request casefiles for the red ones." She flipped over the page and a name caught her eye. "Margie Zello?"

"Yeah," Nester said, turning to his computer and typing. "I already requested the case file on that, and the local PD sent it. She lived in Granite Falls. She was in her mid-fifties and not in great health, but she still died unexpectedly of complications as a result of A-fib."

Laurel chewed on the inside of her cheek. "Do you have the police reports on this?"

"What are you thinking, Boss?" Walter asked.

Laurel stared at the paper. "I don't know. Is she related to Officer Zello?"

Nester typed. "Yeah, she was his mother."

Laurel's neurons fired rapidly. "Abigail dated Officer Zello, and when she dumped him, he kept pursuing her," she said slowly.

Walter's eyebrows rose. "You don't think that she did something? Sure, she didn't want him to bug her, but . . ."

Laurel didn't know what to think. "Abigail's a malignant narcissist, and if he angered her enough, who knows what she'd do." Laurel shook her head. "No, this is too far-fetched. I mean, not even Abigail."

"What if Frank knew something about the case you're building against Abigail?" Nester asked thoughtfully.

"What do you mean?" Walter looked down at the computer guru.

Nester shrugged. "They were dating and intimate during the time we think Abigail was messing with Jason Abbott's head. Plus, Zello provided an alibi for Abigail, right?"

"Yes," Laurel said. "My premise is that she drugged him the night she left their bed to attack Rachel Raprenzi, the reporter. What if he wasn't completely out of it, or what if he's starting to remember things?"

Walter crinkled his papers. "Why would Abigail kill Zello's mother?"

"I don't know," Laurel said. "Maybe he confided in his mother, or maybe Abigail wanted to turn his attention to something other than her case. I can't get into Abigail's head."

"I know your half sister is not a good person," Walter muttered. "But to kill someone's mom just to mess with an ex's head? That's . . ."

"Psychotic?" Nester asked helpfully. "Malignantly narcissistic?"

Walter pressed a hand to his stomach as if it hurt.

Laurel checked out his breathing. It was a little shallow. "Walter, you're overdoing it," she said as gently as she could. "You're still recovering from the bullet wounds. I want you to take the rest of the day off."

"Not in a million years," Walter said. "We are short-staffed, to put it mildly, and we have eight different things going on at once. Why don't I go meet with the Granite Falls PD about Margie Zello's death and then scout around her neighborhood, maybe talk to her neighbors? It's easy legwork, and I can find something to eat while I'm out."

Laurel had never been in charge of teammates before,

but now their well-being was her responsibility. "You can do that tomorrow. Abigail isn't going anywhere, and I need you at full speed. Period."

"Fine. Tomorrow, when you let me work again, should I speak with Zello?" Walter asked.

Laurel shook her head. "Not unless we find concrete information. I don't trust him not to go right to Abigail with our suspicions so she can deny them."

Nester groaned. "She sure has her hooks in him."

"Aptly put," Laurel agreed. Her blood started to hum. Maybe she could finally catch Abigail at one of her many crimes.

It was time to put her half sister away for good.

Late afternoon was the worst time of the day. Everybody was safely inside their place of work or home and difficult to reach. It was too light outside—even during storms. Nighttime was better. Nighttime was when prey was more alert but much easier to grab.

The stacks of purple tents took up the entire first shelf of the pantry. They'd been purchased from an old outfitting business at their going out of business sale before the owners retired to the Caribbean. The tents were most likely untraceable. Even if the fabric and manufacturer could be found, the buyer never would be. Cash and a good disguise worked every time.

Sometimes fate intervened, but not this time. This time, the destiny of those horrible men had been inevitable.

In the corner by the tents were stacks upon stacks of Valentine's Day heart-shaped candies in their sweet little boxes. They had been stolen from several places, so they were untraceable as well. Everybody had this kind of candy. They were heart-shaped candies stamped with lies.

So many horrible, horrible lies on them.

The rage inspired by just looking at those candies was nearly unbearable.

Why wouldn't the dead stay buried?

Why wouldn't the pain be banished?

Maybe because there were two more sinners who had to be punished. Two more for certain, and yet what then? There seemed to be so many terrible, awful, horrible men who hurt everyone, who didn't deserve to live. It was good to have a mission, good to have a calling. Sometimes the only thing that could release a soul from its sins was the letting of blood, so much blood. Soon it would be dark, and it would be time to hunt again.

The monitor in the corner flickered and then came back to life. How easy it had been to install the camera outside the officer's home to keep track of him. He thought he was so strong . . . so tough. Yet he was merely flesh and blood, and his torso and neck would be as easy to slice as the rest.

Night was finally beginning to fall and the blessed darkness was descending. How wondrous it was that the darkness arrived so early, even though it was March. The camera perfectly captured the scene as the officer jumped out of his truck and opened the back door to let out his dog.

The dog was cute. He agilely leaped from the truck and ran around on the freezing ice, sliding every few feet. He wandered off to the trees as the officer moved into his garage and removed a shovel to take care of the driveway and the walk to the log home. The snow was thick, and his shoulders bunched as he moved. To most people, he probably appeared powerful.

But he was weak, as only a cruel and uncaring man could be. He deserved the agony he'd experience, deserved to have his heart sliced into ribbons. Into careless shredded pieces as he'd no doubt sliced the feelings of many an innocent victim.

It was convenient to see him home so early tonight, because the urge to make him pay was too strong to ignore. To the outside world, the monster was not visible within the fit officer, but fate always revealed the sinner. It had taken years to get to this point, but the time had come. Perhaps the pain would end with the death of this one. How lovely it would be if the pain would finally end.

Was it possible? Or must this mission continue on forever?

At least this demon had a fairly reasonable routine, although sometimes he stayed late at work. No matter where he was at midnight, he'd be captured and then taken to his final resting place. His dog was always with him. The dog should probably be saved.

But the officer would die in intense pain, as he deserved.

Chapter 31

After seven that night, Laurel jogged out of the office to her car, shivering in the cold evening. Despite the absence of wind, the air was absolutely frigid. She ignited her engine and turned on the seat warmers before backing out and zipping onto the main road as fast as possible. Her phone buzzed. "Snow," she answered.

"Hi, it's Kate." Kate's voice was higher than normal.

Laurel sighed. "What's happened now?" If Norrs was bothering Kate over Jiro's death, then she'd need to hire a lawyer. Laurel had double-checked, and there was no connection to be found between Kate and Jiro. Kate had never heard of the man. "Is it Norrs?"

"No, and this is so awkward, but Kirsti came over, and I think she was drunk. I think she threatened me."

Laurel slowed down so she could better concentrate. "What did she say?"

Kate audibly swallowed. "It was so weird, but she said that if something happened to me or the girls, she'd get all the money. Then she offered to settle for half of the insurance money."

Heat pricked along Laurel's back. "Was it a viable threat?" This was going too far.

"I don't know. It was more her tone of voice than her

words. I'd sound silly making a report." The words rushed out of Kate. "I was polite when I told her to get out, but she had this scary look on her face. You know what I mean?"

"Yes," Laurel whispered, working through the best possible outcome. "I'll make sure you're covered, Kate."

"I can take care of myself and my girls," Kate said. "I'm armed, and we're getting a dog as soon as my shoulder is better. I just wanted you to know in case she tries something."

Laurel forced emotion away so she could think. "I'm paying to have an alarm installed in your home. I'll get Nester on it tomorrow."

"I wouldn't say no," Kate said. Something fell in the background. She sighed. "Gotta go. A volleyball just hit my table. Night." She ended the call.

Laurel took several deep breaths and ran through her available options. There weren't many at the moment, so she'd have to be creative. She leaned over and input a number she'd memorized during their last case.

"You've got Zello," Officer Zello answered, laughing.

A woman giggled in the background, and it took Laurel a moment to recognize Thema Sackey's tone.

"I'm sorry to interrupt you, Officer Zello," Laurel said. "This is Agent Snow."

"Stop it," Zello said, chuckling louder. "Thema, give me a second." He cleared his voice. "Agent Snow, I told you to call me Frank. There's a high likelihood I won't be an officer again. Lately, I'm thinking about becoming a private detective for a certain law firm."

He sounded happier than Laurel had ever heard him. She could tell because his voice was slightly higher and livelier than normal.

She slowed down over a patch of ice. "I don't mean

to bother you, but I might have a job for you if you're interested."

"I am very interested. A job with the FBI?" His words rushed together.

She winced. "Not exactly," she said. At least not yet. "My team is stretched thin right now, and I need somebody on surveillance and protection detail." She couldn't ask Walter to take this on while he was still recovering, and Nester wasn't a field agent. So it was either pull somebody in from the FBI unit in Seattle—which didn't have any free agents—or hire somebody else. Officer Zello seemed like a perfect candidate.

"Are you available?" she asked.

"Absolutely. I'm your guy," he said.

She slowed to a stop at the light. "I need to rely on your discretion completely with this. I'm trusting you, Frank." She chose his first name deliberately.

"You can absolutely trust me."

She would find out whether she could or not. If this worked out, it'd be nice to have a private detective close whom she could hire for other cases. It'd be good to have a support team in the vicinity. "Are you available to begin tonight? I know you're on protection detail for Ms. Sackey, and I don't want to take you from her security."

"I'm free starting right now until I escort Thema from home to her office at 8:00 AM, and then I'm free until she has court at 1:00 PM," he said easily.

She appreciated that he knew his protectee's schedule so well. Of course, it sounded like he was also in a relationship with Thema, but that wasn't something Laurel chose to worry about right now. She gave him Kate's address. "I want Kate Vuittron and her girls protected throughout the night, and they're home now." It was a short-term solution until Kate found a dog and Laurel had the alarm system installed. Laurel would also have another talk with Kirsti. "I'd like for you to surveil the home through the night. I need to know that they're safe. Please don't let them know you're there."

Zello was quiet for a moment. "You want me to watch your own employee?"

"Yes," Laurel said, hoping this wasn't a colossal mistake. "Her family is under a possible threat, but I don't want to alarm the girls too much. I am, again, depending on your discretion."

"You've got it. I'll leave right now because Thema is secured here in her apartment building. I should arrive at the location in approximately two hours. That's the soonest I could get there."

"That's acceptable. Thank you. Please send me the appropriate bill afterward."

"You've got it," Zello said cheerfully.

Laurel's mind had already moved to the next issue. "Thanks," she said, disengaging the call. She glanced at the clock. Dang it. She was running late. She sped up slightly. Even though it had stopped sleeting, the roads were slick with black ice.

She made it to Abigail's subdivision within twenty minutes and punched in the gate code, having memorized it months ago. Her half sister resided in a high-end subdivision with expensive, rather cold-looking homes on five acre lots. Abigail lived all the way to the left at the end of a small cul-de-sac. A forested area took up the right side of her property and extended as far as Laurel could see.

She parked in the driveway and noted that Abigail had left the lights on for her. Taking a deep breath, she steeled her shoulders and tried to calm everything inside her. It was difficult dealing with Abigail, and she needed to be in top form. Finally, she swung her legs from the car and hurried across the walkway and up to the front door.

Abigail opened the door before she could knock. "Hello, dear sister. I'm so glad you made it."

"You didn't give me a choice." Laurel stepped inside and removed her coat and boots.

Abigail placed her coat on a hook on the other side of the door and nudged her boots onto a mat. The smell of something delicious filtered through the open-plan entry/living room of the high-end home. The furnishings were white, gray, or black, the floor cold tile, and the walls a stark white.

Laurel moved automatically to the kitchen with its stainless steel appliances and heavy granite workspace. Abigail had already poured two glasses of wine and no doubt it was of an excellent vintage.

"It's a cabernet," Abigail said, handing Laurel a glass. "You'll like it."

Laurel sniffed the spicy bouquet and then took a sip. Her stomach roiled and she winced. "Where is your phone?"

"Oh, no, dear sister. First we eat," Abigail said. "Then you can listen to every message on my phone. What's wrong with the wine?"

"It just smells funny." Every bone in Laurel's body felt tired, although she knew that was a physical impossibility. Bones didn't become tired. She was experiencing stress, and the physical symptoms were fatigue. "I'm not up to sparring with you tonight."

"That's all right. We won't spar." Abigail took a healthy sip of her drink and returned to the stove, where something was bubbling in a wide saucepan. Her dark red hair was piled high on her head, and she wore a winter-white sweater over faded jeans. "I made chicken cacciatore. It's my own recipe and it's quite delicious."

It figured that Abigail could cook as well as she did

everything else. If the woman had used her brilliance for good instead of evil, who knew what she could have accomplished in this life.

Laurel pulled out a bar stool and sat, pushing the wine glass away. It smelled rancid. She didn't want to lose any of her faculties when dealing with her half sister.

"Have you heard from dear old dad?" Abigail asked, lifting the pot cover and stirring the thick liquid.

As Zeke's daughter, Abigail could call and get any information she wanted, so there was no harm in telling her the truth. "My last phone call revealed that he took a turn for the worse and isn't receiving any visitors," Laurel said. "Thus far, we haven't had a chance to question him."

"Hmm," Abigail said. "I really do wonder if you had the courage to finally stab that bastard."

"Was it you?" Laurel asked, not expecting an answer.

"If it were, you'd never catch me," Abigail said evenly, stirring the pot.

Laurel studied her sister across the island. "You're wrong. I absolutely would catch you. It may take me a while because you're very good, Abigail. But in the end, the truth always comes out."

"Does it?" Abigail tilted her head and placed the lid back on the pan. "I don't know if that's true. If you think about it, the only people who get caught are the ones, well, you catch. Just think of how many you haven't caught."

That thought kept Laurel up at night more times than she wanted to admit.

Abigail hummed softly as she cooked. "How is Huck?"

"He's well." The last person in the world Laurel was going to discuss with Abigail was Huck. "As I said, I'm not up to games. Can we not do it tonight?"

Abigail poured more wine into both of their glasses, filling them to the top. "Is it possible I just want to help?"

"No." Laurel saw no reason to lie. "I don't want wine." She was feeling slightly off balance.

Abigail sighed. "Drink up. Even you have to admit that I have the ability to read people. I can zero in on weaknesses with minimal effort."

"So?"

"You're too different from each other. He's a cozy stay at home and build a family type of guy, and you, well, you get shot at a lot." She removed the lid again and twisted pink sea salt over the fragrant concoction. "Living with you, loving you, would slowly kill him." She added freshly ground pepper. "Or he'd turn on you and you'd fight all the time." Her shudder made a silver necklace dance on her throat. "How predictable."

There was enough possible truth in the words that Laurel's temples began to ache. "Let's listen to the messages," she said. "I promise I'll stay and eat dinner afterward." The idea of eating with Abigail made her want to vomit.

Abigail scrutinized her, her blue and green eyes narrowed. "Oh, very well. Let's get that out of the way and then we can have a nice dinner and chat together. I would love to hear how your relationship with that hunky Huck Rivers is going even though we both know it can't last. I do hope you aren't about to get your heart broken."

"I appreciate your concern," Laurel said dryly.

Abigail tugged her phone from her pocket and slapped it onto the counter, pressing play. The first message was from a woman named Jolene who had heard that the pastor was back in town and had been hurt. She wanted to express her love and prayers and then gave a plaintive plea to be kept up to date. Abigail rolled her eyes the entire time. Laurel just listened.

Message after message came through in a similar vein

until another woman came on, saying, "Hi, this is Julie Rawlingston. I need to tell you that your father is dangerous. I know most people won't be saying this. But the worst thing in the world for any of us is if he truly is back in town. Please inform me when he is out of the hospital so I can make preparations."

Laurel stared intently at the phone. "Who was that?"

"Never met her," Abigail said carelessly. "She obviously knows the pastor better than any of the others."

Laurel made a mental note to text the name to Nester. She would go talk to the woman tomorrow. The next message was from Thema Sackey, asking Abigail to speak with her about Jason Abbott. Laurel lifted her eyebrows.

Abigail shook her head. "Not a chance."

Laurel sighed. "What happened was your fault, too, Abigail. You need to face that."

Abigail just smiled and once again stirred the pot. The next message was from Pastor John, asking Abigail to keep him informed about Zeke's progress. He said that everybody was praying for him.

Finally, there was a message from Walter asking to interview Abigail about the Zeke Caine stabbing. That turned out to be the final message.

Abigail reached for two plates already placed on the countertop. "You know, if you ask me, I would look at Pastor John. He doesn't want to lose control of that church. He's an ambitious guy, and he wants to be famous on television."

Laurel's stomach growled. She'd missed lunch again. "I plan to speak with him. Maybe tomorrow. I don't see him stabbing somebody though, just to keep his church. Plus the Valentine's Day candy angle is odd."

"Ah," Abigail said. "But that detail was made public

on *The Killing Hour*. Speaking of which, how is Rachel Raprenzi? Is she bothering you?"

Laurel gave in and took a sip of her wine. "No, and please don't threaten to kill her again."

Abigail smiled wider. "I may suffer from being overly protective of my little sister, but I have never threatened Rachel Raprenzi." She dished up two plates. "If I had decided to harm her, you would never catch me, dear sister."

Laurel put down her wine glass. "That seems to be the theme of the evening."

Abigail threw back her head and laughed. "Oh, Laurel. That's the theme of our entire lives." She put a plate in front of Laurel.

Laurel gagged and shoved it away. The smell nearly demolished her.

Abigail's eyebrows rose. "Oh, shit."

"What?" Laurel gulped down several swallows and tried to keep from throwing up.

"The fatigue, the paleness, the oversensitivity to smells? Laurel Snow. You're knocked up."

Laurel reared back. "That's crazy."

"Are you late?"

Her head spun, as did the room. "I don't have a schedule. I'm not regular and can go for months without a period." Was she getting dizzy? "Besides. We've always used condoms." When was her last period? It was before she'd left for DC, at least eight weeks ago.

Abigail watched her raptly, her lips partially tilted in almost a smile. "Condoms are only ninety-eight percent effective. Everyone knows that."

Laurel drew in air through her nose. There was no way she was pregnant.

Except . . . it was possible.

Chapter 32

Laurel left Abigail's house as soon as she felt well enough to drive. During the interim, the woman had subtly questioned Laurel about their father's stabbing, and Laurel couldn't shake the thought that Abigail had been responsible. She could see the scenario playing out, but she couldn't quite discern a motive. Sure, Abigail probably hated Zeke as much, if not more, than Laurel did, but killing him would only make things easier for Laurel. That couldn't be one of Abigail's motives.

Zeke had mentioned that he needed to tell Laurel something about Abigail. Hopefully the doctor would allow visitors soon, because the key to Zeke's stabbing lay in whatever he'd seen that night. Perhaps he'd been face-to-face with his attacker.

The idea that Laurel could be pregnant kept swirling around in her head, and she shut it down. She had never been regular with her menses. She'd double-check the next day, but for now, she had to focus on her job.

She thought through the case. They still didn't have enough agents to perform all of the legwork. Even though it was long after supper, she took a chance and dialed the Marshall & Cutting Law Firm. An automatic telephone service answered, and she pressed the buttons for the first three letters of Melissa Cutting's name.

"Cutting," Melissa answered, sounding distracted.

Laurel perked up. "Ms. Cutting, this is Special Agent Laurel Snow. You're working late."

"I often do," Melissa said. "How are you, Agent Snow? It's been a few days." She sounded dry about that, but Laurel didn't see the humor.

"I know."

The woman sighed. "Have you figured out who killed my fellow attorneys yet?"

"We have not," Laurel said. She needed to bring the woman in for more careful questioning. Melissa was now the sole named partner in the firm, another possible motive. "So far our victims have been men, but you should be careful as well."

"I have my own security."

That was good news. "I believe you mentioned that you met Victor and Frederick through your husband, Rich?"

"Yes," Melissa said. "They all knew each other from their teen years, I believe."

Laurel slowed down as several deer ran across the road in front of her. "Did they attend high school together?" she asked, pretending she didn't know their backgrounds.

"Yes. Rich actually attended school with Victor, but not with Frederick."

"Interesting. What about Jiro Makino?"

"I don't believe so," Melissa said. "But I don't really know Jiro's background, so I can't say."

Laurel sped up once the deer had finally finished crossing the road. "Do you know if your husband attended a summer camp with Victor and Frederick?"

"Dunno." Rapid typing came over the line. "What's

another word for bullshit?" Melissa asked mildly. "I'm working on a brief."

"Balderdash?" Laurel asked. "Bunk, gibberish, acka-marackus, malarkey . . ."

"Excellent. I'm going with ackamarackus," Melissa said as the speed of her typing increased. "Wonderful. You're very helpful."

The vehicle skidded and Laurel slowed down as she passed a dark and silent home. Many of the homeowners in Abigail's subdivision spent their winters elsewhere. "Did Rich have any living relatives I could interview?"

"No, sorry. He was an only child, and his folks have both passed on," Melissa said.

Laurel turned out of the subdivision and exited the gate. "I appreciate your help. When would it be convenient for you to come in for a formal interview?"

Melissa sighed. "I don't have time for a formal interview."

"Make time," Laurel countered.

Melissa typed faster. "What's another way of saying I'll destroy you? I need a different word than destroy."

Laurel sped up. "Consume, crush, damage, wreck, annihilate, maraud, mutilate, vaporize."

"Ooh, I like vaporize," Melissa said. "Thanks. I don't suppose you're looking for a job."

Laurel sighed. "I'm not, but I am looking for you to come in for an interview."

Melissa kept typing. "Let me check my calendar . . . All right. I could fit you in next Monday, at seven in the morning? You bring the coffee, and I like a double macchiato."

"I need to see you sooner than that," Laurel said slowly.

"Then you'll have to subpoena me or arrest me. I have to go. What's another way of saying good-bye?" She clicked off.

Laurel rolled her eyes. If she had anything she could arrest the woman on, she'd do it. "Next Monday morning it is," she murmured. Her phone buzzed and she pressed the button on the dash. "Snow."

"Hey, where are you? I'm home and thought you could come by for a late dinner. I'll cook something—most likely a frozen pizza," Huck said.

His voice went right through her, and she again shoved thoughts of a pregnancy away. "I'm headed home now. I could definitely meet for a nightcap." Except she probably shouldn't drink, just in case. But hot chocolate sounded delicious all of a sudden.

Huck chuckled. "Nightcap. Where does that silly phrase come from anyway?"

Laurel stopped at the end of the road and waited for two SUVs to pass by before turning right. "It comes from the time of actual nightcaps, when people wore hats on their heads to keep warm at night. Then folks started enjoying a warm beverage before bedtime, usually something alcoholic. The two habits eventually combined into nightcap."

Huck was silent for a moment. "All right, now I know that. Where are you anyway, Snow?"

"I'm coming from Abigail's."

"You're what?" His voice lowered.

She didn't recognize the tone, but it was different than it had been a moment before. "Yes, I agreed to have dinner with Abigail if she would let me listen to her phone messages. There was no way to get a warrant."

"Are you crazy?" he asked, his voice still low and dangerously soft.

She pursed her lips and mulled over this conversation. "No." It was the correct answer.

"You're not working the Zeke Caine case, remember?"

She winced. "I know, but Abigail wouldn't share those

messages with anybody else, and there was a lead in one of them. I had to go listen."

Aeneas barked in the background. "I can't believe you would take a chance like that. The woman is a cold-blooded psychopath, at the very least."

"She doesn't want to murder *me*," Laurel said. "At least not right now." There wasn't a doubt in Laurel's mind that, if pushed too far, Abigail would certainly try to kill her. But right now Abigail was interested in Laurel. "At the moment, I'm perfectly safe with her, Huck."

His growl sounded oddly animalistic. Interesting. She'd never actually heard a person growl before.

"I can't believe you were so shortsighted," he said.

All of Abigail's warnings tumbled through Laurel's mind. Maybe her half sister was right. Huck wasn't looking for a woman with a dangerous job. "I don't know why you're so angry."

"Then you're not nearly as smart as we all think you are, now are you?"

She might not be good at deciphering subtext, but she could recognize sarcasm when she heard it. "I have a job to do, and if you don't like it, then maybe you should think about that," she shot back, surprising herself by how angry she felt.

"Fine. I will think about it. Drive carefully." He ended the call.

She stared at the dash, shocked. What had just happened?

Huck made it to Laurel's house before she did and waited patiently on her front porch, surrounded by the crazy-looking leprechauns. The lights were on above him, showing that they apparently were on a timer, while the wind whipped the snow through the frigid air.

Aeneas bounded around the front yard, yipping excitedly and chasing shadows.

Huck heard her vehicle before it came into view. He wasn't sure when she caught sight of him, but she rolled up to the garage and parked, stepping out, her movements hesitant.

He hated that he'd caused that hesitancy, but he admired the way she squared her shoulders and strode his way, stopping to crouch and pet the dog. As Aeneas greeted her with a short bark and then kisses to her hand, she didn't laugh. She dutifully petted him and then stood, walking toward Huck.

"Hi," she said.

"I didn't handle that well," he said by way of greeting. "I'm sorry."

Her eyes widened, and then she continued up the stairs. He stood and dusted off his pants.

"I don't think this is going to work," she said.

His heart sank. That's pretty much what he expected. "We can make anything work," he countered.

She stared at him for several long moments and then walked to the door and pulled the key out to unlock it. "Come on in," she said.

His shoulders settled, and he followed her inside the already warm home, pausing to turn and use his hands to brush the snow off his dog before allowing him inside. One of the cool things about Laurel was she didn't seem to mind the dog being around all the time, even if he was snowy.

She removed her coat and boots and then greeted her cat in the living room, petting him and giving him attention for a couple moments. The cat had surprised Huck.

She didn't seem like a cat person but seeing her with the odd feline somehow made sense.

"Have you eaten?" she asked.

"I did," he lied.

Apparently, she had had dinner with Abigail, and the last thing he wanted was food. "I was wrong in the way I responded to you on the phone."

She clicked on the gas fireplace and then turned to look at him. With the firelight illuminating her wild, dark red hair, she looked fragile and small. While the woman could fight and shoot, she was still breakable.

"You should have taken backup," he said.

She lifted her chin as the soft light caressed the high angles of her face. Her blue and green eyes glowed in the near darkness. She was so beautiful, it was hard to breathe.

"I thought you were apologizing," she said.

"I am. I was wrong in the way I approached the situation. You were wrong in going without backup."

Heat flared in her eyes, and he took a moment to appreciate it. She was so logical, it was rare to see emotion take her over. "I'm an FBI agent. I know what I'm doing."

"That woman is your half sister, and she's as smart as you are," he countered. "She's also dangerous, and at the very least, she shaped a killer. I'd bet my bottom dollar she also is a killer."

Laurel threw up a hand. "I agree, but she had evidence I needed, and there was no way she was going to give it to anybody but me."

"Is that all?" he asked, his temper rising again.

"Excuse me?"

For some reason, she had a blind spot when it came to danger. "What degrees does Abigail have?"

Laurel's brow furrowed. "Abigail has degrees in computation and neural systems, social and decision neuroscience, game theory, practical ethics and philosophy as well as biochemistry. Why do you ask?"

He forced his temper to calm. "I asked because I also want to know what degrees you hold."

"You know my degrees," she retorted.

"Tell me anyway," he replied.

Her eye roll was cute. "Fine. I have degrees in bioinformatics, integrative genomics, data science, neuroscience, organizational behavior, psychology, game theory, and mathematics. Like I said, I went to college when I was very young. What is your point?"

Her cheeks flushed with anger. If he told her that she was absolutely beautiful when angry, she'd probably hit him. He took a deep breath. "Are you sure that you're not trying to see who's smarter?"

"Excuse me?" she snapped, her chin shooting up and her fingers closing into a fist.

He held up one hand to ward her off. "Just listen to me for a second. You're used to being the smartest person in any room, and finally, there's somebody as smart as you. Are you sure you're not playing her game just to see if you can outwit her?"

Laurel looked down at his dog, looked over at her cat, and then bit her lip. "I don't know. I never thought of it like that."

Yet another thing he really liked about her—she was extremely reasonable. "Maybe you should think about it," he said. "Tonight you took a risk, and I understand why you took it, but it might not have been the smartest thing to do."

She tilted her head. "Maybe not, but Abigail doesn't want to hurt me right now."

It was the "right now" part that got him. The cat meowed, and she leaned down to pick him up, snuggling him against her chest. "I don't know that I'm girlfriend material," she said softly, not meeting his gaze.

"Is that you talking, or Abigail?" he retorted.

She jolted. Then she frowned, looking years younger. "It may be something Abigail said," she murmured thoughtfully.

Yeah, that's what he figured. "If you have doubts about us, come to me, but don't let whatever she's saying get into your head. We both have to be smarter than that."

"That's a good point." She dropped her gaze down to his feet. The cat meowed and scrambled to get free, and she let him go. "I don't know what to do about us."

He moved for her, reaching her quickly. "I have an idea." Then he kissed her.

She sighed into his mouth and then wrapped both arms around his neck and kissed him back.

He ripped off her shirt and licked across her jaw as she frantically yanked his shirt up. Ducking his head, he let her remove the material before ripping off her bra.

"Hurry," she whispered, pulling his belt free.

Gladly.

In a tangle of clothing and limbs, they made it to the sofa, both nude. He fumbled for the condom in his pants on the floor, tore it open, and rolled it fully on, brushing his fingers across her sex.

"I'm ready," she said, reaching for his hair and yanking him down to kiss her.

He took his time entering her, making sure she was ready. Then he was moving. Hard and fast, holding on, making up. He'd try to find reality in the morning, but in this second, he felt like he'd finally found a home.

So he kissed her again and stopped thinking.

Chapter 33

Huck insisted upon accompanying Laurel to Sunrise Camp, and she was grateful for the company during the five-hour drive. Their lovemaking the night before had calmed her when it came to their relationship, but she couldn't stop thinking about her conversation with Abigail. Was there a chance she was pregnant? She didn't share her thoughts with Huck because at the moment she just couldn't focus on the possibility. It was highly likely that she was not; her entire adult life she had been so irregular that she had gone months without experiencing her menses. Even so, she should probably buy a test.

She received a text from Officer Zello that all had gone well at Kate's house the night before and the girls were at school while Kate was in the office. He had to go escort Thema to work and would await further instructions.

Perhaps she could hire him as a consultant until additional agents were assigned to the unit. She felt she was building a good team here in the wilds of the Pacific Northwest.

They stopped for breakfast on the way and reached Sunrise Camp at just about noon. While it was warmer in the southwestern part of Washington State, the weather

was still drizzly and chilly. Not quite the bone piercingly
frigid air of her mountain town, but cold enough to be
miserable.

Her phone buzzed again. "Snow."

"Hi, it's Nester and Walter," Nester said.

She smiled. Yes, it was a good team. "You're on speaker."

"The warrant just came in for Abigail's lab at the college," Walter said, raising his voice as if he thought he
should speak louder to reach them.

Huck snorted.

Laurel sighed. "We're five hours away." She couldn't
wait that long.

"I'll execute the warrant, Boss," Walter said.

She frowned.

Huck caught her look and slowed down before turning
off the main road. "Walter? Do you mind taking Ena with
you again? I want her to have more experience in the field."

Laurel smiled her thanks to him. Walter was good at his
job, but everyone needed backup.

"Sure," Walter said cheerfully. "She's a smart officer, and
I'm happy to help her out. We'll call in if we find anything."

"Thanks," Laurel said, ending the call. "I appreciate
that," she murmured to Huck.

He shrugged. "Ena does want more fieldwork. This is a
good thing."

They reached the far side of the quiet lake after driving
over dirt roads riddled with potholes that obviously had
not been taken care of for several years.

"How long has this place been closed down?" Huck
asked.

"About a decade," she said.

Huck maneuvered around a downed tree, having to
drive into a meadow on the side. "Looks like it."

Between clearings, thick forest lined both sides of the

dirt road. They reached an entrance to a long driveway that was bracketed by a pine gateway. On each side of the entranceway, pine logs stood tall, connected by rusted metal brackets to a pine arch. Dangling from the center of the arch was a sagging Sunrise Camp sign that swung in the breeze. It must have fallen from the other side, as it was now hanging perpendicular to the ground.

Laurel shivered. A dilapidated fence extended from both sides of the gateway with most of the boards broken down and crumbling.

"Nice place," Huck muttered, driving through the gate and winding around several curves in the dirt road.

Soon the lake became visible through the trees. It was an unfathomable gray, reflecting the bulbous clouds above them. Several weathered, crumbling cabins appeared to their right, all missing windows. A couple had their roofs crashed in. Bushes and vines covered most of the wood.

He turned left and drove along the lake until they reached the main hub of the camp, which was a white clapboard building fronting the lake. Most of the paint had peeled off, and the few steps leading up to the door were missing or broken.

Laurel looked at the angry lake. "I bet this was an enjoyable place to spend the summer when the property was maintained."

Huck pulled to a stop and cut the engine. "I don't know. This place creeps me out."

Laurel opened her door and stepped down to the marshy ground. The wind whistled harshly through the trees and ruffled her hair. She shivered.

He let Aeneas out of the truck, and the dog bounded toward the water despite the rain quickly dampening his coat.

"Is the guy supposed to meet us?" Huck asked, looking around.

Laurel glanced at her watch. "Yes, we said noon, and it's five after."

As if from nowhere, a man ambled around the other side of the main building, or what was left of the main building. Laurel jumped and Huck immediately pivoted, noticeably putting his body between the guy and Laurel.

"Hello?" Huck sounded threatening.

"Hi." The man moved closer. "I'm Bernard Johnson. You must be Special Agent Snow." He angled his head to look beyond Huck to Laurel.

"Yes. Hi, I'm Agent Snow. It's nice to meet you, Mr. Johnson. Thank you for agreeing to show us around the camp," she said quickly.

Bernard Johnson had to be about ninety years old. His hair was a thin gray and his body tall and wiry. He was probably about six foot seven, but he hunched over as if suffering from osteoporosis. His eyes were black and his nose craggy. He pressed very thin lips together. "You're late."

"Sorry about that," Laurel said, shivering in the wind. "The road wasn't in as good condition as we'd hoped."

Johnson shook his head. "I know. It's a crime how they let this place go. It was so vibrant when the kids were here but . . ."

"Why did they?" Huck said, looking around. "I can imagine in the summer this would be a pretty nice lake."

"It is," Johnson said. "There are no motorboats allowed, so it's just fishing and quiet water sports. All water sports should be quiet." He clacked what had to be dentures together, his face pinched.

Huck planted his foot on the bottom step and the wood instantly gave way. "Why did they let the place fall into disrepair?"

Johnson sighed heavily. "The camp was run by Old Man Tucker, and when he died, the entire property went into a trust for his bratty kids. One's in Silicon Valley and the other's gallivanting around, I don't know, Europe or somewhere. They didn't want anything to do with the camp and just abandoned it. They wouldn't sell the property because I think they figured it would become more valuable through the years."

"It probably has," Laurel said, looking around. "We heard that it recently sold."

"Yep, which is good 'cause I'm about ready to call it quits. I live down the way so I've been kind of taking care of this area, but I'm retired, and I'm done with it. Every once in a while I got to shoo raccoons out, and sometimes kids come here to party, so I got to call the cops on them. I'm sick of it."

Laurel angled her head to the side. "I'd like to look inside, but I'm thinking it's not that safe."

"Oh no, you don't want to go inside. You'll go right through the floor. I can tell you this was the main hall where they had meals. The offices were to the side. All the kids stayed in the cabins."

"Tell me about the kids," Laurel said, looking toward the crumbling cabins.

"Most of them were okay. I helped run the place, you know. I did most of the water sports. Sometimes they got some bad seeds, but you know, for the most part kids are all assholes."

Laurel swallowed.

Johnson threw up his gnarled hands. "I don't know why anybody would have kids. They do nothing but ruin your life."

"Do you have children?" Huck asked mildly.

"Oh heck no. I never made that mistake," Johnson said.

Laurel pushed her sodden hair out of her face. It was probably a good thing the grouch hadn't had kids. She turned and walked toward the water where Aeneas was bouncing around and kicking at rocks. "Did anything illegal happen here? Anything bad?"

"No," Johnson said following her. "We had a couple kids almost drown, but that's just because they were stupid. We saved them each time. Some of the kids snuck in booze, but you know, normal kid stuff for the most part."

As she reached the water's edge, a structure down the shore caught her eye. Partially hidden by trees, it was another crumbling, once-white building with a steeple. Awareness pricked through her. "Is that a church?"

Johnson followed her gaze. "Oh, yeah. That was the Church of the Lake. A lot of people in the city would come out to the church in the summer. They liked to spend time at the lake, and it was a seasonal church. We'd get a rotating group of clergy. It was a lot of fun."

Laurel turned and started walking toward the church. It appeared to be in better shape than the camp. "People don't use the church any longer?"

"Nah. They built a much bigger and nicer one about half an hour away that's over on Looney Lake. With the camp closing down, people just don't come this way very often. They'd be trespassing to get to the church, to be honest, and I don't know . . . when the camp ended, so did the church."

"What's going on?" Huck asked. "Why the interest in the church?"

"I don't know." Laurel walked closer to the church. "Can we go inside?"

Johnson coughed and wheezed when he spoke. "Yeah. It's in a little bit better shape than the lodge. You can go inside. I go in there every once in a while and talk to God."

Laurel wondered if God listened to this old grump. Probably. She walked up the stairs and pushed open the door. The heavy wood creaked loudly. She couldn't help the shiver that took her body as she walked inside. Worn pews led up to a light oak altar that had been damaged by moisture.

The space was too quiet, as if just waiting for life. Dust mites swam in the chilly air, and the wind cried through the rafters.

"Offices are this way," Johnson said.

There was one doorway to the left that revealed an office as well as stairs leading down.

"What's down there?" she asked.

"It used to be the playroom for the little kids during sermons. You know, you get a bunch of little kids, they're screaming and wailing. We put them in the other room."

Laurel opened the door wider.

"Let me go first," Huck said, checking out the first step. "All right. It seems sturdy enough." He flicked on the light switch, and nothing happened.

"Oh, we don't got no lights," Johnson cackled. "But here, I got a flashlight." He moved to the lone desk in the room and rummaged in the bottom drawer to hand Huck an industrial-sized flashlight.

Huck accepted it. "Thanks." He flicked it on and started down the wide, surprisingly well-kept stairs to a lower room. Laurel followed him and fought the urge to reach for his jacket. Eerie was the right way to describe the entire structure.

When they reached the bottom, Huck looked around and whistled. Laurel followed his gaze. Desks and chairs were scattered around along with discarded toys that included Barbie dolls and teddy bears. At the far end was what looked like a reading nook with mats on the floor, colored walls, and a colored ceiling with silver stars. The mats were purple, the walls were purple, and the ceiling was purple.

"Oh," she said quietly.

Huck flashed the light up to a window that was at the top of the wall at ground level. A window well was filled with rocks wet from the rain.

"Yeah," Johnson said. "Some of the kids from the camp would sneak in that window and come down here to do dirty business. I'm telling you, damn kids."

Laurel turned around. "They'd come in here and have sexual relations?"

"Oh, yeah. One of the last years of the camp, there were these three girls who got sent home." He pointed to scratched markings in the wall. One had five slashes, one three, and one seven. "They had a contest one year. Can you believe it? To see how many boys they could lure down here. Those girls deserved to be kicked out."

Laurel's pulse rate increased. Fascinating. She studied the area until the dampness and smell of mold became too much. "Let's go," she said, turning to walk upstairs and through the church to the dreary day outside with the men following her. Once in the meager daylight, she pulled a photocopy of the camp picture from her pocket and unfolded it. "Do you recognize any of these kids?"

Johnson snorted. "So many kids went through this place. I seriously doubt it." He squinted to scrutinize the photograph. "Well except for that one."

"Which one?" Laurel asked.

Johnson pointed. "That dude. He's running for city council. Yeah, he was out here about a year ago wanting to buy the property. I believe he entered into the bidding war but didn't win it."

"Who's that?" Huck asked.

Laurel tried to make more connections in her mental murder board. "Councilman Swelter."

"Guess we're talking to the councilman again," Huck said.

"Absolutely." She thanked Mr. Johnson and hurried to the truck, where she shed her outerwear and tried to wring the water from her hair.

Huck loaded Aeneas and then tossed his coat in the back and jumped in the front. "Let's get out of this creepy place."

She wiped water off her face and pressed speed dial on her phone.

"Smudgeon," Walter answered.

"Hi. I was wondering how it was going at the lab."

"We just got here," he said. "We had to find somebody to unlock the door for us. There's a quadruple lock on the thing."

That sounded like Abigail. Laurel's breath quickened. She couldn't wait to see what was in there. "We're still five hours away but take pictures of everything. We'll head right there when we get back into town so I can view the photographs."

"You've got it," Walter said. "Hey, the door's opening."

Something rustled and then a loud boom came over the line.

Huck hit the brakes and looked at her phone.

Another boom echoed so loudly that Laurel leaned away from the device. Panic rushed through her. "Was that an explosion? Walter!" she yelled.

There was no answer.

Chapter 34

Laurel careened into the hospital reception area with Huck right behind her. She nearly slammed into the desk where a young woman, probably in her early twenties, looked up. She had several piercings in her face.

"Can I help you?" she asked.

"Yes, I'm Special Agent Laurel Snow." Laurel flipped out her badge. "One of my agents was brought in, Walter Smudgeon." She had been on the phone with Nester during the drive back, but he hadn't been able to report much.

He turned the corner. "Hey, Laurel."

"Nester." She hurried past the reception area and reached him, grabbing his arms. "Is Walter okay? What happened?" She could barely breathe.

"Right now, all we know is that it was an explosion," Nester said. "Agent Norrs and his team immediately went out there when I called in the officer down, although it took them some time to get there. They've taken control of the scene."

"How is Walter?" Laurel wanted to shake Nester.

"He's all right," Nester said, patting her arm. "Come on. Let's go back."

She walked rapidly with him to reach a familiar-looking

room. Oh no. Was it the same one Walter had stayed in after he'd been shot? Her stomach whirled and she fought the urge to throw up.

Walter sat up in bed with bruises and burns visible down the side of his face and his arm. "Hey, Boss," he said. "I'm fine. Take a deep breath. You look like you're about to pass out."

Laurel's gaze swung to Ena, who sat in a chair. She had a lump on her forehead, but otherwise appeared fine. "What happened?"

"The place was rigged to blow," Walter said.

Laurel wanted to put her head in her hands. Why hadn't she thought of that? Of course, Abigail would have booby trapped her lab. Laurel hadn't had any idea that Abigail knew how to use explosives, but it was Abigail. She would never want anybody to find her research. Laurel swayed.

"Yo, Boss. Sit down," Walter said.

Nester not so gently pushed her into a chair.

Laurel looked around, a dull ache centering behind her left eye. "Where's Huck?"

"I'm right here." He walked into the room. "I was checking with the doctor."

That was a good idea. Laurel hadn't even thought of that. She took a deep breath. "Walter, what happened?"

"We got the warrant. We went to serve it. Took a while to find a guy who could unlock the door," Walter said, telling her what she already knew.

Laurel's head dropped. "I should have thought when you told me that there were so many locks. I should have thought."

"It's not your fault." Huck put a heavy hand on her shoulder. "You can't think of everything."

Yes, she could, and she should have thought of this.

"Walter, you've been healing so well. I'm so sorry about this."

"I'm fine, Boss," Walter said. "The doctor gave me a clean bill of health. The blast tossed me across the hallway, and I hit the other side. I got a little bit burned. I didn't even make it inside the lab."

"He saved my life," Ena said earnestly. "He covered me with his body and then we both smashed into the wall." She leaned over and patted his arm. "I guess not all men are bad."

Huck rolled his eyes. "Ena, get a grip."

The woman smiled at Walter with stars in her eyes.

Walter shifted his weight and reached for what looked like tapioca pudding from a table next to him. "You know, I kind of missed this stuff," he said cheerfully.

Laurel's mind spun. "So you were injured but not badly?"

"Yeah," Walter said. "Thank goodness, right?"

Laurel couldn't imagine if Walter had been seriously injured again. "Yes. Tell me how soon the explosion happened."

Walter frowned. "The maintenance guy unlocked the door and then got out of my way. I opened it. I couldn't even take a step inside before I was flying through the air."

Laurel put her index fingers against her eyebrows and pushed up to counteract the migraine that was trying to kill her. "So the explosion was meant to scare you and probably destroy all evidence, but not kill you."

Walter paused with the spoon halfway to his mouth. "I guess that's fair. Otherwise, it would've been rigged to blow once somebody was inside, correct?"

"Correct," Laurel said, bile rising in her throat.

Huck caught on before anybody else. "Your theory is that Abigail thought you'd be the one eventually executing a warrant if we found this place."

Laurel nodded.

"Ah," Walter said. "She didn't want to kill you."

Laurel's head spun. "Not right now, anyway." She took out her phone and dialed Norrs.

"Agent Norrs."

"It's Snow." She cleared her voice to sound more authoritative. "Are you still at the scene?"

A whirring of some sort of mechanical device trilled through the line. "Yeah. I've been here about four hours," Norrs said. "Thank God nobody was killed. This place went up like you wouldn't believe."

"I believe it," Laurel said. "Is there any evidence left?"

"No. The explosion caused a fire hot enough that everything melted. We think there were chemicals in here. According to the university, it was a storage unit for a couple of the science labs." He muffled the phone and yelled out instructions before returning. "We're in the older part of campus that's rarely used, and there are no cameras here."

Of course. She had to tread lightly here. "Jason Abbott told us it was Abigail's lab."

Norrs snorted. "She has her own lab. Why are you listening to a serial killer, Laurel? Give me a break, would you?"

"You don't find it suspicious that Abbott directed us to that lab and the minute we tried to open the door, an explosive detonated?" she asked. "Abbott claimed that Abigail experimented on him in that lab. The one that just blew up, destroying all evidence."

Something crunched as Norrs no doubt walked over rubble. "There's nothing left in this lab. As far as I know, Abigail is not an expert in explosives. According to my guy, whoever did this knew exactly what they were doing."

"Meaning what?" Laurel asked.

"Meaning the explosion created a fire that destroyed

everything but didn't kill anybody. It would've taken an expert to place these devices at exactly the right places."

Laurel slapped her head. "Your girlfriend is a fucking genius."

Nester jolted and then smiled.

"Agent Snow, you've obviously had a fright today," Norrs said. "Why don't you take care of your teammate, and I will handle the scene."

Could he sound any more condescending? "Fine," Laurel said, ending the call. What a moron. She stood. "Walter, are you sure you're okay?"

"Yeah, Boss, I'm fine. In fact, I'm just waiting for my discharge papers and will be right back to work tomorrow. Your sister didn't want to kill anybody this time, which was a good thing for me."

Huck shook his head. "There's no evidence. We won't be able to tie her to this."

"Where's Kate?" Laurel asked.

Nester looked up from his computer. "She was here earlier but had to go pick up the girls at school, and I guess they were going to get a dog."

"Good. I need you to arrange for an alarm system for her home as soon as possible. I'll pay for it." Laurel tapped her finger against her lips as she mulled over the situation and tried to ignore the fact that Walter was back in a hospital bed because she'd sent him into danger without thinking. "Also, please get ahold of Kirsti Vuittron and tell her she needs to come in for an interview tomorrow. If she doesn't, I'll find her."

Nester's eyebrows rose. "I take it those two items are related?"

Laurel nodded. "Yes. Kirsti showed up drunk on Kate's doorstep." It was too bad there was no way to get Melissa

Cutting to come into the office at the same time. "I know I'm dumping a lot on you, Nester, but I also need you to track down Councilman Swelter. We can't force him into an interview, but can you casually ask him about his attempting to acquire the Sunrise Camp? I find it odd."

"I can call him," Walter said, finishing the pudding. "I'm not doing anything else in this bed."

"No," Laurel choked out. "You're going to stay here and recuperate. Period." She stood. "I need to use the restroom. I'll be right back."

She walked out with everyone watching her and moved down the hallway to lean against the wall for a minute, shutting her eyes and putting her head back. This was her fault. Walter had been nearly fatally shot. He'd finally healed, and she had sent him into danger again.

"This isn't your fault," Huck said by her side. She jumped. She hadn't heard him approach. "You did your job, Laurel. Walter did his and he is going to be okay. You can't take that on."

It was her first time leading a team and the responsibility felt overwhelming. What if something had happened to Walter? They'd had three cases together and he'd been injured in two. "I just need a second," she said, feeling hollow.

"Okay," Huck said. "I'm going to double-check on Ena and make sure she's all right. Physically she's okay, but she's new to the field and this has to be freaking her out a little."

"All right," Laurel said.

When he disappeared around the corner, she turned and maneuvered to the rear of the hospital where the pharmacy was located. She took a deep breath. Then she walked inside and purchased a pregnancy test. It was highly doubtful she was pregnant, but she had to know. She quickly strode to the public restroom near the reception area and went inside to use the test.

The box said to wait for three minutes after she urinated on the stick, so she placed it on a paper towel on the counter and watched it. She couldn't look away. Slowly, the first line came into view, which showed that the test was working.

She held her breath and stopped thinking. For the first time in a long time, she quieted her mind and refused to allow thoughts through. She imagined space. She imagined darkness. She imagined the sky at night without stars, just making her mind go blank. At least several minutes passed before she looked at the test and saw the second line.

She was pregnant.

Chapter 35

Laurel started the fire in the fireplace as her cat slept lazily near it.

Huck was shoveling outside while Aeneas played. Her hands were sweaty, but she stood by the heat for a moment. Then, without anything else to do, she turned and sat in the chair nearest the sofa.

She'd asked Zello to keep an eye on Kate's house for another night, and the man had seemed eager to make money. So that was at least one concern off her mind.

Huck stomped inside, kicking off his boots and coat as Aeneas ran into the kitchen to slurp noisily from a water dish she'd put out last time he'd stayed. "You hungry?"

"No." She clasped her hands in her lap.

His gaze wandered over her, and he cocked his head. Snow melted in his thick, dark hair, making the strands curl beneath his ears. In his dark T-shirt, he looked broad and strong. "What's up?"

She took a deep breath. "We need to talk."

One of his dark eyebrows rose. Sighing, he lumbered over, his socks marred by several holes. "You're not going to talk about dumping me again, are you? If so, I have to tell you that I like you. A lot. Maybe more than like." He grinned.

When she didn't smile back, his smile slowly slid away. Then he sat on the sofa and reached for her hand, leaning toward her. "What's up, Snow?"

This was more difficult than she'd realized. "I haven't been feeling well."

His gaze swept her face. "You are pale. Are you ill?"

She shook her head. While her vocabulary was extensive, she was experiencing difficulty finding the correct words. "I'm pregnant," she blurted out.

He froze. "Excuse me?"

"I took a test at the hospital, and I'm pregnant." She couldn't breathe.

His jaw went slack. "You've been home less than two weeks."

Oh. Good point. "I'm probably about eight-ish weeks pregnant." When his jaw dropped, she hastened to continue. "I've never experienced regular menses, so I didn't realize I was late. Very late." She looked lamely at snow falling outside the window. "This is a shock."

Huck looked toward the fire, his rugged features handsome even in profile.

She watched the storm, her brain feeling sluggish for once.

They were quiet for several moments with the only sound being the hum of the gas fire and the tumultuous wind beating against the windows.

Finally, Laurel cleared her throat. "I'm uncertain about the protocol here."

Huck's cheek creased as he looked back at her, his eyes a bourbon brown. "Protocol?"

"What to do," she said, swallowing.

"Ah. Well, here's a start." He reached over and plucked

her from her chair, settling her on his lap before extending his legs and planting his feet on the messy coffee table. "This is unexpected, but it's good news. I want this baby and I want you."

Something inside her settled. She hadn't realized her chest had been constricted. She breathed out, her lungs feeling capable of inflating fully again. "I want this baby and I want you, too." Those were good words. Simple and yet strong. His heat surrounded her, and for the first time all day, she felt safe. "There's a lot to consider."

He leaned back and cuddled her close. "Yeah, but not all tonight. Right now, let's just take a moment and sit with the fact that there's a genius inside you probably already calculating the best time of day to be born. Okay?"

She smiled, finally feeling lighter. "Statistically, there's no guarantee that my progeny will have a genius IQ, though there is a good chance." She needed to buy books on pregnancy and babies. Though she'd created and run a nonprofit for preemies for years, she'd never really learned much about them. "Abigail said you'd want to marry a kindergarten teacher."

Huck's dark brows drew down. "I would?" He cocked his head. "My kindergarten teacher was a really cool gray-haired lady we all called Grams. I don't want to marry Grams."

"That's not the point," Laurel murmured.

"I know." He ran a comforting hand down her arm. "When I see my future, I see you, Laurel."

She didn't know how to do this. "I'm scared." For the first time in her life, she let a man see her vulnerability.

He kissed her on the nose. "Babies are terrifying. I'd be worried if you weren't scared."

She leaned back to get a better look at his face, and he met her gaze directly. "Really?"

"Absolutely." He kissed her, sliding her to straddle him, going deep.

Desire rushed through her, and she returned his kiss before planting both hands on his cheeks and then wrenching his face away. "Wait a minute." This was wild. Should she think for a moment?

"Why? Are you feeling okay?" His eyes had darkened.

"Yes." In fact, she felt incredible. So why think herself out of the moment? She wanted to be right here and right now with Huck Rivers. So she leaned in and kissed him again, enjoying his response.

He stood, lifting her with him and holding her tight. "It's not like you can get more pregnant." With that, he strode toward the stairs and her bedroom.

Laurel chuckled, her heart warming.

For now, she chose to enjoy the moment. Tomorrow would come soon enough.

Laurel's phone jolted her from a dream-filled sleep in which Abigail chased her around a mountain wielding a sharp knife. She fumbled for her phone, acutely aware of the heated body next to her. Her body was sore and satiated after several rounds of sex with the captain the night before. She pressed a button. "Snow," she said, looking toward the window. It was still dark outside.

"Hey, Laurel, it's Kate."

Laurel sat up and tried to focus. "Kate, is everything okay? Are you and the girls all right?"

Kate chuckled. "Yes, we're fine. A call came in from the Whatcom County Sheriff's office. They have a body."

Laurel wiped sleep out of her eyes. "Why did they call you?"

"At night, I have calls transferred to me instead of the

Seattle office. I figured it was better that way," Kate said. "They called us because they have a body similar to the ones that were on the news, and they didn't know what else to do."

Laurel pushed herself from the bed and reached for her jeans. "Okay. Text the address to my phone."

"You've got it," Kate said. "Do you want me to call in Walter?"

"No," Laurel said, looking over her shoulder as Huck slid from the bed and reached for his jeans. "I'll take Captain Rivers as backup. You don't have to awaken Walter."

Huck looked over his very bare and broad shoulder and gave her a wink. It wasn't right for any man to look that good in the morning. His hair was tousled, and a strong shadow of whiskers covered his hard jaw. In the barely there light, his eyes were a mellow bourbon color. Laurel rolled her eyes and reached for her sweater. It was a chilly morning, and it probably wouldn't warm up much through the day.

"Kate, would you also send me the contact information for the Whatcom County Sheriff?" she asked as she pulled her hair into a ponytail, noting sore muscles in very interesting places. The night had been . . . energetic.

"I sent it with the info. You should be getting the text now."

Laurel's phone had already buzzed. "All right, I'll see you at the office later today."

"Be careful," Kate said. "This thing's getting way too weird."

Laurel couldn't agree more. "Bye," she said.

Huck hurriedly got dressed and used the restroom. "It's nice that I didn't have to argue with you about taking me as backup."

She moved to brush her teeth. "Actually, you have fast

reflexes and you're handy in any situation. You're also a very good driver." If he drove, she could text and coordinate with her team. But perhaps she should let them sleep until after she'd taken a look at the scene. She jogged downstairs to feed her cat while Huck took Aeneas outside and started the truck. She grabbed her coat and hurried out with her weapon and her laptop bag, climbing into the vehicle. Soon they were on their way with Aeneas snoring in his crate behind her seat.

Laurel engaged the navigation system. Her stomach was rolling around again. "We should arrive in about an hour and a half," she said.

Huck looked at the falling snow, his gaze mellow. "The roads are pretty icy. It may take a couple of hours. I'll take 530 to I-5 and go north. It'll be the best-cleared path." He glanced her way. "How are you feeling?"

She wrinkled her nose. "Nauseous but not too bad." It was so odd to think of a life growing inside her. "Did you always intend to have children?"

He shrugged. "When I was engaged a long time ago, I figured we would. Then when I thought it was just Aeneas and me until the end of days, I gave up that dream. But I'm excited about this now. Still taken aback but happy. You?"

She examined her thought processes and emotions. "I never really thought about it, to be honest. Now that we're here right now, I'm excited and nervous and should start researching obstetricians."

He nodded. "Let's get that appointment scheduled soon."

"I will. For now, this case," she said, pressing the button. The phone rang several times.

"Sheriff Willis," came a low female voice. Something crackled over the line. Wind?

"Hi Sheriff. It's Special Agent Laurel Snow. You called my office?"

The sound of wind whipped across the phone. "Oh, hi Agent Snow. Yes, we found a body in a tent in one of our alleys."

"What color is the tent?" Laurel asked.

"It's purple and the victim has been stabbed many times. There's Valentine's candy scattered all around the victim's face and forced down his throat. I've been watching the news and knew this was your case."

Laurel reached forward and turned on her seat warmer. "Yes. The MO sounds like it matches several of our cases. Thank you for calling. Do you have the body secured?"

"We're having a pretty bad rainstorm right now. I've had officers stretch a tarp over the tent, but the wind is really something else. Our county coroner is here and wants to take the body. Our crime scene photographer is also here and has photographed the scene. I don't think we should wait for you. How far away are you?"

Laurel glanced at the clock. "We're at least an hour and a half." It was important to get the body out of the elements in case there was any trace evidence left. "Go ahead and release the body to your coroner. But then I would like him or her to release the body to the Tempest County coroner, who has been performing the other autopsies."

"Fine by me," Sheriff Willis said. "I'll wait here for you at the scene. I assume you want to witness it yourself?"

"I do," Laurel said. "Have you identified the victim?"

Willis coughed several times. "Sorry about that. Fighting a cold. No, we don't have an ID yet. The coroner will print the vic before she releases the body to Dr. Ortega."

Laurel glanced at the clock. Sunrise wasn't for another couple of hours, so there'd be no natural light for a while. "You know Dr. Ortega?"

Willis chuckled. "Everybody knows Dr. Ortega. He's a great guy."

That was the truth. "We'll be there shortly." Laurel disengaged the call. "Do you think it's too early to call in my team?"

Huck glanced at the dash. "Five in the morning is early."

True, but she was dealing with murder.

Chapter 36

The crime scene was creepy as hell. A low mist hung over the street almost down to the pavement in the back alley of an industrial zone. Rain pattered down, which would be all right if the wind wasn't bent on destruction. There were a few stores dotted around, but otherwise, the place was cold and vacant. The purple tent stood out like a beacon in the middle of a fairly clean alleyway behind a strip mall.

Huck stood to the side and watched as Laurel surveyed the entire scene, walking it and then bending down to look inside the tent. From his vantage point, he could see the heart-shaped candy smushed into the blood. Definitely creepy.

Even so, his mind was on his personal life for once. He wished his dad were still alive. He would have loved the idea of being a grandpa. For now, Huck kept an eye on Laurel as she worked the scene. He'd been falling for her since the first day they'd met, but he'd planned to take it very slow as he brought her into his world. She was hesitant with relationships, and he figured it was partly because of her big brain and partly because she'd been raised without a dad. The baby changed things.

He was responsible for them both now, which was a sentiment Laurel might not appreciate. Or maybe she would. It was impossible to read her sometimes.

Sheriff Willis, a tall blonde probably in her fifties, was patient as she showed Laurel around and answered any relevant questions. So far it appeared that they didn't have an identity on the victim.

Laurel walked to the end of a warehouse building, which was vacant at this hour. The sun failed to lighten the mist in any way. She looked both ways. "There's no church."

"Excuse me?" Sheriff Willis called out.

Huck watched as Laurel looked around. There were warehouses on either side of the street. Frowning, Laurel ducked her head and fought the wind to walk across the street. She squinted and pointed at a smaller building that was sandwiched between the two much larger warehouses.

"Sheriff Willis," she called out. "What is this in the middle here? What is this place?"

Huck walked out to the street to look back at the metal-sided building that now concealed the purple tent and crime scene. All of the businesses were dark at this hour.

Sheriff Willis ducked her head and ran across the street to stand next to Laurel. She looked across. "Oh, that's DRIFTWOOD COMMUNITY CHURCH. Their sign was stolen last week."

Laurel's expression smoothed out. "But it's a church? In the center of this industrial area?"

"Yes," Willis said. "It's a small nondenominational church, and they play really loud music. I've had a couple of complaints at night. They had a sign that said 'DRIFT-WOOD COMMUNITY CHURCH' lit up real pretty. I don't know who stole it, but I will find out."

"That's fine. I just wanted to make sure that a church was located in the vicinity," Laurel murmured.

That was a fact that even Rachel hadn't dug up. Huck checked out both directions on the road to make sure nobody was coming, but the quiet street was abandoned at this time of morning. As he stood there, the wind cut through his jacket as if it was made of feathers. Man, it was going to be a cold day. He saw Laurel shiver, but she didn't complain. Instead, she took out her phone and photographed the scene from every direction.

He fought the urge to take off his coat and plant it over hers in front of the other officers. But he'd get her back into the warm truck as soon as he could.

The sheriff's phone tinkled a merry tune, and she pulled it from her coat pocket. "Sheriff Willis," she answered. She listened for several beats. "Got it. All right, thanks." She clicked off. "The coroner fingerprinted the victim, and his name is Mateo Perez."

Laurel's eyebrows lifted. "Does that mean anything to you?"

Willis shook her head. "No, but Dr. Bloomsburg said that Perez was a probation officer with Skagit County. I never met him."

Huck looked around. "So he works in Skagit County and lives in Whatcom?" Skagit County was located between Tempest County and Whatcom County. Whatcom bordered Canada. "Do you have a home address for him?"

Willis nodded. "Officers are already on scene. They found the officer's dog safely locked inside the garage, and so far, no sign of a struggle."

Huck walked back to the tent and crouched down, aiming his flashlight inside. "Have you been able to count how many heart-shaped candies are present with each body?"

Laurel shook her head. "They've been too smashed to determine, but Dr. Ortega thinks there were approximately forty at the first scene, fifty-two at the second, forty-seven at the third, and just ten at Zeke Caine's scene. But I believe those just dropped from the attacker's pockets."

"Hmm," Huck said. "So there's no consistent number."

"No," Laurel said. "I already thought about that. They're all candies from those square boxes, but the lab hasn't gotten back to me with any more information than that. As you can see, there aren't an equal number of any particular color, as far as we can tell. A lot of them were compromised by the blood." She pulled out her phone, punched a couple of buttons, and lifted it to her ear. "Hi, Nester. I'm texting you a victim's name, Mateo Perez. He was a probation officer in Skagit County. I want to know everything about him within the next hour." She paused. "Really? That was fast. Thanks." She clicked off.

Huck shoved his hands in his pockets. "What now?"

She shivered in the heavy wind, dialed, and lifted her phone to her ear again. "Hi, Officer Zello. I know. Frank. Are you still in position?" She listened and then shoved her free hand into her pocket. "Great. Nobody cruised by or showed any interest in Kate's house last night?" Her face cleared. "Thanks. Bring a bill by the office when you get the chance—I don't need you to watch her any longer. They're installing her alarm today." She ended the call and pushed her hand and phone into her other pocket.

"Laurel?" Huck asked.

She focused again on the crime scene, her nose red from the wind. "Now we meet with the entire team for a profile and a plan. It's time we found this butcher."

* * *

Laurel checked with Agent Norrs to discover that Zeke Caine's condition had been downgraded to serious, but he still refused to meet with anybody. It was as if he wanted to frustrate her. She had to get Walter in to speak with him, and soon.

For now, she stood by the two case boards at the far end of the conference room with her team settled around the opulent table.

At the far end, Nester typed out notes on the laptop in front of him. Walter, burns on the right side of his face, had taken the position to Nester's right, and Kate, her arm still in a sling, sat across from him. Laurel's team was wounded.

Huck and Ena, whom she also considered part of the team, were out on a call.

"All right," Laurel said. "I thought we should do a run-through of the case. Here's what we have." She pointed to the five photographs taped to the victim board. "Four of the five victims were found stabbed in a purple tent with candy shoved down their throats—all near a church. Victor Vuittron was the first killed. He was a lawyer at Marshall & Cutting. Frederick Marshall is our second victim, and he was a partner at the firm. The only named partner still standing is Melissa Cutting. She's a suspect."

Nester looked up from the computer. "Are there other partners?"

"Just junior partners and associates, and we need to speak with all the ones we don't have on record yet," Laurel said, her thoughts flowing as she worked through the case with the team. "The third victim is Jiro Makino, a filmmaker who made videos for Swelter and Vuittron as well as the law firm. In addition, he had connections to the first two victims from childhood."

Laurel used the end of a marker to tap Zeke's picture. "The fourth victim, the only one still alive, is Zeke Caine. We have not drawn a connection between Caine and the other three victims as of yet. Also, while there was spilled candy on the ground around him, there was no purple tent to be seen. Of course, this kill was interrupted when I arrived on scene."

It helped to say everything out loud for her team. "The fifth victim is Mateo Perez, who was a probation officer from Skagit County but lived in Whatcom County. There's a good chance he knew at least one of the lawyers. That is one of the things we need to track down today. There's no connection between Mateo and Caine that we know of."

She moved to the suspect board. "On the suspect board we have Melissa Cutting, who is now the only remaining named partner of the law firm. We've conducted a background check on her. There are hints that she might have been having an affair with Victor Vuittron."

"What about connections to other victims besides the two lawyers?" Nester asked.

Laurel made a notation beneath Cutting's picture about seeking a warrant for financial records. She didn't have probable cause yet, and that was a goal. "Thus far, we haven't found a connection between Melissa Cutting and Zeke Caine. She might've met Makino during the filming of a promotional spot for the firm, but she is not included in the footage. There's also a chance she met Perez if Victor Vuittron worked with him, but we have no evidence so far confirming either supposition."

"We're looking at all of the attorneys at the firm, since anybody could've had dealings with him." Walter took a long drink of coffee from his oversized mug. Unlike weeks ago, it was black without creamer. "However, we don't have much, do we?"

"We're getting there." Laurel pointed to the next photograph on the suspect board. "Next is Kirsti Vuittron, Victor's widow. She was most likely having an affair with her personal trainer and seems to have had several in the past."

Laurel moved down the board. "Here we have Thema Sackey, who is a junior associate at the firm. She was having an affair with Victor Vuittron, and she had an earlier relationship with Frederick Marshall. In addition, she is featured in the firm's promotional film by Jiro Makino. Thus far, we haven't unearthed a connection between her and Perez or Caine. However, again, Perez was a probation officer, so it's possible they crossed paths at some time."

There was no doubt Zeke Caine was the outlier here, but it was possible Mateo Perez was as well.

Laurel studied the perfectly posed picture of the councilman. "Next, we have Councilman Swelter. He, Victor Vuittron, and Frederick Marshall attended a summer camp together as teenagers. Jiro Makino was also a camper. We've warned the councilman that he could be in danger, and he is taking precautions. He's also a suspect."

Nester grimaced. "Councilman Swelter is dodging my calls about his attempt to buy the camp. I'll keep trying."

Laurel appreciated the effort. "Victor was running for a council seat against Swelter, and they definitely didn't like each other. Jiro also made a campaign film for Swelter and then refused to do a second one because he started working on Victor's campaign. Thus far, I don't have a connection between Perez or Caine and the councilman."

"He looks smarmy," Kate said.

Laurel nodded. That was an apt description. "I think the

key is the summer camp but don't want that theory to cloud our vision. The church there had a purple playroom, and our victims are found in purple tents. It could be a co-incidence, but it'd be a big one. The key must be this camp."

She tapped the picture of the campers that had been taped to the board. "It's a little blurry and it's difficult to make out features. I don't see Zeke Caine or Mateo Perez, but both are bald now, and many years have passed. We've been unsuccessful in tracking down anybody alive in this photograph except Councilman Swelter. I need him to help us now. I want to know if Perez or Caine are in this picture. That would tie all the victims to the camp."

Kate snorted. "I thought Councilman Swelter didn't like cops and refused to help."

Laurel looked at his picture. "I'll have to persuade him."

Walter cut Kate a look, his eyebrows raised.

"What?" Laurel asked.

Walter shifted closer to the table. "Nothing, Boss. It's just . . . you're not . . . all that charming."

That was true. Laurel flashed a smile. "I'm not trying to be charming." She turned back to the board. "There's a possibility that the Zeke Caine attack"—she pointed to the picture of her father— "was unrelated to the other four, considering he survived."

"Yes, but didn't you interrupt the killer?" Walter asked quietly.

Laurel fought a shiver. "I might have, but he has no connection to the other victims or camp so far, and there is a possibility that somebody else wanted Zeke dead. I'm tracking down a woman who left a message on Abigail's phone. He has harmed women in the past, and he disappeared for five years, so he probably has more enemies than we know, including Abigail Caine."

"She always pops back up, doesn't she?" Kate muttered under her breath.

Laurel had taped a picture of Abigail on the suspect board. "I don't believe she had anything to do with the other four deaths, but I think we should keep an eye on her for the attack on Zeke Caine. I am a suspect as well, which is why Walter is handling that aspect of the investigation."

Walter whistled. "I've got you."

"We are getting closer. This subject is what we'd call a mission killer, and the mission will never end. Even if his or her original targets become victims, this killer will find another mission," Laurel said, feeling the clock ticking down on the next murder.

"Do you think it's a woman?" Nester asked.

Laurel looked at the suspect board. "I don't know. We have a blank slot here for a serial killer who randomly chooses these men because of their age, their success, or some other quality we haven't discovered."

"Like Jason Abbott," Nester said.

"Yes." Jason Abbott had hunted successful women on the Internet, stalked them, and then killed them. Laurel tapped the end of the marker on the board. "A broad profile would be of a subject who has a problem with men. The killer leaves Valentine's candy around the head and shoved down the throat of the victim. Valentine's Day symbolizes love and the heart. Candy suggests romance. I think this is someone who is angry at men, considers them liars, and feels betrayed. That could be why the heart-shaped candy is shoved down the throat after they've been stabbed to death."

Kate leaned back in the white leather chair. "That's a broad range of people."

"I know. The suspect is between twenty-five and fifty,"

Laurel murmured. "Strong enough to stab somebody repeatedly and drag a heavy body off a truck and into a tent."

Walter pushed away from the table. "Okay, so what's the plan?"

Laurel took a deep breath. "I would like you to learn everything you can about these five churches. See if there's any sort of connection between them as well as between the victims and the churches. I don't want to miss anything."

"No problem," Walter said. "I'll start with the closest one and work my way out."

"I thought you could also drop by and see Melissa Cutting at her place of work. Take her by surprise?" Laurel didn't want to wait until it was convenient for Melissa.

"Sure," Walter said cheerfully.

Laurel turned to Nester. "Keep on the labs about the tent and the candy. In addition, we're still waiting on the phone dumps for Frederick Marshall and his wife. Those should have come in by now."

Nester nodded. "Yeah, there was a holdup in DC, but I can dump the phones now. I had to update my program and it's almost finished. I'll get those to you today."

"Good, thanks. Also, there should be something on the paint chips found on the victims' heels. And I really need you to track down that truck we saw the night Thema, Kate, and I were fired upon."

"You've got it," Nester said.

Good. Who had been the intended target? The shooter had missed and would most likely try again.

Soon.

Chapter 37

After a frustrating afternoon in her office during which Councilman Swelter avoided her calls and Zeke Caine refused to see law enforcement officers, Laurel once again tried to get an appointment to meet Julie Rawlingston. The woman said she regretted leaving a message on Abigail's phone but still agreed to meet with her in an hour, saying she didn't have a lot of time.

Laurel also needed to make an appointment with an OB-GYN. She wanted to start researching medical credentials in the area. For now, she had to find a killer.

Maybe she'd have better luck with the councilman by using a different strategy. Fighting the urge to cross her fingers, Laurel input another number and reached Eric Swelter's secretary. "Hi, this is Special Agent Laurel Snow. I need to speak with the councilman now, or I'm coming down to City Hall. Unfortunately, where I go, the media follows," she said.

The woman sighed. "Fine. Just a second."

"Councilman Swelter," he answered.

"Hi. It's Agent Snow."

"I don't have time for this, Snow," he burst out.

She stretched her neck, not bothering with charm. "You're probably in danger."

"I know, and I have a protection detail. If you'd do your job and find the maniac shoving candy down the throats of men, I'd really appreciate it."

Laurel dug deep for patience. "Then help me. I know you are very busy, but I have a photograph of you and several teens at Sunrise Camp. I need you to identify all the kids for me."

He snorted. "I don't remember half of those kids."

"If you see the picture, you might. I could drive it out to you if you like, or I could email or text a copy to you."

His sigh was long-suffering. "Fine. Email me a copy, and I'll see what I can do."

She started typing on her keyboard to send it. "Why did you make an offer on the Sunrise Camp property?"

"I thought it'd be a good investment," Swelter said, sounding bored. "Before Frederick was viciously murdered, he worked on my portfolio, and we decided I should invest in real estate. The corporate retreat market is booming right now, so I looked for a place to buy, and that one came up. I remembered having some fun there. It's unfortunate I lost the auction."

Was it as simple as that? "What dirt did Victor have on you?"

The councilman was silent.

"I'll keep digging until I find it."

He groaned. "You're impossible. It was nothing—just a tax mix-up. Frederick fixed it, I paid a fine, and it went away. Dumbass Vuittron wanted to use it against me, because nobody wants a councilman who doesn't pay his taxes. Geez, Snow. Try to find the real criminals, would you?"

She'd double-check his statement with Melissa Cutting,

but it sounded true. Now that Vuittron was dead, Swelter didn't have anything to worry about, so why lie to a federal agent? "Councilman Swelter, I really do appreciate your help on this, and as soon as we solve this case, I'll make a statement to the media that you were not a suspect." Of course, unless he was the killer.

He was silent for a moment. "I would appreciate that. It would probably be very helpful for my campaign if it looks like I was harassed, and then you apologize."

She hadn't said she'd apologize, and there was no way the guy had been harassed. "So you'll take a look at the picture?"

"I will. I have several meetings, but I'll look at it this afternoon and name everyone I can. I don't have a lot of faith, though. I attended multiple summer camps, and I honestly didn't make many friends."

That wasn't a surprise. "Thank you."

He ended the call. Laurel stood and reached for her laptop bag, hurrying down the hallway and pausing at the computer room. "Any news?"

Nester cleared his throat, his gaze flicking across the screen. "The ballistic and casing reports just came in, finally. The bullets recovered after you, Ms. Sackey, and Kate were shot at were from a 9mm Glock. There's no hit in the system." He typed rapidly and read the screen. "And the shots fired at you at the church the night you interrupted the killing of Zeke Caine were from a Smith & Wesson 9mm. It doesn't pop in the system either."

"The bullets don't match, so we might be dealing with two entirely different attackers," she said.

It was time to meet yet another woman who hated Zeke Caine.

* * *

Julie Rawlingston lived about twenty miles away from the Genesis Valley Community Church up a long gully that fronted Last Crow Creek. Her A-frame cabin had been stained red at some point, but the elements had faded the wood to a burnished pink. While her long driveway and sidewalk had been shoveled, piles of frozen snow lined both sides of the walkway, which had iced over. Laurel slipped several times before reaching the front door. She knocked.

The door was opened almost immediately by a fortyish woman with long black hair and stunning green eyes.

"Hi, Ms. Rawlingston. I'm Special Agent Laurel Snow." Laurel took out her badge to show to the woman.

The woman accepted the badge and studied it carefully. Then she looked up and studied Laurel's face. "It's uncanny. You and Abigail could pass for twins now that she's no longer hiding behind wigs and contacts. I saw her not too long ago in town."

Laurel forced a smile. "Yes, we share similar coloring," she said.

"Well, come in," Julie said, stepping back and allowing Laurel to walk into a living area that held one sofa and two chairs drawn up close to a wood-burning fireplace. A sliding glass door led to a deck outside, in front of the creek. The smell of freshly baked pies wafted in the air. "Can I get you anything?"

"No, I'm fine. Thank you," Laurel said.

"Please have a seat." Julie pointed to one of the chairs.

Laurel took a seat, waiting for Julie to do the same. "I listened to the message that you left my sister." She purposely called Abigail her sister, even though the words nearly stuck in her throat.

"I know." Julie looked down at her hands. She was a

tall woman dressed in a long skirt with a bright green sweater. "I shouldn't have left that message. It was unkind, considering Pastor Zeke was attacked."

"I don't know him," Laurel said. "What I do know of him isn't good. I've heard bad things."

Julie's eyes widened and her shoulders settled. "You have?"

"Absolutely," Laurel said. "In fact, I would like to discover where he's been these last five years, because I doubt he was doing anything legal." It wasn't like her to reveal facts to a possible witness, but she had to establish some sort of rapport to keep Julie talking.

Julie clasped her hands together. "You're so right. He's a dangerous man and . . ." She looked toward the creek outside.

"Did he hurt you?" Laurel asked.

"I don't like to talk about it."

Laurel searched for the right words. "It's all right. You can tell me confidentially."

Julie sniffed. "That's all it can be. I used to help out at the church when Pastor Zeke was still there, and one night we drank some wine together. I helped write one of his sermons." She paled.

"It's all right," Laurel said.

"It's not all right. I don't remember anything after that. I woke up in the morning naked in his office. There was a blanket over me, and we'd definitely had sex."

Laurel's chest ached. "If you were passed out, it wasn't sex," she said gently.

Julie sighed and her hands shook as she reached for a pillow to hug against her torso. "I know, but it's his word against mine, and I don't know what happened. I was confused so I went home and took a shower." Her voice broke but she rushed on as if she wanted to get it all out. "I just stayed at home for a couple of weeks. There's no physical evidence. Even if there was, he would say it was consensual."

"Is that why he left?" Laurel asked.

"No. That was a good three years before he left," Julie muttered.

Laurel thought about the last decade, about where Zeke might've gone. What crimes he might've committed. How was there no record of him anywhere? "Do you think you were drugged?"

Julie nodded vigorously. "Yeah. I know I was drugged, now. At the time, I was just befuddled and confused and kind of scared."

Laurel felt for the woman. Zeke Caine was definitely a predator. "Are you aware of any other instances with women in the church?"

Julie shook her head. "No, sorry. But it's something I've never talked about, so it's probable that there are other victims out there. I've had a lot of counseling the last couple years, which is why I can talk to you about it, but I'm not going to file a report and go to court or anything like that. There's just no evidence, other than my word, and I'm in a good place now."

"I understand."

Julie sniffed. "Plus, apparently somebody else wants him dead. It's too bad they didn't succeed."

Laurel winced. It was because of her that the killer hadn't succeeded. She might hate Zeke Caine, but she couldn't be anybody other than exactly who she was. She'd done her job and she'd saved his life. Now it was time to put him away. "Ms. Rawlingston, I hate to ask you this, but where were you the night that Zeke Caine was stabbed?"

Julie chuckled but the sound lacked mirth. "Oh, believe me, if I had stabbed that bastard, I'd be happily screaming it from the rooftops. I was at my boyfriend's house." A light pink dusted her cheekbones.

"Could I have his name and address, please?"

"Sure. His name is Phillip Planten, and he's an accountant with Planten and North." Julie reached for an envelope in a stack of mail on the sofa table and a pencil to scratch out a name and a number. "He's an honest guy, and I was with him all night. We went out to dinner and then I stayed at his place. He doesn't have security cameras, but I'm sure you could probably see us on a road or something. At least that's what happens on television."

Laurel smiled. "Yeah, we can look at CCTV sometimes, but we'll see." She didn't get the feeling that Ms. Rawlingston was lying. At least there were no indicators of it. "Are you familiar with Victor Vuittron or Frederick Marshall, who also went by the name 'Ricky'?"

"Mmm. No to Frederick." Julie looked up at the ceiling as if searching her memory. "I did see Victor a couple of times at the church, but we didn't speak or anything."

"How did you know his name?"

Julie shrugged. "I heard it somewhere. Maybe the pastor used it."

"How about Matteo Perez or Jiro Makino?"

Julie frowned. "No, I've never heard of them, either. Why?"

"I'm just asking," Laurel said, switching topics before coming back to the church. "Where did you grow up?"

Julie's face lost the pinched expression. "I grew up in North Carolina and moved here about twelve years ago, with a guy. He was a river guide named Jordan Phillips. We broke up shortly after moving here. Last I heard, he was up in Alaska doing deep sea fishing, but I liked it here, so I stayed."

"Did you ever attend any summer camps in the Pacific Northwest?"

"No," Julie said, her brows furrowing. "That's really a weird question. Why would you ask me that?"

Laurel looked at the three pies cooling on the countertop. "It's all routine, I promise you. Why did you leave that message on Abigail's phone?"

Julie's hands fluttered in the air. "I don't know. I heard that the pastor was back, and I knew that Abigail had returned to town, so I wanted to warn her. Rumor has it that he sent her away for most of her childhood, so I thought perhaps she didn't know what a beast he could be. It was silly, I'm sure."

"No," Laurel said. "I think it was kind of you. Have you met Abigail?"

"Oh, yes," Julie said, brightening even more. "When she was dating Pastor John, she attended the church quite regularly, although back then she was a blonde, unlike now. When they broke up, she stopped coming to church. I was always intrigued by her. She's not the warmest of people, but for a while she seemed to make Pastor John happy, and that mattered to me."

"I see," Laurel said. "Thank you for your time. I don't really have any more questions." She stood and waited until Julie did the same. "Oh, just real quick, have you ever met Melissa Cutting or Kirsti Vuittron?"

"No."

Laurel sped up her questions. "What about Eric Swelter?"

"The councilman?" Julie winced. "No. He seems like a real jerk. Have you seen his campaign ads? The guy is . . . what's the word?"

"Smarmy?" Laurel supplied helpfully.

Julie chuckled. "Yeah, smarmy. That's exactly right. That Swelter is smarmy." She grinned. "Not that I have to worry about it since I don't live in Seattle, but for some reason I get all their campaign ads."

Laurel made sure the ice was off her shoes. "Yeah, me too. What about Thema Sackey? Is that a name you know?"

"Thema? Sure. She attended the church with Victor Vuittron several times."

Laurel paused. That was surprising. "Thema and Victor attended church together? He was recently married to somebody else, correct?"

Julie's eyes widened. "I didn't know he was married. I thought they were a couple. You know. A May to December romance, considering the age gap."

"Do you know how long Thema attended the Genesis Valley Community Church?"

"No, but now that I think about it, the first time she appeared, Pastor John acted like he'd known her for quite some time. I'm afraid that's all I can tell you."

Laurel moved toward the door. "Thank you. By the way, do you own a 9mm handgun?"

"No," Julie laughed. "I'm a pacifist. I don't believe in guns."

Laurel opened the door. "What do you drive?"

"A Subaru. Why?"

"Just routine questions," Laurel said. "Thank you again for your time." She hustled outside into the cold air, the phone already to her ear.

"You've reached the god of snowboarding, Nester," Nester answered.

"Hey, I need you to do a deeper dive on Thema Sackey before you do the rest. See if she owns any weapons, and trace her childhood the best you can, would you? I want to know about her ties to Genesis Valley Community Church. There might be a connection to Zeke Caine after all, and the other men as well."

She sensed the killer would attack another target soon, but she was zeroing in. Fast.

Chapter 38

As the snow turned to sleet outside and beat against the windows, Huck carried the two full mugs of hot chocolate into his living room, where Laurel was lounging on his sofa, finishing a phone call. It was weird to see her cat flopped over by his fireplace and Aeneas giving him curious looks.

"That's not my fault, Agent Norrs. However, I am going to speak with him." She clicked off and tossed her phone onto his coffee table, which was littered with magazines on topics ranging from hunting to fishing to football. "Zeke Caine is still refusing to talk to anyone," she muttered.

Huck handed her the mug and padded over to sit next to her, stretching out his long legs and propping his feet on the coffee table.

"You require new socks," she said.

He looked down. All of his socks probably had holes in them. Aeneas lounged happily on his pillow over by the fireplace, every once in a while lifting his head to study the cat. Huck had worked on search and rescue training with him earlier, having had the dog track Laurel around the garage into the house. His dog had done a good job.

So he'd played with him for quite a while because that's how the dog was rewarded.

Laurel's phone buzzed and she reached for it, then read the screen and blanched.

"What?" Huck asked.

She looked over. "It's Kate. She said to turn on *The Killing Hour*."

"Oh, wonderful." That was all Huck needed. He reached for the remote and turned on the flat-screen TV, maneuvering to the streaming site. Rachel came up on the screen, her blond hair waving perfectly around her face.

She smiled. "*The Killing Hour* has exclusive information that the Pacific Northwest Violent Crimes Unit has zeroed in on Councilman Eric Swelter as one of the main suspects in the Broken Heart Murders."

"Crap," Laurel muttered.

Rachel's eyes remained serious and her expression somber. "We reached out to Councilman Swelter's office for a comment, but they have not gotten back to us as of the time of airing. Apparently the special agent in charge of the Pacific Northwest Violent Crimes Unit is Laurel Snow, who you might remember as the woman who caught both the Witch Creek Killer and the Snowblood Peak Killer. She's quite talented, and she has narrowed her focus to Councilman Swelter. Allegedly," Rachel added at the end.

"She has an aptitude for drawing conclusions," Laurel mused thoughtfully.

Rachel leaned slightly toward the camera, looking serious in a black suit with a pink shell beneath. "In addition, we can exclusively report that Agent Snow was fired upon in her parking lot last week. As far as we've been able to determine, Councilman Swelter's whereabouts were unknown at that time. Again, we did reach out for a comment but have not heard back."

Huck frowned. "She's skirting slander there." But just on the edge—she hadn't said anything untrue.

Laurel stretched her legs to gracefully place her feet on the coffee table. She barely reached, and her blue socks looked new with no holes.

Rachel kept her somber expression in place. "The fourth in the Broken Heart Serial Killer's spree is none other than Pastor Zeke Caine, a beloved leader of the Genesis Valley Community Church, who fortunately survived the attack. Coincidentally, we just learned that he is also Agent Snow's father."

Heat flashed through Huck's chest. "How did she find out about that?"

"Her sources are impressive," Laurel said, watching intently.

Rachel's eyes gleamed. "As you know, the other victims of this terrible killer are Victor Vuittron, Frederick Marshall, Jiro Makino, and Mateo Perez."

One by one, pictures of the victims came up on the screen.

"Finally," Rachel wound down, "while we don't know what this killer is going to do next, we do know who will probably stop him. Special Agent Laurel Snow, we're counting on you."

Rachel seemed to shift uncomfortably in her seat, but Huck had learned long ago that her every movement was choreographed. "Here we go," he muttered, just waiting. His breath caught in his lungs and his muscles stiffened.

"Unfortunately, there's more to this family drama. In an exclusive interview that will be filmed tomorrow morning, we have arranged to interview none other than the Witch Creek murder suspect, Jason Abbott." Rachel's chin dropped in what might appear to be a regretful look. "Mr. Abbott is alleging that Dr. Abigail Caine, Agent Snow's sister, drugged him and basically triggered the killer inside him. So stay tuned tomorrow for more about this situation."

The show went to commercial. Laurel groaned and put her head back on the sofa.

Huck winced and turned the channel to an old sitcom. "At least she's not going after you any longer."

"For now," Laurel murmured. "I have no doubt she'll switch her focus at any point to get ratings."

"Agreed," Huck said, sighing heavily.

He regretted ever dating Rachel, much less asking her to marry him. In fact, he couldn't exactly remember the details that had led to that night. It was probably a good thing she'd turned on him for a story as soon as she could. That had been a narrow escape.

Laurel's phone dinged and she reached for it, looking at the screen and then exhaling as if she needed to calm herself. She clicked the speaker button. "Hello, Abigail."

"Hello, sister. Did you just watch *The Killing Hour*?"

"I did," Laurel said.

Abigail chuckled. "I am more than happy to take care of that woman if you want."

Laurel looked down at the phone. "Is that a threat?"

"Of course not," Abigail said smoothly. "I would never threaten anybody. You know that. Did you tell Huckalicious that you're his baby mama?"

Huck stilled.

Laurel sighed. "Go away."

Abigail's chuckle was throaty. "Just call me if you need help." She clicked off.

"You told her?" Huck asked.

"Of course not. She guessed by looking at me, which is creepier than I can describe," Laurel muttered.

Huck took a deep breath. "I don't think there's any doubt that she's the one who threatened Rachel and partially strangled her, is there?"

"Negative," Laurel said, looking up at the TV.

Huck sighed. "It's unbelievable that you two share DNA."

"You're telling me," Laurel said, uncharacteristically using a colloquialism.

He wanted to protect her from all harm, but the best he could do was help her to relax. "Why don't we just watch the TV and drink our hot cocoa?"

There was no other way to assist her right now. Maybe having a night off and getting rest would be good for both of them. She snuggled into his side, sipped her cocoa, and pretended to watch the television show, and then another. He could almost feel the brain waves coming from her mind as she worked through the case. He said nothing, knowing she needed silence to be able to do so.

After a couple more mindless sitcoms, he flopped his feet on the wooden floor and stood, heading for the dog. "Let's go to bed. I'll take Aeneas out first."

Her phone dinged again, and she jolted. "What now?" Reaching forward, she lifted it to her ear. "Snow." She stopped moving. "Are you serious? When? Yes. I'll be right there."

Huck paused near the fireplace. "What happened?"

"Jason Abbott attempted suicide earlier this evening. He's at the hospital now." She stood and started toward the door. "I suppose you're driving?"

* * *

Tempest County Hospital was three times the size of the Genesis Valley Community Hospital, and the parking lot was nearly full. With Huck on her heels, Laurel barreled into the hospital waiting area to find Walter already chatting with the young man behind the intake desk.

He saw her and straightened. "Hey, Boss. Kate called me. I think she's trying to make sure I'm still your partner."

Laurel reached him. "Of course, you're my partner." She flipped out her badge to show the receptionist. "What is Mr. Abbott's status?"

"His status?" Haylee Johnson careened from around the corner with a cup of coffee in her hand. "His status is that he tried to kill himself and it's all your fault." She looked down at the coffee cup and her bicep muscles tightened.

"Whoa," Huck said, stepping in front of Laurel. "You throw that, and it's battery. I'll arrest you in a heartbeat."

Haylee looked up at him with tears streaming down her face. Her nose was red, and her hair was a wild mess around her shoulders. She wore brightly patterned workout leggings and a worn green sweatshirt as if she'd run out of bed when she'd gotten the call. "I'm not going to do anything, but this is your fault."

Laurel focused on Walter again. "What's his status? Have you heard?"

"Not yet," Walter said. "The doc said that Abbott sliced his wrists with a piece of metal he somehow managed to get hold of. They found him in time, though."

Haylee started wailing.

"Knock it off," Walter said, not unkindly. "Get a grip on yourself. The guy's a serial killer. You seem like a nice person. Move on."

Laurel studied the young woman, her mind ticking through facts. "Haylee, do you own a gun?"

"No," Haylee sobbed. "I should get one, though. It's a dangerous world out there."

Laurel couldn't deny that.

"What are you driving these days?" she asked

"I told you I've been hanging out with my cousin, who wasn't charged for yelling at you, by the way. He drives me around in his blue Subaru." Haylee sniffed loudly.

Laurel looked at the receptionist, not really caring if the cousin had been charged. "Can we see Mr. Abbott?"

"Not until the doctor comes out," he said. "Sorry."

"That's all right." Laurel turned back to Haylee as Huck edged to the side. Was he positioning himself to intercept the young woman if she attacked? "Haylee, I know that your aunt works at Marshall & Cutting."

Haylee threw up her hands. "My aunt owns the law firm. What is your point?"

"I'm wondering if you've ever met Jiro Makino or Mateo Perez."

Haylee sniffed loudly. "Who?"

"They're both men in their fifties. Jiro was a filmmaker, and Mateo a probation officer."

Haylee angrily wiped tears away from her face. "I'm not an actress, and I've never been on probation, so no, I don't know either of those men." She shuddered and then held a hand to her stomach as if she were in great pain.

"What about Zeke Caine?" Laurel asked.

"No, but he has the same name as your evil stepsister," Haylee spat out.

"Half sister," Laurel corrected.

Haylee frowned, her face scrunching up. "You are such a bitch."

The young woman had issues, but Laurel couldn't see her being organized enough to plan the killings of the four men. She had no doubt that if Haylee had a gun, she might impulsively shoot it, but she wouldn't just drive into a parking lot and do it. She wouldn't acquire a gun on her own.

"Can we call your aunt to come and get you?" Laurel asked. It was surprising that Melissa Cutting hadn't already tried to help Haylee. The young woman needed distance from Jason Abbott.

"I already did." Haylee's shoulders slumped as if all the fight had deserted her. "She should be here in a few minutes to get me."

Laurel tried to think of the right thing to say, but Haylee needed to wake up and chart her own path. Instead, Laurel focused on Walter. "Were you able to meet with Melissa Cutting earlier today?" While the woman hadn't been available to meet with Laurel until Monday, Walter sometimes had a way with witnesses.

"When I showed up at her office, she fit me in like I hoped," Walter said. "I traced her movements at the times of the attacks, and she actually has an alibi for both Jiro and Mateo's murders. I have it all documented so I can show you at the meeting tomorrow."

"Excellent," Laurel said, crossing off suspects in her mind.

A forty-something-year-old doctor walked out with a tablet in her hands. She was about six feet tall and had short black hair and earnest green eyes.

"Hi, I'm Special Agent Laurel Snow," Laurel said, showing her badge.

"I'm Dr. Curate. What can I do for you?" the doctor asked in a no-nonsense tone.

Laurel stood taller in her flat boots. She should buy some with heels. "I'd like to see Jason Abbott."

"He said he wouldn't see anybody without his lawyer present."

Haylee perked up.

"Where is his lawyer?" Laurel asked.

"She's been called," Dr. Curate said. "However, Mr. Abbott is sedated and won't be able to speak with anybody until tomorrow, so you might as well go home and come back at a better time." She turned briskly on white tennis shoes and strode away.

"Huh," Walter said.

Laurel turned toward the exit. "I like her."

"This is all your fault," Haylee yelled.

Huck sighed. "Get a new line, would you?"

"It's her sister's fault," Haylee said. "Dr. Caine did this on purpose. She went to see Jason today and whatever she said made him do this."

Laurel paused. "What did you say?"

Haylee glared.

Laurel looked at Huck, then back at Haylee. Her heart rate increased. "Did you say that Abigail visited Jason today?"

"Yes," Haylee said, dissolving into tears again.

"Holy crap," Walter muttered.

Laurel nodded. "She would've been a visitor and not an attorney or medical professional."

"Oh," Walter said, brightening. "That's right. Her visit would've been videotaped."

"Absolutely," Laurel said. "I'll meet you at the jail."

Chapter 39

It had been surprisingly easy to gain access to the recording of Abigail Caine's visit with Jason Abbott. Huck pushed his chair next to Laurel in the small interrogation room with the monitor set up on the far wall as Walter sat next to him.

The idea that they could finally catch Abigail in some sort of manipulation had his blood racing. She was both arrogant and impulsive, and those weaknesses were finally going to take her down.

The techs had some trouble with the screen, so he took a moment to make sure Laurel was all right. "Did you eat today?" he asked.

Walter cut him a quizzical look.

"Yes," Laurel said, still watching the screen. "Plenty of protein." She gave up on the screen and looked beyond Huck to Walter. "Did you discover anything interesting when you investigated the churches?"

"No." Walter shrugged. "Nothing that would tie the victims or suspects to the churches. I'll keep trying, though." He straightened his green tie. The guy looked like he'd lost weight, and his coloring was better than Huck had ever seen it. "Also, I had some extra time, so I went and talked to Margie Zello's neighbors."

Huck frowned. "Who's Margie Zello?"

"Officer Frank Zello's mom," Walter said. "She died unexpectedly, kind of, which kept Zello occupied and away from Abigail."

That's right. Zello had been her alibi for the attack on Rachel Raprenzi. Huck looked at Laurel. "You don't think—"

Walter cleared his throat. "Ms. Zello was cremated, and her house has already been cleaned out. She was renting." He glanced at the frozen screen. "Most of her neighbors didn't know anything interesting, but one lady, a busy-body named Florence, said that Ms. Zello had a female visitor every few days or so. A blonde with sunglasses who always wore dowdy clothing."

Ah, shit.

"Did you show her a picture of Abigail?" Laurel asked.

"Yeah, and I showed her a picture of Abigail as a blonde, but Florence just wasn't sure." Walter shook his head. "Even if she identified Abigail, there's no proof of a murder. Ms. Zello had A-fib, and everyone accepted that as contributing to the cause of death."

Huck frowned. "Why would Abigail kill her ex-boyfriend's mom?"

"We're thinking either Zello confided in the mom about doubts he may have had, or perhaps Abigail just wanted to distract the guy. Who knows? She seems to enjoy killing or at least creating a challenge for Laurel," Walter mused. "It's all a game to her."

Laurel sighed. "We'll never know now because Margie was cremated."

The screen came alive to show the small interrogation

room. Jason Abbott looked surprisingly confident in his orange jumpsuit with his handcuffs attached to the bar on the table. He was growing a beard, and with his dark hair, it made him look almost studious. A broad guard stood close to the door, his belly falling over his belt.

Abigail wore a cherry-red skirt with a white shell and a matching red jacket along with what appeared to be four-inch black heels. She walked inside confidently, her shoulders back and her chin up. "Jason, I'm sorry I haven't been to see you, but I didn't think it was a good idea," she said smoothly, pulling out a chair and sitting.

He glared at her.

She'd worn her hair down, letting the dark reddish curls cascade over her shoulders. Her face was finely angled like Laurel's, and her heterochromatic eyes were shockingly similar to her sister's. Yet their hearts and minds were opposites. Her very manner and bearing were different from the kindness and intelligence he could see in Laurel.

Abigail sighed. "You wanted me to come visit you, but I can leave if you prefer."

Jason looked toward the door and then back at her. "Why did you do this to me?"

Her eyes widened. "Do what to you? You know I tried to help you work through your issues."

"My issues?" He exploded, jerking on the chain. It rattled loudly, metal against metal. "You shot me full of drugs and then provoked me to go on a killing spree."

Abigail's facial expression smoothed out, but a small smirk still lifted her upper lip, which was painted red to match her suit. "Provoked you to kill? That's the silliest thing I've ever heard. The only thing I gave you were vitamin B shots, and you know it. Why are you still lying to yourself?"

He looked down at his hands and then back up. "I'm not lying." For the first time, he didn't sound so angry.

Abigail reached out and patted his hand. The beefy guard standing by the door stiffened. "Oh, sorry," she said, pulling her hand back. "I forgot. No touching." She sighed. "Jason, I'm so very sorry I was unable to help you. But your issues, they were too much. Remember how you felt about your mother, what she did to you, how she treated you?"

Jason hunched down in his chair.

"Now look at you," Abigail said. "You're like a caged animal. There's no way out."

His gaze cut up to her. If anything, he slumped even more. "There's no way out," he repeated.

She talked to him for about twenty minutes longer, sounding sympathetic, but brutally painting the stark reality of his life. Finally, she looked at her watch. "I'm so sorry. I have to go. I have a meeting with several PhD candidates at my school, all women, all very smart. They'll be hugely successful in this life, I believe."

Jason didn't even look at her any longer. He just stared at his hands, which had stopped moving.

Abigail stood and clip-clopped toward the door. "It's funny how the educated and intelligent women always win, isn't it? You have a good day now." She opened the door and smoothly exited the room.

Laurel pushed a button on the remote, and the screen froze on an image of Jason Abbott looking somehow as if he'd lost six inches in height and twenty pounds in those thirty minutes.

"Wow," Walter muttered.

"That was probably the most manipulative thing I've ever seen, and yet she didn't really do anything wrong,"

Huck murmured. "There was absolutely nothing actionable on the video."

Laurel sighed. "He was supposed to be interviewed about Abigail by *The Killing Hour* tomorrow morning. Abigail couldn't let that happen, could she?"

Huck's gut ached. He'd spent his life in the service and then as a cop, before becoming a Fish and Wildlife officer. During that time, he'd seen predators in every form, including human.

The woman in the red skirt was deadlier than all of them put together, and she had her sights set on his woman and unborn child.

Deep in a dreamless sleep, Laurel jolted upright when her phone buzzed. She looked at the clock to see it was two in the morning.

"What now?" Huck muttered, sitting up next to her. They'd stayed the night at his place.

She fumbled for her phone and hit the button. "Agent Snow." She ground her palm into her eye. This pregnancy was messing with her cognitive abilities and making it difficult to focus.

"Agent Snow. It's Agent Norrs."

Her stomach sank. "Agent Norrs, what's going on?"

"I wanted to let you know that Councilman Swelter's house was broken into tonight, or rather this morning."

She blanched. "Is he all right?"

"Yes, the councilman is fine. He had two alarms. The first was actually cut. The second blasted out long and loud enough that the police immediately headed to his residence, sirens blaring."

Hope rose within her. "Did they catch the burglar?"

"No, sorry," Norrs said. "They didn't. Witnesses

described a blur running away, but nobody could even give me height, weight, sex, or anything. Whoever it was did drop some Valentine's Day candy on the way out. Must have been loose in a pocket or something. So it's definitely our guy."

Laurel sighed. "Or girl," she muttered. "It could be a woman. Are you sure the witnesses couldn't identify anything about the person?"

"No. It was dark and raining hard, and nobody saw anything."

"What about CCTV? Councilman Swelter surely has cameras in his home, right?"

Norrs sneezed and then came back on the line. "He did, but the feed was cut. Believe it or not, they were the older, cheaper kind that are easy to tamper with. Swelter's kind of an arrogant ass," he whispered.

"Yes, I've noticed," Laurel agreed.

Norrs cleared his throat. "Are you getting any closer on this?"

"Yes, I am. Now that the councilman has also been attacked, a pattern has emerged. Could I speak with him?" she asked.

"No, he was taken to the hospital to be checked out."

Laurel frowned. "Did the assailant get near him?"

"No." Norrs's voice lowered again. "I think he wants the press, and he refuses to speak with us until tomorrow."

Laurel smacked her hand against her head. "He's going to the hospital just to get press?"

"Oh, yeah. If you want to ignore it, I wouldn't turn on the TV. This guy really likes the cameras."

Laurel rolled her eyes. Huck started to get up from the bed, but she shook her head. "We're not going anywhere," she whispered.

"Oh, good." Huck settled back in.

"Agent Norrs, I appreciate your giving me a call," she said. Everything went back to that camp. She had to figure out who those other campers were. If she had to sit all the next day in Swelter's office, she would.

The sounds of light traffic came over the line. "There's another thing," Norrs said. "Zeke Caine has agreed to speak with you and your sister. That's it. He won't talk to me or anybody else."

Laurel bit her lip. "I'd rather speak to him alone."

"That's not what he wants," Norrs said. "That's also not what Abigail wants. You might want to do something for your sister just this once."

As far as Laurel was concerned, her sister was a murderer. "What time?"

"I don't know. When the doctor clears it, the hospital will give you a call. It'll be later today for sure," Norrs said. "I would like for you to record the meeting, but I don't know if Caine will allow it."

"All right. I'll do my best," Laurel said.

"Thanks," Norrs said. "Also, what do you think about dinner this weekend? The four of us."

The last place in the entire world Laurel wanted to be was around her sister, especially now that she was pregnant. "I don't think so, Special Agent Norrs. I don't know how else to explain it to you."

Norrs was silent for a moment. "All right. Abigail wants me to be patient with you, and so I will, but at some point you're going to have to cut her a break. Maybe it'll be tomorrow when you both face your father." He ended the call.

Laurel slowly placed her phone back on the night table.

"What's up?" Huck asked.

She snuggled down and rolled into his arms. "Swelter

was attacked, but not really. He's fine. He's at the hospital. Nobody got a view of the assailant, and apparently good old Zeke Caine wants to meet with Abigail and me at the same time tomorrow."

Finally.

Chapter 40

Laurel spent a frustrating morning with her team as everybody reported in on the status of their investigations. They were good, and she was impressed, but nobody had any answers that helped her. The churches didn't connect to one another or the victims, and the interviews at the law firm hadn't revealed any new information. In addition, it appeared as if Kirsti Vuittron had hired an attorney and didn't want to speak with them unless she was arrested.

There was nowhere near enough probable cause to arrest the widow.

In her gut she knew that everything tied back to that camp. She called Councilman Swelter several times to no avail. After she met with Zeke Caine, she was driving to Seattle to find that jackass.

In addition, she'd tried to call Thema Sackey to talk about Thema attending church with Victor, but only reached the lawyer's voice mail.

Laurel's phone buzzed, and she answered a call from the hospital notifying her she could see Zeke now. Her ears rang. No doubt adrenaline was coursing through her body, so she took several deep breaths to calm herself as she walked down the hallway. Stress hormones couldn't be good for the baby. "I'm going to the hospital," she told Kate.

"I'll walk you down so I can get a desperately needed latte." Kate hopped off her stool and followed her.

Laurel reached the bottom vestibule. Should she tell Kate about her pregnancy? Not yet. For now, the news was just for Huck and her. "Kate? How are the girls doing?"

Kate sighed. "It's up and down. We're seeing a therapist, and they have a lot to work through. Vic wasn't a good father the last few years, but he was still their dad. They're mad, angry, and confused. Like me."

Laurel leaned in and hugged her. Being a parent seemed fraught with difficulties. "How's Viv?" The poor girl never should've seen her father like that.

Kate shook her head. "She's having nightmares, which isn't unexpected. So is Ryan. I think this has brought them even closer together, and that wasn't really what I wanted."

It seemed there wasn't a lot of control in parenting. "You're doing a wonderful job with those girls, Kate."

"Thanks." Kate's smile was sweet and grateful. "I'll see you in a couple of hours." At Kate's nod, Laurel strode outside into the snowy air.

She drove to the local hospital, her mind turning with thoughts. Her mother would be home in just a few days, and she'd have to tell her that Zeke Caine had returned to Genesis Valley. She wasn't looking forward to the discussion and was appreciative of the reprieve. When she reached the hospital, she hurried inside, flashing her badge at the grumpy receptionist. The one at the county hospital had been much more pleasant.

Finally, the receptionist allowed her beyond the reception area and down the hallway to room 112. Laurel reached the door and pushed it open, steeling herself before moving inside. Zeke Caine sat up in the hospital bed, one IV attached to his arm with several liquid bags pouring in. He was pale and bandages peeked from the neckline of his gown.

"Laurel, thank you for saving me," he said, "Apparently, I owe you my life."

"I don't want your life," she said, striding inside and standing near the counter.

He gestured to one of two chairs. "Please, have a seat, and I do not consent to a recording of this conversation."

"I don't need to sit, and your refusal of recording does not surprise me," she said. "Who stabbed you?"

His gaze ran over her face. "It's remarkable, really, how much you look like me."

"I don't," she said. He was bald and pale, and although they did have the same eyes, he was tall, whereas she was not. "What do you remember about the night of your stabbing?"

His smile reminded her of Abigail's, and a shiver went down her spine. The door opened behind her, and Abigail walked in.

"There you are," Zeke said. "I called over an hour ago."

"I was at the school," Abigail said evenly, looking from Laurel back to their father. "Isn't this a nice little family reunion?"

Nausea rolled in Laurel's stomach. "Where have you been the last five years, Zeke?"

"Oh, here and there. You can call me father if you want."

"I don't," Laurel said.

His gaze hardened.

"Now, Laurel . . ." Abigail moved closer to stand next to her. "We're one big happy family now, aren't we?" Her tongue flicked out to lick her bottom lip, and her eyes gleamed. "Where have you been, Zeke?"

Zeke somehow sat straighter in his bed and his nostrils flared. "I would think you'd be nicer to me, Abigail."

"Why is that?" Abigail asked.

Zeke looked down at the bandages visible on one of his arms. "You know exactly why."

Laurel looked from Abigail to Zeke, and then back again. "Abigail?" she asked.

"I have no idea," Abigail said, her smile one that Laurel couldn't interpret but that made the hair rise on the back of her neck.

Laurel focused on Zeke. "I'm an FBI agent. If you lie to me, I will arrest you." His smile slid away. "Did Abigail stab you?" she asked directly.

Abigail playfully slapped Laurel's arm. "Now, Laurel, what a silly question."

But was it? There were undercurrents upon undercurrents in the room, and Laurel couldn't read any of them.

"I was hoping we'd have a civil reunion," Zeke said, looking at them both. "It's remarkable. You could be twins. Well, except for the height."

Laurel didn't let any expression cross her face. It didn't make sense, but she truly resented the fact that Abigail was at least four inches taller than her.

"Abigail, haven't you missed me?" he asked. "And Laurel, don't you want to know me?"

Laurel took a barely perceptible step toward him. "I want to put you in jail," she said honestly. "You're a rapist and a criminal, and you deserve to face justice."

His lips turned down. "That makes me incredibly sad."

"Oh, I missed you," Abigail said, the scent of her expensive perfume competing with the smell of bleach in the small room. "But I won't again. I won't miss next time."

The door opened again, and the doctor walked in. "It's

time for you two to leave. I agreed to a short visit only. My patient needs to rest."

"I really do," Zeke said, pulling the covers up a little bit more. He looked at Laurel. "You and I will discuss our relationship later. I'm looking forward to it." His gaze then flicked to Abigail. "And you and I will continue the discussion we began the other night. It won't end the same way, my dear daughter."

Laurel had to get the truth. "Did she stab you?"

"I'm done," Zeke said.

"You have to go, now," the doctor said, ushering them toward the door. Abigail walked out first and Laurel followed her, winding around until they reached the reception area.

"Do you want to accompany me to lunch?" Abigail asked cheerfully.

"No." Laurel tried to wrap her mind around the entire situation. She wasn't one to go on instinct, but that interplay had cemented the truth in her mind. "You stabbed him, trying to duplicate the Broken Heart Killer, didn't you?"

Abigail laughed. "Of course not."

"Did you shoot at me?" Laurel asked. "You stabbed him and then shot at me?"

Abigail leaned closer for a moment. "Now Laurel, if I shot at somebody, don't you think I'd hit them?" She walked gracefully away toward the exit. "But you are my sister, aren't you? I'd never hurt you."

"Wait," Laurel said.

Abigail turned, her multi-colored eyes stunning. "What can Auntie Abigail do for you?"

Laurel's stomach lurched. No way would her child be

subjected to this woman. "Have you worn your blond wig lately?"

Abigail looked down at Laurel's still flat stomach and then back up. "Why? Are things already boring with Huckalicious? Are you looking to role play?"

Laurel just stared at her.

Abigail rolled her eyes. "Why do you ask?"

"You wore the wig and visited her, and one day you just killed her, didn't you?" Laurel whispered. "Mrs. Zello. Why?"

Abigail's chin lowered. "Why would I murder a nice lady like Margie? Just because her son was a nuisance? Don't be silly."

Oh God, she *had* done it. And she was proud of it. Laurel wanted to vomit. "Did she know something about your attack on Rachel? Did you want to hurt Officer Zello for being persistent? Or did you just want him distracted for a while so you could solidify your relationship with Special Agent Norrs?" Her voice trembled, but she couldn't hide her reaction.

"If I had done such a dastardly deed, I would've had my reasons, and you wouldn't ever be able to catch me." Abigail slowly smiled.

That was it. This was all a game to her. "Abigail," Laurel whispered.

The smile widened. "Let me know if you want to borrow the wig. It's fun playing at being somebody else for a while." With that, Abigail turned and strode out into the storm.

Laurel remained still for a moment and then pivoted, rushing for the nearest restroom to vomit.

Chapter 41

Laurel spent the afternoon drinking ginger ale, reviewing case files, and revisiting every step of the investigation while her head felt like it was wrapped in cotton. The confrontation with Abigail and Zeke that morning had impacted her intensely. No doubt hormones had flooded her system and then disappeared, which had left her feeling fatigued and uneasy. Plus, she was worried about the baby.

Even so, there was now no doubt in her mind that Abigail had stabbed Zeke, so he was not one of the victims of the Broken Heart Killer. She was even more certain the connection was Sunrise Camp. For now, she must put aside the horrifying thought that Abigail killed Mrs. Zello and set the explosives that had harmed Walter. After Laurel found the Broken Heart Killer, she'd focus all of her energy on Abigail.

After five, she excused her team and went back to her office to eat a granola bar for dinner, unable to stomach anything more substantial. Huck was working late on another poaching case and said he'd swing by the office and fetch her for a late dinner around seven. For now, she let the quiet center her as she drew connections.

"Excuse me?"

Laurel jolted and looked up to see Ena Ilemoto in her doorway. "Ena, hi. What can I do for you?"

Ena hesitated. "I was wondering if Walter was still around?"

"No. I sent him home." Laurel stretched her neck.

Ena's face fell. "Oh. I thought we were going to meet for a drink." A light peach crawled across her cheeks.

Laurel's temples ached. "Walter probably missed the subtext." She could relate. "Did he expressly say you'd meet for a drink?"

"No." Ena chuckled. "I'll get ahold of him later. For now, if you need any legwork done, please call on me."

"I will. Have a good night." Laurel turned back to her notes. There was quite an age gap there, but it'd be nice to see Walter happy. She reached for her phone and dialed Thema Sackey again. Too many connections led to the young woman.

"Sackey," Thema answered.

"Thema, this is a Special Agent Laurel Snow, and I've been trying to get ahold of you. I would like you to come in for an interview tomorrow, please."

The sound of a zipper being engaged came over the line. "Sure," Thema said. "How about now? We're both obviously working late, and I would like to speak with you about Jason Abbott. I'm leaving his room at the hospital now. Are you free?"

"Yes, I'm available now," Laurel said, taking her weapon out of her laptop bag and tucking it into her waistband, just in case. "Feel free to come on by."

Wind whistled through the line, as Thema no doubt walked outside. "I'll be there in about fifteen minutes," she said, her voice at a higher pitch than normal. "We have to do something about Jason. There is no question in my mind that Abigail Caine manipulated him into attempting suicide. The man needs help, not prison."

"I look forward to speaking with you," Laurel said. There was no question in *her* mind that Jason Abbott belonged in a prison cell for the rest of his life. She continued going through the case files and then reached for her phone again.

"City Hall," a chipper voice answered.

"Hi, this is Special Agent Laurel Snow with the FBI. You're working late."

The woman giggled. "It's a new community outreach program where we answer phone calls until seven every night. It's good overpay, to be honest."

It was also convenient for Laurel. "I see. I need to speak with Councilman Swelter. His assistant told me earlier that he'd be back in the office around six this evening, once he finished giving all of his interviews." The guy had been on the television all day, talking about his near miss with death. In truth, he hadn't even seen the assailant.

"Just a sec. Let me see if he's in."

A shuffling sounded and then a loud click echoed. "Good evening, Agent Snow. Did you see me on the news earlier?"

"You hit every channel," Laurel said, placing the phone on her desk and pressing the speaker button so she could reach for the photograph. "Now how about you help me out, so I don't have to also speak with the media and tell them you were nowhere near danger last night?"

"I have a feeling that's extortion," he said.

If anything it'd be blackmail, but actually it was just her telling the truth. "You can help me or not, but the sooner I catch this killer, the sooner you get to write your bestseller about your brush with death," she said reasonably.

"Fine," Swelter said as the sound of papers being shuffled came over the line. "Okay, I received your stupid picture." He whistled. "Wow, I was a good-looking kid. All right, let's look at this thing."

Finally. Anticipation zipped through her. Laurel flattened the old photograph on the desk. She'd already written Swelter's name above his picture and had done the same with Vuittron, Makino, and Marshall. "Zeke Caine is not in here anywhere. Is he?" she asked.

"Never heard of the guy," Swelter said, chewing ice.

Laurel tried to ignore the loud crunching. "What about a Mateo Perez?"

"Oh, yeah, Perez," Swelter said. "I forgot all about him. Weird dude. He was like the hall monitor, always telling on people. He's the third guy from the left in the second row."

Laurel squinted and wrote the name above it. "Okay, I can see that." Now she could, although the facial features were much different. Time had not been kind to Perez. He'd had a thick head of hair when he was a teenager. "Let's start with the counselors," she said.

"All right, I'll try, but I don't remember very well." Swelter identified three out of the six. "You know, I think I did one of the older counselors, but I don't remember her name. She's the third one from the right. Wait a sec. Her name was Ginger something. Yeah, that was it."

Finally. The more information she garnered from him, the more people she could seek to identify the remaining campers. She noted Ginger's name above her picture. "Do you remember a last name?"

"No. But she was very bendy, if I remember right." His chuckle made her want to punch him in the nose.

She drew in air and settled herself. "All right, let's attempt to identify the teenagers in the second row."

He remembered maybe half of them, and he wasn't sure about many of those. "I'm sorry. I went to a lot of camps." He slurped something. "Do you drink, Agent Snow?"

She used to and probably would again in seven months. "Not really. Why?"

"I thought maybe you and I could have a drink sometime. Even though I'm not a big fan of cops, I can't get your eyes out of my mind. I even looked them up. Do you know how rare it is to have heterochromatic eyes with a burst in one of them?"

"Yes." Of course she knew. They were her eyes. "Back to the case?"

There was the sound of liquid pouring into a glass. "You didn't answer me. How about you and I have dinner sometime. Or just drinks?"

"Thank you for your kind invitation, but I'm seeing somebody at present." Actually, she was having a baby with somebody, but she wasn't going to share that with this dullard.

He snorted. "So? If you change your mind, let me know. After this recent spate of news, I'm going to climb a lot higher than just the city council." He gulped loudly. "I don't recognize the first couple of kids in that next row. Sorry about that."

"That's fine. You're doing a good job," Laurel said. At least he'd moved on from asking her out to working with her. But she needed him to concentrate before he drank too much of whatever he had in that glass. Every new name gave her a new avenue to pursue. Since all four of her victims had attended this camp, she was definitely on the right path, but she needed him to verify her theory, and she didn't want to lead him there. "Was there a church nearby?"

"Oh, yeah," Swelter said. "There was definitely a church nearby. We had to attend every week, but we went even when we weren't asked to do so." He snorted loudly. There was something in his voice.

"Could you tell me why your voice just lifted?"

He was quiet for a moment. "You really don't catch much, do you?"

"Councilman Swelter, please work with me," she said.

He crunched more ice. "Fine. Yes. Church of the Lake was right next to the camp. The church had a playroom that you could get into through a basement window."

"You used this playroom?" Laurel asked. So she *had* been on the right track.

"Yeah, you know, for kids during church services and stuff, except that's not how we used it."

Laurel straightened. "Really? Tell me about this playroom. Please describe the room and the colors in the room, if there were any."

"Oh, man. Let's see. There were thick mats on the ground and a starry night painted on the ceiling. The entire room was dark."

Laurel stiffened. "What do you mean dark?"

"It was purple. The mats were purple. The walls were purple. Even the starry night was purple. When we were in there, it was like being on the moon or something."

So the space had always been purple. "Or a tent?"

"I guess. It was a great place to have sex. The mats were cushy." He gulped something loudly. "Why? What is it about the church?"

She wrinkled her nose. What the heck was he drinking? "I don't know yet. Was there Valentine's Day candy around?"

"No," he said.

She looked again at the pictures. "You mentioned that you and Victor Vuittron didn't like each other back when you were teenagers. Why was that?"

"Oh, yeah, that. Well, I was seeing this girl, and he slept with her in the purple room, too. I was feeling betrayed by him 'cause he was my buddy and all. But then it turned out she slept with a lot of guys."

Laurel scanned the photograph again. "She did?"

"Yes. It turned out she and a couple of the girls at camp had some sort of contest going on. I don't know. It seemed kind of wrong in the church and all. But then again, I had a good time, if I remember right."

Movement sounded down the hall and Kate appeared with Thema, who was dressed for court in a green suit and black blouse. Officer Zello stood behind her in dark jeans and sweatshirt. He motioned a question mark.

"Just a sec, Councilman," Laurel said. "Kate, go home—I'll see you on Monday."

"No. If you're here, I'm here. Period." Kate turned and strode back down the hallway.

Laurel sighed as Zello made another question mark in the air. "What do you need, Officer Zello?"

"Frank. Just Frank. I was going to go grab some coffee," Zello said. "I wanted to make sure that my protectee was secure. Do you two want anything?" He nudged Thema with his hip.

They were a cute couple. "She's secure," Laurel said.

He leaned down to whisper something in Thema's ear.

Laurel tried not to roll her eyes and focused on her

phone, which was lying flat on the desk. There was a time and place for noodling, as her mother once said. "Councilman, what was the name of the girl? Is she in this picture?"

"Oh, yeah," Swelter said. "Let's see. Oh, there she is. She's the fourth one from the right in the front row. God she was pretty, wasn't she?"

Laurel looked at a cute blonde with freckles across her nose. "Yes, she was. What was her name?"

"Oh, man, what was her name?" Swelter muttered. "Wait a sec. That's right. Her name was Margie. Margie Zello."

Chapter 42

Everything inside Laurel froze. She looked up to find Officer Zello pointing a gun at her. He gently shut the door and motioned for her to end the call. She clicked the button, cutting off Swelter.

"I really wish you hadn't discovered that," Zello said, looking down at the photograph.

Thema backed away from him. "What are you doing?" Her eyes widened.

Laurel took a deep breath and barely kept from placing both hands on her abdomen.

Zello kept his focus on Laurel. "You're very good at your job, aren't you? All I wanted to do was protect you."

Thema gasped. "What is happening?"

Laurel leaned back in her chair, trying to keep the weapon at her waist hidden from him. "The four victims, Vuittron, Perez, Makino, and Marshall, they all slept with your mother? Did they rape her?"

"No," Zello blasted out. "But they might as well have. They were old enough to know better. They were old enough to know that she could get pregnant. They told her words of love. All she wanted was to be loved. All she wanted was someone to care about her. They used her in that stupid church." His eyes widened and a flush darkened his handsome cheeks. Even his mustache twitched.

She glanced at the closed door. Kate was the only one left in the office, and she couldn't let Kate get hurt. She'd have to be quick when she went for her weapon.

Zello grabbed Thema by the hair and yanked her in front of him, pressing his gun to her ribs. "I know you're armed, Agent Snow. Please take your weapon out."

Laurel calculated her odds, and they weren't good, even though she didn't think he'd shoot them both in the office. If she could get free of the desk, she might have a chance to fire. Slowly she removed her weapon and placed it on the desk near the computer. "Was one of those men your father?" she asked.

"Yes," he spat. "They deserved to die. They told her wonderful lies with beautiful words about hearts and candy. They had to pay."

"How long have you been planning this?" She tried to gauge the distance between them.

He must have pressed harder against Thema because she rose up on her toes and winced. "I don't know. I grew up with my mother telling me all about my father and how he told her that he loved her and that she was the most wonderful woman in the world, and then he just disappeared on her. She never gave me a name."

"I'm sorry about that," Laurel said, trying to reach him. "But Thema is innocent."

Zello swallowed loudly. "Every Valentine's Day, we'd buy candy, and she'd read from the hearts. She'd say that some people didn't get to live those words. She didn't get to live them. He used her. She was sure he used her. I asked her so many times to contact him, but she always said no." His eyes widened. "It was their fault she couldn't trust. That she couldn't love."

Laurel gingerly pushed herself away from her desk. "Maybe she was embarrassed, Frank." She used his first name on purpose. "It's possible. It sounds like she and her friends were in a competition that went too far that summer. She might have been embarrassed to call your father and just wanted to have a good life with you. More than likely she didn't know who the father was and didn't want to go through the ordeal of trying to find out."

"No," he hissed. "It was their fault we were all alone. Now I'm all alone."

"Because your mother died," Laurel whispered. "How did she die?"

He was crying harder. "She had A-fib . . . that's why she died."

"Was there an autopsy?" Laurel needed to get closer to her gun.

He frowned. "No. Why?"

"Is it possible Abigail killed her? That she gave your mother something that caused a heart attack?"

He wildly shook his head. "Of course not. Why do you hate her so? Abigail is kind and lost and confused, just like my mother. I told her all about Mom, and she related to her story. She said she felt like they were the same person but in different times."

That was the sickest thing Laurel had ever heard. Abigail had most definitely manipulated Zello, and there was a good chance she'd killed his mother. "Did you confide in your mother about the night Abigail attacked Rachel Raprenzi?" Laurel whispered.

Zello straightened. "If Abigail did so, and I'm not saying she did, then she was just trying to protect her sister. You." He yanked a folded-up piece of paper from his back pocket and threw it on the desk. It slowly opened, the paper worn to reveal a printout of Abigail from her college website. "I keep her with me at all times, even though she's too lost to understand she belongs with me. She needs me. I'd never abandon her like those boys did my mom."

Realization dawned on Laurel. Killers often reacted to an inciting event, and the death of the woman he'd always wanted to protect must have spurred him on. "Did you and Abigail speak about the lying men who might've been your father?"

"No," he said. "I found my mother's diary in her belongings after the funeral. She listed everybody who had taken advantage of her that summer and described the church and the playroom in great detail. They all had to die. I wasn't going to let them have great lives after they abandoned me like that, after they told her flowery words, and then just used her."

Thema struggled a little. "Frank, you're hurting me, and I know you don't want to hurt me." Shock had widened her eyes and her left eyelid was twitching.

"I don't want to hurt you," Zello said, tears filling his eyes. "I want to protect you. I want to protect all of you from these terrible, terrible, horrible men. I've tried. I tried to protect Abigail."

"How so?" Laurel asked.

He loosened his grip on Thema's body. "I protected her from the last killer. From Jason Abbott. Maybe from you as well, since you obviously want to hurt her. You're as vulnerable as she is, but you're a trained agent, and she's just a lost little girl. All I want to do is love her, but she threw me away, too. You know why?"

"Why?" Laurel asked.

"Because of your father," Zello spat. "He treated her

wrong, and so she doesn't know how to love. It's his fault, not hers."

Laurel could argue that point, but now wasn't the time. "You didn't stab him though, did you?" she asked. Was there a chance that she'd read the room wrong earlier this morning in the hospital with Zeke and Abigail?

"No, but I would have. I'm going to when I find him," Zello said. "Come around the desk, Laurel. We're all going to walk out of here. If you don't want your pretty receptionist shot in the head, you'll come with me."

Laurel stood. Her knees trembled, but her mind calculated the most effective way to take him down. She had to protect Kate and this baby, as well as Thema. She reached the edge of her desk.

Thema coughed. "Did you shoot at us the other day?"

"Yeah," he said, his chest expanding and his eyes glittering. Was that pride? "I needed to scare you and thought Laurel would put me on protection for the receptionist so I could stay close to this case, but instead, I was hired by you, Thema. I thought you were pretty, and then I figured I might actually start a security business, so luck was on my side, as usual." He snorted as if bragging now. "I collect vehicles and have several trucks. You hit one of them that night, Laurel. I had to drop it over a ravine where it'll never be found."

"Frank? Are you really going to kill us?" Thema's voice wavered.

He sighed. "Yeah. I don't want to hurt you, but I can't stop my mission. I guess there has to be some collateral damage."

If Laurel could just get Frank's gun pointed away from Thema, she could take him down.

He reached behind himself and opened the door. "We're going to walk out like this. First you, Laurel, and then I'll be plastered up against my sweet little protectee here. If you do anything, I'll shoot her first and then you, and then that receptionist. Do you understand me?"

"Yes," Laurel said. Her best bet was to take him on the stairs. She wasn't quite sure how to get the gun pointed away from Thema, but if she could push him just right, gravity would take care of the rest.

"Let's go," he said calmly. Way too calmly.

She took a deep breath, then strode out of her office and down the darkened hallway where she could hear Kate talking on the phone to one of her girls. A lump settled in her stomach. She had to get Zello out of the office before she made a move, and she had to somehow protect her baby at the same time. She'd never, in her entire life, felt so vulnerable.

She walked slowly as if trying to ward off inevitability. How could she get by Kate without Kate knowing something was wrong? Suddenly a body burst out of the computer room and slammed Zello against the wall. Plaster flew in every direction as the sheetrock protested loudly and cracked.

Thema Sackey flew across the hall and a gun fired. She screamed and ducked to the ground, scrambling to flatten herself on the wooden floor.

Laurel turned to fight, just in time to see Huck punch Officer Zello in the wrist. The gun dropped to the ground, and then Huck followed up with three more sharp punches that threw Zello into the conference room. He landed on the heavy glass conference table and the glass shattered, flying in every direction. He screamed, fighting wildly, and Huck kicked him once in the jaw. Zello's head fell back into the golden base with a hard thunk. He slumped into unconsciousness.

Huck looked wildly around, his hands in fists and his jaw set at a furious angle. "You okay?"

Laurel stared at the bloody killer on the ground. The world swayed around her, but she took a deep breath. "Yes." She turned and helped Thema Sackey up. "Are you okay?"

"No," Thema said. "Of course I'm not okay. How could anybody be okay?"

Kate stood at the end of the hallway. "I'll call an ambulance," she said.

Huck tugged Laurel into his side and kissed her head. "I'm glad I got hungry," he said, his body strong and warm next to her.

"Me, too."

Chapter 43

Laurel finished filing the paperwork for the Frank Zello murders at around noon on Saturday, wanting to forget all about Zello and his victims for at least a few days. Unfortunately, there was no way to tie Abigail to Margie Zello's murder, at least not right now.

The woman was evil, and Laurel still believed that evil always lost. Somehow.

Huck was down in his office filing paperwork as well and then they were going to play hooky for the rest of the weekend. Her mother would be home on Monday, and Laurel wasn't looking forward to telling her that Zeke Caine was back in town, but Deidre was strong, and she was smart. She would be okay. They would figure it out together.

Officer Zello was now in the county jail being held without bond. He'd suffered a broken jaw as well as lacerations from the shattered table, but he was still well enough to give a full confession. He had considered it his duty to do so.

She wondered where he'd gone wrong. His mother might not have been the most loving person, but he'd grown up in a fairly stable environment. How he'd turned to killing upon her death, Laurel didn't quite understand yet. She would need to meet with him, if he would agree, so she could learn. Everything she learned would help her find the next killer.

"You have a visitor," Kate called back.

"I told you to take the weekend," Laurel yelled.

"I will leave when you leave," Kate bellowed.

Laurel shook her head. It was nice to have a friend, and even better to have such a loyal guard dog as Kate at the end of the hallway. They were both trying to decide if Viv should do an internship with the unit considering the danger they'd been facing. But after the most recent incident, the deputy director was releasing funds to increase their security. They were going to set up cameras as well as an automatic door that Kate could open with a button from upstairs. It would be a fairly safe environment if they did it right.

Thema Sackey walked back and paused in Laurel's doorway. "Hi," she said.

"Hi," Laurel said, looking at the young attorney. She wore jeans and a University of Arizona sweatshirt. "How are you?"

"I've been better," Thema said. "I'm leaving. I'm packing up and heading back east."

Laurel straightened. "You are?"

"Yes, I . . . it's time," Thema said. "I . . . between Victor and then Frank, I obviously need to go be by myself for a while and not date anybody."

It was probably a good idea. "I can understand that," Laurel said. "Are you going to be okay?"

"I am. I'm going home to my family. I just want to say thank you for saving my life."

Laurel grinned. "I was doing my job. And, to be honest, I also thought you were a suspect."

Thema's smile was slow, but humor blended in her eyes. "I know."

"I'm glad you're not a killer," Laurel said. "By the way, I had a witness tell me that you attended the Genesis Valley Community Church several years ago."

Thema's gaze lightened. "I actually attended churches all over Tempest County when I first came to town. I wanted to find the right place for me, and so I tried many different churches for about a year. I liked Genesis Valley. I went for a while, but I stopped attending until recently when Victor and I started attending together."

"So you knew Pastor Zeke Caine?"

Thema frowned. "Yes. I thought he gave a great sermon. But there was always something about him that . . . I don't know." She looked down at her feet.

"Tell me," Laurel said.

Thema sighed. "There was just something off about him. I can't explain it. You know, he had a great voice. He had terrific cadence, but when he looked at you, it was just like there was nothing behind his eyes, you know?"

Laurel fought a shiver. "I think I do," she said. "Sometimes it . . . I'm not that good at reading people, but every once in a while I'll see somebody, and it's like a light wasn't turned on inside them."

"Exactly," Thema said. "That's how I felt the few times I spoke with Pastor Caine. I don't know. I guess that's part of the reason I moved on to the next church. I returned later with Vic when I'd heard that a new pastor had taken over."

"I think you actually have good instincts, Thema," Laurel murmured. "You just need to listen to them."

Thema nodded. "Yeah. I don't know who'll be representing Jason Abbott going forward, but I'm sure you'll receive a notice. I'm glad I'm out." She patted the doorframe. "I have to go. Good luck, Agent Snow."

"Thanks, Thema. You, too."

Thema turned and strode away.

Laurel's phone buzzed and she sighed, lifting it to her ear. "Snow."

"Hi, Agent Snow, it's Melissa Cutting. Congratulations on closing the Broken Heart Killer case."

"Thank you."

Melissa cleared her throat. "I'm giving you a heads up that I'm taking the Jason Abbott case, so I'll have two cases against you, my niece's and his."

"Lovely. What's another word for 'talk to my lawyer'?" Laurel ended the call and returned to work, humming as she completed paperwork until her phone dinged again. "Snow," she said absently.

"Agent Snow. Hi, it's Walter."

Her unit needed to learn how to take a weekend off. "Walter, I told you to go rest or have fun or do anything but work."

"I know, but I popped by the hospital to question Zeke Caine for you. I thought maybe man-to-man I might get something out of him."

She dropped her pen onto the pad of paper. "Did you?"

Walter sighed. "No. In fact, Boss, I hate to tell you this, but he's gone."

She stopped cold. "What do you mean 'he's gone'?"

"He's not here. He wasn't discharged, but he's gone." Paper crinkled. "He left a note."

Laurel sagged against her chair and pressed one hand to her abdomen. "What does the note say?"

"*My dearest daughters, you have both disappointed me greatly. I will see you very soon.*"

Laurel's head dropped. She'd be more frightened if Zeke

didn't want to retake his position at the church so he could be famous and rich. Even so, the note did sound like a threat. "Thanks for trying. Let's worry about him next week."

"You've got it. See you Monday." Walter clicked off.

"Are you leaving yet?" Kate called back.

"Yes, she is," Huck said, emerging at the end of the hallway and heading toward Laurel's office.

Laurel perked up. She was starving and needed to get away from work and killers for the rest of the weekend. "Are you ready for lunch?"

"I am."

She collected her belongings, then tried to keep up with the captain as he hustled her down the hallway. Apparently he was ready for a day off.

He pulled her into him at the reception area and kissed the top of her head. "Let's go have some fun."

"I agree," she said. "Kate, go home. Go goof off. Do something enjoyable."

"Gladly," Kate said, following them down the stairs and outside into the sunny day.

Huck kept his arm around her. "I was thinking. Now that you've saved me and I've saved you, what do you say we take a vacation together? Somewhere warm and away from murder, poachers, and snow?"

She slipped on the ice and then regained her composure. "Go away together? Are you ready for that?"

He lifted his shoulder. "Sure. With our crazy careers we should take every moment, don't you think?"

It was a sweet sentiment. Warmth bubbled through her.

"We should also think about something more permanent, considering we're starting a family." He walked beside her to his truck. "We have a dog, a cat, and now a baby on the way."

She'd never thought she'd have any of those items, and now she understood that saying about someone's heart feeling full. Oh, realistically, a heart could not have feelings, but her chest still felt warm and wonderful. "Our lives aren't easy." Unless one of them quit their job, they'd never have easy. Even if one did, life would be full of challenges.

"Who wants easy?" At his truck, he turned her to face him. "I'll go as slow as you need, Laurel Snow. But at the end of all this, it's going to be me and you and whatever family we decide to create." He leaned down and kissed her.

She returned the kiss, leaning into him. That sounded like a plan.

Explore the world of Rebecca Zanetti in digital format!

WARRIOR'S HOPE
The Dark Protectors

New York Times **Bestselling Author**
Rebecca Zanetti

**An explosive love triangle comes to its passionate
conclusion and decides the fate of battling nations
in award-winning and *New York Times* bestselling
author Rebecca Zanetti's Dark Protectors . . .**

As the only female vampire ever born, and the heir to
two powerful immortal families, Hope Kayrs-Kyllwood
has always felt the weight of fate and destiny. Now her
heart is torn between two men and two different futures.
It's a choice between duty and love, peace and war, with
the fate of everyone she loves hanging in the balance.

As the leader of the Kurjan nation,
Drake has always known that mating Hope is the best
path to avoiding war. He's counting on her to know
the same. . . . Paxton has been Hope's best friend
and protector since they were children. He would kill
and die for her without a second thought. In fact,
he's always known that would be his path . . .

With deadly factions at her heels, Hope must decide
whom to trust and where her loyalty lies—before the
choice is taken away from her . . .

**Don't miss these exciting novels by Rebecca Zanetti,
coming soon!**

ONE WHITE ROSE

New York Times Bestselling Author
Rebecca Zanetti

**Information is power,
and those who control it live like gods.
In my world, billionaires play deadly games of insult
and influence, where magic is the dirtiest weapon
of all. Here, even a powerful princess can be
swallowed by the darkest of shadows . . .**

They christened me Alana—
and while the name means beauty, beneath that surface
is a depth I allow very few to see.
I'm sole heir to Aquarius Social, a media giant about to
succumb to an unseen enemy. My father's solution is
to marry me off to the son of a competing family.
My reaction? Not a chance. Now I have just a week
before the wedding to change my fate.

Who knew the unforeseen twist would be an
assassination attempt and an unwanted rescue
by Adam Beathach, the Beast whose social media
empire is driving Aquarius under? The richest, most
ruthless of them all, he protects his realm with an iron
rule: no one sees his face. When he shows himself to me,
I know he'll never let me go.

Adam may think he can lock me in his castle forever,
but I'm not the docile Beauty he expects.
If the Beast wants to tie me up, I'm going to take
pleasure from every minute of it . . .
and we'll just see who ends up shackled.

FROSTBITTEN
Deep Ops

New York Times Bestselling Author
Rebecca Zanetti

"ZANETTI IS A MASTER OF ROMANTIC SUSPENSE." —*Kirkus Reviews*

Enigmatic.
With a wildly gifted mind,
and a wild head of hair to match,
petite powerhouse Millicent Frost is brilliant when it comes to gadgets and electronics—less so with people. After an attempt to bust a bank scam goes awry, Millie is in hot water with Homeland Security and targeted by lethal enemies. In the midst of the trouble, she heads home to help out with the family hunting and fishing business. But when their rival competitor and Millie's ex is murdered, she's the number one suspect . . .

Irresistible.
Former Marine turned lawyer Scott Terentson devotes himself to getting his clients out of tricky binds. A loner, the last thing he wants is to belong to any team, yet the Deep Ops group considers him one of their own— and he pays the price by getting shot at by their enemies. Now Millie is seeking his help—just as he's dealing with a brutal fail regarding a recent trial. Both are a headache, yet he's drawn to Millie in spite of himself. They're opposites, but maybe the old adage is true . . .

Electric.
Working together, Millie and Scott
soon have more on their hands than they bargained for as the danger escalates—along with the sizzling heat between them. And when a disappearance is thrown into the mix, all bets are off . . .